Jane Wenham-Jones lives by the sea in Broadstairs, Kent. Her short stories and articles have appeared in a wide range of women's magazines and national newspapers and she has contributed to the Sexy Shorts charity anthologies. She writes a monthly advice column for *Writing Magazine* and a humorous weekly column for the *Isle of Thanet Gazette*, her local paper. Jane has appeared on radio and television and is regularly booked as an after-dinner speaker. *One Glass is Never Enough* is her third novel.

www.janewenham-jones.com

Also by Jane Wenham-Jones

Perfect Alibis
Published by Bantam Books
Available from Accent Press Ltd
ISBN 0553813730

Raising The Roof
Published by Bantam Books
ISBN 0553813722

Praise for *Raising The Roof*
and *Perfect Alibis*.

"Thoroughly enjoyable and full of deft, sparky humour"
Jill Mansell

"Laugh out loud funny." **Lynne Barrett-Lee**

"Frothy and fun!" **Woman's Own**

"… the story you've always wanted to read about
infidelity – and how to get away it" **Cosmopolitan**

"Original and lots of fun!" **B magazine**

'This comic novel is a perfect read for bored gossips"
OK! Hot Stars

"Does risk-free mean guilt-free?...Convincingly drawn."
Daily Mail

"It's great fun" **Heat**

"A great read!" **Best**

Published by Accent Press Ltd - 2005
ISBN 1905170106
Copyright © Jane Wenham-Jones 2005

Printed and bound in the UK by
Clays Plc, St Ives

Cover image © Dynamic Graphics Inc.

For Wendy Carr and Jacqui Cook
With love and gratitude xxx

Acknowledgements

I raise a glass to:

Dr Mike Cardwell, Lawrence Shaw and Alex Ochs, who answered my queries on medical matters – human and canine; Chris Carr and Fred Davies for lending me their wine lists and Hamish Marett-Crosby and Phillip Silverstone for their expertise on same. Lorraine Dilnot and PC Ken Pickett from Kent Police who were so helpful and the lovely Rikki Arundel, who generously shared her insights. John and Catherine Leech from the Balmoral Wine Bar for letting me prop it up and Patrika Salmon for her encouragement.

Lynne Hackles, Maureen Devlin, Trish Maw and Lynne Barrett-Lee for being the sort of friends every writer needs. Everyone on the ME List – ditto. Katie May for sisterly support. Mike Pearce for his weather eye, Karen Hodgson for being a pal and Nige Derrick, because I forgot him last time (sorry Nige!). Thanks as always to my family – especially my son Tom for his inspiration – and all who made The Harpers Experience what it was…

Finally, and for just about everything else, I am hugely grateful to Teresa Chris, Rachel Loosmore and Hazel Cushion. Thank you so much. The drinks are on me!

1. Bollinger Special Cuvee

*A fine Champagne. Fresh and vigorous, bursting
with potential.*

Welcome to Greens. Kiss. *Welcome to Greens.*
  How lovely to see you. Kiss. *Welcome to Greens.*
  Welcome to Greens. Kiss. *Now under sparkling new
management.* Kiss. *(Whoops – don't know her.)*
  *Please help yourself to a complimentary glass of Fleur
de Lys – our specially-selected house wine in red or white.*
Kiss, Kiss. *(Mmmn. Ooh yes...) Welcome to Greens. (Oh.
That must be his wife glaring.)*
  Do come in. Kiss. *A warm welcome to Greens. Kent's
Premier wine bar and...*
  "A bottomless money-pit run by three mad women who
don't know what they're doing." Victor pushed his way to
Gaynor's side, holding a glass of champagne high in front of
him. He hadn't brought her one. She grimaced. A supportive
husband was such a boon in business.
  "Good evening!" Gaynor fixed a blonde just coming
through the door with her biggest smile. "Welcome to
Greens." She gave Victor a sharp nudge with her elbow.
"Could you take over for a moment, darling? Just got to pop
to the loo…"
  Let him chat her up. Gaynor needed more alcohol. So
far, she'd ushered in what felt like five hundred people – all
on a quick snort of Bolly and the tiny glass of Chablis she'd
managed to grab when Sarah, one of her two new business
partners, wasn't looking.

1

"You're not allowed to get pissed till later," Sarah had said. (For someone about to open a wine bar, she could be very boring about drinking.) "You're meeting and greeting! Your job's to look lovely and make them feel wanted."

Hmm. Gaynor could have done with a bit of that herself. She stepped sideways to let more people through, looking at the back of Victor's glossy brown head as he moved forward to shake hands with a tall man in a suit. She sighed. She'd been so looking forward to this and she should have been feeling marvellous. Instead, this odd feeling kept welling up inside her, making her want to rush away and hide somewhere.

They'd worked so hard for tonight, she and Sarah and Claire. Six weeks ago, when they'd bought it, the place had been run-down and filthy with only three old drunks propping up the bar.

It had been hard to imagine, then, that it could look like this, but Claire was a woman with a vision. With military precision, an army of builders and a frighteningly long list of Jobs-to-be-Done, she'd led them firmly through the battle of creating it.

Now Greens had reopened in all its freshly-stripped floor boards and newly-painted glory. The bold Mediterranean oils – sun-drenched squares of bright yellows and blues against the white walls – set off the huge terracotta pots, the dark beams, the delicate fronds of the deep-green palms.

Beneath the varnished oak canopy above the bar, rows of sparkly wine glasses twinkled in the spotlights. Gaynor listened to the chink of many more amongst the buzz of voices and laughter from the clusters of beautiful people jostling for every square foot of space. Faint strains of the high, sweet voice of Norah Jones came through the speakers, almost drowned out by the hum of chatter below. They'd known they'd be busy – but nobody had expected this.

They were six deep at the bar. Gaynor could see Sarah and Jack's heads bobbing about as they moved rapidly to and fro serving. She started to wriggle through the hot crush of bodies so she could get to the fridge.

Every few seconds someone stopped her.

"What a transformation!"

"Gosh, I didn't recognise the place."

"Fabulous wine list, darling – did it take ages to choose?"

It had taken several near-terminal hangovers. Claire had been in touch with every wine supplier in the country, it seemed, and the cases of samples had reached the ceiling. One night they'd tasted so many mid-range Cabernet Sauvignons Gaynor couldn't say it, let alone pick one.

"Lovely place you've got here!" Someone grabbed her arm. "And what we want to know is …" It was a dark-haired woman with mad eyes and an alarming amount of eyeliner. "Are you going to do Sushi?"

"Not sure about that." Gaynor slid her wrist from the woman's grasp and edged away. God knows who she was. Sushi?

Claire and Sarah had spent hours poring over recipe books discussing the menu, but she didn't remember raw fish appearing on it. Claire was for free-range, organic, 'kindly-killed' meat. Gaynor had snorted at the incongruity but Claire, a fierce vegetarian, had been serious. "People will expect steaks," she'd said regretfully, "but we can at least choose where we get them from." Sarah talked of beautifully simple pasta dishes, colourful salads and delicious soups – everything made from scratch. Gaynor looked up at the blackboard where she'd earlier written up a list of sample dishes, in coloured chalks. She'd felt so excited. Wow, she'd thought, hugging herself inside, as she carefully drew the outline of a long-stemmed wine glass in green, I own part of this…she looked back at Victor on the door. If only she felt she could share it.

As she pushed her way through to the bar, she felt two hands close over her buttocks. She squealed and swung round. Local stud, Danny, was grinning. "Hello, gorgeous – phroor –

you look horny in that dress." Someone shoved past behind her and she was pushed up against him. He pulled her closer.

Gaynor's heart sank. Danny was tall and good-looking with curly blond-brown hair, shiny hazelnut eyes and very white teeth. Much fancied and with more notches on his bedpost than Greens had wineglasses. He was the last person she wanted to see. She glared at his sun-tanned features and dazzling orange and green designer shirt. "For God's sake!" She glanced anxiously towards the front door. "Victor's over there."

"It's OK – he's not looking. He can't see my hands anyway." He raised his voice to be heard over the noise and Gaynor squirmed away from him, frowning. She could only move a few inches without squashing the people behind her. She began to slide sideways. He caught hold of her again and put his mouth against her ear. "I want you."

"Charmed I'm sure," she said, twisting her head, trying to see if Victor was still occupied.

Danny was still pressed close. "When am I going to see you? It's been weeks since…"

"I've been busy with this place – took ages to get ready. Painting, cleaning. We had to…"

"It's done now. Thought the other two were going to run it."

"They are, but I have to help too. I'm going to be hands-on sometimes."

"I want to be hands on all the time." His fingers were sliding up the hem of her dress.

"Danny! The place is full of people I know."

"But they aren't looking. Remember when we…"

"Get off!"

She dived between two waiting customers and through the gap in the bar, nearly colliding with Claire, who was coming through with a tray. She stepped back again.

"I'm bringing up more meatballs," Claire cried, as Danny pushed his crotch against Gaynor's thigh. "This is fantastic. If all these people just come in once a week each…"

4

"Yeah, great." Gaynor wanted her wine. She scowled at Danny and slid round behind Jack, their young and enthusiastic barman. He eased out a champagne cork with an expert flourish, turned and grinned at her.

"Hello, sweet-pea."

"I need a drink."

"You're the boss." He put the heavy bottle of Bollinger in an ice bucket and reached up for two flutes from the shelf above. "What shall I get you?"

Sarah swung round. Her pale skin, against her shock of red hair, looked whiter than ever.

"We're rushed off our feet here," she hissed. "Can't you do something useful instead? I need to go and check on the children. Mum's supposed to be in charge – better make sure they haven't trussed her up or anything. There's been some very funny noises coming through the ceiling."

She shovelled ice into two tumblers as Gaynor laughed affectionately. "Come off it! You can't hear a thing down here with this lot."

Jack draped an arm around Sarah's shoulders on his way to the till. "Everyone's entitled to a little paranoia." He gave her a squeeze. "But I'm OK here if you want to go up."

Sarah made a face. "In a minute. There's people waiting to be served." She turned a corkscrew deep into a bottle of burgundy. "Gaynor, can you go and collect some glasses?"

"Yep, sure." Gaynor opened the fridge and grabbed at the Chablis bottle she'd opened earlier. There was about an inch left in it. Damn. Sarah would notice if she stood around opening another one. She hesitated, then emptied it into the largest glass she could find and topped up with house dry before Sarah turned round.

"You OK?" she asked her old friend and now fellow wine-bar-owner.

Sarah gave a sudden smile. "I think so. Just about."

It had been a mad few weeks for all of them, with painters and electricians and plumbers and tilers and floor-sanders and God-knows-who crawling about the place. Not to

5

mention Claire having them on twenty-four hour squad duty on the cleaning front, during which Gaynor had actually been forced to don Marigolds herself. But for Sarah, a newly-single mother with three kids to look after, a house move to the flat upstairs and all the ex-marital stuff to deal with… No wonder she looked permanently exhausted.

But she'd scrubbed up well tonight. You wouldn't know she'd scurried upstairs to get ready just before the doors opened. She'd lost weight in the last couple of months and the red silk shift suited her. She'd slapped on enough concealer beneath her huge green eyes to cover up the dark circles unless you got very close.

"You look great." Gaynor smoothed her hands over the hips of her own little glittery black dress. There'd been a point when she'd thought they'd be opening up in filthy jeans and paint in their hair. It was five o'clock before the electrician solved the mystery of why the cellar was plunged into darkness every time someone opened the upstairs fridge, and the plumber finally departed.

The ice machine was still balanced precariously on a beer crate and the glass-washer refused to work for anyone. But they were open. Gaynor had finished arranging the flowers mere minutes before seven and Sarah, Claire and Benjamin – a young trainee chef hastily recruited from the local catering college – had finished the food seconds later. There'd been little time to savour the moment – a quick mouthful of champagne and they'd flung open the doors.

Sarah turned to serve someone. "We got there in the end, eh?" she said, over her shoulder.

"Do you have any English wine?" The speaker was fifty-five and bore a striking resemblance to Ann Widdecombe. She was looking straight at Gaynor.

"We tried a rather nice one in a little vineyard near Canterbury," her tweedy husband interjected helpfully.

Gaynor shuddered. "I'm not actually serving," she said, squeezing back into the mêlée. "Our lovely bar-hand Jack will be with you shortly…"

Victor seemed happy enough on the door. Gaynor found space for a moment by the open brick fireplace, balancing her glass on the thick beam of mantelpiece. She saw a neighbour waving at her and waved back. She should be circulating. She was supposed to sparkle. That's what she was good at. "It'll be right up your street," Sarah had laughed. "Kissing all and sundry."

But it was hot and noisy and her heart wasn't in it.

She could feel the wine zinging its way around her bloodstream – there'd been no time to eat since breakfast – and she longed to curl up in a corner.

A group of twenty-somethings laughed loudly next to her. She pressed her fingers against her ears and then released them. In and out, in and out, as she'd done as a child, hearing the roar of voices swell and recede in dizzying waves.

Her step-daughter Chloe appeared, in a cropped white T-shirt and low-slung raspberry silk combat pants.

"What are you doing?"

Chloe was beautiful. She had an almost oriental look with her almond eyes, pale face and dark lips. Gaynor had been mesmerised by her creamy teenage skin when she'd first met her, not believing that anyone could have cheeks so pore-less, so smooth they looked airbrushed. At twenty-seven her complexion was still perfect. She was tall, like her father, with Victor's strong chin and confident movements. She commanded attention like he did. People turned their heads to watch Chloe.

"Nothing. You look lovely," Gaynor said, gazing into Chloe's glass at a deep pink liquid that matched her pants. "Cranberry? Bet you've got a large vodka sneaked in there."

"No, I haven't."

"Well, you should have."

Chloe put her arm through Gaynor's. "It's so fab. Shame Ollie had a bloody client."

Gaynor smiled. Not to her it wasn't. There was nothing wrong with Oliver but since he and Chloe had moved in together things weren't quite the same. Gaynor loved Chloe.

But on her own. She liked staying up late with her after Victor had gone to bed. To drink wine, talk about clothes and shoes and hair and – sometimes – why Victor could be such a funny bastard.

Chloe would tell of the parties she'd been to and who was bedding who in the TV company where she worked. They'd paint each other's nails, do each other's hair, meet for lunch or cocktails when Gaynor went to town.

In Harvey Nichols – the two of them scooping up lipsticks – the decade between them disappeared. Gaynor smiled inside when she thought of Chloe holding up the latest eye-lift wonder-gel. "Dad's credit card?" she'd asked mischievously. The saleswoman had thought they were sisters!

"Why's Dad grumpy?" Chloe nodded towards the door.

"Probably because I've left him there and he's got to be nice to people."

Chloe frowned. Gaynor knew what she was thinking. Why should that be a problem? Victor had made a whole career out of being nice. He was Mr Smooth, Mr Charisma. Flattering a few over-dressed middle-aged blondes was right up his street.

Gaynor glanced over to where he was shaking hands at the door. In his dark suit, he looked every inch the successful executive he was. Tall, self-assured, clean-cut. With his charming, almost apologetic smile, the lock of hair that curled across his forehead, the even, slightly boyish, features, he could always endear himself to women. They watched him stoop to kiss a small brunette in a red dress. For a mad moment Gaynor thought about telling Chloe. Once, she might have done. Once, when they saw each other a lot, when they used to giggle together behind Victor's back, when they sometimes really did feel like sisters. Until Chloe met Oliver. And something changed.

Chloe was gesturing around her. "You've made it lovely. What's this Claire like? Will you all get on?"

Gaynor took a mouthful of wine. "I think so. Anyway, I'm not involved in the day to day…"

They'd worked it all out. Gaynor would put up a third of the cash and be a sleeping partner. "I'll come down and circulate," she'd said – seeing herself perched at the bar, champagne glass in hand – "and Victor and I will get all our friends down, but I can't do things in the kitchen or anything."

Sarah had laughed. "No, I wasn't visualising you doing the washing up, don't worry."

"Claire's very efficient," Gaynor said now, remembering the spreadsheets and the PowerPoint presentation she'd prepared for the bank, the decisive way she'd dealt with the solicitor and the accountant. And a little scary, she added silently to herself. "She's got all sorts of systems worked out. We're going to…"

"Oh well, that's good." Chloe had lost interest already. "I've got tomorrow off, did Dad tell you? I thought we could have lunch and stuff – catch up properly." She gave a sideways smile. "I might even stay another night. I've got so much to tell you."

Gaynor made herself look pleased. The further achievements of Oliver the Oracle no doubt. But her heart sank. Victor was home tomorrow and she'd wanted to talk to him. If Chloe stayed it would be yet another chance for him to avoid her, another lost opportunity to confront him about what she'd found...

She switched on her bright voice. "No, he didn't. I've hardly seen him." And he barely spoke to her these days anyway. "But that's great, great. That'll be fun."

She'd have to do it after Chloe had gone to bed. She glanced across the room. Victor had disappeared. She took another mouthful of wine and then a deep breath. "I'll have to go back on the door."

"Who's your friend?" Danny blocked her path.

"My step-daughter."

"Hi." Chloe looked at him coolly.

9

"Catch you later." Gaynor shot a warning look at Danny and made her way back to the entrance. She hoped he wasn't going to make trouble. Things were complicated enough as it was.

And her glass was empty again. Gaynor sighed.

Welcome to Greens. Kiss. *Welcome to Greens…*

"Well," said a spiky blonde to Sarah at the bar. "I see our Gaynor's not worried about mutton and lamb…"

Sarah looked from her to Gaynor on the door. "She looks wonderful, doesn't she? Wish I had her body."

The blonde examined her nails. "She's got nothing to do but go to the gym all day. We could all be like that if we didn't have to work."

Sarah lifted a tray of glasses. "You a friend of hers, are you?" she asked sweetly. "Gaynor's done a lot to get this place up and running."

True, most of it had been on the phone to the fabric department of John Lewis, she thought, but she wasn't going to have this old shrew running her new business partner down. "Excuse me."

She dodged behind Jack and turned to serve the next couple. Gaynor might not be too hot on the practical stuff but she was perfect at this sort of thing – air-kissing everyone, greeting each new guest as if they were the most important of the evening.

Sarah smiled as she watched Gaynor thrust her chest out a fraction as two blokes walked in on their own. She wondered if she knew she did it. One of them kissed her on the mouth, his hand lingering for several seconds on her bare back. Gaynor smiled up into his eyes. Sarah shook her head. If only they'd flock round her so easily.

She thought of her mother's words earlier. "You won't find it so easy now, you know. At your age everyone's paired off." Her mother had sighed. "When I think of that lovely house…"

That lovely house with the repossession order on it. With the unpaid bills piling up on the window sills, the detached garage housing the car with the overdue HP payments. That house…

"And you nearly forty…"

Sarah was thirty-seven. Though first thing that morning, she could have passed for ten years older, she thought ruefully.

"Bottle of Bud, please, darlin'" The young man the other side of the bar could probably have been her son. If she'd got pregnant at fourteen, like half the other girls at school, he could be her grandson. Well, not quite. But he could have given her a grandson by now. If not two.

Over at the door, Gaynor turned and caught Sarah's eye – her eyebrows raised suggestively. Sarah shook her head.

"Do you want a glass for that?" she asked the boy.

He shook his head, and put the neck of the bottle to his mouth.

Sarah gave a small smile. Of course not.

It was late and nobody new was likely to arrive now. Gaynor headed back to the Chablis. Sarah was polishing glasses, talking to Seb, a friend of Claire's naughty brother Neill. With their tight T-shirts and bleached-out jeans, both young men looked more like pop-stars than city bankers.

Sarah had her school-teacher face on. "I'm much too old for you – I've got three children."

Seb laughed. "I wasn't thinking of marriage, I was thinking of giving you one."

Sarah rolled her eyes but also flushed. Gaynor moved round behind the bar and gave her a small prod. Sarah brought her foot up and poked Gaynor back with the toe of her shoe.

"How very kind of you," she said dryly to Seb. "I'll bear it in mind if I don't get any better offers tonight."

"Oh yessss," Gaynor said, looking at Seb's behind as he wandered off in search of more willing prey. "Just what you need – a nice, firm young body…"

"A toy-boy?"

"I wouldn't say no."

"You never do."

Gaynor jabbed at her with a long nail. "That's not a very nice thing to say. I thought you and Jack were going to get it together."

"Don't be silly – we're just mates. Though I think he might have got a bit of a crush on me, actually. We were having a little banter earlier…" Sarah laughed self-consciously. " I think he'd quite like to take me to bed."

"Of course he would. Bloody hell, he's nineteen – he's going to be gagging for it all the time."

"Yeah, but he's a bit frightened of us."

"Rubbish. Go and give him one – he'd be terribly grateful."

Sarah shook her head. "I'd be grateful – it's been that long."

"You didn't get anywhere with…?"

"He's not interested."

They both turned and surveyed Richard, who was sitting on a bar stool looking pained. Gaynor could see he was a good-looking bloke in a quiet civil-servant, might-still-live-with-his-mum sort of way, but she couldn't understand why Sarah viewed him with such longing. He'd clearly had a personality bypass and it was no surprise to her he'd never been married. But Sarah insisted he wasn't gay, that he lived on his own in quite a big house, earned mega bucks in some important job at Pfizer, the pharmaceutical company, and that lots of women would fall over themselves to get him to bed.

Hmm. As far as Gaynor was concerned, he should think himself jolly lucky someone like Sarah would look at him twice, and he should have been falling over himself to woo her! So far, however, Sarah reported sorrowfully, he barely appeared to have noticed her.

"Hmmm," said Gaynor out loud, weighing up the options and making a snap decision. "Jack AND Seb – shag both of them."

Sarah laughed. "Is that what you'd do?"

The last of the stragglers had gone and they were sitting in the courtyard. Tea-lights and lanterns flickered among the hanging baskets and tubs, throwing soft shadows up the whitewashed walls and over the trails of greenery. In the fairytale light the pansies and geraniums had lost their sharp crimsons and purples and looked dark and velvety. It was after one but the air was still warm and sultry. Or perhaps she was just full of alcohol. Gaynor breathed in the scent of the sweet, heady jasmine that climbed among the ivy and surveyed the various bottles and glasses littering the wooden tables. She looked around at the faces in the candlelight and felt a surge of pride and pleasure.

"Isn't this lovely?" she said, waving an arm around her. "Isn't it all wonderful?" She was slurring slightly and Victor frowned at her, but who cared. She took a large swallow of Pinot Grigio – it was the fourth different wine she'd had this evening; she'd just drunk what was open – and raised her glass to the others. "To us!"

"To us!" Claire, leaning back in her chair with Jamie, her partner, perched on the arm of it, raised her own drink. "It went so well, didn't it?"

Jamie squeezed her shoulder. "After all that!" he said.

Neill, sitting on the paving slabs, his back against the wall, sucked on a large joint before handing it across to Seb.

"Yeah, you really had your knickers in a twist earlier didn't you, Sis?"

Claire pulled a face at him.

Sarah laughed. "When that water started dripping through the bloody ceiling…"

Claire poured another glass of wine. "He's coming back tomorrow, our so-called plumber, and I'm not letting him out of here until he's checked every pipe in the place. And there's still the hanging sign…"

She pulled a notepad towards her, suddenly frowning. "There's a hell of a lot to do. It's going to have to be all hands to the pump during the day until this is all sorted. She looked at Gaynor. "You're around tomorrow, aren't you? There's still some cleaning…"

"I thought we were going to court for the full licence."

"You don't need to come – it's only me and Sarah."

"I want to support you both."

"It's only a formality. We've got the protection order and nobody's going to object to us now. So who cares if we sell a few spirits too?" She nodded at the tumbler in Victor's hand. "People like to have a choice." She looked back at Gaynor. "And someone needs to be here when the deliveries come."

"Chill, Sis." Neill shook back his floppy brown hair, blew out a long stream of smoke and closed his eyes. "I'll do it. You don't want to give yourself high blood pressure. You've only been open a day."

Claire screwed her mouth into a sarcastic pout and wrote more on the list. "No danger of that," she said tightly.

Neill gave her a languid smile. Victor, glancing at Gaynor over the top of his Scotch, raised his eyebrows in an infuriating gesture that said, "Oh dear! Trouble already?" She ignored him.

"So how's life with you, Chloe?" Sarah spoke brightly.

Chloe looked across at Victor and giggled, putting her hand over her mouth, uncharacteristically girly. Then her eyes flicked to Gaynor's. "I was going to tell you both tomorrow," she said.

Gaynor swallowed the last of her wine and poured another glass. As if they couldn't guess. Ever since Chloe met Oliver and her idea of a thrilling conversation had moved from Crème de Mer and Manolos to pensions and quality of life, she'd known it was only a matter of time.

"What's that, my darling?" Victor was smiling indulgently at his daughter.

"Oh, I don't know. Ollie should be here really…"

Gaynor cringed inside. What, to go down on one knee in front of them all? Only Chloe would upstage their opening night by announcing her engagement. This was supposed to be a celebration. A toast to the opening of Greens and their brave new enterprise. Now they'd have to gush over her and Oliver – probably look at the wedding dress samples and swatches for the colour scheme Chloe would whip from her handbag.

"Oh, go on." Sarah was smiling at Chloe encouragingly.

Chloe lowered her eyes for a moment. In the candlelight, her oval face looked exotic and feline. It held an odd mixture of self-conscious shyness and smug pride. She sipped at her drink for a moment before answering.

As Gaynor looked at the juice in her step-daughter's hand, it all fell into place. Her stomach flipped coldly and the walls seemed to roll downwards.

Now there was real triumph in Chloe's eyes. For a moment Gaynor wanted to lunge at her, clap a hand across those wine-coloured lips to stop her saying it.

"I'm pregnant."

NO.

"Oooooh." The chorus of approval roared in Gaynor's ears.

"Champagne!" Victor was standing up, taking his daughter in his arms.

The room shifted and blurred. Gaynor stood up too. Thinking she could do it. Could move quickly, speak brightly, add her noises of pleasure. But as she opened her mouth and tried to summon the words, something else welled up inside her in a sickening swirl. Panic-struck, she stumbled across the courtyard and into the corridor, hearing Sarah's voice exclaiming in delight behind her.

She just made it to the loo before she threw up.

2. Rheingau Riesling

A heady number with lingering aftertaste.

"Nurofen Plus," said Sarah, handing Gaynor two of them with a pint of water. "You should have taken them hours ago."

Gaynor, slumped at the kitchen table in the flat above Greens, amongst the used mugs and cereal packets, groaned deeply. "I was out cold."

Sarah, still in her dressing gown, hair on end, shook her head pityingly. "Forward planning. I set the alarm for five-thirty just so that I could swallow them down and get another hour's sleep before this lot did my head in. And now we're out of milk."

She held up an empty plastic container. "This is your fault!" she said crossly to her eldest son, Luke, who'd wandered in in a pair of boxer shorts. "Couldn't you have left enough for cereal?"

The boy shrugged.

Sarah handed him her purse. "Get dressed and go to the newsagents – two pints. Make that four!" she yelled after him as he slouched off. "Thirteen, and he eats more than me and the other two put together. Take your eyes off him for a second and the cupboard's bare."

Ten year-old Charlie was still holding the Weetabix and – quite clearly – a grudge. "He always drinks it all," he said darkly.

"What about toast?" Sarah asked him. She nodded at Gaynor. "You'd better have some, too." Gaynor shuddered. Charlie shook his head.

"I want Ready Brek..." Bel appeared in the doorway looking sleepy-snuggly in her pyjamas. Gaynor held out her arms to the little girl.

Sarah sighed. "Come on, you two!" She clapped her hands, wincing in a way that told Gaynor the dawn pain-killers hadn't quite done the trick. "Get your clothes on – Luke will be back in a minute."

They disappeared. Sarah sat down at the table and put her head in her hands.

"Bloody hell." She looked up again. "How come you're here so early, anyway?"

"I didn't want to see Victor and Chloe."

She'd woken feeling like death, and slid quietly out of bed, praying for Victor to stay asleep while she staggered downstairs with an armful of clothes. She knew she looked a complete mess. "Can I have a shower here?"

Sarah waved an arm. "Sure. If you can find it."

Gaynor drank more water and looked around her at the piles of packing cases and half-filled black sacks. "It's going to be fabulous," she said encouragingly.

"Ugh. One day. If I ever get straight. I am so sick of living with cardboard boxes. Have you seen the lounge? Have you seen their bedrooms?"

"You'll make it lovely."

Sarah had that knack – wherever she lived felt like home. Even her last house had been the sort of place you never wanted to leave. OK, it was terrible and stressful for her, all the business with Paul. She said the atmosphere was dreadful but still, to Gaynor, there'd been that feel. She'd loved it, admiring all the details that Sarah got exactly right. The colour of the curtains, the angle of a throw on a sofa, the placing of a pot in a fireplace, the tossing of a cushion in an old wicker chair.

Once Gaynor had thought it was a matter of interior design. She'd go home dissatisfied, thinking that she, too, should have a yellow kitchen or deep red walls. She remembered going to Sarah's one dark winter's afternoon when the fire was lit, lamps were glowing in corners, and the kids were playing on the floor. She had felt this huge wash of emotion. She'd sat on a stool in the kitchen watching Sarah slowly turning onions in olive oil, lowering chicken joints into an earthenware casserole dish, one hand stirring, the other reaching down to stroke Bel's hair as the child wound her arms around her mother's leg.

Gaynor had sniffed the air, fragrant with herbs and wine and realised all at heart-punching once that it was nothing to do with the colour scheme or the position of things – it was that sense of Home. That comfort that came from people belonging together. Her own house was beautiful – everyone said so – but it was just that – a house. An arrangement of rooms. There was no warmth...

"When am I going to have time?" Sarah raised her voice. "Charlie! Bel! Get dressed!" She looked at Gaynor. "Why didn't you want to see them?"

Gaynor swallowed. "Victor will have a go at me – he was really cross. Said I'd made a fool of myself. And I can't face Chloe."

Sarah put a cup of coffee down in front of her. "You were ill, that's all. Weren't you?" she asked searchingly.

"I drank a bit too much but…"

"You drank a lot too much but I've never known you be sick before."

"No, well I was upset."

"So what was the problem?"

It lay like a brick, hot and heavy in her stomach. The words were hard to say.

She saw Sarah's eyes flit anxiously to the clock but she still leant over and squeezed Gaynor's arm. "I thought you'd decided you didn't really want any."

"I have. Well, I sort of had. I'm not sure I'd be any good with a baby. Which is just as well since I can't anyway. But I don't want her to have one…"

"But she was bound to want to, wasn't she?" said Sarah, reasonably. "How old is she – twenty-seven?"

18

"And I'm going to be a bloody grandmother at thirty-eight!"

"Only a step-one. It doesn't count. Is there really no chance of you getting pregnant?"

"I don't know – I'm due to see the gynae bloke this afternoon, funnily enough." She picked up her mug and put it down again. "Bloody hilarious in fact. Perhaps I'll cancel. Do Claire's jobs instead. I don't think Victor wants one any more, anyway. Not with me. You should have heard him last night…"

Sarah raised her eyebrows. "Perhaps Victor was upset by Danny. You really ought to have a word with that man," she went on evenly. "Anyone watching would think you were having an affair."

"Well, we're not!"

"Have you told him that?"

She felt better after she'd showered and got some make-up on, or as better as was possible with a thumping head and chronic dehydration. Sarah gave her a mint. "Don't breathe anywhere near the magistrates, will you?" she said with a grimace. "You smell like an old drip tray."

The hearing for the full licence was that morning. Only Sarah and Claire would be licensees but Gaynor wanted to watch. She knew it was just a rubber stamp – they'd already opened, after all, and as Claire said, who would mind them selling the odd gin and tonic as well as wine? But Greens Wine Bar felt like the only good thing in her life right now and she wanted to be there for the official seal of approval.

"What time have we got to be there?"

"It starts at ten. GET DRESSED!" Sarah rubbed vigorously at her damp hair, as she bellowed down the flat's hallway at Charlie. She groaned as she glanced in the mirror. "Look at the state of me, and I don't know what I've done with the bloody dryer."

Gaynor pulled Bel on to her lap. "Shall I do yours, sweetheart?" she asked the little girl as she began to plait her

19

hair. Sarah's still stood out in a bush. "Comb it flat," suggested Gaynor hopefully. "It'll look all right."

"Mr Darling wants us there by nine-thirty." Sarah turned to the clock despairingly. "I'm never going to make it now. You get over there and tell Claire I'm on my way."

"OK." Gaynor fastened a pink scrunchy round the end of Bel's braid and gave her a kiss. "Be good for Mummy, eh," she said, getting to her feet as Charlie came back in still trouser-less. "I'll leave you to it then," she said hastily to Sarah, whose expression indicated a court appearance for infanticide rather than licensing. "I'll save you a good seat and get the popcorn in."

"It'll be boring," warned Sarah.

"I can take it!"

Anything, Gaynor thought, was better than going home.

Sarah tried to remember what it was like to have a life like Gaynor's where you just rose, showered, dressed, picked up your handbag and left, without the daily battle over the last portion of Frosties, the fruitless search for matching socks, the dull thud of one child's head being pulverised by another.

The boys, after a final session of rolling on the floor, were in school uniform, at last but Bel still had no shoes on. "Can I have pony wallpaper in my bedroom?" she asked angelically.

Sarah forced a smile. "I'm sure you can. Charlie and Luke have to choose their decorations too." She gave her hair a last comb, finished putting on her lipstick and looked at her watch. "Come on now, boys. We're already late for school and I've got to get Bel to Grandma's."

Charlie scowled. "I don't want to share a room with him. I want to go back to our house."

Luke gave a belch. "I don't want to sleep near you either, you muppet."

Sarah handed Charlie his lunch-box, fighting to keep her voice calm. "You know we can't do that, darling. It's been sold."

Charlie dropped the box. It thumped on to the floor, springing open, depositing a cling-filmed sandwich, crisps and chocolate. An apple rolled away into the doorway. Charlie kept his eyes fixed defiantly on his mother.

"I want Dad back."

Claire was thinking about her father too. She'd tried not to care when her brother Neill had brought the news that Dad was 'too busy' to come to the party. She was still trying now. It was, after all, to be expected.

It was a perfect summer morning. The tide was in and glittery small waves foamed white against the sand while fishing boats bobbed against the jetty in fetching postcard manner. She watched her two Airedales, Henry and Wooster, charge ahead of her along Viking Bay, bounding excitedly for the bits of driftwood she lobbed them, shaking themselves at the water's edge. The breeze blew Claire's hair across her face. Up on the jetty, the harbour master waved.

Neill's friends thought they were mad to live in Broadstairs.

"You've got to be joking, mate" – Seb was the most vocal – "living all the way down there – arse end of England!"

Seb and his cronies found the two-hour commute to work a cause for great amusement and derision. Sometimes Jamie got tired and dispirited too, and said perhaps they should think about moving closer to town. But Claire, watching Henry and Wooster chasing the waves, knew she wouldn't want to live anywhere else. Especially now.

She'd done all the moving she ever needed to do, she thought, recalling the endless pubs of her childhood. Her father was always looking for the next challenge. The next broken-down nicotine-stained dump to transform into a humming haven of warmth and noise. Before they moved again.

"Don't you get fed up with it?" Claire had once asked her mother. "Don't you want to settle?"

And her mother had smiled that placid, accepting, I'm-only-the-little-woman smile that always set Claire's teeth on edge. "Well, sometimes I think..." she'd begun vaguely, pushing back her wispy hair, leaving the sentence unfinished as she always did if a subject were contentious, and going straight to "You know what your father's like..."

Claire did. He'd raised his thick eyebrows when she'd told him she was buying Greens. Given a small amused shake of his head. "Good luck to you, girl," he'd said. But later, after they'd all had lunch, when Claire's mother was bustling about clearing plates and dishes, he'd taken Jamie aside and begun to give advice. Telling him about profit margins and stock levels and the importance of knowing who your customers were.

"I'm the one who's buying it," Claire had said furiously. "It's going to be mine. Jamie will still have his job."

Jamie worked in a Japanese clearing bank in the city. Seb, Neill's friend, was one of his workmates. That was how she'd met him. He'd been white with fatigue and hangover after a heavy night celebrating Neill's birthday in the pubs and clubs of Southend before coming back to breakfast in The Three Crowns, the family's inn, where Claire's mother had sprung dutifully from bed at 6 a.m. to provide egg, sausage and bacon.

"Do you like working here?" he'd asked Claire later as she laid up tables for lunch, and she'd smiled at him. It was the first time anyone had enquired.

She remembered her father's face when, two years later, after The Three Crowns had been swapped for the Anglers Arms in Broadstairs and her father's interest in that small seaside town had already waned, she'd told him she was staying on. "I'm twenty-three, Dad, I don't want to work for my parents for ever." She and Jamie had bought a house together. She'd had a series of jobs locally before becoming assistant manager of the Grand Hotel, and then, within a short space of time, became Manager, when the previous job-holder dropped to the floor with a coronary while trying to placate an irate guest whose breakfast hadn't been up to scratch.

It was on a bright morning like this that she'd first noticed Greens was for sale. She'd walked down past with the dogs and stopped and pressed her face against the window. There were three or four dirty pint pots on the bar and an empty Bacardi bottle. On the table nearest the bay, an ashtray was filled with dog ends. She'd looked at the peeling brown paint longingly as the dogs strained frantically at the leashes in her hand. She wanted it so much it hurt.

It would have gone on hurting if fate hadn't delivered Sarah to the hotel kitchen, needing to make extra money by doing some evening shifts as chef. Sarah had worked for Claire's family before – when they ran the Anglers Arms. Claire remembered how good she'd been – even her ultra-critical father had been impressed. Sarah had salvaged enough money from the wreckage of her marriage to afford a small house, Claire could talk the project up at the bank but still they needed more. Then Sarah produced Gaynor.

Claire whistled for the dogs. She knew lots of people would think her mad going into business with two women she didn't know well but Sarah was a fantastic cook and Gaynor looked the part. Between them they'd stumped up the necessaries. Gaynor had done bugger-all in the frantic run-up to the opening, save overseeing the upholstery and choosing the blinds, but she'd certainly pulled in the crowds on the night. Though she drank too much. And Sarah had those children. Claire shuddered. Why anyone would want a baby growing inside them when they could just buy a dog was beyond her.

She clipped the leads back on to the Airedales' collars and started back up Harbour Street, through the narrow flint arch and up the slope. Near the top she stopped outside Greens once more and put her face to the glass again. Saw the gleaming pumps and polished tables. Stepping over the road, she surveyed the fresh green paint and hanging baskets. The illuminated hanging sign that would stand out from the top of the road as you looked down the hill was still to go up, but it was all looking good. She looked critically at the olive lettering across the front. Maybe one more bunch of grapes there…

But it was theirs. Mine, she thought as she walked on. She was going to build it up beyond all expectation. Make it a huge success. Show them all. Especially her father…

It was a minute to nine as Sarah braked sharply on the zig-zag lines outside the St Katherine's Primary School gates. Late again, despite her best intentions. It wasn't really Gaynor's fault. Yes, she'd turned up unexpectedly but there'd still been the usual skirmishes involving lost PE kit and trying to communicate via Luke's newly-acquired Neanderthal grunting and Charlie's downright belligerence. She made a point now of walking her second son right into the playground and kissing him. He wiped his cheek in disgust. "Ugh, lipstick!"

Two other mothers hurried past with their heads down. Why was it when – just for once – she was wearing a skirt and jacket with make-up on, nobody gave her a second glance, yet when she turned up in her pyjamas with her hair unwashed, trying to skulk in the car and just tip Charlie on to the pavement, everyone was queuing up to speak to her?

"Hi!" she called brightly to Roderick, chair of governors, father of four immaculate and brilliant children, dapper as ever in his suit and black umbrella, who generally regarded her with repulsion. "Lovely morning!"

He looked curiously from her to the leaden sky, evidently not recognising her.

"Hello there." She tried again with Fiona-perfect-hair – who sported the full foundation and blusher ensemble with matching accessories even when waving the children off on a four a.m. school trip – hoping the woman would notice her own attempt-at-coiffured locks.

Fiona cringed beneath the jacket she was holding over her head, not even looking at Sarah, as she cried, "Must dash!"

So must they all. Sarah looked at her watch. She'd failed Mr Darling on the nine-thirty front but had followed his enjoinder to dress smartly. Which had clearly been aimed only at her, as Claire had been power-suited in crisp black and white at the time, hair twisted up on top of her head, glasses on for the serious look, while Gaynor had dripped with her customary jewellery and glittery heels. It was her own stained tracksuit bottoms he'd been looking at.

So here she was, done up to the nines trying to look every inch the cool business woman. The rain was hammering down on her windscreen as she pulled up outside her mother's.

"Quickly!" she said to Bel. "There's Grandma at the door." But Bel's mouth had gone into a square. "I've left Rosie!"

"Never mind, you'll see her later." Sarah's heart sank as the child went rigid and folded her arms. "I want her now!" she wailed.

"Why didn't you remember her, then?"

"She's only four." Her mother had appeared on the pavement in a headscarf. "No wonder she needs some security after…"

"Yes, OK!" Sarah snapped, watching her mother's lips clamp together. "Look, I'm going to be late." She attempted to haul Bel out of the back seat, feeling the rain drumming down on to the back of her neck. "Rosie will be fine, darling. You've got lots of other toys at Grandma's…"

"I want Rosie!" Bel screamed.

"It wouldn't take long just to pop back…" Her mother had pushed past her and was halfway in the car and patting Bel's leg. "Sshh, darling, Mummy will fetch her…"

"I can't. There's no time." Sarah scowled at her mother. She was behind enough already without going back to collect a bald, smelly rag-doll with one leg hanging off. "Get out of the car right now, Isobel…"

"Just let her calm down first." Her mother patted on, apparently oblivious to the rain soaking into her back.

It was flattening Sarah's hair, running in streams down her face, no doubt taking most of her make-up with it. She wiped at her cheeks as her mother, never one to let a little weather deter her from a crisis with a grandchild, wedged herself more firmly into the car and cooed. "Shall we make fairy cakes, poppet?"

Sarah looked at her watch. "Mum, please!"

The minutes were ticking past. Bel upped the volume of her cries as Sarah, finally managing to elbow Granny aside, dragged the child out by the arms, carried her through the downpour and deposited her on the doorstep. "I'm sorry, darling." She kissed the top of the sobbing head. "I've got to go."

Her mother sighed. "I've got my patchwork circle at three, remember."

"I'll be back by then."

Somehow. As well as the list of jobs awaiting her at the wine bar, she had to go shopping, iron Charlie's cub uniform, clear up the kitchen, buy Luke the cricket helmet he'd told her this morning he needed for tomorrow...

But right now she had to get the hell over to Margate. Which was only a few short miles away especially if you cut up through St Peters and on to the long straight road past the hospital. Here she could put her foot down and be there in minutes. Unless... Sarah swore loudly. She slowed abruptly to twenty miles an hour looking despairingly at the traffic in front of her. After all the weeks of trying to buy the wine bar, the hours she'd sat up late swotting up on the drinking laws to get her certificate, the trials and tribulations they'd had raising the money they needed, now everything could be delayed because there was a dead body on the road.

She tugged anxiously at her hair. The inevitable funeral procession – undertaking was Thanet's second largest service industry – was still a mile from the turning to the crematorium. Sarah looked at the snake of cars and sighed. Was there really any need for fourteen different drivers to miss appointments? Once you were in your box, what

26

difference would it make if someone slid past at more than five miles an hour?

The car in front was driven by an old boy in a hat. No chance of him overtaking, then, even if he wasn't following a hearse.

She stretched out a hand and scrabbled in her handbag on the front seat, confirming what she feared. Her mobile was still at home on the kitchen table. Probably no credit on it, anyway. She could feel Claire's disapproval. Perhaps even her doubts. Her thinking that, even on a day as important as this, she, Sarah, new business partner extraordinaire, was late again.

But at least Gaynor would be there. Dizzy she might be, but Gaynor could explain.

3. Mavrodaphne
Deceptively sweet with overtones of plum.

Gaynor, sitting at the back of the magistrates court, imagined her husband's face appearing above the dark wood panelling of the dock.

Victor Warrington, you are charged with an act of gross unfaithfulness with person or persons unknown. Evidence for the prosecution:.

1. Putting the phone down rapidly when your wife enters the room.

2. Staying away overnight even more than usual.

3. Being in possession of a receipt from a nightclub when you say you hate them.

4. Having a generally shifty air when questioned.

Gaynor thought about what she'd found. She'd wanted to show Sarah but there was no time this morning. Sarah had said they'd have a coffee afterwards, before Gaynor's hospital appointment with the consultant.

Sarah would probably try to explain it away, but how could she?

I would like to draw the court's attention to exhibit one. A shirt worn by the accused clearly showing...

"Where's she got to?" Claire shifted irritably beside her.

"She was just dropping the kids off and then coming straight over."

"She'd better be here soon. If we're next…"

"I'll ask!" Dumping her bag on the floor, Gaynor stood up, swung past two red-faced men in tight suits and approached the usher.

"Greens Wine Bar?" she enquired. "Are we next?"

He jerked a hand at her and nodded towards the bench, black cape flapping. "QUIET!" he mouthed, frowning.

Gaynor went and sat back down. "Did PC Whitehouse say anything?" she whispered to Claire, looking fondly at the policeman sitting at the front of the court. *Mmmm*. What was it about uniform?

Getting out her make-up bag, Gaynor began to apply another coat of mascara, forcing thoughts of her traitorous husband aside and allowing herself a delicious moment of picturing the PC standing over her, loosening his tie with hands shaking with lust… "Damn!" she said out loud, as the ensuing tremor caused her to poke herself in the eye.

"SHHHH!" The usher by the door put a finger to his lips. Gaynor pulled out a tissue and watched the object of her fantasy addressing the magistrates.

Claire shook her head. "Not surprised he's objecting to her," she said out of the side of her mouth. "Look at her! Nineteen!"

On the stand was a pale, skinny girl who looked about twelve. She continually bit her lip and pushed lank dirty-blonde hair out of her eyes as the landlord of the Horse and Gristle made an impassioned plea for her to become a licensee of his premises. There was no-one else. His wife had left him, his manager had absconded with the Bank Holiday weekend takings and his chief barmaid had never recovered from her hysterectomy. The three magistrates looked rather glazed.

"And it was him who said –" the landlord's huge frame swivelled to look at the policeman, "that there had to be two of us. And," he finished, jabbing a finger, "she don't lack experience."

PC Whitehouse was big on experience. Gaynor remembered the interview he'd given Sarah and Claire, demanding to know the full extent of theirs. She'd sat in a corner flashing him smiles. He was completely gorgeous and she'd rather regretted that she hadn't been subjected to his stern line of questioning herself.

"Huh," muttered Claire, as the landlord ended on a resounding crescendo of woe, involving imminent closure of his business and personal bankruptcy if Lanky wasn't approved. "Can just see her dealing with a punch-up!"

"How long will they be?" asked Gaynor as they all rose for the magistrates to retire. She jiggled her keys. "I'm going to have to put another ticket on the car."

Claire glanced back at the clock. "God knows. But let's hope they take ages. You really don't have to stay," she added, "since you're not going to be on the licence." Gaynor imagined her sending up a short prayer of thanks. Claire might be pleased to have her as an investor but Gaynor was under no illusions as to what she thought of her abilities. Roughly the same as Victor's view, probably – that Gaynor could certainly fix a piss-up in a brewery, but that was about all.

"I want to support you." Gaynor was adamant. "You and Sarah."

Claire sighed impatiently and looked at her watch again. "Where IS she?"

At that moment, Sarah appeared, visibly breathless, hair damp.

Gaynor waved – glad she'd arrived before Claire got any more twitchy – and tried once again to catch PC Whitehouse's eye. But only Jonathan Darling, solicitor to the licensed trade, nodded unsmilingly in her direction. She pushed open the heavy door and went down the stairs of the court building and hurried out across the square to her car.

She didn't want to miss anything. This was the last link in the chain of events that had started the day she'd met Sarah in the High Street, looking white and exhausted. She hadn't seen her for weeks but, that day, Sarah had hugged Gaynor, pulled her into La Joules for a cappuccino, and spilled it all out about Paul and the messy end to her marriage. Finishing with how she and Claire had this idea about buying Greens, making it a proper wine-bar, filling it with the wealthy and glamorous of Broadstairs. Gaynor, who remembered it as a filthy, dark bar where only those with tough stomach-linings dared to tread, had looked at her wide-eyed.

It would be perfect, Sarah had explained. There was a flat above for her and the children, but she and Claire just couldn't raise enough money between them. Gaynor had felt that strange excitement inside. Told Sarah how she was looking for something to do, now the boutique where she'd worked had been sold. "You know," she'd said, already wondering how to best persuade Victor. "I've always fancied owning a wine bar…"

Shit! She'd arrived in front of the parking meter before she remembered why she'd only put an hour on it in the first place. She looked into her purse and swore again.

By the time she'd been to the bakers and cajoled them into providing the right coins (Notice: sorry we cannot give change for parking meters – Gaynor homed in on the only bloke and secured a handful) and belted back up to Court Two, Claire and Sarah were standing up at the front and Jonathan Darling was in full spiel.

"Miss Claire Banks…publican's daughter…lifetime's experience of the licensed trade…" Gaynor tried to close the door quietly.

"Ms Sarah Cartwright…" Gaynor stopped as the door clunked loudly shut. The magistrate in the middle, an elderly tortoise-necked man with a shiny bald pate, squinted at the papers in front of him. "Cartwright?" he queried.

Sarah leant forward. "I've recently changed back to my maiden name…"

Jonathan Darling spoke over her. "Cartwright, formally Stanford," he said briskly, as the tortoise adjusted his glasses. "Ms Cartwright is a chef with considerable catering expertise and proven experience in the running of …"

Gaynor's heels clattered across the wooden floor. Several people looked round.

"And Mrs Warrington, the third investor who will be a sleeping partner – she and her husband are well-known in the community – is at the back of the court…"

31

He turned his head a fraction and inclined it to where Gaynor was sliding into her seat. She gave the magistrates a small wave. They ignored her.

PC Whitehouse rose from his seat. *Mmmm* all over again. Gaynor wondered if she'd get a mention from him, too. She held her breath as he stood up.

"No objection," he said, and sat down again.

"That's that then." Jonathan Darling shook hands with Claire. "So you're open now?"

"Oh yes. Last night. It was terrific. We were…"

"Splendid. Now the problems really start eh?"

"Ha, ha," said Claire as they walked away. "He thinks because we're women we're not going to cope." She smiled. "But we'll show 'em, eh?"

"Course we will!" Gaynor flipped her handbag on to her other shoulder and bestowed a huge smile on the usher who'd reprimanded her earlier.

Sarah swallowed.

"I know she's right," she said to Gaynor when they were installed in the Wine Lodge over the road with, respectively, a large coffee and a hair of the dog. "I know we've got to start trading before we miss the season but we're really not ready."

"It was good last night."

"Yes, but that was a party. When we're open properly, people will expect it to be professional. We still haven't got enough staff and it's all very well for Claire to say we'll manage, but if you have a busy night when the bar's full and the restaurant is packed then you do need… are you listening to me?"

"Sorry?"

Sarah stopped, exasperated. "Look, Chloe is pregnant – you're not going to change that but you might be able to change what happens to you. Why don't you talk frankly to this guy this afternoon and see what can be done, and then go home and tell Victor how you feel and how much you want a baby. He may think he's past all that but I'm sure once you were actually pregnant…"

"It's not going to happen."

"You don't know that."

"Look!" Gaynor picked up the carrier bag she'd collected from the car and emptied the contents on to the table. "Victor's shirt! Which he'd put straight into the washing machine so I wouldn't see it. Which I wouldn't have, if I hadn't wanted to wash my denim skirt and needed to check there was nothing in there that might turn blue…" She pushed the shirt towards Sarah. "It's got lipstick on it!"

Lipstick! If it hadn't hit her hard in the solar plexus, if it hadn't made her heart pound, then she might have laughed at the sheer, ludicrous, cliché-ridden, bad-movie melodrama of it all.

"Hang on. Don't jump to conclusions." Sarah frowned. "There could be a perfectly reasonable explanation."

Of course Sarah would say that – good friends are duty-bound to try to make you feel better even when the evidence that you should be sitting in a darkened room, eating lots of chocolate, is overwhelming.

Especially when they don't know the full story.

"It doesn't mean a thing," Sarah went on confidently. "You know what these advertising types are like – kiss anyone. I expect some silly girl was doing the luvvie bit and missed. Happens all the time, I remember I once kissed…"

"On the inside?" Gaynor picked up the shirt and waved it at her. "Look!"

They both did. There, indisputably, on the inside of Victor's pale green fine Egyptian cotton shirt, was an unmistakable smear of red lip gloss.

"Could it be something else?" Sarah asked hopefully.

"Like what?" Gaynor held out the cloth for Sarah to examine. "And it even looks like a bit of foundation as well. The bitch has had her whole bloody face in here. Inside my husband's shirt. What was she doing?"

"Perhaps," began Sarah slowly, clearly calling on her deepest creative skills. "Perhaps one of his clients spilled red wine down her white top and Victor, being a gentleman…"

"Always smarming over anyone who spends money with him, you mean."

"Being considerate, whipped off his shirt and let her wear that while her top was being sponged down. And she had a load of slap on and some of it came off when she put the shirt over her head."

Gaynor looked at her. "You believe that?"

"Or," said Sarah, inspiration striking again, "they've just won the Estee Lauder account and they were feeling the texture of the make-up – you know so they could write some really good lines and Victor just…"

"Decided to rub some of it on the inside of his clothing. Come on! You know it doesn't add up."

Sarah put a hand on Gaynor's arm. "It doesn't constitute grounds for divorce, either."

"He's always staying away. I found a bill from a nightclub – Victor, in a nightclub! He finds fault with me all the time, he never wants to talk, he…"

Gaynor stopped. She thought she could tell Sarah anything but it stuck in her throat.

Sarah spoke gently and calmly, as if Gaynor were one of her children. (There were times, Gaynor thought ironically, when she almost wished she was.) "Then you've got to talk to him. Don't shout or scream or accuse him – just ask."

Gaynor snorted. "Yeah. Good evening, darling! Who are you shagging?"

Sarah sighed. "Look, he might not be shagging anyone. He might just be tired or stressed. Worried about something at work. The nightclub was probably with a client – you know Victor, you say yourself he'll do anything to win an account."

"Then why did he tell me it was a boring dinner at Langhan's and he went to bed early?"

"I don't know, but perhaps he forgot, or knew you'd take the piss. You could be imagining a whole lot of things here.

You know how it is – once you get worried about something your imagination can run riot. Why don't you just sit him down and pour him a drink and make him a nice meal and say he hasn't seemed himself lately and you're concerned about him and is there anything worrying him?"

Gaynor smiled. "Is that what you did when you found out about Paul and The Bimbo?"

"No, I went through his pockets, read his phone bill and then beat it out of him with the sink plunger."

"And I really don't want to go to this appointment," Gaynor said as Sarah hugged her. "I've been putting it off and off `cos I'm due for a smear this time."

She looked at Sarah, suddenly stricken. "Oh God, I hate smear tests, really I do."

"Well nobody likes them," said Sarah. "But I'd rather have one than a filling."

Gaynor shook her head. "I wouldn't." The mere thought gave her a wobbly feeling on the inside of her knees. Made her wake in the night, sweating and counting speculums. "They hurt me, they really do."

Sarah squeezed her hand. "I'd suggest a large vodka and two Nurofen, but, in your case," she said, looking at Gaynor's empty wine glass, "you'd better just take the pain-killers."

She rummaged in her handbag. "If you just swallow these down and relax, you won't feel a thing…"

4. Irouleguy Blancs

An earthy concoction with bitter aftertones.

"OUCH!"

Gasp. Squirm. Yuck. Gaynor grimaced. She was distinctly light-headed, and wanted to put her head between her knees. Trouble was a bloke she'd never met had got there first.

"Ugh! Aggh! Errrk!"

He lifted his head for a moment and sighed.

"If you could just try and relax!"

I am bloody trying. Gaynor stuffed her fist into her mouth.

Mr Bradley-Lawrence – Consultant Gynaecologist F.R.C.O.G and unfeeling bastard – extended a pin-striped arm towards the nurse. "Bigger speculum please!"

"Eeegh!" The yelp she'd tried to muffle made its way through her scrunched knuckles and her thighs, generally better-known for having a will of their own in the opening department, clamped themselves tightly shut.

"Actually," Mr Bradley-Lawrence said wearily, "a bigger one can be more comfortable. One doesn't have to open it so far..." The reassurance was too late. Gaynor fell back against the pillows, head swimming, the room transformed into a dizzying array of black and white spots. *Breathe! Swallow. Breathe! In, out. In, out.*

"That's better."

He bent forward again, his head twisted sideways. She noticed that he too had come out in a light sweat.

"If you could just move your shin," he said tightly as he leant closer and she shrank away up the bed.

"OW!"

He gave another long, loud sigh as the nurse sprang forward and took Gaynor's clammy hand in hers. More out of duty than compassion, Gaynor felt, having already inferred from her tight-lipped expression, that she thought squirming and whimpering just because you had a cold piece of steel and half somebody's arm rammed up inside you was an indication of the worst sort of weakness.

"Don't know how you'd manage childbirth," she quipped sourly – clearly the sort with a pelvis like a bucket, who'd just lifted her leg and let her own children drop out while barely pausing in scrubbing the front step.

"With difficulty, I expect." *Oh God, don't cry.* "Can't I lie on my side?"

Mr Bradley-Lawrence made an impatient noise in his throat.

"I can't see it in that position."

Old Peterson could. He always took smear tests like that. Encouraged her to curl up, hugging her knees while he deftly went in from behind. By the time she'd got her mouth open to shriek, it was all over. "I've been doing it for forty-four years, dear," he'd said calmly.

But he'd retired. Mr Peterson, who'd patted her so kindly on the shoulder, who'd sat and made small talk about his azaleas for twenty minutes and then said; "Well, shall we have a little look, dear?" and went to wash his hands, humming, waiting patiently while she disappeared behind the curtain, had gone.

Now it was pin-stripe! The tall, thin, unsmiling Mr Bradley-Lawrence, who moved nowhere without a hatchet-faced nurse two paces behind, who had probably concreted over his entire garden so he didn't have to bother with greenery at all, and whose pager beeped at regular intervals throughout.

She saw him glance longingly at it lying on the desk, its flashing screen clearly infinitely more interesting than an overwrought, weeping patient, old enough to know better.

Then he turned back to Gaynor.

"Try a cough."

"Sorry?"

The nurse gave up on Gaynor's hands and grabbed a knee.

"Cough!"

"Ahem."

"There!"

"Eeek-ouch-ughhh!"

He was back in and Nurse had one whole arm wrapped round Gaynor's thigh. She smiled manically. "That's it, just relax!" (Was she mad?)

Mr Bradley-Lawrence poked and prodded. "Nearly done…"

Christ! There was a nasty, burning pain.

"Ouch, ouch!"

"There!"

Mr Bradley-Lawrence straightened, handing the glass slide to the nurse who had let go of Gaynor's hand and was disdainfully proffering a tissue.

He looked at her briefly then away as she scrubbed at her face. God, what was it with internals? It was the only time she ever cried.

"I think we got enough that time," he said heavily. "You can get dressed."

"You have a retroverted uterus," he said when they were once more safely divided by his desk. "Back-tilting womb," he added, as if she wouldn't possibly know what he meant. "That's what makes it difficult to get hold of. But you shouldn't be that sensitive."

It sounded like an accusation.

"They've always hurt."

He looked at a sheet of paper in the folder in front of him.

"Hmmm. Any pain on intercourse?"

"Umm…"

What intercourse? She wasn't having any. It was weeks since Victor had touched her in bed. If he was here and not at endless client dinners which necessitated him staying over in town, then he was either asleep before she got to bed or stayed downstairs until she was. Gaynor knew Victor well enough to know he was avoiding her. Why? Her stomach contracted to a tight ball of misery.

She recalled Sarah scraping the barrel of marital excuses. Victor was fretting about something, or exhausted by the long hours he worked…

But more likely, thought Gaynor bitterly, he's permanently shagged out `cos he's doing it four times an afternoon with someone else.

"Sorry?" Mr Bradley-Lawrence was frowning at her, waiting for the answer to his question.

His biro tapped against his notepad. The nurse made a show of shifting her large bottom on the chair in the corner to remind everyone she was still there.

"Er, no." The last time she'd had sex it hadn't hurt. Actually the last time she'd only nearly had sex, and that was a blur. She squirmed at the memory.

"Hmmm." Mr Bradley-Lawrence was still peering into the cardboard folder. Gaynor twisted her head to try to peer with him.

He closed the folder abruptly and looked at her, his fingers knitted together as if in prayer.

"You don't think?" she suddenly asked, hearing her voice wobble slightly, "it could be the menopause? "

Please don't say yes. I am not ready for hot flushes and thinning bones and the slow shrivelling of my womb. I want to be young and fertile and ripe a little longer. I want…

He cleared his throat. "It could," he said slowly, "be any number of things."

Bastard! Say I'm too young!

"Or nothing at all." He looked hard at her for a moment, clearly assessing her neuroses and hypochondria ratings and coming to an unflattering conclusion.

"What I should like you to do," he said, getting brisk, "is to keep this chart for six months and then come and see me again." He pushed a sheet of paper across the table towards her.

"It's very straightforward..."

Things often were, when you came down to it. If it looked as though Victor was having an affair then he very probably was. Gaynor lowered herself gingerly into the driving seat of her car. She'd promised Sarah she'd go back to Greens for a couple of hours this afternoon but she really just wanted to go home and get into a hot bath.

She looked at the carrier bag on the seat beside her. And she wanted to tackle Victor. If that was possible, with Chloe hanging about. At the thought of Chloe her stomach turned over again. No doubt Victor would be glad to have his daughter there. It was a good excuse not to talk and to contrive separate bedtimes. Her whole body felt strung out, her nerve endings humming with a restless energy.

"Any loss of libido?" Mr Bradley-Lawrence had asked, clearing his throat.

Unfortunately not.

The bar was a veritable mass of libido-inducing muscle. A huge and rather tasty number in shorts was piling up planks of wood, aided by a young suntanned one. *Mmmm.* Sarah was polishing glasses, Claire had a folder under her arm and was frowning at a small mournful-looking man. He indicated the piece of pipe in his hand and shook his head sadly. "I don't know what we're going to do about this."

"We're going to fix it, I hope," said Claire briskly. "Gaynor, there's a flow-chart on the wall downstairs, showing jobs to be done and progression of tasks. I've colour-coded them so all the red jobs have to be completed first and then…"

"Hi!" Gaynor turned a big smile on Mr Huge.

He looked her up and down appreciatively. "All right?"

"You could make everyone tea." Sarah pushed pint pots further back on the shelf. "That would be really helpful." She turned and looked at Gaynor. "How did you get on?"

Gaynor pulled a face. "I'll tell you later." She set off down to the kitchen. "Ugh. Mugs are a bit gross," she called up the stairs.

"Try hot water! You'll find a bottle of green stuff by the sink – it's called washing-up liquid …"

Sarah nudged Gaynor in the ribs as she stood administering sugar to Muscle Man.

"Don't forget Sam."

Gaynor looked around her.

"Outside," said Sarah. "Claire thought one more bunch!"

Gaynor went out on to the pavement. An old bloke, in a paint-splattered denim shirt was up a ladder, dabbing a small brush at a cluster of purple grapes beside the dark olive lettering of the Greens name.

Gaynor preened at the bottom with her tray. "Would you like one?" Fresh from a bit of light flirtation with the other two, she giggled fetchingly. He didn't look down.

"One what?" he asked flatly.

"Cup of tea?"

"Not stopping."

"Suit yourself," Gaynor retorted, not used to her charms being so blatantly ignored. "Sign looks good, anyway." He didn't reply.

"You're doing us a hanging one, too, aren't you?" she enquired. He came down the ladder and walked past her back into the bar. He spoke to Claire.

"The bracket's rusted right through up there – you'll need a new one before I put the other sign up or it'll land on

41

someone." He put the little brush, bristles upwards, in his top pocket. "I'll be back when it's done."

"Oh." Claire frowned. "Do you know anyone who…" But he'd already moved towards the door.

"No," he called over his shoulder.

"How long…"

Sam kept walking. They watched him cross the road.

"Damn." Claire frowned. "I was hoping he'd be finished by now."

"What's his problem?" Gaynor said, as Sam disappeared under the arch into the alleyway beyond.

Claire shrugged. "Brilliant sign-writer. But not very communicative. Jamie! Jamie." She flapped her list at her boyfriend as he tentatively put a foot out of the door. "Where are you going? We need a blacksmith!"

Jamie stopped and sighed. "I haven't eaten all day."

Claire nodded towards the packet of biscuits Sarah had bought for the builders. "Have one of those."

"And poor old Henry and Wooster are shut in," Jamie added hopefully.

"Oh." Claire nodded grudgingly. "You'd better go home then."

"You are not hungry, Charlie. You can't be." Sarah surveyed the biscuit wrappers, crisp packets and remains of a take-away pizza adorning the floorboards and wished she'd ignored the blood-curdling screams and not ventured up to the flat at all.

She'd wanted the kids to stay at her mother's longer – on her own she could just about stand sleeping among cardboard boxes, stripping wallpaper till the early hours and being woken at dawn by the plumber hacking the grimy tiles from the bathroom, but with the kids it was a nightmare. She'd managed to get their bedrooms habitable and there was finally hot water but their whole lives were piled in packing cases from floor to ceiling and the kitchen was still grim and cooker-less.

Anything more complicated than a bowl of cornflakes and she had to run down three flights of stairs. And her children – as Charlie reminded her mutinously now – were growing, in constant need of nourishment, and didn't get nearly as much to eat here as they had at their grandmother's.

"But they miss you," her mother had said weakly, clearly frazzled from the rigours of the three of them battering each other.

"How's Dad coping?" Sarah had asked.

"From the shed," her mother replied with feeling.

So here they were, running riot amongst the wreckage. Sarah gathered up plates and cups and items of clothing and tried to restore order, aware that there were less than two hours to opening time and Claire needed her in the kitchen downstairs. "Charlie, put that bat down, Luke, stop winding him up. Bel – leave Scarface alone now, he doesn't want to wear a party dress."

Bel stuck her lip out. "He does."

"He does not," said Sarah, looking at the long-suffering ginger tom. If it wasn't enough to have three permanently starving and belligerent children going wild they'd now been adopted by a war-torn feline of enormous proportions who'd already made his presence felt by swapping a dead mouse for the cold chicken she'd foolishly left on the sofa. He was now dressed in fluffy pink. Judging from the lumps out of him he could take on the biggest and ugliest in town but was amazingly restrained when four-year-olds stuffed him into an Easter bonnet with matching socks.

"I need you to be good for me tonight," she told them all for the fourth time. "You've got to do exactly what Susannah says." She paused, silently praying that the sixteen-year-old daughter of her mother's neighbour, who seemed so willing to baby-sit, was up to the challenge. "I can't keep running up and down the stairs when we've got customers. Not when I'm cooking."

"How many customers will you have?" Bel adjusted the ribbon beneath the cat's chin and looked up at her mother.

The little ripples of anxiety Sarah had felt all day rose up in a great wave. "I don't know yet!" Claire seemed supremely confident she would cope but, to Sarah, it felt like a long time since she'd worked in a professional kitchen.

"Will there be a hundred?" Bel beamed at her.

Sarah tried to smile back. Please God, I hope not.

Please God let Chloe have gone home. Gaynor drove slowly along the esplanade towards North Foreland, composing her lines.

"You'll just have to talk to him," Sarah had said as she left the bar. "Calmly!"

She would be calm. When she'd decided what to say. She ran through the options.

Victor/darling/you bastard

I am worried/mortified/hopping mad

That you may be tired/stressed/dipping your wick

I'm sure you have a good explanation/excuse/one of your fat lies for this lipstick...

She turned the car on to the open cliff-top road and crawled past the iron railings and electric gates and stone lions of her neighbours, frontages. She remembered when they'd first moved in, how she would drive slowly like this – looking at each house, amazed that she lived here. Incredulous that one of these imposing, detached residences was her home.

It was a pretty house. Built in the 1920s by a local architect, it had low gables and mullioned windows, with a cottagey look, although it was very spacious inside. Gaynor had never lost her sense of wonder at being able to look though the windows and straight out over the sea.

Victor's Jag was on the gravelled driveway.

Gaynor pulled in next to it and got out. Once she used to be so excited to come back here.

She walked across to the heavy oak door and slid her key in the lock, turning it slowly, pushing the door quietly open, hoping maybe she could creep upstairs…

"Ah, here she is!" Victor appeared in the beamed hallway. "We've been waiting for you." He frowned: "Why didn't you have your phone on?"

"Oh!" Gaynor pulled it out of her handbag. "Turned it off when I went to see the gynae bloke. Forgot."

She followed him into the kitchen. Chloe was perched on a stool against the breakfast bar. Victor looked from her to Gaynor.

"Chloe's got to get back, after all."

Chloe giggled. "Ollie's being a bit over-protective."

"And as you didn't make lunch and Chloe wanted to see you –" Victor's voice was pleasant but his eyes were flints as they flicked towards Gaynor "– I thought we'd have a little celebration before I take my daughter to the station."

Gaynor looked at the bottle of Moet in an ice bucket. White cloth in perfect ironed folds laid across the top, three crystal flutes waiting beside it. A small dish of olives, one of nuts.

Victor popped the cork with a flourish. "We can drink it even if you can't," he joked, nodding at Chloe as he poured.

"Oh, I'll have a little one." Chloe was flushed with pleasure, smiling at her father, catching Gaynor's eye. "Thank you, Daddy."

Gaynor did the best she could. Raised her glass, then crossed the kitchen and put her arms around Chloe to hide her face. "It is marvellous, such good news, is Oliver excited? Of course he must be. Are you feeling well? Not sick at all? I didn't ask you how far gone you are – when's it due?"

Her voice rattled on gaily like a train, only faltering at the last. At the thought of that moment when Chloe would…

She chinked glasses with both of them. "Congratulations!"

She stood under the shower and squeezed a little more Grapefruit Body Grit on to the sisal sponge. She scrubbed briskly at her thighs, using circular movements, as recommended in the best magazines, guaranteed to dispel

45

cellulite and boost the circulation. She did it automatically, moving up over her buttocks, across her abdomen.

In the kitchen earlier, Chloe had passed a hand over her perfectly flat stomach. "I hope I'm not going to put on lots of weight."

Gaynor had a sudden vision of Chloe in a few months, her face filled out, bump swelling beneath some designer maternity dress, looking radiant. The vision she'd once held for herself.

She scrubbed harder, working the sponge into her upper arms as the hot water hammered against her back.

Of course Sarah was right – Chloe was young and healthy and doing what women did. She should have known it was only a matter of time. Something Gaynor didn't seem to have much of.

At your age. That's what Mr Bradley-Lawrence had said "At your age, with a history of endometriosis…"

"It got better."

"You took a course of Danol which was apparently successful at the time…"

"Dreadful stuff – made me fat and spotty. But it did the trick." She'd laughed.

Mr Bradley-Lawrence hadn't. "Endometriosis has a habit of recurring. It could be that this has happened now. You are tender in the same sites."

Victor had taken Chloe to the station. Back into the ever-loving arms of the Oracle. She'd hugged Gaynor as she left. "I must bring Ollie down to see the wine bar really soon."

"That would be lovely." And then she'd wander among Gaynor's friends, telling them her good news, Oliver beside her, his arm in hers, happy and proud…

Victor had jiggled his car keys. "He'll have to start working hard now he's going to be a father."

Chloe's eyes had narrowed. "He works hard already – he's doing really well."

46

But not well enough for Victor. Nothing was ever good enough for him, these days.

"So?" Chloe had popped an olive between her lips and bitten it in two with perfect white teeth "How's the wine bar today?"

"Yeah, great. It still needs a bit of work. We had the guys in to start building a proper cool-room in the cellar and the new windows are…"

Victor had laughed. Sneered. "Place is a complete wreck. Falling down everywhere you look."

Gaynor forced a smile. "It's a listed building. It needs a bit of work here and there but at least we're open."

He'd talked over her. Once he'd have listened. Once he'd been lovely. Had encouraged her to make something of her life. To see what she could achieve. Once he'd even seemed proud.

"Back soon," he'd said tightly as he left.

She'd be waiting for him.

Gaynor wrapped herself in a big towel and rubbed at her hair. Even if Victor did still want a baby the chances seemed remote. This afternoon Mr Bradley-Lawrence had snatched her dream from her and slowly shredded it.

"It is a disease particularly prevalent in women who have not had children. And, as I said, at your age …"

"I still want them!"

He'd raised his eyebrows. "I must tell you that if endometriosis is present your chances are significantly reduced. As you will be aware…" His voice had droned over her talking of hormone levels and scar tissue and effects on fallopian tubes.

"But I could still have a baby."

"You could. Anything is possible. But I must impress…"

Gaynor had stopped listening. There was only one phrase burned on her mind.

Anything is possible.

*   *   *

He came in banging the door.

She was in a towelling robe, sat in the breakfast room, rubbing body lotion into her legs. She'd drunk the rest of the bottle of champagne and had worked herself up for a full confrontation. Her insides were a tight knot of outrage and apprehension. She heard him in the kitchen – the chink of ice cubes, the glug, glug of Scotch being poured. He appeared in the doorway, tumbler in hand. Here we go.

"Where were you?"

"You know where I was. At the gynaecologist's."

"All day?"

"No – I was in court this morning and then…"

"Where did you have lunch?"

"I didn't. I had a drink with Sarah and then…"

"Oh, so you can spend time with Sarah but you can't come home and see my daughter when you'd promised to."

"I didn't promise. We were having a meeting about Greens and…"

"Pah!" Victor swirled his ice-cubes about and swallowed his Scotch in one. "How do you think she felt?" he asked aggressively.

"How do you think I felt?" Gaynor's voice rose. Victor's brief and disastrous marriage to Marie, Chloe's mother, had already ended by the time Chloe was a year old. He'd barely seen her until she was a teenager and never went to a huge effort to keep in touch now. It was Chloe who made all the running and Gaynor who ensured Victor responded. Yet he managed to take on this air of the devoted father and somehow make Gaynor feel selfish. She looked at him. "Aren't you even going to ask how I got on this afternoon?"

He looked back with contempt. "You'll tell me anyway."

"I won't bloody bother!" she cried, wounded. "You're not interested. You've got rather more pressing things on your mind, haven't you Victor?"

His mouth tightened. "What's that supposed to mean?"

"You know very well."

"No, I don't, Gaynor. Try speaking plain English – I know it's not always easy for you…"

She felt herself flush. "You supercilious bastard. I know what you're up to. You should have been more careful if you didn't want to be found out."

For a moment she thought she saw alarm in his eyes, but he said, sounding bored. "What are you talking about?"

"You! Your bit on the side. This woman you're shagging!"

He laughed. "I'm not 'shagging' anyone."

"Certainly not me!" It was out before she could stop it. All at once a humiliating wave of self-pity came up into her throat. She swallowed it.

He didn't answer, just gave her a strange smile and went across to the table in the corner and refilled his glass.

Recklessly she ploughed on: "You never come to bed at the same time as me anymore. You never…"

"Yes, I do. You're usually drunk and pass out."

"That is not true! I don't drink any more than you do and the other night I kept calling you to come up and…"

"I had work to do. We had a big presentation in the morning."

"More like you're getting it somewhere else."

"You're being ridiculous."

"Well, prove me wrong then!" Part of her wanted to break down and beg. *Take me to bed now. Love me, hold me, look at me. Give me a baby like Chloe's got. Listen to me, for God's sake...*

Instead she ran upstairs. Fetched the shirt still in its carrier bag from the bedroom floor. Brought it downstairs and hurled it at him. "Explain that!"

He examined it calmly. "What is it?"

"It's make-up! Lipstick, foundation. From some bloody woman's face. That she's obviously had all over your clothing."

Victor looked at her coldly. "No woman has been anywhere. I have no idea what this is or how it got there but I am not having an affair. And perhaps if you were less neurotic and a bit more reliable I'd …"

"I know there's something going on. What about that nightclub?"

"What nightclub?"

"You had a receipt from it when you'd said you'd been…"

Victor's expression was now thoroughly hostile. "Oh, so you're going through my things now, are you?" he said, with quiet fury.

"I was looking for some change." For a moment she faltered, then looked again at the shirt lying between them.

"There's something going on, Victor!" She was yelling now. "You don't want to sleep with me, you're always away. You're secretive…"

"And you're paranoid." His voice was low and angry, but he didn't look at her as he left the room.

He went upstairs. She heard his footsteps cross the bedroom above. Was he going to sleep in one of the guest rooms tonight, like he did last time they'd had a row? Any excuse to keep away from her!

She went into the kitchen and got a bottle of Pinot Grigio out of the fridge. She poured a glass and breathed deeply. She was shaking all over. So much for staying calm. She'd try again when he came down. *Victor, I'm sorry I shouted. But I do feel…*

He appeared in the doorway with an overnight bag.

She looked up, startled. "Where are you going?"

"Town. I was leaving at five tomorrow morning anyway. Might as well go now."

Gaynor moved towards him. "But I want to talk to you."

"I think you've said enough."

"Victor, look!" She knew she sounded desperate. "There's obviously a problem between us here."

He looked at her coldly. "No, Gaynor. Not us. You are the one with the problem."

"We need to get an overview. Find out where the problem is."

Mr Bradley-Lawrence had pushed the chart across the desk. They'd both looked at it. Gaynor with her usual blankness at anything scientific or vaguely technical. He with the long-suffering expression of the expert dealing with the terminally thick.

She was to keep a record of her monthly cycle. You filled in the little boxes marked "Flow" – shading in half a box if it was very light, two boxes if it was average, three to four if it was really quite heavy, and the entire six if it had gushed all over the sofa.

Then there was the pain graph where you noted whether it was a couple of paracetamol, a glass of wine and grit your teeth sort of day or the get paralytic, give up completely and go to bed with a hot water bottle variety. And finally a small white daily space in which one recorded one's 'feelings'.

Gaynor had looked at him questioningly.

"For example," he explained, suddenly more cheerful than he'd been for the entire appointment. "Feelings of depression, stress, tearfulness, anxiety…" He smiled for the first time. "That sort of thing…"

Gaynor curled up on the sofa, wearing pyjamas, her arms around a cushion. She'd tried to phone Sarah but she was 'very busy' in the kitchen, Claire had told her. Her best friend Lizzie was still away in India. Gaynor was halfway through the bottle of wine and the house seemed big and empty and lonely. She looked miserably at the chart. Start it today, he'd said. She surveyed the little boxes.

Flow: none
Pain: none
How I feel today...

Gaynor took a swallow of wine and pulled her dressing gown more closely around her. Victor had gone off to London to stay God-knows-where with God-knows-who. Chloe was pregnant. Gaynor wasn't.

How did she feel? She picked up a pen.

Bloody awful...

5. Petit Chablis
A provocative little number with hidden bite.

"Gaynor! Not like that!" Claire moved rapidly and grabbed at the bottle of San Miguel that Gaynor was pouring into a tall glass. "You need to tip it."

"Sorry." Claire spoke to the guy the other side of the bar, shaking her head at the inches of froth. "Gaynor's still training."

Gaynor laughed. "They can't get the staff."

The guy laughed too, winked at Gaynor. "Oh, I think they can…"

Claire pulled a square of paper from a small pad and got down a fresh glass. "Take that down to the kitchen, will you?" she asked Gaynor, as she began to pour the beer herself.

Gaynor ran down the stairs and pushed open the swing door. Greens had been open a week and as usual the kitchen was hot, the air pungent with the smell of garlic. Sarah stood in a blue and white striped apron stirring something at the huge hob. Benjamin, in a white apron, was stacking plates into the dish-washer. Gaynor pinned the paper on the notice board above the stainless steel work tables.

"One tomato, peppers and mozzarella panini and a bowl of…"

Sarah swung round, her mouth a tight line of annoyance. "Not more bloody paninis. What's wrong with these people? Is it national fucking panini day or something? Tell Claire there'll be a wait – the machine's so bloody slow. Tell her to make them have lasagne – I've made all these bloody

53

lasagnes and salads –" She waved an arm to indicate a row of earthenware dishes piled high with ripe tomatoes, onions, crisp green lettuce, couscous and coleslaw. "Why can't they order something I can put in the microwave?"

Gaynor stepped back, momentarily thrown by the fury in Sarah's voice. Benjamin, she noticed, had his head well down. He was a strange boy in some ways – obviously terribly intelligent with an old-fashioned, almost formal way of speaking. She'd already asked herself why he wanted to be working in a kitchen; now she wondered how he would cope with one so volatile and full of hormones. She tried to lighten things and laughed. "Glad you're enjoying yourself, anyway."

Sarah glared. "It's OK for you, hanging over the bar up there with all the blokes admiring your cleavage."

Gaynor turned away. She'd taken ages to get ready, choosing her clothes carefully, trying to find an outfit that was sexy yet sophisticated, pretty but practical. She thought she'd hit it just right with the low-cut stretchy top and hipster jeans, hair off her face in a clip, chunky silver jewellery. Then Victor had told her she looked like Bet Lynch.

"I'm sorry!" Sarah walked through to the cellar and her handbag. "I've got a splitting headache." She pulled out a foil card of pain-killers and popped two into her hand. "And I feel dreadful. You couldn't check on the children could you?"

"Sure." Gaynor saw no point in telling her that Charlie and Bel had been down three times already and – seeing Claire's growing irritation – she'd loaded them up with crisps and after-dinner mints to keep them from doing it again. "Shall I bring you a drink?"

"Just a lemonade or something. And, Gaynor?"

"Yes?"

"Don't you drink too much either."

Why ever not? Upstairs, Gaynor smiled at Mr San Miguel who'd already bought her a glass of Chablis. If customers wanted to get her drinks, what was wrong with that? More money in the till, which should please everyone, and she was a much better barmaid is she wasn't too sober.

Mildly inebriated, she forgot about Victor being horrible and Chloe having a baby and was sparkling and welcoming, making the punters feel this was the place they most wanted to be. A lot of those walking through the door were down to her.

She'd invited everyone she could think of to the first night and since then had put cards through the door of every business, shop and des. res. property in Broadstairs. By the time they'd bought Greens there were only two customers left and one of those was the owner, Fergal, a drunken Scouser with a gammy leg and a good line in belching and falling over.

The other one was here now. A man of fifty or so with thinning hair, unbuttoned shirt and patchy chest, he'd first put in an appearance the day before the opening-night party. Gaynor remembered the way he'd winked at her with the sort of half-leer that suggested he might be in mid-circuit around the town's full range of hostelries, and then headed determinedly towards the bar, lurching slightly as he skirted a bar stool, laid down his paper and rested his elbows on the counter. He'd smiled lopsidedly and leant his red face over the bar to Sarah.

"Open yet?"

"Seven tomorrow." Sarah had turned on a smile, clearly longing to ask if he really thought she'd be serving in a paint-splattered man's shirt and rubber gloves, to the backdrop of frenzied hammering from below.

"Ah yes." He paused. "I thought I should come and introduce myself." He held out a meaty hand. "Neville Norton at your service."

Sarah had removed a Marigold and pressed the damp palm. "Pleased to meet you."

He nodded. "I'm one of your regulars you know…"

"Lovely." Sarah's face was a picture of polite interest. "Well, we look forward to welcoming you later."

"I am," he enunciated with care. "A bit of a character around here…"

Gaynor had clapped a hand over her mouth to stop herself giggling but Sarah's smile did not falter. "I'm sure you are."

He stopped, looking at her, eyes rolling. "Fergal and I," he said, trying to slide a buttock on to the stool and managing at his third attempt. "Go back a long way…"

Gaynor, snorting, had disappeared round the corner where Claire was securing invoices with a bulldog clip. "Who the hell is that?"

Claire had shut down the lid of her lap-top. "That," she said, snapping an elastic band around the cash books in front of her, "is fifteen grand's worth of goodwill."

He was a little more sober this time. "You're looking very lovely this evening," he told Gaynor, almost without slurring. "I would like a glass of your very finest house red, and a black coffee."

Grrr. Gaynor had so far avoided mastering the coffee machine – it looked far too complicated – so she smiled and took his money and waited for Claire to come back from serving the Panini Eaters who were sat in the restaurant area. It looked lovely back there – half a dozen heavy wooden tables along the walls with bench seats and smaller tables in the middle. All had flickering candles and a small spray of freesias. It looked relaxed yet intimate – the sort of place she'd have chosen to go and eat herself if she wasn't the owner of the joint. The thought still gave her a warm glow.

Claire slapped a pile of menus back on the shelf under the bar. "OK, they've all got drinks, let's teach you how to use this thing."

Hmm. Gaynor would have preferred Claire to just do it for her but Claire was in full staff-training mode. Twenty minutes later, Gaynor delivered two cappuccinos to the kitchen.

"She made me keep doing it till I got the froth right," she complained to Sarah. "Too much head on the beer, not enough on the coffee. Ever get the feeling I'm not a natural?"

Sarah was smiling again. "You're fine," she said. "What you lack in froth-levels you make up for with innate charm. And a great cleavage," she added with a wink. They both laughed.

"Sorry Benjamin – does that embarrass you?" Sarah nudged at him as he stood chopping onions. "That's the trouble with female bosses."

"We'll be sending you out for tampons next." Gaynor giggled. "You know I always thought it would be so nice to be a hot-shot businesswoman with a male secretary I could send out on little errands. Would it make you squirm, Benjamin? Could you go to Ann Summers for me?"

Sarah laughed. "Don't! Poor Benjamin. Don't you go giving in your notice now will you? I need you! I'll protect you from her. Hey, though, talking of Ann Summers – did I tell you what Suzie bought me as a flat-warming present?"

She rummaged in a cupboard, producing a pink cardboard box. She pulled off the lid.

Gaynor looked at the contraption inside and grinned. "Why's it down here? Are you going to beat the eggs with it or something?"

Sarah laughed. "Or the double cream. I don't want the kids getting hold of it, do I? Charlie would take it apart, Bel might do something unspeakable to the cat."

"What *do* you do with it?"

They both examined the strangely-shaped mauve plastic. "I'm not entirely sure," said Sarah, "but Suzie says it was last year's top seller."

Benjamin coughed. "This is quite surreal," he said, beginning to snap the stalks from a pile of mushrooms.

Sarah shrieked with laughter. "Sorry Benjamin! This happens when you share a kitchen with a bunch of frustrated crones."

"Oh, it's absolutely fine. I'm not embarrassed at all," he said, in his precise way. "I've got an older sister," he added solemnly.

"I might need to borrow this." Gaynor was still twisting the vibrator in her hands. It might be her only chance of a sex life the way things were going.

"Gaynor!" Claire's voice resounded down the stairwell.

Gaynor thrust the box back at Sarah. "Whoops – stand by your beds!"

The bar was filling up. A group of girls came in and bought champagne. Gaynor recognised one of them as an ex-customer of La Bonne Femme – the boutique where she used to work. She couldn't remember her name but knew she always spent a lot. She made a point of going over to their table for a chat. They were happy and giggly.

"The guys are joining us in a minute." The girl from the boutique rolled her eyes in mock martyrdom. "It's Alistair's birthday!"

Gaynor had no idea who Alistair was but he clearly knew how to enjoy himself. He arrived minutes later, a tall red-haired Scotsman, who ordered three more bottles of Bollinger, paid cash and told her to keep the change.

"Come and have a wee glass with us!" he called as Gaynor collected empties from the next table. She was about to when Claire came past her, expertly balancing several plates of pasta.

She jerked her head. "You've got a customer."

Gaynor turned her head. Sam the sign-writer was sat at the bar.

"A coffee, please," he said, barely meeting Gaynor's eyes. Claire stopped on her way back through with a tray of used glasses and went over to him. "The hanging sign's brilliant – thank you very much."

He nodded. He looked younger tonight, Gaynor thought. Bigger, somehow, more muscular. She imagined that, with his piercing blue eyes, thick fair hair and square jaw, he must have been quite striking once. Cheered by the attentions of the Birthday Boy, she felt suddenly flirty and frivolous.

"What sort of coffee would you like?" She leant forward a little and smiled. "Cappuccino? Espresso? Latte? I've been given the full low-down tonight. Or do you want to be my first customer for the double chocolate mocha surprise?" She winked at him. "The surprise is, I don't know how to make it!"

Further along the bar, Mr San Miguel laughed appreciatively. "I'll have two of them then, darlin'" He'd got a bit more vocal with each beer and was now looking rather red. He'd been joined by Neville Norton who'd bought a bottle of Cote de Rhone and asked for two glasses. Neville guffawed too, pouring his new pal a drink and swaying slightly.

Sam regarded her impassively. "Just a coffee."

"Black? White?" She wondered why he disliked her so much. Was she losing her charms? Her husband stayed away to avoid her, and this guy who she'd hardly met wouldn't even look at her. Was she destined now only to be attractive to the Neville Nortons of this world?

And why was it that when someone didn't like her – even someone she couldn't give a stuff about – she still felt the need to keep trying for approval? She knew it was stupid but couldn't help herself. She made a fuss of piling sugar and biscuits into the saucer and laying the coffee before him solicitously, with her hugest, most beguiling smile. "Hope that's OK for you."

He returned her gaze without a flicker. "Thank you."

"I'm going to get a smile out of him if it kills me," she said to Sarah who had taken her apron off and come upstairs. "You done down there?"

"Leave the poor bloke alone." Sarah poured herself a glass of Frascati. "Yeah, more or less. I've left Benjamin to finish off and do the floor."

"Richard's here."

Sarah's face brightened. "Is he?" She smiled at Gaynor. "I am sorry about earlier – it gets a bit fraught in the kitchen sometimes."

"No problem. I popped up to the flat. Luke's watching a video but the other two are asleep."

Sarah gave her arm a squeeze. "Thanks."

Claire was serving now so Gaynor went back to see the birthday group and the nice blonde girl who she'd remembered was called Terrie, and Alistair who was now singing along to *Best of the Nineties* and who held his arms out as Gaynor started to gather the empty bottles.

"It's my birthday – who's gonna dance with me?" He leapt to his feet and swung her round by the waist. "Come on baby…"

Gaynor laughed and twirled with him, feeling suddenly light-hearted again. They did a jerky, giggly circuit of the bar, almost knocking over a stool. Mr San Miguel clapped. Gaynor came to a breathless halt by Sam. "Want to dance with me?"

He shook his head.

"I will!"

Gaynor turned to see Danny grinning at her. He put a hand on her hip and drew her towards him. She wriggled away. "Got to clear up, really," she said.

"Boring!" he called after her. He leant on the bar and turned the full force of his smile on Claire. "A glass of champagne please, gorgeous."

Within five minutes, Danny had joined the birthday group and was sitting very close to the blonde with the tiniest dress. Sarah, it seemed, had made progress too. She was sitting on a bar stool at the side near the door, her glass on the narrow ledge that ran the length of the room, perched next to the elusive Richard who did actually appear to be talking to her.

Gaynor, who had had too much of Alistair's champagne, grinned across at her and raised a thumb in approval. Sarah pretended she hadn't seen but Gaynor saw her mouth twitch as she sipped demurely at her wine and listened attentively to whatever Richard was explaining so earnestly.

"Glasses, Gaynor?" Claire handed her a freshly-washed ashtray to put back on a table. "Check the others, will you?"

Gaynor cleared the wine goblets around Sam and made a display of emptying his ashtray. She noticed he smoked tiny roll-ups. She picked up his tin of tobacco and wiped a cloth underneath it. As she put it back, she draped a friendly hand on his arm. "OK there?"

He stiffened under her touch. "Yes, thank you."

And then, knowing it was madness, but carried away on an alcohol-induced wave of who-cares, she said:

"Have you got a problem with me?"

He looked up. "No. Why should I have? I don't know you."

"But you don't like what you see."

His blue eyes bored into hers. "I don't have feelings either way." He swallowed the last mouthful of coffee and jerked his cup back into its saucer. Then he stood up, picked up his tobacco, lighter and book.

She stepped back. "I'm sorry if I've upset you."

"You haven't."

Gaynor could see Claire looking over and frowning. "Stay then," she said desperately to Sam. "Stay and I'll buy you another drink."

"No, thank you, I have to go."

"Go on." She took hold of his arm.

"No!" He shook himself free.

Gaynor dropped her hands to her sides, feeling as if she'd been slapped.

Sam's voice was curt as he headed for the door. "Goodnight!"

Gaynor sat on a box in the cellar blinking back the ridiculous tears that had sprung to her eyes.

"Come on," said Sarah. "Every other bloke in the place would give their right arm for you. Why are you getting upset over one odd hermit? What's really wrong? "

"Everything." Gaynor put her head in her hands.

Sarah sat down on a beer crate next to her. "Look, things always seem worse when you're drunk or tired." Sarah looked exhausted herself. "Is it Victor? What's happening?"

"God knows. He's still away all the time."

"But in fairness," said Sarah, running a hand through her mop of hair, "he always has been away. He works in London – he's stayed away ever since I've known you."

"This is a different sort of staying away." Gaynor knew she sounded childish and petulant. "He won't talk to me and I know there's something going on."

"I keep telling you to talk to him."

"Don't you think I've tried?"

"Is he home tonight?"

"Yes, but…"

"Can one of you come and help?" Claire appeared with a tea towel in her hand.

Sarah sprang to her feet. "Oh God, sorry."

"Come on," she said to Gaynor. "We've got to clear up."

Gaynor emptied the last of a bottle of Pinot Grigio into her glass. It was hardly worth saving. The last customer had gone and just the three of them were left. She'd been given the pumping to do which involved a lot of thrusting with a device like a balloon pump that extracted all the air from half-filled bottles. "Keep going till your arm hurts," said Claire by way of instruction.

"How did you get on with Richard, then?" Gaynor picked up the last bottle of red and raised her eyebrows at Sarah. "You looked pretty cosy from here."

Sarah busied herself rinsing the filters from the coffee machine. "He asked me when my night off was, actually."

"And?"

"And I said we're closed Mondays and he said, perhaps we could go for a drink…"

"Hey!"

"You know," said Claire, coming up behind them with a tray of mixers. "I was thinking, we'll have to stay open on the Monday of Folk Week. The town will be heaving. Can't turn down an opportunity like that. Though it's going to be a real marathon if we're to do these breakfasts and lunches …"

"Breakfasts?" Gaynor raised her eyebrows.

"Yes, it's all they had left and we want to be on the programme. We get a free ad then, too. So we're Poetry Breakfasts. As far as I can tell, we just have to do some scrambled eggs or something while various Folksy types stand up and spout their stuff."

She shrugged as Gaynor pulled a face. "Well, I think we need to be part of it if we can. Digger from the Nickleby says he takes more during Folk Week than he usually does in a month." She leant down and began to slot bottles into the rack beneath the bar. "So, if you can manage some shifts, Gaynor… I've made a chart on the computer for the whole eight days. I'll be putting it up shortly."

"It's going to be a nightmare," said Sarah. "We'll be open from eight a.m. till midnight. Don't know when we're meant to do anything else."

Gaynor looked at her. "What about the kids?"

"They're staying with Mum. My poor Dad will be hiding down the garden again."

"I think," said Claire, fixing her eyes on Sarah and not looking at Gaynor at all, "that we ought to draw up some staff guidelines. You know things like time-keeping and not drinking behind the bar."

Gaynor gave the Rioja a last pumping and rubbed her arm. "Is that directed at me, by any chance?" she asked, taking a swallow from her glass and forcing a smile.

"No, no, not at all," said Claire hastily, "though I do think we need to set a good example. I mean I don't think it gives a good impression if staff are swigging away behind the bar, and the till is always the first thing to go. That's when the wrong change gets given out and…"

Gaynor leant down and got a fresh bottle of white from the fridge. "OK," she said, "I've got the message."

She walked across the little square opposite the bar and up the winding path to the esplanade. She felt tired and heavy and chilled. As she closed her denim jacket across her chest her breasts felt tender. She looked at the moon, thought about howling at it and did a little mental calculation. Maybe that was why she was a bit doo-lally today. Her cycle! She suddenly remembered she hadn't filled in Mr Bradley-Lawrence's chart for days.

She walked past the dark bulk of Bleak House, its turrets black against the night sky. Funny to think of Charles Dickens beavering away there at David Copperfield. Another book she'd never read. They'd done *Great Expectations* at school – she'd liked that – but somehow most of the classics had passed her by. When Victor wanted to be nasty he would jibe at her lack of education. He'd pick up whatever she was reading and say "What's this?" as if it were the worst sort of transgression to be reading romance.

"Perhaps if I got some at home…" she thought sourly. She walked past the two fisherman's cottages and the old wooden shelter overlooking the sea. Then her heart jerked in fear. A tall figure appeared out of the darkness of the shelter and blocked her path. She gave a small scream, the sound coming out of her mouth before her brain had registered who it was.

"Jesus – you frightened me!"

Danny laughed. "Bit jumpy, aren't we! Thought I'd give you a lift home."

"Didn't you score then?"

"Didn't want to. I only have eyes for you!"

"Yeah, yeah."

"I wanted to save you a walk."

"It's OK, thanks – I need the exercise."

His eyes shone in the street light as he regarded her with amusement. "You look cold to me. You're shivering. Come on, the car's just over there."

"I'd better not. Victor…"

"It's just a lift – I won't drive you to Joss Bay car park and jump on you." This dark area on the top of the cliff just past where she lived was a hot spot for groping couples. Danny looked Gaynor up and down and grinned. "Much as I'd like to."

"I've missed you," he said, as he started the engine of his red Porsche Boxter. He'd had a black one last time, she was sure. "I used to like our little chats."

Gaynor didn't reply. She fastened her seatbelt and sat with her handbag on her lap, grateful to be driven the rest of the mile home but slightly apprehensive.

"How's the bar going?" he said conversationally.

She glanced sideways at him. He was attractive and good company, had a bob or two. No wonder women fell at his feet. But now – he would always make her feel uncomfortable.

"Do you want a coffee at my place on the way?" he asked hopefully as he got to the end of the seafront and headed towards North Foreland .

"I'd better not. Victor will be waiting for me."

"Mmm, if I was him, I certainly would be."

"Can you stop here?" She sat up straighter as he prepared to swing round into her road. She didn't know if Victor would really be up, but if he was, the last thing she needed was to roll up in Danny's car.

"Sure thing." He pulled into the side of the road. "You know where I am if you ever want to pop round," he said, leaning out and putting a hand on her knee. "If you want to take up where we left off…"

She wandered along the grass verge opposite the inky sea and turned into her driveway. She'd already seen that the bedroom light was still on. She looked up at it now in hope. Victor awake and waiting for her? She crunched her way over the gravel. Perhaps that would put right the shameful embarrassment of what she'd put herself through with Sam this evening. Danny might want her but then he was hardly choosy. The expression on Sam's face was still burned hotly on her memory. She cringed as she thought about it.

But perhaps Victor would have come back to her. Perhaps tonight when she got into bed…

She could see Mr Bradley- Lawrence's chart now:

Tits – sore

Ego – bruised

Marriage…?

The light above her was abruptly switched off as she got her key out.

Marriage – no change there then…

6. Cabernet Sauvignon
Intense flavours with surprising bursts of fruit.

There was a queue at the gift shop entrance outside Bleak House. Women fanned themselves, children grizzled, a couple of red-faced men in shorts guffawed loudly. It was hot! The beach was packed. Gaynor had walked along the jetty, looked at the screaming kids and hordes of summer Saturday chip and ice-cream eaters and dived into the relative calm and coolness of the wine bar. It was quiet in here – a couple sat in the window eating Greek salads, two or three more sat around the bar. Including, Gaynor noticed, Richard, who was reading his paper and studiously ignoring Sarah who stood behind the bar with a tea towel in her hand. "I didn't expect to see you till tomorrow," Sarah said, surprised.

"Just passing. Victor's still away." Gaynor shrugged. "Where is everyone?"

"Enjoying the sunshine, where I should be." Sarah sighed and looked at her watch. "I'm going to take Bel and Charlie to the beach as soon as we close. You OK?"

"Sure."

Down in the kitchen, Claire was instructing Benjamin on the art of portion control. "About this much," she said, wielding a large knife above the cheeseboard. "Fully booked for food tonight!" she said to Gaynor over her shoulder.

"That's good." Gaynor waited until Benjamin was artfully arranging grapes on the wooden platter. "It's all going well, then?"

She felt a bit guilty at how hard Claire and Sarah were working. The hours were endless and though the deal had been that they would run everything and Gaynor need only help out when she wanted to, she felt she should be doing more.

"Shall I come down and help this evening?"

Claire flashed her a sudden smile. "That would be great, actually. I didn't realise quite how many staff we would need. Really – anything you can do…"

"I'd love to."

She might as well. It was either that or another night alone in front of the TV. For a brief moment she thought of offering her services right now but the washing up loomed over Benjamin's shoulder and, knowing Claire, she'd have her in Marigolds in no time. Gaynor went back upstairs. "Can I do anything?" she asked Sarah.

Sarah looked around. "Not really," she said.

Gaynor thought of the children waiting upstairs. "I'll finish off if you like," she said. "You can take the kids to the beach now."

Sarah held out her arms. "You're a life-saver."

Gaynor kissed the top of Bel's head as she came through the back of the bar, carrying a bucket. Charlie puckered his own lips.

"I'm going to dive off the end of the jetty," he told Gaynor proudly.

"Goodness," she said. "Don't bang your head on a rock."

Sarah rolled her eyes. "Don't say that or he probably will. We've practically got our own chair at A & E as it is." She smiled at Gaynor. "Thanks again for this."

"No problem." Gaynor waved them goodbye and bent to stack more glasses into the washer. And it really wasn't, she thought, straightening again as the Greek salad couple approached to pay their bill. In here, working behind the bar, she felt as though she had a role and a purpose. She was useful and wanted. Neither of which seemed true at home. "Thank you," she said as she handed back a credit card and acknowledged the tip with a smile. "Thank you very much."

She said goodbye to Claire, crossed the road and wandered up the path towards the clifftop. As she reached the top and the two white cottages just past Bleak House, she slowed and looked. The garden of the nearest one was fantastic. Usually she walked straight past, but today Gaynor stopped. She didn't know the names of all the flowers but it was the sort of garden she loved best: banks of hollyhocks and delphiniums, a hotchpotch of lavender bushes and lupins, sweet peas, and a tangle of honeysuckle and ivy growing up the wall. The sort of garden that looked as if it just happened and which probably took three times the work of the tulips-in-rows creations. She remembered going to the Royal Horticultural Society gardens at Wisley and seeing the meadow with its long grasses and wild flowers. "Can't we do that at the bottom of the garden?" she'd asked Victor. "Get some wild flower seeds and just sort of scatter them?" He'd looked at her pityingly.

A large grey cat leapt up on to the wall beside her making her jump. She felt a jolt of recognition. She reached out a hand to stroke him and he arched his back, lifting his head for her to caress his throat as he purred deeply. "You're beautiful," she said.

"He's a rascal."

She hadn't heard the speaker come up and this time the feeling of recognition was far less pleasant. Sam the sign-writer was standing a yard or two away, wearing faded shorts and a short-sleeved shirt, bare brown feet in worn leather sandals. Oh God. Gaynor's insides shrivelled into an immediate cringe. She'd had no idea he lived here – she'd have walked round the roads behind if she'd known.

Her toes curled as she remembered draping an arm around him. How bloody embarrassing. What could she say? *I don't usually behave like that?* (Even if patently untrue) *Sorry to have brought my revolting self into your line of vision again so soon?* (His look of horror the other night would stay

69

with her forever.) *Thank you, my ego is suitably wilted so excuse me while I sprint home and put a Tesco bag on my head?* (My husband would no doubt approve.)

Or what?

In the end, she heard herself say, in a high, false voice sounding like the wife of the Chairman of the Rotary Club when Victor had been called upon to give an after-dinner talk on the power of advertising, "He's lovely. Burmese isn't he?"

Sam nodded. "He is."

"My God-mother had one when I was a child." Gaynor gave a silly little laugh. "Exactly the same colour. Blue, is it? He was called Sidney," she added, feeling stupid.

"This is Brutus," said Sam. Brutus rubbed himself against Gaynor's arm. They both looked at him in silence.

"Your garden's lovely, too." *Well done, Gaynor, Oh Queen of the adjectives.* Why didn't she just say goodbye and walk off?

He looked around at it. Leant out and plucked a deadhead from a fuchsia bush.

"I love forget-me-nots," she said desperately. He nodded.

"We've got a gardener but we call him Dig-`em-up. Dig-`em-up Don. He worked for the council for years and that's all he knows. He used to put in all the plants in rows and then three months later..."

"He dug `em up again," Sam finished for her and suddenly smiled. He looked completely different.

"Yes, that's right." If Victor could hear her, he would tell her she was twittering. "He put in a load of forget-me-nots once. They were gorgeous – they'd just started to look really good – you know, spread out – and I came home and found them on the compost heap. He said they always did that in June."

Sam's smile had gone. "It's a mentality," he said. "There are a lot of people like that." He nodded at a cloud of blue. "They self-seed if you leave them. Why don't you do the garden yourself?"

"I'd be no good at it. I'm too impatient. And you have to keep doing it, don't you? It's like housework. The moment you've finished, it's time to do it again. Very tedious."

He raised his eyebrows. "Do you have someone to do that, too?"

"Yes. I'm a spoilt, rich bitch." She gave another self-conscious laugh.

He didn't reply – just looked at her.

She felt uncomfortable. "Look," she said, stroking Brutus, studying the back of his collar, feeling her face heat up. "I'm sorry about the other night. I was drunk and I was... I'm sorry."

"Do you want a cup of tea?"

"What?"

"Come in – I'll bring it out."

He opened the gate for her, not looking at her as she walked through. He indicated the chairs and table on the small patio outside the open door to the cottage. The locals called them the Fishermen's Cottages but this one was long and low with large picture windows – a sort of chalet bungalow. Inside she could see a leather armchair. A table piled with books.

"Um, no milk, please."

He stopped. "Darjeeling?"

"Yes, thank you."

He went inside. Brutus had disappeared too. She wished she could have him on her lap to stroke – to give her something to do. Instead she fiddled with her bracelets. She felt like a child left outside the head's office, waiting to be reprimanded.

He came back carrying two mugs. Put one on the table in front of her, sat down opposite. She felt them both waiting. She looked into her tea, wishing she'd gone home when she had the chance.

"I'm sorry, too." He sounded gruff, angry almost. "I behaved badly. I'm not proud of it."

71

She felt embarrassed. "No, I'm the one... Throwing myself at someone I'd barely met. I was a bit upset and I hadn't eaten and..."

"You needed a hug." His mug had a spoon in it. He began to stir slowly. She sat motionless, stiff with surprise.

"And God knows, I've been there. I should have been gentler." He looked up and met her eyes properly for the first time. "The thing is that it's so long since I was in that situation, I've forgotten what to do."

She needed to get on safer ground. She laughed, in best coquettish fashion. "I can't believe that. I'm sure hundreds of women have thrown themselves at you in your time."

He laughed too, without humour. "Not for a very long time."

"Well, that just shows it's never too late."

"I think it may be."

"How old are you?" she said without thinking.

"Fifty."

Bloody hell. He was only two years older than Victor. When she'd first seen him she'd thought him much more. Looking at him now, she saw that while his eyes were bright and young, his face had a lived-in, been-there look, whereas Victor's always looked smooth and pampered. She faltered. "And your wife?"

"Dead."

"I'm sorry."

"No need to be. Some time ago now."

"Have you got children?" She didn't know what else to say – she was locked into it now, asking inane questions, making conversation.

"Yes, two. It was hard on them when their mother died. Hard to see someone suffer like that."

"Was it cancer?"

"Yes."

She wanted to go. His blue eyes made her uncomfortable. But her mug was still full, she'd only been

72

there a few minutes – she didn't know how to get up and leave.

"So have you always been a sign-writer?" She took another mouthful of tea and smiled.

"No."

"Chatty, aren't you?"

He looked at her hard and she felt herself squirm. "The long answers aren't very entertaining. What about you? Are you married? Do you have children?"

She made her voice chirpy. "Yes and no. To both parts of the question. I am married but it doesn't feel like it. I can't have children but I have a step-daughter. She's pregnant." She didn't know why she'd told him.

"Is that why you needed a hug?"

He showed no inclination to talk about himself but by the third cup of Darjeeling he knew a lot about her. For all his monosyllabic grunting, he had a way of listening, of looking at her as if what she said mattered. A way of asking the one incisive question that would cut to the heart of the matter. She wouldn't have believed she could tell a stranger so much. Somehow, barely realising it, she told him there were problems between her and Victor, her feelings about Chloe and Oliver and how, although she'd had loads of casual jobs she'd never really found what you'd call a career, and her new and extraordinary pleasure in buying a share in Greens and being part of something. He nodded.

It was as if, she thought, looking at this strange, remote man in his soft faded clothes and two days of stubble, some curious mixture of sympathy and pain etched on his face, it was as if he cared...

She kissed him when she left. It was what she did. She went into automatic – thanked him for the tea, leant up and kissed his cheek. She would have kissed both of them but she was stalled by his rigid face. He didn't bend towards her to return the gesture. Just held himself very stiff and straight. Even his skin felt cool. She stepped back, rebuffed, feeling as foolish as when she'd arrived. Then he touched her arm. "It's me," he said. "It's not you, it's me."

She looked at him, confused. Strange words, she thought. As she wandered home along the cliff top, oddly unsettled, she realised they were the very opposite of what Victor would say.

7. Piesporter Michelsberg
Delightful bouquet, with a sour finish.

But what Victor actually said was 'sorry'. Which seemed to surprise them both. He went away for a week to Thailand to shoot a hair gel commercial on a white sandy beach and came back more smiley and relaxed than she'd seen him for months. He arrived bearing perfume and a red silk dress. "I haven't bought you anything for ages," he said. "We should go shopping."

Gaynor was overjoyed to hear this – not just for the thrill of getting new clothes, though that was pretty good – but because shopping had always been Victor's way of showing love.

He might get grumpy in the supermarket when the queues were too long and the sales staff too slow but he had always been wonderful about buying clothes. She had been amazed by him in the early days. Whereas other boyfriends had sighed and complained and gone outside for a fag whenever she wanted to spend more than thirty seconds deciding on a garment, Victor had entranced her by not only waiting patiently while she tried on a dress but by suggesting further combinations of separates she hadn't even thought about. He would move about the shop, grasping handbags and boots to match, picking up earrings, holding tops against her to see how they might complement trousers, charming assistants to seek out further colours and styles from their secret stock in the back.

They both adored the scene in *Pretty Woman* where Richard Gere took Julia Roberts shopping, both getting pleasure from small exclusive boutiques where there was a lot of fuss, and if you were lucky, a bit of creative input too. When Gaynor had worked in La Belle Femme at the bottom of Broadstairs before the owner had sold up, and before she'd fallen in love with the idea of Greens instead, Victor had toyed with buying it.

"Attention – that's what women want," he'd say. "Give them a glass of champagne, offer them a Belgian chocolate, make them feel special on a squishy sofa, bring out clothes just for them…"

The advertising man in him came out in full force over the selling of things female. In her darker moments, Gaynor suspected that it was because he thought of them as simple creatures, easily swayed and seduced by a bit of shiny packaging and ribbon.

But today it suited her just fine. Victor had driven her up to London early with the promise of a long and glorious retail tour. They'd stopped off first at the Soho Square offices of Ezekiel, Bradbury, Thomas and Davenport advertising agency where Victor was Creative Director. "I just need to pop in briefly," he'd said apologetically. "Then I'm all yours."

Ziggy, Victor's assistant, made her a coffee. She was wearing a very short skirt, fishnet tights and thigh-length boots, beneath a shiny top made mostly of safety pins. "Some fab gear out there at the moment," she said, hearing Gaynor was going shopping. "Check out 'Simply Dead' – really wicked boots."

Gaynor smiled, not having a clue where or what the place was. "I like your hair," she told the girl. Last time she'd seen Ziggy, she was blonde and spiky. Now her hair was pink and orange, long down one side and cropped on the other. Gaynor noticed she had a ring through her lip these days, too. She smiled to herself. However funky her own look appeared to be in seaside Broadstairs, Ziggy always made her feel ancient.

Laurence, the Art Director, sauntered in, all designer jeans and sunglasses. "Oooh, the very gorgeous Mrs Warrington." He kissed her on both cheeks. "How are you, darling? We haven't seen you for such a long time…" They all seemed perfectly friendly and normal. Victor looked relaxed as he wandered off to see someone upstairs, obviously not worried about leaving her to chat. As though he had absolutely nothing to hide…

And perhaps he didn't, she thought, looking around his office with its bright red square-edged sofas and framed stills from his TV campaigns all around the white walls. From what Laurence had been saying, they really were all working flat out. Ziggy still seemed to treat Victor like an elderly uncle, she couldn't detect any frisson there.

Perhaps, after all, she'd been leaping to conclusions.

"Ready?" Victor stood beaming in the doorway. "Shall we hit that plastic?"

By the time they stopped for lunch she was the proud owner of a short Miu Miu skirt, a pair of Prada boots and a long Donna Karan dress in some amazing black fabric that looked like fluid rubber and took ten pounds off her. "Not that you need it to," said Victor gallantly, quite taking Gaynor's breath away. He was usually the first to make a quip when she'd put on a pound and she certainly felt herself to be less than her toned best at the moment.

Recently, with the wine bar, she'd been to the gym less and with Victor away so much, it was easier to eat kettle crisps dipped in houmous than make a salad for dinner. But, "you're looking good," he said, and Gaynor looked at him with grateful love.

"After this," he said, "we'll check out Selfridges and see if there's any bits and pieces there you'd like."

"What about you?" asked Gaynor. "You haven't even bought a shirt!"

It was a joke between them. Victor had hundreds of shirts – in every shade of linen and silk and cotton. For a moment, it stabbed at her – the still-unexplained stain on one of them. She'd momentarily forgotten and she wondered if he'd thought of it too, but he laughed easily. "Perhaps I'll get one later. What are you going to have?"

They were in The Ivy. Victor came here a lot and was blasé about the place but for Gaynor it was still a peculiar thrill to look around and celebrity-spot. She'd never got over the excitement of spotting Michael Parkinson – for whom she'd harboured a passion since she was sixteen – holed up in a corner, and bumping into Barbara Windsor coming out of the Ladies.

She looked at the menu. She knew the deeply trendy thing to do was to order mineral water and Caesar salad with no dressing or croutons but she hadn't had breakfast and was starving. "The hamburger?" she said.

"Whatever you want, sugar."

She looked up. He hadn't called her that for a very long time.

"Bottle of Macon?" Victor was still surveying the wine list.

"Yes, lovely."

She sipped at her water as Gary Rhodes sat down at the table next to them. "Is that Nicholas Parsons over there?" she asked Victor in a whisper. He grinned. "Thank you for bringing me," she said happily. "Thank you for this."

"You deserve it," he said. "You've been working hard in that wine bar of yours." She glanced at him in surprise. "You've done well," he went on casually. "I didn't think it would work out – thought it was a bit ambitious – but…well it has." He paused while the waiter poured wine, then picked up his glass and chinked it lightly against hers. "Good for the three of you!"

She felt pleasantly tipsy as they went up the escalator in Selfridges. Victor had left her to drink most of the wine. He was still being lovely. He had his hand under her arm now, guiding her to the designer department.

"Are you OK now?" she asked, emboldened by alcohol and the away-day feel of it all. "Are you better with us?"

He gave her elbow a squeeze. "I've been stressed at work," he said. "The Stay-free Hair-gel campaign, you know, it was tricky. Lot of balls to juggle."

He brought her to a halt by a steel rack and an emaciated shop assistant with purple hair.

"What about this?" He held up a skinny black top by Joseph. "Would you like it?"

He bought her jeans and perfumed candles and Yves St Laurent body lotion with a scent to die for. She held his hand as they wandered along with their carrier bags. She felt warm inside. He'd come back.

"Want anything in here?" His voice was casual as they came upon the lingerie department. Her heart rose. Once too, this had been a ritual. He buying or she secretly selecting something to surprise him with. He held up a confection of cream lace. "Why don't you try it?"

In the changing room, looking at herself in the pale silk slip, she felt tremulous. It wasn't the raunchy gear he'd once have tempted her towards – this was more sensual and romantic – but it was good enough for her. If he wanted her to buy this then surely he wanted to make love to her again. She ran hands down her slippery hips, turned sideways to see the outline of her breasts, checked the flattering cut over her stomach. It would be as it once was. They would go home and she would parade for him in her new clothes. Leaving this till last…

She emerged to see him already at the till, paying for something. She saw him look anxiously round and she shot backwards. A surprise! She mustn't spoil it. By the time she came out for the second time he was standing nonchalantly near the changing rooms, holding her many carrier bags.

"Fit OK?" He smiled at her.

She nodded.

There were opportunities, of course, on the way home, to say all sorts of things. She looked at his dark profile as they sped along the M2 and she ran through them mentally. There was Chloe's baby and Gaynor's lack of one, Victor's previous strange and disparaging attitude to her buying a share of Greens and the nagging truth that organising an advertising campaign for hair-gel – however ground-breaking and innovative its staying power and wet-look properties might be – could not, in all normal circumstances, really account for twelve weeks without sex.

But they'd had a nice day, he'd held her hand and bought her presents, listened to her as if she had something to say for the first time in a long time. So Gaynor kicked off her mules, put her bare feet up in front of her, leant back, lowered the window and enjoyed the feel of the wind through her hair. Victor looked sideways at her. In a bad mood he might have frowned, fretted that some residue of coconut foot balm was going to besmirch the walnut perfection of the Jag's dashboard, but now he just smiled.

So she decided to leave her entire agenda of unanswered questions until later. Until they'd made love and she was snuggled in his arms. Until the last lost fragment was in place and they were together again.

She'd hung up her new clothes and had a bath. She wondered – with all the nervous excitement of a first date – what quite to do now. Should she put on the new cream thing? Or keep her robe on and wait for him to produce whatever he'd bought for her earlier? So far he was putting on a very good show of watching the news and yawning loudly. He'd suggest an early night very soon.

She wondered where he'd put it. She knew she should wait but she was filled with thrilled curiosity. He'd insisted on looking after all the bags and carrying the shopping upstairs for her and had obviously secreted it away then. She opened a few drawers and then his wardrobe.

There at the bottom, tucked round the corner where you'd never see it unless you opened both doors and pulled out his ever-ready overnight bag and several pairs of shoes, was the stiff paper bag with the familiar logo. She paused for a moment to listen but there was no sound on the stairs – he was still obviously comfortably ensconced in the TV room with his bottle of claret.

Grinning to herself, she knelt down and pulled the bag on to her lap, easing out the beautifully-wrapped package, unfolding the fragile paper carefully, so she could return it to its pristine state and Victor would be none the wiser.

Her fingers felt for the satin or silk that would be nestling beneath the tissue and she half-wondered if she should put it on anyway, hide it away under her dressing gown, go downstairs and say: "Hey Victor, let's take that wine to bed..." before whipping open her robe. Perhaps she could wear a pair of high heels too, suspenders even...

She lifted the contents gently from their luxurious wrapping, still smiling. Then she froze, as she got a proper look.

Oh God, Victor. Her heart felt huge. Rage and misery and fear shot through her, making her nerve ends jangle. After their lovely day together, after her thinking it might all be all right again. Gasping, she began to wrap the package back up, fold upon fold, sticking back the shiny gold embossed seal, pushing it back into the bag, back into the dark reaches of the closet from which she wished she'd never drawn it. She felt sick, hot, cold, stupid, angry.

She sat on the edge of their bed where she had imagined their passionate reconciliation and listened dully to the TV downstairs where her husband sat, oblivious to what she had just seen. And she had just seen it. There was nowhere for him to go this time.

Even Victor couldn't talk his way out of this one.

8.South African Pinotage
Rich and complex with confusing endnote.

"Well, did you confront him?" said Sarah, sorting through a big plastic tray of vegetables in the wine bar kitchen. "Fuck it, there's not enough avocados here – we're bound to have a run on them now."

Gaynor shifted her position on the biggest chest freezer. "No, I didn't. I couldn't bear to. All that grief he's given me – all those years of prodding me and saying – 'putting on a little bit round our middle are we?' After all that, he's buying lingerie in a size sixteen! He's screwing a fat cow!"

"Marilyn Monroe was a size sixteen," Sarah reminded her. "And don't you think you could just be adding two and two together and making four hundred and ninety six? Perhaps he brought the wrong size by mistake. You know how hopeless men are – Paul wouldn't have had a clue what size I was – he could just as easily have come home with an eight or a twenty-four. And you know Gavin, that dopy friend of his? He went to Germany on a business trip, spent eight hundred pounds on a red leather suit for his wife – said to the girl in the shop 'she's about your stamp' – and it was three sizes too small. Carla was furious – said it was gross in any case but at least it might have fitted…"

"For God's sake," said Gaynor furiously. "I don't want to hear about Carla or bloody Gavin or you telling me I've made a mistake again. I KNOW Victor has another woman. OK? I KNOW. And if I ask him then he'll come up with some smarmy, bloody, smooth-talking excuse of the sort you keep suggesting and he'll just make out I'm paranoid again." She breathed deeply and clenched her fists. "I could kill him," she said painfully.

Sarah heaved a sack of potatoes to the end of the kitchen, pausing briefly to put a hand on Gaynor's knee. "So what did you do?"

Gaynor looked at her miserably. "Nothing. I just went into – you know, automatic, like nothing had happened. Sort of pretended it hadn't. I put it back where I'd found it and I went downstairs and after a bit he said – shall we go to bed and I, I just…"

"And how was he? I mean did he, did you…"

"Yes."

Oh yes – Victor had made love to her again. If you could call it that. She'd had the feeling they had both been somewhere else. She was in the bottom of his wardrobe, shrieking why oh why – who are you, you curvaceous witch? And he – well, who knows where he was.

It was a careful, civilised, decorous act after which he'd fetched her another glass of wine and been solicitous about tucking the duvet around her shoulders. She was left confused and empty and dissatisfied. Victor went to sleep the moment he laid his head on the pillow and left very early the next morning.

"You have to find a way to sit him down and talk to him properly," said Sarah, tipping carrots on to the stainless steel work surface. She picked one up and sliced the top off it. "Just tell him how you feel."

Gaynor got down from the freezer and began to pace up and down the quarry tiles. "That's what everyone says, isn't it? Every counsellor, every magazine, every bloody radio phone-in. Sit down and talk to him!" She put on a mocking sing-song voice. "As if it's that's easy. But what do you do if he won't talk? If he tells you to shut up, or changes the subject? If he walks out of the room, or drives back to London? It's all very well in theory, but some men won't talk. Some men won't even listen."

"I know," said Sarah, deftly peeling. "I do know, but I can't think what else to suggest."

Gaynor changed the subject. "How was your drink with Richard?"

Sarah looked at her sympathetically for a moment then shrugged. "Lovely. We had a really nice time. How many words has he spoken to me since? Think a of a number between one and five!"

"Perhaps he's playing it cool."

Sarah pulled a face and gouged out a channel along the length of the carrot in her hand. "I don't want him to play it cool. I want to be given the chance to, thank you very much. I want him in here bringing roses and chocolates and champagne – asking hopefully if I might have an evening free…"

"In your very overcrowded diary…"

"Which has 'get very sweaty in kitchen' down for four nights a week and 'stand behind bar looking vacant" for two more!"

They both laughed. Sarah turned the carrot over and scored it three more times.

"What are you doing to those?"

"Giving them fluted edges."

"Looks like a lot of palaver."

"It is. Why don't you do some – take your mind off things." Sarah held out a peeler.

"You'll have to make him jealous," said Gaynor, looking at the piles of vegetables with distaste. "Flirt madly with all the customers."

"Like who?"

"Doesn't matter who." Gaynor half-heartedly pulled the peeler along a carrot. "Or have a passion with Jack. Or Benjamin!"

Sarah snorted. "Not that I'd want to cradle-snatch or anything."

"Richard needs to see how alluring you are."

"Hmmm – I'd like to see how alluring I am. Especially after a six hour stint in here. I'm surprised Benjamin can keep his hands off me."

"Did I hear my name spoken in vain?" Benjamin appeared in the doorway, a crash helmet under his arm.

Sarah blushed. "Gaynor's being silly," she said.

Gaynor put the peeler down. "Gaynor's off. Here, Benjamin – help make these carrots look pretty. I'm no good at this stuff."

"She means she's bone idle," said Sarah but Benjamin was already tying his apron strings behind him.

"It will be my pleasure."

Upstairs, Claire was polishing the brass bell they used to ring time. "Want a job?"

Gaynor shook her head. "Not especially. But I'll be back later," she added placatingly, as Claire went on rubbing. "I'll do something then." She still wasn't entirely sure of Claire. Could never quite work out what lay behind the business-like exterior.

Sarah came up the stairs behind her. "Can you come in early tonight, Gaynor? Get set up with Claire so I can stay upstairs a bit longer with the children? Charlie's being very difficult – I think I'm just not spending enough time with him. Or any of them. I mean of course they all love Grandma and Susannah the baby-sitter is terrific but..." She sighed. "Luke's monosyllabic, and poor little Bel – she's with my mother so much she's practically forgotten what I look like. I'm going to have to –"

The phone jangled loudly, interrupting her. Gaynor leaned over and picked it up.

"Good morning, Greens." She listened for a moment. "Hello? I'm sorry do you have a cold or are you trying to be obscene? Pervert," she said, banging the phone back down. "Could hear someone there but they weren't speaking."

"Gaynor, for goodness sake," said Claire crossly. "That was probably a potential customer on a bad line."

Gaynor shrugged. "They'll have to phone back, then."

Sarah looked worried. "Or it could be..."

"What?"

"Someone did that the other day. And there was a funny message on the answer-phone yesterday morning when I came down. Just a sort of breathing, snuffly noise."

"Why didn't you tell us?" Gaynor asked. "Let's hear it."

"I erased it – didn't think much of it at the time. But now I wonder…"

"Could be anything." Claire was brisk. "Might be some saddo – heard that three women have got the place, or it might be a wrong number from someone with adenoids."

"When I went riding as a child," Gaynor said, "the riding school was always getting funny calls. It was all that stuff about girls on horses. I was out once with my friend Karen and this guy exposed himself to us."

Sarah raised her eyebrows. "Were you scared?"

"No – all the little kids were crying but we were pretty fascinated really."

Sarah shook her head. "I might have guessed."

"Anyway, one of the other kid's fathers went to the police and they said the ones who flash it about are the last ones to do anything with it."

"Nobody's flashing anything yet," said Claire firmly. "Let's put it down to a wrong number or a bad line, eh?" She stared meaningfully at Gaynor.

"Sure." Gaynor glanced at Sarah, who was still looking troubled. "Probably never happen again anyway."

Sarah hugged Gaynor at the door. "See you this evening then, yes?" She smiled. "You're much better at flirting with customers than I am."

Gaynor looked at her. "Think I'm losing my touch, actually."

Sarah squeezed her arm. "What are you going to do about Victor?"

Gaynor shifted her handbag to the other shoulder. "I don't know yet. Just keep watching him, I suppose. There was the lipstick and now I've seen this. But I'll wait for something else. Something he really can't wriggle out of – 'cos I'll have the proof."

"And what will you do then?" asked Sam quietly, looking past her out of the window, relighting one of his minute squashed-looking cigarettes with a battered-looking Zippo. He ran a hand down Brutus's spine as the cat prowled along the arm of his leather chair. "If you go all out to find out what he's doing and you do prove he's being unfaithful, then you need to have thought about what you're going to do next."

"Well, I'll…" Gaynor put down her teacup and walked over to the window. "I'll confront him."

"I thought you'd done that already," he said mildly.

"Yes, but this time I'll have proof and he won't be able to deny it."

"And then?"

She looked away from him. "I don't know yet. I suppose it depends what he says. I've got to catch him first. I've got to find out where he goes and who he sees. I even phoned up a detective agency." She laughed self-consciously. "But they wanted an absolute fortune to follow him and I couldn't spend that sort of money without him knowing about it."

"You don't want to touch them, anyway," said Sam. "There are other ways of finding out. But first you have to be sure you really want to know."

"What ways?" Gaynor asked. She looked at a sketch for a greengrocer's sign that was propped on Sam's drawing board. It was a mass of bananas and cherries.

"Because once you find out," he said, "if there is anything to find out, you can't un-know it. And sometimes, there are some things that are better not to know."

"What ways? How can I catch him?"

"Put on a wig and follow him yourself?" Sam gave up with the lighter and dropped the dying cigarette end into an ashtray.

Gaynor looked at him. "Seriously!"

Sam sipped at his tea and considered her for a moment. "Depends how far you want to go," he said slowly. "There's always a paper trail. Credit card statements, mobile phones, mileage on the car... a judicious phone call or two to work can turn up a lot – you can find out all sorts with a little probing. And then – you can turn up where he is and see what you find, though I wouldn't advise it."

Gaynor looked at him and suddenly smiled. "Were you a private dick yourself before you were a sign-writer?"

"No, I was a policeman."

"I wasn't a very good one," he said, when they both had more tea. "I didn't fit in very well." He coaxed a new roll-up into life. "I could do the hard man act but my heart wasn't in it. Spent too much time wanting to ask 'Why?' I was supposed to just lock 'em up and get on with the next one but when you pick up a little sixteen-year-old drug addict who's become a tom to get her next fix or a twenty-five-year-old black guy who's spent more than half his life in custody and gets picked up weekly and the dull fury comes off him in waves, you do stop and wonder what the hell it's all about."

Gaynor smiled wryly. "You weren't a policeman round here then?"

He gave an answering shrug of amusement. "I was in the Met."

"My grandfather was in the police," she said.

He looked at her with sudden interest. "Was he? Your mother or father's side?"

"My father's."

He gave a bitter sort of laugh. "And what did your father do?"

"Became a geography teacher."

"Good for him."

"It wasn't good for him. He spent his whole working life in a state of deep depression or rage or despair or all three."

"And what did your mother do?"

"Tried to hold it all together."

"Have you got siblings?"

"A brother."

"What does he do?"

"You like to know your job descriptions, don't you? When he's taking his medication he works for Reading council in the IT department. When he's not, he stays at home to traumatise my mother. Or runs off somewhere saying he'll kill himself."

Sam gazed at her and his eyes were suddenly full of something she hadn't seen there before.

"That sounds very difficult for everyone."

She sat down on the arm of the sofa next to his chair. He'd picked up the small wooden sign he'd been painting when she arrived and balanced it back on his knees. Now he took a fine brush from the table, dipped it in paint, and began delicately filling in the tiny scales on a little blue fish peeping out from a frond of seaweed.

"Is he younger than you?" he asked, his head bent.

"Yes, David's thirty-five now. It's sad, you know, really he's a sweet, gentle person. I always wanted to protect him when we were younger, stop my father yelling at him. But he's very difficult when he's ill. It's hard not to lose patience. Of course he can't help it – but it's so wearing. He becomes paranoid and obsessive – you can't reason with him and it's a nightmare trying to get him to take his drugs again or get him anywhere near a doctor. We've had to have him bundled screaming into an ambulance before." She shuddered.

Sam carried on painting but his voice was soft. "Seen a bit of that myself. Bad enough when you don't know them. Must be awful if it's someone close."

Gaynor bent down to stroke Brutus, who had wrapped himself around her legs.

"Yes." She gave a brittle laugh. "Childhood was lots of fun – there was always someone weeping or wailing or threatening to cut their throat. My poor mother had to try and pacify them both and of course whatever she did, it was never enough…" She stopped as Sam laid down his paintbrush.

He put the sign carefully on the floor and reached out a hand. His fingers were warm and dry and surprisingly smooth as they closed around her wrist. He squeezed it gently, looking at her with sympathy and understanding.

"No wonder you want so much attention."

9. Côtes du Rhône

Poetic on the palate, peppery and dramatic.

"More eggs and smoked salmon!" Claire shot through the swing door into the wine bar kitchen and grabbed at a tray. "God, it's bedlam up there."

She slapped a sheet of paper down on the steel work surface and picked up the plates of bacon. "We're almost out of fresh orange juice and the coffee machine just can't keep up!" She kicked at the swing door. "And Gaynor…"

Sarah pushed back the hair from her face. Claire didn't have to say any more. Gaynor hadn't been put on the planet to be a waitress – Sarah could picture her upstairs now, wafting about with plates of breakfast, never sure who had ordered what; but nobody oozed more charm when things went wrong, nor, come to that, got bigger tips. Last week she'd managed to empty a plate of avocado prawns into some guy's lap and forgotten to give him and his mate any cutlery whatsoever to eat their main course with, and he'd still left her ten quid.

Today they were busier than ever. It was nearly the end of Folk Week and they were all exhausted. They'd been there since seven and opened the doors at half-past, letting in the first eager beavers who wanted to get a ringside seat for the Poetry Breakfasts which began promptly at eight under the guiding hand of Veronica, a leading light in the Broadstairs Poetry Ring and beater of the drum (literally) for the right of every individual – however un-lyrical – to bring his or her verse to the wider audience.

Upstairs, Gaynor frothed up milk at the coffee machine and watched as Veronica spread her knees beneath a midnight-blue kaftan adorned with mirrored moons and stars and stuffed a small set of bongos down between them.

"Can we begin?" she called in a high quivering voice. She began to beat the drums with the flat of her hand. "As always," she cried, "when I pass the drum, stand up and share…"

It was the same lot every morning and the drum always started its circuit at a serious-looking young man with spots and long hair, called Darwin, who would rise to his feet and spout whatever he'd written yesterday. The actual poetry – though largely incomprehensible – was bearable, Gaynor thought, but his tortured explanations of why he'd written it, which usually took twice as long as the recital, were mind-numbing.

"I was moved to compose this yesterday afternoon when I was particularly struck by a piece of flint juxtaposed against chalk in the light of a rock pool…" he droned.

Gaynor smiled at the other poets beginning to shift and twitch while Veronica gazed on rapturously.

"Thank you Darwin," she said reverently when he'd finished and Gaynor carried cappuccino and toast over to the table beside her. "Keep the beat going. Pass it on."

Gaynor went back behind the bar as the drum was thrust towards a tall gothic-looking woman in purple. Veronica beamed. "Ah, Serena – what have you got for us this morning?"

"Thank God that bloke with the stammer's not here today," Gaynor said to Claire, as she loaded a tray with coffee cups. "I thought the poor bastard was never going to end."

Claire gave a sudden giggle. "They were still here at lunchtime." She consulted her pad. "Gaynor, have you brought up the muffins for table eight yet? And there's a couple of tables need clearing. Oh heavens, and that bloke who wants the cheese omelette is waving his arms again. Yes, how can I help you?" She turned as more people approached the counter. "Six teas? Coming right up…"

It was not ten yet and already Gaynor felt unbearably hot as she belted up and down the stairs with plates of eggs and warm rolls, trying to keep up with the never-ending stream of requests for teas and coffees. "Whose idea was this, anyway?" she growled at Claire when they got a minute's respite.

"We can't afford to turn any business away at the moment," said Claire crisply. "This week's a gold mine for us – we've got to make the most of it."

"I know, I know, but I'm knackered already." Gaynor took a foot out of its mule and wiggled it about. "My legs are killing me."

She was supposed to stay on all day. They were open until midnight. Jack and a couple of the students were coming in from lunchtime to do the bar and waitressing but Claire had said they might still need Gaynor if they were very busy. And she could hardly refuse when Sarah and Claire had been here the whole time.

"Thanks, I would appreciate it," said Claire as Gaynor assured her she'd stick around. "I shall probably have to help Sarah and Benjamin in the kitchen later. I just hope to God the new washer-up turns up today."

Gaynor snorted. The last one – a cheerful-looking girl with a nose stud and plaits, called Melody – had left after three weeks saying she couldn't manage the stress.

"Stress!" Claire had fumed. "I'll give her bloody stress."

Gaynor had seen Melody later wandering along the jetty wrapped round a boy in a leather jacket. "I think shagging holds more appeal than scrubbing," she said to Claire now. "Ooh, talking of which…"

A tall tanned guy with a tight T-shirt and very white teeth was leaning over the other end of the bar. "A bottle of Bolly and some freshly-squeezed orange-juice." He smiled at Gaynor.

"That's more like it," said Gaynor to Claire as she filled a champagne bucket with ice. "I could do with some of that myself."

"We're out of oranges," said Claire. "You'll have to send Ben up to the greengrocers. And," she added, with her best head-mistressey look. "Don't you dare. We need you upright!"

And upright Gaynor was, up and down stairs, backwards and forwards into the restaurant. The minute the breakfast crowd had cleared, another started coming in for lunch.

"If I go up and down these stairs once more…" she said to Jack who was managing to look incredibly cool and laid-back despite dozens of people around the bar. He threw a bottle of Bud up into the air and deftly caught it again. "Good for the thigh muscles," he said, grinning.

"Bollocks," replied Gaynor.

Jack winked. "Who knows, might be good for them, too."

It had quietened a bit by five although there were groups lingering in the restaurant and clusters of drinkers sitting around tables in the bar. Through the open door, Gaynor could hear Irish folk songs coming from one of the pubs up the road.

She watched families walking up Harbour Street from the beach, trailing buckets and towels and whining children. The hot sun had softened and the shadows were beginning to lengthen. A group of bare-chested boys in shorts walked by swinging cans of lager. Catching sight of Gaynor in the doorway, one of them yelled "Nice tits!" and the rest erupted into laughter.

"Isn't it past your bedtime?" she called back. "Twats," she said, as Claire collected glasses behind her.

Claire straightened, the tray of empties balanced against her hip. "That reminds me," she said in a low voice. "There was a horrible answer-phone message when I opened up this morning. I didn't tell Sarah – she was upstairs and I didn't see the point of worrying her."

Gaynor nodded. "What did it say?"

Claire began to carry the tray back towards the bar. "I couldn't make it all out but it was abusive. 'You're an ugly old dog', something like that."

Gaynor picked up a couple of pint pots. "So someone's got the hots for one of us."

Claire gave her a grin. "Bound to be you, then!"

Gaynor grinned back. "And he's probably got a very small one and can't even get that up."

"He wouldn't be able to if I got hold of him," said Claire. "He'd withheld the number, of course."

Gaynor nodded again, thoughtfully. "I suppose we're going to get that sort of thing – a bar run by women…"

She stopped as a forty-something blonde wearing too much eye make-up leant across the bar. "Excuse me, is there something wrong with the Ladies? The door's been locked for ages."

Gaynor went out into the corridor with her. "Shouldn't you have more than one?" the woman enquired. "In a bar this busy?"

"There's not really room for any more." Gaynor tried the door handle. She could hear water running inside. "I expect she'll be out in a minute!"

"She's been ages already."

As Gaynor knocked on the loo door for the second time, she was joined by a small anxious-looking woman with greying hair tied back in a scarf. "I'm her mother," she said, agitated. "It's my daughter in there."

She pushed her face up against the scrubbed pine. "Nicola! Come out now, darling. Please come out."

Claire appeared behind her. "What's happening?"

The blonde in the corridor was shifting from foot to foot. "Is she going to be much longer?"

"Use the Men's." Claire was short. "It's just the same."

The mother turned beseechingly to Gaynor. "We must get her out of there. Can you break the door down?"

A tall, thin, man in cord trousers and a baggy shirt came in from the courtyard. "I've looked outside – the window's tiny."

"What exactly is the problem here?" Claire frowned at the mother who was wringing her hands. "What do you think your daughter's going to do?"

Neither parent answered her. Several more women filed into the passageway. "You'll have to use the Men's," Claire said over her shoulder.

"Look we're very busy here," she called, raising her voice." She rapped sharply on the loo door. "Can you come out, please? There are people waiting!"

"No!" The mother clapped her hands to her face. "Don't shout at her."

"I'm trying to run a business here!" Claire turned on her heel and stalked back into the bar.

Gaynor followed a few minutes later. "They want us to call the police or the Fire Brigade and get her out. They seem to think she's having some sort of turn in there."

"Bloody hell," Claire muttered. "OK, we'd better do something – we don't want her carried out of here, do we? Not exactly a good recommendation."

She spoke to the small brown-haired girl behind the bar. "You OK here for a moment, Kate?" Kate smiled. She was down from Leeds University for the summer and seemed to smile at everything. Claire looked at Gaynor. "Let's see what Sarah says."

She went down into the kitchen with Gaynor behind her. Sarah was pulling things out of the big fridge. "Some nutty girl's locked herself in the loo," Claire said. "The mother wants the emergency services called in."

Sarah looked up, wiping her hair back from her face with the back of a plastic-gloved hand. "Oh joy," she said. "Well, you'd better then. Try and find out what we're dealing with."

But back upstairs the mother was in full negotiation at the keyhole while the father was standing on a chair in the courtyard so he could deliver his own brand of persuasion through the tiny window to the Ladies. This mainly consisted of him barking: "Come out right now, you're upsetting your mother," at regular intervals.

"Have you called someone?" The mother sounded desperate.

"I was just going to ask you…" Claire began, as the door slowly opened and the mother started shrieking. The girl stood quite still in the doorway – a long black, greasy curtain of hair falling across her face, eyes cast downwards, holding her hands out in front of her. They were red and livid, already starting to blister.

"Oh my God," Claire muttered. She ran back down the corridor. "Ice!" she shouted to Kate. "Bring ice!"

The ambulance bloke was matter of fact. "What medication is she on?"

Gaynor heard the mother say Olanzapine and a name she didn't recognise and begin to recite dosages in a low voice. Gaynor's stomach went into a tight ball.

The ambulance man nodded and put a blanket around the girl's shoulders. "OK, my love, let's get you along to the hospital." He spoke again to her parents. "History of this sort of thing?"

The mother turned furiously on Claire. "How could you have the water so hot?"

Her husband pulled her towards the door. "We'll deal with it," he said. "We'll get on to Health and Safety."

"We've been fully checked," said Claire tightly. "It's all within guidelines."

"We'll see about that," said the father. "Have you seen the state of her hands?" He turned to his wife. "You go with her, I'll follow in the car. We'll do the complaints procedure later."

Gaynor's heart began to pound. She felt the adrenalin race through her body, sending shocks to her fingertips.

"It's not our fault," she cried, as customers fell silent and listened. "Your daughter burned herself deliberately."

"She shouldn't have been able to." The father stopped and faced Gaynor. Over his shoulder, she watched the girl climb into the back of the ambulance and her mother follow. The father spoke coldly. "I shall be taking it up with the Environmental Health department. That water should have been…"

Gaynor gave a hiss of frustration. "And if she'd smashed the mirror and then slashed her wrists with the broken glass? Would that have been our fault too?"

He turned on his heel. "I'm not listening to this!"

Gaynor was screeching. "Would it? Your daughter's ill. If it's anyone's fault, it's yours! You shouldn't have left her alone. You shouldn't have brought her in here. It's your responsibility – don't you dare blame us…"

"Gaynor, that's enough!" Claire had a hand on her arm.

"No, it's not!" He was going out of the door. Gaynor wanted to run after him and shake him. "They make me sick – blaming everyone else but themselves. She's mentally ill. She's self-harming." She raised her voice and yelled after the father's retreating back: "If she'd stabbed herself with one of our steak knives would you get Health and Safety in to say they're too sharp?"

"Stop it, Gaynor!" Sarah had come upstairs and was standing next to Claire. "We'll get it sorted out. Don't say anything else."

"Bloody hell!" Gaynor swung away from them, went behind the bar and pulled a bottle of Pinot Grigio from the fridge. "Jesus!"

Kate had stopped smiling.

"Are you OK sweet-pea?" Jack asked.

Gaynor glared at them both. "NO!"

The voices had started up again in the bar. It was five to six. Gaynor glowered at the knots of Happy Folkers who sat about drinking, as a guy walked in with a guitar and a Labrador dog.

"OK if I busk a couple of numbers?"

"Sure." Claire walked round the bar and smiled down at the animal.

"We don't allow dogs unless you're blind." Gaynor poured herself another drink. Claire frowned at her.

"It's fine, really," she said to the man. "You go right ahead."

"Give us all a treat," said Gaynor sourly.

Claire came back behind the bar, her voice low. "Look, I can see you're still upset, Gaynor, but you can't take it out on the customers."

"He's not a customer. He's just going to make some ungodly racket, while his mangy mongrel lies on the floor and licks its balls."

"Don't be so silly." Claire glared, her voice annoyed. "If you can't behave, I think you'd better go home."

Gaynor tossed the rest of her drink down her throat and banged the glass down sharply. "Don't worry, I'm going."

"It makes me so fucking angry." She paced up and down in front of Sam's piano. She'd found herself going there almost without thinking. There was no point going home. Even if Victor had been there, which he wasn't, he'd hardly have cared.

"What does?" Sam asked quietly.

"People blaming other people. That girl stood in there with her hands under the hot tap until she had to go to hospital and her bloody parents say it's our fault."

Sam reached up for his tobacco and pulled out a cigarette paper. "They were frightened. It's a natural reaction to look for someone to pin the blame on – it helps one make sense of it. Poor kid."

Gaynor stopped. "Poor kid?" Her voice was aggressive.

Sam put a tiny pinch from the pouch into the paper and began to roll. "She's obviously in a bad way," he said calmly.

Gaynor began walking about the room again. "Yes, she probably is, but it's always the poor depressive we feel sorry for, isn't it? The poor old flake. My mother used to cut out articles about depression. Try and make me read them so that I'd feel sorry for my father or David or whoever was currently staring at the ceiling muttering. Bought me a whole damn book on it once. How to treat a depressed person. *One*, do not tell them to snap out of it. *Two*, remember they cannot help it…"

Sam closed the lid of the piano. "They can't. We can't. I've been there, Gaynor. The depressed person often feels a lot of guilt because they feel they should be able to pull themselves together. It's an illness, Gaynor. It's just the same as…"

She scowled at him. "I know it's a fucking illness. My mother told me every day of my life. But however much you know that, however much you read, you still have to actually cope with it. You still have to put up with that person being like that day in and day bloody out. I used to want to shake David. I used to want to say: 'get a bloody grip!' Don't givel me that crap about it being like telling the man with the broken leg to skip down the High Street. I know that! OK? I bloody know it!" She was trembling.

Sam sat down. "I wasn't going to say anything like that. What about your father? Did you want to shake him too?"

"Huh." Gaynor tossed her head contemptuously. "I'd lost interest in him. Which made us about equal."

Sam flicked at his Zippo lighter and lit his little roll-up.

"One in four," said Gaynor bitterly. "One in four of us suffer from depression. That means three-quarters of the population have a hell of a lot to put up with."

She stopped and held up the bottle of Chardonnay she'd grabbed on her way out of Greens. "Do you want some of this?"

He shook his head. "No thanks."

"Don't you ever drink?"

"Sometimes."

"Don't you like it?"

He smiled. "Sometimes. I used to drink whisky. But I gave it up when I realised it didn't make any difference."

She looked at him. "It makes a difference to me. It makes me feel better."

"Doesn't look like it from where I'm standing."

She glared at him. "You don't know how I'd be if I was sober. Well I am sober, sort of."

He laughed. "You're about as sort of sober as I'm sort of flying around the room. Come here." He sat down on the sofa and patted the space beside him. "Come and tell me why this has upset you so much."

She felt calmer after another glass of wine. She refilled the goblet Sam had found her and watched him rhythmically stroking Brutus, who purred like an engine.

"Do you get support?" asked Sam quietly. "What does your husband say?"

"Victor? Oh not much. He's charming to my mother on the rare occasions he sees her. Polite to my father. Can't understand what David's all about. Thinks he's a bit of a nuisance. What's he doing still living at home at his age, etc. I don't think Victor gives it much thought. Why should he?"

"Because they're your family."

"My family." Gaynor took a mouthful of wine. "Doesn't feel like it much. I used to see David a lot. We were very close. But it's been a while now. I should get up there one weekend, I know I should. My mother phoned, she said David hasn't been very good. I said I'd see him. I have been thinking about him but what with the wine bar and Victor, and then Chloe's supposed to be coming down soon…" She trailed off.

Sam's voice was reassuring. "You can only do what you can do."

"The thing is." Gaynor looked at him, stricken. "The truth is – I don't want to go."

Sam nodded. "I can understand that," he said slowly.

"Can you?" She jumped up from the sofa. "There was one time – David was in hospital and there was this woman there waiting to see her sister. The sister had had ECT – she'd had it about six times, it was the only thing that ever worked and the woman said they just struggled along and she'd be OK for a while and then she'd gradually get worse till she had to have some more…"

Gaynor stooped and picked up her glass. "And this woman, she said to me, you could be in for a long haul so don't sacrifice yourself. Just give what you have to give because other people's depression is a black hole. That's what she said. She said you could throw your whole life in there." Gaynor made a sudden sucking noise like waste being swirled away down a pipe. "And it would swallow you all up and still never be enough…"

Sam leant out and took her hand. Gaynor felt her chin wobble. "That's what my poor mother has done – chucked her whole life in and they've gulped her down. You know she's sort of washed away now – if you look at her, she looks like she's had all the life sucked out of her. Last time I saw her she was wearing this awful droopy beige cardigan. I got cross – said why didn't she put on some colours for a change…"

Sam pulled her down to sit beside him again. "Do you miss her?"

Gaynor made a contemptuous noise. "Didn't really ever have her to miss." For a second she had a lump in her throat.

Sam was speaking very softly. "You look as though you need to cry."

She swallowed more wine. "Nah, I don't really do that."

"Perhaps you should."

She shook her head. "I haven't cried for a long time. I feel like it sometimes – you know, the tears come into my eyes." She gave a short laugh. "I grizzle a bit but I always stop. I never cry properly. I wouldn't sob. It always seems such a lonely thing to do."

"Doesn't have to be." Sam was rolling another cigarette.

"I thought you said you were giving that up."

"I am – that's why I'm making small ones."

"Small? That one's hardly worth it – it's going to be over in one puff."

"When I got ill," he said, ignoring her, "I cried for the first time in years and years and years. And then I started to recover. One of the doctors told me after Eleanor died, not crying's not good. If you can't cry, you're in trouble."

He ran his tongue along the minuscule sausage of paper. "Tell me more about your mother. What about when you and David were small? Was she around then?"

"Yeah. She was around. She was always around." Her face tingled. "She was there but she was taken up with other things. I mean she was good – she looked after us and cared for us but my father was awful and somehow…" Gaynor stopped. She felt as though she was ready to split apart with all the unexpressed, half-formed feelings she couldn't articulate. Her fingers closed up on themselves. "It's too long ago. I can't explain."

He took hold of one of her hands, slid a thumb into her tightly bunched fist and gently unwound her fingers again.

"Let it out," he said.

She shook her head, shuddering.

"You're having a hard time," he said. "Victor, Chloe, worrying about David…" He took the wine glass from her other hand and put it down on the table next to him. Then he put his arm around her. She had the peculiar sensation of watching herself, sitting there, holding herself so rigidly. Then her face turned into his shoulder. She felt him patting her back as though she were a child. "That's right," he was saying soothingly. "Let it all out…"

She opened her eyes and looked curiously at the ceiling and then woke properly with a jolt. It took some seconds to remember where she was. She lay in her T-Shirt and pants, shivering beneath the quilt. There was nothing much in the room apart from the double bed. White walls, a chest of drawers. Sam had pulled the curtains across but the dawn light came through the gap in the middle, making the room grey with half-light.

There was a glass of water on the bedside cupboard. She sat up and reached out for it as all at once everything came back – a kaleidoscope of images: her shouting in the wine bar, snapping at Claire, falling sobbing on Sam. Her head ached. She remembered staggering across the room, telling Sam she felt sick.

A stab of anxiety and shame hit her in the solar plexus so hard it made her cry out. She rocked herself in the bed, desperate to shut out the feelings. The door opened and Sam came in. He was still dressed in the same green polo shirt and faded shorts he'd had on last night. "It's OK."

He sat on the edge of the bed, touched her shoulder. "It's OK," he said again.

"No, no it isn't." She began to thrash about, one hand clutching her stomach. "I feel awful, I feel terrible." She was shaking. "I feel ill."

"Are you cold?" For a moment she thought he was going to get into bed with her, offer to warm her up. For a moment she wanted him to. But he went out of the room and came back with a towelling robe. "Sit up and put this on." It was huge. She put her arms in and tried to lift her body up to get it round her. He tugged at her. "Get out of bed."

He drew it round her as though he were dressing a child and tied the cord. Then he lifted the covers and she climbed back beneath them.

"I'm sorry," she said.

"Move over."

Yes. He was going to get in to bed with her. She suddenly wanted that more than anything else. With a start she realised she wanted to be held by him, made love to, kissed, caressed…

She held out her arms as he slid, still in his clothes, beside her – but he put his arm around her, pulling her head on to his shoulder. Heat shot through her body and she pressed against him, her hand moving across to stroke his stomach. His hand stilled hers. Moved it gently and firmly away, folded it back against her body, and hugged her closer.

"You go back to sleep," he said, stroking her hair. "You're all right now."

She lay there in his warmth, caught between disappointment and gratitude. Wrapped in the comforting roughness of the towelling, her face buried into his shoulder.

"Don't you want me?" she asked, feeling tears well in her eyes again.

"Shhhh." He cradled her in both arms. "I'm looking after you," he said. "You sleep."

"I can't," she said. But, somehow, the painful knot in her stomach loosened and, safe in Sam's arms, she did.

10. Australian Shiraz

Inviting aromas, rich and spicy
with a disappointing finish.

Gaynor sat in a chair outside Sam's back door, still wearing his dressing gown, eating the toast he'd made her. The garden here was nowhere near as big as in the front. There was just a small patio area with a square of lawn and a few tubs.

All the glorious colour was in the front but Sam had led her out here, presumably thinking she shouldn't sit in another man's bathrobe in full view of the streams of Folk fans and locals wandering along the cliff top to the town.

"Won't Victor have phoned home?" Sam asked. "Won't he be wondering where you were?"

Gaynor shrugged. "Probably not. He can phone my mobile if he's worried, can't he." She pulled a face. "But he won't be. And I don't much care if he is."

She smiled at Sam. She felt strangely peaceful in an odd, pummelled, washed-out way. Like she'd walked twenty miles and just got out of a hot bath or woken after a night of very good sex.

Which she hadn't. She didn't know how long he'd stayed in bed with her. When she'd woken next, the room had been full of bright sunshine and she'd been startled to see from the bedside clock that it was almost eleven. She'd come downstairs to find Sam reading the paper. He'd got different clothes on and had shaved. He'd looked up as if her being there was quite normal. "Tea?" he'd asked, matter-of-factly.

Now he looked at her seriously. "Come on. Be sensible. You'd better get home."

She looked at him coquettishly. "Are you throwing me out? Have I overstayed my welcome?"

He sat down in a garden chair opposite her. "Don't be silly. I'm thinking of you. I don't want you to get into trouble – sounds as if you've got enough complications there already."

Gaynor crunched at the last corner of toast and stretched. "I feel better. I feel very philosophical this morning."

"That's because you've had an emotional release. But the facts haven't changed. You've still got a marriage that needs sorting out."

Gaynor pouted. She thought about him climbing into bed with her and wished he'd put his arms around her again. "Torchlight procession tonight. Do you like Folk Week or are you glad it's nearly over?"

"I don't know. Don't know much about it."

She looked at him in surprise. "What – don't you go to anything? But you still see it and hear it – you can't really avoid it living here, can you?"

"It's the first year I've been here. I've seen the old Morris dancers wandering about – I heard a couple of guys playing in your bar the other night…" He shrugged.

"Oh, I thought you'd lived here ages."

"No."

"Let's go tonight," she said brightly. "I'm not working – Kate and Jack are both on. And Claire's brother Neill and his mate Seb are staying – they'll help if things get frantic. Let's wander around the pubs and see the procession. You'll love it – it's a great atmosphere."

Sam raised his eyebrows. "Is that a good idea? Should you be walking around with a strange man who's not your husband?"

Gaynor shook her head dismissively. "It's Folk Week – there'll be thousands of people out and nobody will take a blind bit of notice. Anyway," she went on, "I'm allowed friends aren't I? He obviously has them!"

"And do you?"

She looked sideways at him. "Are you asking if I have affairs?"

"I suppose I am, though it's none of my business,"

"Well I don't. I think people think I do. I'm quite flirty and cuddly and I mess around sometimes – well, you know that –" She felt herself blush. "But I've never – you know."

She felt all at once guilty and compelled to tell the truth. She gazed at the scarlet mass of red geranium that burst from an old chimney pot on the paving stones and took a deep breath. "I nearly did once. I was drunk –" she laughed self-consciously "– again and this guy I've known for ages – he always tries it on – he's very good-looking and all the women fancy him and, I don't know – Victor was away and being awful half the time anyway – it was when he started getting all these funny moods and Danny, he was just sort of there…" She stopped and met Sam's eyes, appealing to him to understand. He looked back calmly.

"I was out with my friend Lizzie," Gaynor went on, "and she's worse than me! We ended up at Lizzie's flat with Danny and his mate Pete, and Danny made it very clear, you know. I was flattered and I very nearly but…"

"Is he the one who was waiting for you the other night out there?" Sam jerked his head backwards towards the front of the house.

She looked at him, alarmed. "Were you watching?"

"I just happened to look out of the window and I saw him spring out at you. I was a bit concerned – I just watched for a moment in case you needed any help. But you seemed to know him so – " He shrugged.

"Yes, he gave me a lift home. Nothing happened…"

"As I said, it's none of my business."

"No, but I'm telling you it didn't. I feel bad about the way I behave. You know – I still feel awkward about that first night with you in Greens. I always wake up in the morning and cringe at myself, but I don't know – when I've had a drink I…"

He picked up her mug. "You're as you are. No point beating yourself."

"You didn't like it much."

"It was a bit of a surprise!" He smiled. "And I'm a miserable old git. But no harm done. The only one you seem to hurt is yourself. More tea?"

He went inside. She sat in the sunshine and drew her feet up on to the edge of her seat and hugged her knees. She felt peculiar. There was something of the confessional in talking to Sam. Part of her felt a huge urge to tell him all her sins. To hear his soothing tones telling her she was all right really – even if she knew she wasn't.

She suddenly wanted to tell him everything...

But she smiled brightly when he came back. "What made you come to Broadstairs, then?"

He put a fresh tea down and sat next to her, gazing down the garden.

"We used to come to Margate when I was a child. When I came out of the police, I was in a bad way. Debra, my daughter, she suggested we came down here for a day out – she was trying to cheer me up."

Gaynor laughed. "By coming to Margate? Who needs enemies when you've got relatives?"

He smiled wryly. "She meant well. But it wasn't as I remembered. I didn't feel comfortable there at all. But then we drove over here. Just by accident really – just drifted along the coast. Parked on the jetty, had a wander about – Debra wanted fish and chips – and then we came up here and this was for sale..." His voice was distant, almost as if he were talking to himself.

"It was the garden." He was staring down at the flint wall at the bottom of the small patch of grass. "It was completely overgrown and neglected but I could see what was there." He shook his head. "I told Debra I wanted to make an offer on it. I barely looked inside the house."

"What did she say?"

"She told me to think about it. I said I had."

"So," he said, suddenly brisk again. "I sold up and came down here. Nothing to keep me in London any more. My son Joe's abroad, teaching English in Italy, Debra's got her own life – she's very capable and independent – and property prices down here were a fraction of up there. I swapped a flat for this!"

"How long ago did your wife die?" Gaynor felt hesitant, wondering whether Sam would keep talking or suddenly clam up again.

"Six years ago, nearly. Debra was sixteen, Joe two years younger. Terrible age to lose a mother. Well, any age is, I suppose."

"Is your mother alive?" Now she'd started questioning, Gaynor couldn't seem to stop.

He shook his head. "No. Neither of them are now. I think that's what cracked me up. There was Eleanor dying and having to hold things together for the kids and working all sorts of hours and then my father died and my mother just fell apart. I dealt with that – I had to – but after she'd gone, I fell apart myself. And then –" he gave an odd bitter laugh "– the kids had to look after me. Well they didn't have to – I told them to get on with their own things but they were wonderful." He sounded suddenly moved and stood up, picking up their mugs and her plate.

"I expect that's because you'd been wonderful to them," said Gaynor. "I can imagine you being a lovely father." She suddenly felt all emotional again and turned gratefully towards the cat. "Oh look – hello, gorgeous."

A sparrow that had been perched on a tub flapped away in alarm as Brutus sprang up on to the arm of her chair and stepped on to her lap, back arched. She stroked him and he rubbed the side of his face into her with pleasure.

"Where've you been?" Sam dropped his free hand on to the back of the cat's head and he purred deeply. "You been down the jetty scrounging again? He came back the other day reeking of fish," he said in an ordinary voice. "Knew straight away what he'd been up to." He moved his hand to Gaynor's

110

shoulder. "And that's what they'll say about you if you don't go home!"

She stood in the kitchen doorway once she was dressed, watching him rinse the breakfast things.

"So, shall we go out tonight?" she asked shyly.

He slotted a plate into the plastic drainer. "If you're sure it's OK."

She nodded. "It's OK. I'll go home and get sorted out. I'll come back at eight or something…" She hesitated for a moment and then crossed the room, put her arms around him and hugged him. "Thank you for having me."

A flicker of amusement crossed his face; his hands were wet and soapy but he raised one eyebrow as he squeezed her back with the crook of one arm. And she found herself smiling too. And wondering for a mad moment, as a frisson ran through her, what it would have been like if he really had…

The house felt strange and empty as if she'd been away a long time instead of just one night. Chloe had left a message on the answer-phone at ten the night before. Gaynor looked at her untouched bed and suddenly felt a stab of guilt – what would Victor say if he knew she'd spent the night in another man's, however innocently? Suppose he'd phoned the wine bar and Claire had told him she'd gone early? She shook her head. He wouldn't do that – he'd try home and then ring her mobile. But there was never much signal down at the bottom of the town there so if he couldn't get through…

As she looked at it, the phone rang again, making her jump.

"Where've you been?" Chloe demanded.

Gaynor felt herself spluttering: "When? What do you mean?"

"I called last night and this morning. Dad's mobile's been switched off the whole time and yours…"

"I was working in the wine bar. Didn't get home till the early hours," said Gaynor, making a snap decision to lie through her teeth and hope for the best. "I was late up this morning – must have slept through the phone or been in the shower or something. Victor's away – there's a big presentation up in Edinburgh – some radio station pitch or something."

"Oh!" Chloe sounded displeased. "I wanted to see when Ollie and I could come down."

"Well, anytime," said Gaynor with forced cheer, adding, "when Victor's back of course. I don't know what…"

"And why's his phone switched off?"

"I really don't know."

But it was a very good question, thought Gaynor, dialling the number herself. The answer-phone cut in at once. She slammed down the receiver ready to slap that robotic-sounding operator – she'd heard enough of her lately to last a lifetime.

On impulse she dialled EBDT.

"His daughter's been trying to get hold of him," she told Ziggy, not wanting to sound too desperate.

Ziggy was unfazed. "They've got back-to-back meetings all day," she said brightly. "You want me to get him paged at the hotel? Or I'll get hold of Laurence?" Gaynor relaxed. So he was at least where he said he was.

"Don't worry, I'll catch him later." Gaynor made her own voice sound casual.

"Should all be over by about four," said Ziggy. "They're on the 18.10 back to Heathrow."

"Oh yes," said Gaynor, as if she knew already, although her heart began to beat a little harder. "And where is he this evening? He did tell me but…"

There was the tiniest pause. "Not sure I've got that down," said Ziggy. "Dinner with the client, I'm pretty sure…"

Yeah, right, thought Gaynor. So why not stay up in Edinburgh another night and have dinner there? Ziggy didn't know where Victor was going, that was the truth. But playing

112

the good secretary, she was prepared to cobble something together.

"I think it might be at Crystal's," Gaynor said, pretending to remember. Ziggy sounded relieved. "Could well be," she said cheerily. "Have a good weekend yourself."

Oh sure, Gaynor thought as she put the phone down. If it was work on a Friday night then why didn't Ziggy know about it? And if it wasn't, then what was he doing that was more pressing than coming home? They'd be clear of the airport by 7.30pm – plenty of time to get back to Broadstairs if he wanted to.

But as she showered, scrubbed and exfoliated, smoothed scented body lotion along her limbs, took extra care with her hair and make-up and dithered over what to wear, she realised that she was quite glad he hadn't. Because, right now, she wanted to go out with Sam.

He'd showered too. He was wearing a soft denim shirt and smelt of soap. She suddenly wanted to feel his arms around her again, to put her head on his shoulder once more.

"You look nice," he said.

She looked down at her pink jeans and cropped T-shirt and ran a hand across her stomach. "I've been wondering whether to get my belly button pierced."

He screwed up his nose. "I wouldn't."

She stood in the garden as he locked his front door. The air was soft – she could smell the jasmine that climbed up the side wall. The sea opposite was oily smooth, the evening sun gleaming on it. All her senses suddenly seemed heightened – colours were vibrant, sounds clear, smells evocative; even her skin felt sensitive. She looked at his fingers as he dropped the keys into his pocket, knowing he couldn't but wishing he would take her hand. He walked along a yard apart from her, seeming awkward.

"So," he said as they wound down the path to the jetty, behind knots of holiday-makers, "where are you taking me?"

"There's a great group on in the Frigate," she said. "We'll start there?"

But from the jetty, beyond the Coastguard's with its crooked walls and beams and white rendering, she heard the dancers. Tinkling bells and mellow chords from the accordion sounded above the large crowd. She glanced up at Sam and saw he was looking that way too.

'Do you like Morris dancing?" she asked hopefully, already feeling uplifted by the music that floated across.

He nodded thoughtfully. "There's a sort of innocence to it, isn't there?"

The jetty was packed. Families sat on benches eating chips in paper, couples wandered entwined, children were pushed in buggies or carried on shoulders, babies slept in slings. Lying the length of one of the benches a huge bearded man was snoring, his pewter pot lying empty on his ample stomach. "He's had a good day," said Sam.

Everyone seemed to have done. Gaynor smiled at a toddler shrieking with glee from her father's shoulders, watched the knots of tanned youngsters with their plastic glasses of beer and Bacardi Breezers. She jerked her head at Sam to follow her and began to edge her way through the crowd until they came to the inner ring surrounding the dancers.

A large woman in a voluminous patchwork dress smiled and pushed her children in front of her so Sam and Gaynor could squeeze in and get a view of the six big men in their baggy white blouses, green neckerchiefs and red trousers. She'd always been taken with Morris dancing. These were big men but they fell lightly on their feet, the bells strung around their knees jangling as they skipped too and fro, the accordion played by an old guy in coat tails, his brown wrinkled face split into a grin beneath his battered top hat.

Gaynor looked happily at Sam, enjoying the familiar scent of sea and beer, watching the dazzle of colours in the evening sunshine.

"And how many years have you been doing this?" he asked as they dropped coins in one of the yellow buckets prominently rattled before them and wandered back along the jetty.

"A fair few. I've been in Broadstairs ten this summer."

"What brought you?"

"Victor. After he rescued me from the gutter."

Sam raised his eyebrows. "Is that your appraisal of what happened, or his?"

She flushed. "Oh it's just a joke he makes. I was working part-time in a nightclub, living in a grim old bed-sit in Kilburn. I think he fancied himself as Rex Harrison – whisking me away from it all! The first month I moved down here was August – and Folk Week."

She remembered how enchanted she'd been. By the beach and the jetty, the little back streets, the white-washed cottages. How lucky she'd felt. How grateful…

They were still some distance from the Tartar Frigate but already she could hear the music pulsating through the open door of the old flint pub. As they reached it, she glanced through at the packed bodies.

She laughed. "Are you ready for this?"

"Mmmn," he said, uncertainly. "The music sounds good…"

"Come on then. What do you want to drink?"

The heat and noise hit them like a warm wall. Gaynor began to wriggle through the solid mass of drinkers towards the bar. The odours of ale and suntan lotion, sweat and excitement mixed with the cigarette smoke that hung in a blue haze beneath the low beams. Over to her left, a group were belting out an Irish jig. She saw Sam's head standing out above the crowd but the players were almost hidden from view. Still the music scorched the air, vibrated through the ancient floor boards and up into her feet. She already wanted to dance.

By the time she'd been served, Sam was near the front. He turned and saw her coming, pushing a shoulder and arm towards her, drawing her through to stand beside him. "Look." He gestured, taking his beer, pointing to where the fiddle player, his eyes closed in some sort of ecstasy, crouched low over his bow, the strings blurring in a dizzying cascade of notes. The guitar man swayed to his strumming and the thud from the bodhran set her body twitching. She moved rhythmically to the music, tapping her foot, rocking gently against Sam.

He appeared transfixed, standing quite still, watching. As the number ended and the pub erupted into fervent applause, he clapped hard, then turned and gave her a huge smile.

"He's good on that fiddle," he said when they'd retreated outside for air at the end of the first set.

"I haven't heard you play your piano yet," Gaynor said, perching on the wooden railings that edged the jetty and looking out across the beach.

He shook his head dismissively. "Oh, I'm rusty now. I wasn't bad once but..." He shrugged. "Life goes in other directions. There was never time – always too much else going on with the kids and stuff. I tried to get Debra to play – she was good when she was young – seven, eight years old. The teacher said she had a real aptitude but she lost interest." He smiled. "Debra's very clever but she's efficient rather than arty. Know what I mean?"

Gaynor fiddled with one of the plastic cups they'd been given to take drinks outside. "I'm neither. I always wished I'd played an instrument. David used to play the violin but my father put him off. Couldn't stand the sound of him practising."

"You look artistic to me. Your jewellery, your clothes and things. You strike me as creative."

"No, I'm not really."

"What are you good at, then?"

She flushed again. "Nothing." She took a swallow of her drink, stung. It sounded like the sort of thing Victor would say.

116

"Hey!" He touched her arm. "I didn't mean it like that. I meant, genuinely, tell me about what you are good at, where your talents lie."

"I don't have any."

"I don't believe that."

They passed Greens on their way up Harbour Street. Gaynor could see it was filled to bursting point, bodies crammed together behind the glass of the large front window, groups standing on the pavement outside. She felt a moment's tug of guilt, thinking of Sarah and Claire trying to deal with all those people, but she had phoned Sarah earlier and Sarah had said it was still OK.

"Do you need to go in?" Sam asked. She hesitated for a moment, then shook her head and led him on up the hill to where a duet of keyboard and sax were playing at The Nickleby.

It wasn't so hot in here but their bodies were still crushed together – the length of her arm was pressed against his. She felt the reverberations of the music run through her. She stole a look at his profile; he was standing very upright, looking directly ahead, watching the group intently. She looked at his strong features, the set of his jaw. There was something very 'straight' about him – honest. Like you'd know where you were. Quite different from Victor – she was beginning to wonder if he ever said anything she could believe. She looked at Sam's fingers curled around his half-full pint of beer. The same pint he'd been holding for the last hour, while she'd had several glasses of vile pub wine.

She found herself thinking of those hands touching her. She realised with a shock how much she wanted him.

When they left, the light was fading but the air was still warm and soft. Gaynor felt strangely cocooned amongst the floods of revellers, hooting and laughing as they jostled for their places on the pavement for the torchlight procession. She watched young girls in minute skirts and loud boys in baggy jeans and yawny-eyed children wearing illuminated headbands sparkling red and green and fractious parents trying to keep hold of them. She felt light and happy.

A never-ending stream of people poured along the High Street, holding plastic beer mugs or ice creams, candy floss or burgers. Minute by minute the throng on the pavements grew thicker. Clusters of foil balloons bobbed above the heads and the air was filled with the cries of children either pleading for one or wailing after getting their wish and then letting it slip from their fingers.

Vendors carried armfuls of flashing headgear and pushed trolleys of sticky toffee apples. The air was filled with the smell of fried onions from the hot dog cart. Gaynor felt all at once that stimulation of being part of a crowd and the comfort of being lost in one.

She put a hand on Sam's arm. "OK?"

He moved aside to let her stand in front of him at the edge of the road, so she'd have a better view, nodding at her.

From the top of the High Street lights shone. "They're on their way, Mother," came a loud northern voice a few yards away. A couple of policemen made their way along either side of the road. "Move back, please. Keep in."

And then the police van with blue lights flashing and reflecting off the shop windows came past, followed by a dragon. Eight feet tall and black-cloaked, it made a show of peering into the crowd, snapping its jaws, stooping down low to bring its long teeth up into children's faces to much squealing and adult laughter. Coins were slotted down its throat and it swung on, followed by the first of the torch bearers, holding up their flames high into the night.

Troupes of dancers in costume stopped and twirled to the strains of an accordion. A fire-eater slid a burning taper into his mouth and roared out flames, then more Morris dancers, and jesters with bells on their toes, and harlequins, came jauntily down the hill. On the procession swept, full of music and colour and dancing and twinkling lights. Here and there, someone in mufti came by holding a torch and either a self-conscious grin or a slightly bewildered air, as if they weren't quite sure what they were caught up in.

Finally, too soon, the brass band marched slowly past followed by the surge of the crowd as the people-packed pavements burst back into the road.

Sam was grinning. He took Gaynor's arm and then dropped it again, as though suddenly embarrassed. Ignoring him, she tucked her arm purposefully back through his. "It's OK," she said as they shuffled their way behind a sea of people, along Albion Street where the fish and chip queues stretched for miles and the pubs spilled their drinkers on to the pavement. "Nobody gives a shit."

The crowd thinned and they left the noise behind as they walked up the path towards his cottage. She wondered if he was going to invite her in. She didn't want to go home yet. She knew the house would feel big and empty there on her own. Victor had seemed unbothered about missing most of the week – once he had loved it as much as she did, but now he clearly had other preoccupations. She thought of Sam the night before – the way he'd held her and patted her, had made her feel so cared for. She wanted to sit with him again, to talk to him, to feel safe.

They stopped at his gate. He pushed it open and stood there, looking slightly ill at ease. She put a hand back on his arm. "I've had a really good time tonight." She smiled.

He looked at her seriously. "So have I."

She felt a little drunk and reckless. "Oh, look there's Brutus." She used the cat as an excuse to push the gate further open, move past him, cross the front lawn and sweep the cat up into her arms. "How are you, beautiful boy?" She sat down in one of the wooden chairs outside the French doors and put her handbag on the table. "What a fabulous night," she said, kicking off her shoes and shaking back her hair. Brutus wriggled free of her grasp and leapt gracefully from her arms, winding himself briefly around Sam's legs and then disappearing around the side of the house.

Sam stood opposite her, his hands leaning against the back of the other chair. "What are you going to do now? How are you getting home? Shall I call you a cab or … I'll walk you but I don't want to put you in an awkward position…"

She shook her head. "No need for that – I walk home from the wine bar all the time. You don't get much safer than Broadstairs, do you?"

"Probably not," he said. "But lots of women wouldn't do it."

Gaynor shrugged. "Sarah worries about it but it never occurs to me to be at all alarmed. It's funny," she went on, "because I'm afraid of the dark. But only when I'm inside. Outside I feel alive and sort of filled with positive energy walking alone at night. Indoors, though, I have to have the lights on. When Victor's away I have lamps lit all over the place. It makes me feel claustrophobic, otherwise. I imagine things leaping on me…" She risked a provocative smile.

He nodded. "I can understand that," he said straight-faced.

She smiled up at him again. "So I'll be fine but I thought you might make me a coffee first."

"Sure. I was just thinking of you. It's late. Your husband…"

"I've told you, he's away. He won't know what time I get home."

He looked at her for a moment then unlocked the door.

"I don't want to go home at all really," she said when he returned with two mugs. "Look at all those stars."

They both looked upwards at the velvety, diamond-studded sky.

"I know," he said quietly.

She toyed with her teaspoon. "I'd rather stay here with you."

"I know," he said again. "But you're not thinking it through. It's not a good idea."

She felt rebuffed. "You didn't mind last night."

He stirred his coffee, his voice reasonable. "You were very upset last night – I was looking after you. Doesn't mean I felt comfortable with it."

"Oh." She felt all at once foolish and hurt and quite unable to stop herself pushing on. "Oh, so you didn't want me here."

"I didn't say that," he said, in the same calm tones. "Look, you've had quite a bit to drink and you're trying to create an argument where there isn't one. I tried to take care of you last night and I would again. If you really want to stay here you can – the spare bed is made up – but I don't think you should."

"I don't want to stay in the spare bed…" She knew she'd die a thousand deaths in the morning but she was locked into it now. The bold, pushy Gaynor-on-the-pull that sprang to life after a bottle of wine was in full flood, and all sober Gaynor could do was look on and prepare to cringe. "I want to sleep in your bed. I want to make love with you!"

He appeared unfazed. "You feel like that because I've looked after you." He gave a small smile. "A bit like falling for your therapist. It's not real. And," he went on, "you'd feel terribly guilty in the morning and so would I. For taking advantage of your emotional state when you've been drinking, not to mention sleeping with another man's wife."

She glared at him. "Taking advantage of me? How quaint."

"I'm old-fashioned."

"And I know my own mind."

He remained resolute. "And I know mine and I know what would be honourable and what wouldn't…"

"Honourable?" For a horrible moment she thought she was going to cry. "So you're kicking me out and you don't want me."

"I'm your friend and I'm here for you. Do you want more coffee?"

"No, I'm going home."

She picked up her denim jacket and pushed her feet back into her shoes. "Goodbye," she said, as she swung her handbag over her shoulder, knowing she was behaving like a spoiled child, her feelings a mass of hurt rejection and humiliation and a huge, gaping pit of loss.

"I won't bother you again," she said over her shoulder, as she prepared to sweep out.

He put out a hand and grabbed her arm, holding her still for a moment. "I'm here for you," he said. "I'm here and I'm your friend."

He let her go, adding, almost sadly. "Remember that if you change your mind."

11. Chilean Merlot

Powerful-bodied with a mellow aftertaste.

"I am not going to change my mind."

"But why can't I?" Charlie glared at Sarah, his bottom lip stuck out in belligerence.

Sarah held his yesterday's lunch box at arm's length and turned on the hot tap, sighing in exasperation. "Because you don't need it."

"Luke's got one."

"Luke's at high school and travels on the bus. When you're at secondary school I'll get you one." Somehow, she thought. At the moment she could barely keep up with the groceries.

Charlie remained unmoved. "I'm the only person at school who hasn't got one now."

She rinsed and scrubbed. "I know that isn't true."

"It is true."

Sarah shook the drips from the plastic and picked up a tea-towel. "Kieran hasn't got one, nor has Matthew, nor, I am quite sure, has Connor."

"I was talking, said Charlie, with deep disdain, "about the people I *like*."

Sarah packed cling-filmed sandwiches and crisps. Added a Kit-Kat and an apple. Topped it all with a paper napkin that would come back untouched.

"Well, I'm sorry, but you're going to have to wait. Luke didn't get one at your age and even if I wanted to buy you one, mobile phones are very expensive."

Charlie kicked at his school rucksack which was in the middle of the kitchen floor. "That's what you say about everything."

"I'm afraid it's true." And whose fault is that, she wanted to shriek at him. Who left us with no money and only a third share in the roof over our heads?

"I bet Dad would get me one," Charlie said, watching her carefully.

She snapped the lid of the lunchbox shut, banged it down on the table with unnecessary force and turned on him. "You ask him, then," she said, "when you see him."

She was immediately suffused with shame. Paul had made no effort to get in touch with the kids for three weeks now. She knew she should try and phone him, tell him how Charlie, in particular, was missing him. But she shrank from the call – unsure how well she could cope with hearing his voice. Perhaps if he'd had a good day at the bookies or casino he would buy Charlie a mobile – hell, he might buy them all one – but just as likely he'd be morose and aggressive or full of bluster about tomorrow or next week, how that would be the big one…

It must be easier, Sarah thought, if your husband was a straightforward bastard. If he stayed out every night, if he beat you up…

Even Gaynor didn't know the full extent of the problem – she knew they'd had financial difficulties at the end but she thought Paul's business had gone down. She'd assumed that the final straw for Sarah was finding out Paul was sleeping with a blonde cashier from the amusement arcade. Funny, thought Sarah ironically, that somehow that was less shaming than the fact that he'd poured the housekeeping for a week into a fruit machine first.

She thought about Richard. He would never do anything like that, she was sure, though what he *would* do was anyone's guess. She couldn't figure him out. Each time he'd taken her out he'd been lovely – attentive, kind, interested in all she had to say – but between times it was like he'd had a huge burst of regret, realised he'd made the most terrible mistake and just wanted to run for cover.

She wouldn't see him for days and when he did appear he would be behind a newspaper, looking like a rabbit caught in headlights when she went to speak to him. I don't need that, she said to herself in the mirror as she tried to comb her red wiry hair into some sort of shape with which to hit the school run. I don't need it at all.

She looked hard at her face. It wasn't only her hair – rising joyfully to weeks of neglect – that was totally out of control. Her eyebrows needed plucking, there were all sorts of extra lines around her eyes, her skin, always pale, looked white and washed out. She had none of Gaynor's casual glamour or Claire's look of cool efficiency. What did he see in her? And if he saw anything, why didn't he see it all the time?

She yawned. Bel had climbed into her bed at five this morning after a bad dream and she'd only dozed after that. It would be one a.m. before she'd be able to crawl back beneath the duvet. Whatever had possessed her to get involved with this bar?

Because there hadn't been much choice. This way she had a job and a home for the kids. And it was a job she'd enjoy, normally. If she didn't have the children to worry about. If she wasn't so tired…

She rubbed at her temples, flipping open the bottle of painkillers on the bathroom shelf and checking the contents. Her period was starting, she felt bloated and heavy. Oh, for a day in bed!

Bel appeared, Scarface in her arms. Sarah made herself smile. "Teeth?" she asked. "Time to go in a minute." Luke had already slouched off to school, Charlie had disappeared to some corner to mull over the unfairness of life. Sarah had a wine delivery at nine and the butcher arriving shortly after. Then Claire would want to discuss the Specials for the week and no doubt feel the need to run through the accounts in a way that, for all Sarah understood, might as well have been delivered in Swahili.

She wondered whether Claire was regretting going into business with her. She was always friendly and kind but Sarah sensed a contained impatience about her, a disappointment, as if she was slightly bewildered that the Sarah she had got was not the Sarah she remembered from hotel kitchens of the past. This Sarah was more tired and anxious, more inclined to bad temper and forgetting to reorder the tortilla chips when they ran out.

This Sarah, she thought, as she shepherded Bel and Charlie down the stairs and across the empty wine bar, was not the same person at all. This Sarah – who had once run catering operations for the great and good, who had stepped into Claire's family hotel kitchen and organised a whole wedding breakfast for a hundred and fifty guests when the chef threw a tantrum and walked out – was now just a single mother of three, barely keeping her head above water.

"It will get easier," Claire had said, sounding reassuring, the only time Sarah had voiced doubts. Claire had her eye on the future. She saw a chain of wine bars, an empire of stripped floorboards and beautiful people and the money rolling in. Gaynor encouraged her in this fantasy, and why wouldn't she? For Gaynor it was a game – an entertaining diversion, something to take her mind off the fact Victor no longer seemed to give a damn. She hardly needed it to pay the electric bill.

Out of the corner of her eye, the answer-phone was flashing behind the bar. Early, thought Sarah. Was that Gaynor now, in a state over the latest Victor instalment? Claire in overdrive making more adjustments to the week's rotas?

She almost stopped to listen but in the end kept Bel and Charlie moving. If it was Paul, euphoric from a night at the roulette wheel, she'd never get them to school.

"When are we seeing Dad?" Charlie asked at the traffic lights.

"Soon, I expect." Sarah gave him the bright smile she knew didn't fool him any longer.

Charlie looked out of the window. "Where is he, anyway?" he asked in his best offhand tone, that didn't fool her, either.

"Away working, I think," she lied valiantly. "We'll give his mobile a call at the weekend, shall we?"

Charlie didn't reply.

"Mummy," said Bel from the back seat, "can we get another cat so Scarface has a friend?"

The large tom was on the bar when she got back. "Get upstairs or out, you," she said, shooing him off. "If you must live with us, you've got to be civilised about it!" He sauntered over to the fireplace and began to wash himself. Sarah moved behind the pumps to the phone and answer-machine and pressed Play.

One new message, the robotic voice intoned, received at six-fifty-two a.m. Wednesday, September fourteenth...

She idly straightened an ashtray on the bar, frowning as a set of crackles and indistinct mumbling came over the speaker.

What? She hit Replay, bending over the machine to listen to the message more intently.

Her heart began to thump as the words became clearer.

"You won't have that winebar much longer you fucking bitch. I am going to get you..."

"Keep calm," Gaynor said. "It could be directed at any of us." Her mind raced through possible candidates. She could see from Claire's worried frown she was doing the same.

"But I'm the one who lives here," said Sarah, agitated. "On my own with three children. I don't like it."

"Let me listen to it again." Gaynor replayed the message. They all leaned towards the machine straining to hear the words. It was a male voice, sounding slurred, maybe drunk. Gaynor half thought she recognised something in the raspy

127

tones but they'd listened to it so many times that maybe it had simply grown familiar.

"Could it be anything to do with Paul?" Gaynor asked gently. Sarah was still white.

Sarah shook her head. "I've thought about that. I don't think so – it's not his voice and really it's just not his style. I mean he's not that hostile to me. I know it was pretty acrimonious at the end but even so…"

"It could be anyone," Claire said, calmly. "Someone we've thrown out or upset." She turned to Sarah. "Remember that drunk bloke you refused to serve the other night?" Gaynor could see she was trying to be reassuring. "Could be someone like that. Still drunk."

"What about the father of that girl who burned herself?" offered Gaynor.

Claire shook her head. "No, he had a much more cultured voice. And he was just upset at the time – he's never been back to us, has he?"

Gaynor thought about it. "Anyway," she remembered, "the first call had come in that morning, hadn't it?"

"First one?" Sarah looked at them both in turn. "Why didn't you tell me?"

"Didn't want to worry you," said Claire. "It just said 'you old dog' or something. "I didn't take it too seriously. We were busy with the breakfasts."

"I wish I'd known! And why so early in the morning all the time?" Sarah frowned. "Those calls with the breathing. They were left at four or five a.m."

"Night worker?" Gaynor mused. "Or unemployed – sits up drinking? Claire's right – he sounds pissed to me."

"Well whoever it is, I'm frightened," said Sarah.

"We'll deal with it," said Claire, firmly. "I'll phone BT. They must be able to do something."

"He'd withheld the number again," Sarah looked doubtful. "Like before."

"They must still be able to trace it if they want to." Claire was already dialling. She nodded meaningfully at Gaynor. "Get the coffee on."

"Try not to think about it," Gaynor said ineffectually as she handed Sarah a cappuccino. "We've done all we can now – we'll have to leave it to the phone lot and the police."

Sarah tore the top from a sachet of sugar and poured the contents on to the milky froth in her cup. "You really think they'll do anything?"

Claire frowned. "They'd better! BT know the number. They won't give it to us but they said if the police ask for it, then they'll pass it over. The policewoman I spoke to said they'd look into it. I expect they'll track him down and warn him off."

Sarah stirred her coffee. "I want to know who it is."

Claire paused at the top of the stairs. "And we're going to find out."

"Tell me about Richard anyway," said Gaynor when Claire had gone down to the kitchen. "Has he got his act together yet?"

Sarah shook her head. "Not exactly."

Gaynor grinned encouragingly. "You mean you still haven't…"

Sarah pulled a pile of glass cloths towards her and began folding them. "It's not that simple. He's very, well he's sort of…"

"What?"

Sarah ran a hand through her hair. "I don't know really. Ah – customer!" She nodded her head towards the end of the bar.

Gaynor turned and felt a jolt in her solar plexus. Sam was settling himself on a stool and unfolding his newspaper. She hadn't seen him since the night of the torchlight procession three weeks before. Every time she thought about how they'd parted, her toes curled. She'd been careful to walk around the roads behind Sam's cottage instead of past it, missing their conversations but too embarrassed to go through yet another apology for her behaviour.

"One of your fans, is he?" murmured Sarah. "Only ever seems to come in when you're here…"

"He didn't know I was," Gaynor said, too quickly.

Sarah raised her eyebrows. "I was only joking. I expect he spotted your loveliness when he walked past."

"Can you serve him?" said Gaynor in a low voice, trying to huddle round the corner by the optics.

"No, I can't – I've got half a ton of mushrooms down there waiting to be soup. You're the barmaid."

"Please." What must he think of her? Women weren't supposed to get half-pissed and go round propositioning men. What was it about alcohol that sent all her inhibitions flying out the window?

"See you later." Sarah picked up her pile of folded laundry and headed towards the stairs. "Good morning," she said to Sam brightly as she passed.

He looked up for a moment as Gaynor approached. "A coffee please," he said, smiling briefly and turning over a page of his paper. "A white one."

Gaynor filled the steel filter head with ground coffee, wondering what to say as she slotted it into the machine and waited for the coffee to drip through. Breathing in the aromas she frothed up some milk, slowly arranging sachets of sugar and an individually wrapped biscuit, taking her time selecting a teaspoon, delaying the moment when she would have to face him.

But he hardly looked up as she put the cup and saucer in front of him. His eyes flicked only briefly in her direction. He said, 'Thank you,' in a pleasant voice and pushed a five pound note towards her.

Now what? she thought as she got change from the till, caught between relief and disappointment. She'd have to make the first move. She wanted to. Suddenly she wanted him back, wanted his attention, his caring. She wanted to talk to him, wanted him to be her friend.

She put the coins down next to his tobacco. "How are you?" she asked, self-consciously. He put down his newspaper, picked up the pouch next to him and began to roll one of his tiny cigarettes. The sleeves of his brushed cotton shirt were rolled back. She found her eyes drawn to the tightly curled hairs on his brown forearms. "I'm OK," he said easily. "How about you?"

"I'm sorry," she said. "Again."

He finished rolling, dabbed the paper with his tongue, spent some seconds coaxing his old Zippo lighter into life then looked at her with a slow smile. "No harm done," he replied eventually, "as long as you're all right."

She picked up a clean ashtray and wiped it unnecessarily. "Oh I'm all right. Bit mad round the edges, you know."

He gave a grunt of amusement. "Aren't we all."

"How's Brutus?" She put the ashtray back and began to wipe the equally-clean bar.

"A brute. He brought half a herring gull for my dawn offering."

"Ugh." She took a deep breath. "Can I come by and see him sometime?"

Sam smiled. "Sure. You can come and see me, too, if you like."

But in the end she stayed at Greens all day. She felt she needed to be with Sarah, who was clearly still worried by the abusive call. So after they closed at lunchtime, she broke with tradition, donned an apron, and sat on a stool in the kitchen shredding cabbage and grating carrots for coleslaw. Sarah threw her a grateful smile.

"This is what takes the time," she said, chopping onions further down the huge steel table. "People don't realise how much there is to do even when you're closed."

"Perhaps we should make more of it," said Gaynor. "You know, that you prepare everything yourself."

Sarah laughed. "Blakes Frozen Foods was parked right outside the other day, delivering to the chip shop. Claire was outside on the pavement telling him to move on in case anyone thought it was us!"

She looked at the clock and ran a hand through her hair. "Oh God! I've got to get the kids in twenty minutes and I haven't even started the soup yet."

Gaynor swept the last of the raw vegetables into a large bowl and pushed it towards Sarah. Then she picked up a wooden spoon and brandished it. "Tell me what to do…"

Cooking was quite soothing, she thought, as she stirred the creamy concoction of mushrooms, adding a dash of sherry as instructed, resisting the temptation to have a snort herself. What with Victor always in London, she'd got out of the habit at home. She wondered idly what Sam ate. Was he the sort of man to produce meat and two veg every day, just for himself? Or did he survive on cheese and crackers the way she did when left to her own devices? Turning the heat down low on the large hob, she heard Sarah and the children come in overhead. She felt better for seeing Sam. The thought of going to visit him again gave her a warm feeling inside. She could talk to him...

"Come up and have a cup of tea!" Sarah's voice called from upstairs. Gaynor went up to the flat where the two younger children were already sprawled in front of the television. Bel jumped up when she saw her. "Do you want to play shops?"

"Mummy's a bit stressed," the little girl confided as Gaynor paid 2p for four tins of baked beans and got a handful of change. She smiled angelically as she packed the shopping into a crumpled Tesco bag. "It's that bloody winebar."

Gaynor stifled a laugh. "You shouldn't say that," she said. "Bloody is a very, very rude word. If they hear you say it at school you'll be in big trouble."

Bel handed her the plastic carrier. "Luke is very naughty," she explained. "He says it ALL the time."

He wasn't saying much today. Gaynor engaged Luke in a series of grunts when he slouched in from the bus-stop.

"Will you answer properly!" Sarah said sharply. In reply, Luke grabbed the remote control, causing his brother to kick and bellow, while Bel shrieked encouragement.

"I am so sorry." Sarah shook her head as she drained a steaming saucepan of spaghetti in the small kitchen. "It's absolute bedlam at this time of day."

Gaynor smiled. "It's OK. It makes a nice change."

It was true – she found herself enjoying the family noise, the sounds of the TV, the kids scrapping, Bel singing to herself as she rearranged her imaginary window display. She watched as Sarah gradually calmed the chaos and began to relax. Gaynor's own house would be in perfect order, but silent and empty. Eating with Sarah and the kids, reading to Bel, lounging on the sofa watching *Neighbours* with Charlie felt good.

"Hey, we'll domesticate you yet," Sarah said, smiling, as Gaynor carried the supper dishes to the sink. She had Bel on her lap. The child was snuggled into her mother's shoulder and Sarah had her arm around her. Stretching out the other one, she leant up and squeezed Gaynor's hand. "Thank you."

"I'll call the police again tomorrow from home," said Claire quietly to Gaynor as they got ready to open that evening, while Sarah was still upstairs with the kids. "Try and make sure they do something. Are you OK?"

Gaynor nodded. "Yeah, I'm fine." Claire had seemed warmer since Gaynor had come in shame-faced to apologise for her outburst at the end of Folk Week. She'd nodded at Gaynor's embarrassed explanations of why the girl burning her hands had affected her so much. "Families are difficult, aren't they?" was all she'd said, but since then Gaynor had noticed a new concern in her voice. Yet, they didn't talk like she and Sarah did. There was still something private about

Claire – something that stopped Gaynor asking too much. "How's Jamie?" she tried now.

"Oh, he's fine." Claire moved around the front of the bar, lighting the candle on each table. "I hardly ever see him! And Victor?"

Gaynor switched the lights on over the wine racks.

"Hardly see him, either."

Claire gave a short laugh. "What are we like! Here – I'm putting that new Shiraz on the Specials board tonight. See if you can shift some?" She came back behind the bar and rummaged in a box next to the fridge. "Oh, and if those two buffs come in droning on about letting wine breathe again, I've got this." She held up a small funnel-shaped object. "As recommended by Michael Winner in the *Sunday Times!* Michael Caine's supposed to have one too."

"What is it?"

"An aerator! Ah, the very chap to try it on…"

Claire grinned as Neville Norton, already flushed, pushed open the door. "Good evening, sir, would you like a glass of your usual claret – with our new innovative oxygenating service?"

Neville blinked across the bar, bemused, as Claire selected a large glass and poured wine through the little plastic gadget. It sprayed out like a small fountain, sending forth a shower of fine red droplets that filled the glass at a rate that was clearly too painfully slow for Neville. He was visibly twitching. Gaynor laughed. "That'll go down a storm at last orders when there's twenty people waiting."

Claire laughed too. "They also do one that plays God Save the Queen!"

It was busy for a Tuesday night. Most of the front tables were filled with couples or small clusters of friends. A table of fourteen – an impromptu night out for the 'Fishing Club', they told Gaynor – hadn't booked, but came in on the off-chance. Claire had to disappear downstairs to help Sarah and

Benjamin in the kitchen, leaving Gaynor alone to man both bar and restaurant.

"I'm sorry," said Claire breathlessly, coming up to hand round starters while Gaynor served the small crowd that had appeared at exactly the same moment the kitchen buzzer sounded. "It was dead last week. Ah Jamie! Just at the right time..."

Claire's boyfriend – still in his suit from the train – was despatched behind the bar. Gaynor, carrying stacks of dirty dishes downstairs, paused and smiled at him. He looked young and tired. "Long day?" she asked.

Jamie yawned. "I was up at five."

But he still got home to see Claire in the evenings. Didn't feel the need to live in town half the week to recuperate. As she came back up to the bar, Gaynor wondered how long it would be before Victor suggested staying up in London permanently. She knew many people would think she had a blessed life, with her lovely home and no money worries and this bar, and she herself sometimes felt guilty for not being happier, but...

"...and a white wine and soda."

"Sorry?" She looked up to see a young couple looking quizzically at her. "I'm so sorry," she said again, realising she'd been staring into space. "What was it you wanted...?"

"Takings are well up this week," said Claire, deftly emptying the till, when the last customer had left at the end of the evening. "That big table left you twenty quid, Gaynor."

"Stick it in the pot," said Gaynor. "You two share it."

"Don't be daft." Sarah leaned over the bar and pulled the tip jar towards her. "There's lots in here – we'll split it between all of us. Here Benjamin..." she leant out and pushed a couple of notes into the boy's hand as he came past, with his crash helmet under one arm. "We like it when Gaynor's waitressing don't we – all the blokes cough up double."

"Charming," said Claire, smiling, as Benjamin left after gravely thanking them all. "Nobody ever tips me, then!" She pushed a wad of notes into a cloth cash bag. "I'll just go and put this in the safe. Then shall we have a drink? Jamie will be fast asleep by now and I've been sent some new samples to try."

Sarah pulled the blinds down and turned the lights low. The three of them sat on stools at the bar, a bottle of Australian Chardonnay, a white Rioja and a Chilean Merlot lined up in front of them.

"Ugh," said Gaynor, sipping, swirling and putting down her glass in disgust. "Tastes German."

"I rather like it," said Sarah, swilling the Chardonnay about.

"That," said Gaynor, prodding her, "is because you have no taste. You liked that awful Rosé stuff they sent us. It's all sweet and fruity. All these new world wines are the same."

"Yeah, it's nothing special." Claire wrinkled her nose. "But it's what people like. I was reading Wine Buyer Monthly. Guess what the top-selling supermarket wine is?"

"Leibfraumilch!"

"Worse than that!"

"Nothing's worse than that. Ummm...Bottled cat's pee?"

"Lambrusco!"

"Ugh! Yuck! Wouldn't clean the loo with it! This is nice, though." Gaynor poured a large glass of the Rioja.

"Didn't even know there was a white one."

"It's quite expensive…"

"I'll just finish this, then." Sarah giggled as she poured more of the Australian white into her glass.

"I don't care about white wine at all, really," said Claire, opening the Merlot. "Apart from champagne, of course."

"Of course!" Gaynor put her glass down and looked at Sarah. "Are you getting pissed there?"

Sarah giggled again. "Maybe – I hardly ever seem to drink these days. Funny, isn't it – surrounded by the stuff all day. I suppose it's like working in the kitchen. Puts you right off food. All this booze and I barely touch it."

"Doesn't have that effect on me," said Gaynor, taking another mouthful of Rioja.

"We've noticed!" Claire grinned and took a sip of her own wine.

"It's odd, isn't it," said Gaynor, "how different we all are. Claire here, so efficient and you, Sarah..."

"Yes?" Sarah raised her eyebrows, her face mock-threatening. "Be careful now."

"No, really." Gaynor waved her glass around expansively. "I mean we are really different people and Claire and I didn't even know each other to start with and we've all got such varied lives and situations yet..." She looked around the dimly-lit bar, breathing in the warm, smoky, end-of-night aromas, feeling a sudden rush of love and appreciation. "We work ever so well together, don't we?" She suddenly wanting to hug them both. "We..." She paused, struggling to think of the right word. "We... complement each other..."

Claire smiled.

"Yes," grinned Sarah. "I think that T-shirt really goes with your eyes..."

Gaynor kissed them both as she left and stepped out into the dark street. "You sure you're going to be OK walking?" Claire asked. "My car's just up by the church."

Gaynor nodded. It was nearly 1 a.m. but if Sam's light was still on, she'd take it as an invitation. Victor was away of course and she didn't feel like going home to a cold, empty house just yet. She felt keyed up, slightly drunk, and she wanted someone to talk to.

Sam didn't look particularly surprised to see her. While he went to put the kettle on, she told him about the funny calls.

"Will the police do anything?" she called, as she sat on his sofa, wriggling her toes. "Oh, my bloody feet. I hope I'm not going to get varicose veins with all this standing."

Sam came in from the kitchen. "Depends who you get, what else they've got on their desk, how much fuss you make."

"Sarah's pretty rattled by it."

"I expect she is. I know it's not much comfort if she's on her own there, feeling scared, but it's very unlikely, the sort of profile to make a call like that, would actually do anything."

"That's what I told her, but you know…" She shrugged.

"Yes, it's nasty." He handed her a cup of tea.

"I should have brought you some wine."

"Hardly ever drink it and you look like you've had quite a bit already."

"Not that much. A couple of customers bought me one – I had a couple more when we were clearing up…"

"I do hope," she said later, with a smile, "we get interviewed by some strapping young constable. I like a man in uniform."

"Authority figures, eh? From what you've told me about your father, hardly surprising."

She grinned at him. "I wish I'd seen you in yours."

"It was very ill-fitting."

She looked at his hands wound around his mug, at his shirt, the way he trailed his fingers down Brutus's spine as the handsome grey cat jumped on to the arm of the sofa.

She was in that peculiar place again, where she knew exactly what she was saying, but was touched by that sense of abandon only several large wines could bring. "I expect it would still have done it for me."

He turned his head to look at her.

She took a mouthful of Darjeeling. "Sorry – you don't want me to flirt with you, do you?"

He smiled ruefully. "It's very appealing." He looked down again as he stroked Brutus, who was now stretched out along the length of his thighs. "I'm attracted to you too, Gaynor. When I first met you, I didn't think you were my type at all." He looked up and grinned. "You scared the life out of me! But once we talked properly – once I got a glimpse of the real you…"

He was serious again. "When I talk to you – for the first time in a long time I feel alive inside. I've missed you in the last three weeks. I'd started to look forward to you coming round – hoped that you would. You're such a funny mixture – sophisticated woman and wayward child. I want to look after you, protect you."

Her heart was beating hard – she wanted to curl up with him, feel his arms around her again, his voice making soft soothing sounds as she buried her face in his shoulder. He went on stroking the cat, his voice even and measured.

"But you're married and, frankly, I'm afraid. I don't want to be falling for you – don't want to feel need or be out of control. It's so long since I've been near a woman there's all sorts of waking up to do and I can feel it happening already but I don't want to come round like Rumplestiltskin only to find you reconciled with your husband and me sitting here with a cat for company feeling bitter and lonely. That's why I can only be your friend. I can give you a cup of tea and a hug when you're down, but nothing more."

She felt a lump in her throat. She wanted him to hold her hand. She wanted to lean out and take his. She tried to keep her voice steady but heard it wobble. She said: "But, sometimes, I think I might want more."

He smiled at her sadly.

"But sometimes, Gaynor, we can't have everything we want."

12. Sauvignon Blanc
Robust and forceful with a penetrating nose.

"Hello, sweetie!" The tall figure on the. doorstep posed dramatically against a backdrop of blue-grey sea, clouded sky, and the black iron railings of the front gates, before sweeping into Gaynor's hall, beaming. "I'm back!"

Lizzie threw her bag to the floor and her arms around Gaynor, jewellery jangling.

"I can see that," Gaynor said, hugging Lizzie hard. She stood back and grinned with pleasure, taking in the familiar, bright, kohl-ringed eyes, the long glossy mane of black hair with its red henna-sheen, the mass of silver bangles and coloured glass beads. Lizzie had a deep tan and had lost weight. Above the quarter-length embroidered jeans, a cheesecloth top was tied, exposing her brown stomach. A red jewel winked there, matching the red-painted toes peeping out of her worn leather sandals.

The whole place suddenly seemed bright and energised.

Gaynor hugged her again. "You look great. Did you have a good time?"

"Bloody fantastic. Touch of Delhi-belly, but nothing terminal."

"Good – where's my present?"

Lizzie kicked at the big leather holdall at her feet. "In there. Where's my drink?"

"It was wonderful," Lizzie said, putting her glass down, shaking off her shoes and lying the length of Gaynor's sofa. "Had to slum it a bit at the end when I ran out of money but I had a brilliant time. I met the most amazing people." She sat up and grabbed her wine again, grinning wickedly. "Really amazing."

Gaynor smiled. "So you got shagged, then."

"Mmmn, did I?"

"Brought him back with you?"

"Him? There was more than one!"

Gaynor laughed. Lizzie prided herself on her ability to love `em and leave `em. "Don't want any of that messy love stuff," she'd say. "As long as they're good in the sack and don't hang around, I'm happy."

Lizzie propped herself up on one elbow. "There was one, though. This guy Ravi – he was travelling about too. We spent a few days together. He was a sweetheart. I mean I wouldn't want to spend the rest of my life with him – he's a bit of a dope-head, full of stuff about the crystals and catching your dreams, out in India in his search of his spiritual home, you know the sort of thing – but we had a great time. And he was really good to me when I was ill. One night, I'd got this terrible cold. I was streaming and coughing and spluttering and blowing my nose constantly – it was all disgusting and I looked delightful. Shiny red hooter, little piggy eyes, hair needed washing, every man's dream. I woke up in the night and I was groping about for tissues, my nose running like a tap and he turned over and put an arm out and stroked my back. He said: "Are you OK?""

Gaynor looked at her quizzically.

Lizzie nodded. "That's it, just – are you OK?" She took a big mouthful of wine. "He wasn't even properly awake, you know, he was all sleepy, but he reached out and checked I was all right." She shook her head, as if bewildered, and looking for a startling moment as if she might cry. "He sounded so concerned. And I thought, that's what I miss out on being single. It's not the physical stuff." She paused and laughed. "You can get that anywhere – it's someone being there in the middle of the night and looking out for you."

They were both silent for a moment. Gaynor thought about Sam with a sudden pang. Then Lizzie laughed, her old flippant tone returning. "It's what you married people get in compensation for not having sex any more."

Gaynor reached out for the bottle and topped up both their glasses.

"Not necessarily," she said. "Some of us don't get sex OR anyone giving a damn." She suddenly felt tearful herself.

Lizzie sat right up and looked at her. "What's wrong? Is there a problem with Victor?"

"Hmmm," she said, when Gaynor had finished and they'd both got new drinks. "Never mind Saint Sarah. I'm with you, honey – no smoke without fire. Sounds to me as if the bastard's up to no good at all, but we need to find out for sure."

"How?" Gaynor asked miserably. "You know what he's like – he always comes up with an excuse and just makes me feel stupid. The teddy thing disappeared from the bedroom and after a few days I did tell him I'd seen a package and asked him what it was. He got all funny at first and then he said it was a present he'd bought for me but he'd taken it back 'cos he'd made a mistake. And then he went on about what I was doing in his wardrobe anyway and made me feel all guilty for being jealous and suspicious."

Lizzie looked sceptical. "So if it was a mistake, why didn't he bring it back in the right size then, huh?"

Gaynor shrugged. "I don't know. He said he wouldn't bother next time if I was only going to be paranoid."

"Pah! I like Victor," said Lizzie. "He can be lots of fun and I'm fond of the old bugger, but he's a slippery sod, isn't he? All those years creating beautiful lies with which to dupe the unsuspecting public – it's bound to give you a certain flair for deceit. And if he keeps staying away…"

Gaynor frowned. "There was one time when he'd told me he was staying in Scotland overnight but I found out he'd come back to London early evening and could easily have come home, but he didn't."

Lizzie sat up straighter. "And? Did you tell him you knew?"

"Oh yes. But he had an answer, of course. Said he'd needed to have a debriefing with Laurence." Gaynor could hear him now. He'd seemed perfectly relaxed about being asked. "We got away sooner than we thought in the end," he'd said. "But it was such an intense two days, I just needed to get my head together – talk it through while it was all still fresh. We had a bottle of poo and a bit of dinner and I hit the sack. I thought you'd be working anyway." He'd smiled at her apologetically. "And I didn't fancy the crap of getting home on a Friday night from town."

It had sounded perfectly plausible. Victor had looked her straight in the eye. "I did believe him," she said now to Lizzie. "But, I don't know – something still doesn't feel right."

Lizzie considered. "What about having him followed?"

Gaynor gave a wry smile. "I thought about that. I even phoned up an agency I found in the yellow pages, but do you know how much it costs? And Sam said…"

"Sam?"

"He's just a bloke I know – he did the sign for the wine bar and we've sort of become friends."

"Friends?"

"Yes, friends," said Gaynor defensively. "You know, we have cups of tea together, that's all, and he's a good listener and I told him about Victor `cos I was a bit upset and – Lizzie, why are you looking at me like that?"

Since the evening after the threatening phone call, she'd made a conscious effort not to flirt with Sam or go there when she'd had too much to drink. But she knew she'd begun to depend on him. Where once she would have twittered away to Victor, now it was Sam she went to with her angsts and preoccupations.

When her mother had called to say David was going through a lot of anxiety again and her father was low, she'd called him the minute she put the phone down. When Chloe had sent pictures of her first scan and Gaynor had been shot through by such exquisite pain she felt her legs would give way, it was to Sam she ran in tears. She opened her mouth to try to explain to Lizzie how he didn't make her feel like an empty-headed bimbo, as Victor was inclined to, how he took her feelings seriously, how he would comfort her and make her feel not only safe and warm but that her feelings were valid. That *she* was, indeed. How, strangely he'd churned up all her feelings up while soothing them. How he'd taught her to cry again…

But she couldn't say any of it.

"He's just a friend," Gaynor repeated.

Lizzie raised her eyebrows. "So why are you blushing?"

Lizzie sat back on the sofa and considered all Gaynor had told her. "So what we have here is a situation where Victor could be playing away and while he is, you want to do the same with Sam?"

"No, it's not that. Sam's lovely. Sam's really good to me but I'm not …"

"Do you fancy him?

"No. Well, yes. I sort of find him attractive but I just feel… I need…"

"You need," said Lizzie decisively, "to know where you are. What time will Victor be back?"

"About eight, he said. Oh God, I said I'd cook."

"Right," said Lizzie, leaping up, "we've got two hours – let's go through his things."

Gaynor looked shocked. "I can't do that," she said half-heartedly, while remembering what Sam had said about a paper trail.

But Lizzie was already opening the door of Victor's oak-panelled study. "Do you want to know or not? Where are his credit card statements?"

"I don't really know where he keeps anything, I don't come in here much." Gaynor hovered uncomfortably by the door while Lizzie pulled open the drawers of Victor's leather-topped desk.

"Where are all his papers and things?"

Gaynor nodded towards an oak cabinet. "There's a load of stuff in there."

Lizzie tugged it open. "He's very organised," she said, flipping through file tabs. "Insurance, life policies, cars, unfortunately nothing headed 'who I'm shagging'. Ah – personal documents – perhaps there's something in here…"

"No, that's our birth and marriage certificates – things like that."

Lizzie was already pulling them out. "Better just take a look in case he's married someone else on the Q T. Hmm, nothing – hey look at you!" Lizzie opened Gaynor's passport. "I'd forgotten you had your hair like that – and look at Victor – what a pretty boy. These must need renewing pretty soon – you both look so young." She grinned.

"Thank you!" Gaynor came across the room, took them from Lizzie's hands and dropped them back into the file.

"Perhaps you should look in there." Lizzie pointed to a file marked 'Bank'. "I don't like to …"

She broke off as Gaynor pulled out a bundle of statements and glanced through them. "Just his current account. Standing orders, cash withdrawals – nothing to tell me anything. I don't know what he does with his credit card stuff. I think one of them is paid for by the company – the one he does all the business entertaining and travel on – and then he's got his own platinum…"

She pulled out a small drawer on the right of the desk. "This is where the receipts go – I give him my shopping and petrol ones for checking against the statement."

She pulled out a bulldog clip with a wadge of credit card vouchers in it and began to sift through them. "There's not much here, just our personal stuff – the Tandoori, Waitrose, garden centre, What's this? Antonio's Hair Factory?"

Lizzie came and looked over her shoulder. "Bloody hell! That's more than I spend on my hair. What does he have done, for God's sake?"

"Dunno. Looked like a trim to me. Still, Sloane Street…"

"Still bloody expensive."

Gaynor dropped the receipts back on the desk. "Look! This isn't going to tell us anything – I bet he takes her away to hotels with him and the agency pays for all that. And probably all their restaurants too – he'll just put it down as business. He always does if we eat out in town."

"What's this?" Lizzie picked up a folded statement from the back of the drawer. "Anything here you don't know about?" She ran her eye down the list. "Duty free goods – perfumery. A hundred and seventy-eight quid!"

"He bought me some on the way back from Thailand."

"What, at that price? How big was the bottle? Perhaps he bought some for someone else too?

Gaynor shook her head. "Maybe, but he came home with a load of stuff for him too – aftershave and lotion and that sort of thing. He likes his cosmetics, does Victor. Go and look in our bathroom – he's got more bottles and potions than I have!"

"The old tart. And when did he last buy you clothes?"

"Two or three months ago – the day we went to London and he got that teddy."

"Nothing since?"

"No."

"No other lingerie?"

"No, I told you. Why, what have you found?" Gaynor's heart was thumping. "What is it?"

Lizzie held out the statement. "Voluptua? Two hundred and ninety-nine pounds?"

Gaynor snatched at the paper. "Where? What's he bought?"

Lizzie shrugged. "I don't know but with a name like that I'll guess it's something sexy."

"Oh, Christ."

"It says Manchester here. Has he been there lately?"

"Not that he's told me. But who knows where he goes!"

"Might be mail order, of course." Lizzie took the statement back and looked closely at it

"But what is it?" Gaynor asked, agitated. " I mean, three hundred quid. A dress? What?" She leant over Lizzie's shoulder. "Look – it was paid for three weeks ago. I've had nothing – it can't be for me. What's he buying? And who for?"

Lizzie reached for the phone. "Only one way to find out."

Gaynor came back into the study. Lizzie was still perched on the corner of Victor's desk with the receiver to her ear.

"What's happening?" Gaynor picked up the empty glasses.

Lizzie grimaced. "Your call is important to us. Please stay on the line. Then Vivaldi's Four Seasons."

"Bollocks."

"Get another bottle open, for God's sake." Lizzie shifted on the desk and crossed her legs. "Ah, a real person at last. Yes, hello Mary-Ann-Speaking, you *can* help me...."

"Couldn't get anywhere really," said Lizzie taking a large swig of her drink. "I tried pretending I was you and my husband had ordered something I was trying to chase up but they wanted an order number and all sorts. I didn't even know your postcode. I said I'd call back – pretended I was concerned about what size he'd chosen." She stopped. "But I did find out what they sell and..." she hesitated, "...I don't see how it could be for you unless he's made a mistake..."

Gaynor looked at her. "Well?"

"Clothes for the fuller figure."

"Bastard!"

"He knows bloody well," said Gaynor, caught between fury and tears. "He knows bloody well what size I am – it's for this bloody hippopotamus he's shagging."

Lizzie crossed the kitchen and poured more wine into Gaynor's glass. "She could just be tall. They said they cater for particularly tall women or women with unusual proportions – big calves, for example. Mary-Ann got quite animated. Explained how they do boots in four width sizes. You measure your leg…"

"Well, she sounds really attractive." Gaynor exploded. "What is he doing? Screwing a six foot elephant with tree trunk legs…" She snorted, half laughing, half crying.

Lizzie sat down at the breakfast bar. "Look, I don't want to wind you up by sounding like Sarah but it couldn't be props for one of his commercials, could it? Remember when they did that pitch for the Exotic Gifts account – he brought all those Champagne Perfume hampers home. We got slaughtered and smelled nice!"

Gaynor looked miserable. "Yes, exactly – he brought them home. If big lingerie and huge boots are part of a bid to win a client, then why not just dump the evidence on the coffee table? I tell you, Lizzie, it's all making sense now. For years he's made comments if I've even put on a pound and yet when we went shopping he told me I was looking good, when I'm clearly bigger than I've ever been."

Lizzie looked her up and down. "Where exactly?"

"He's always used clothes as the romantic gesture," said Gaynor, ignoring her. "He's bought me flowers about three times in our entire relationship and that's because I've asked for them. Chocolates, never. All those calories? You don't want them really do you?" she said, mimicking his tones. "But clothes, lingerie, scarves, shoes – always. If he's got a bird he'll be buying her stuff. That's how he is. What am I going to do," she wailed. "I need to know."

Lizzie opened the fridge. "Let me stay for supper," she said. "What have we got?"

*   *   *

Victor seemed genuinely delighted to find Lizzie in his kitchen.

"You look fantastic," he said, hugging her, "and what's that marvellous smell?"

"She's done her tuna and peppers pasta special for us," said Gaynor, "and we need you to open more wine."

"Looks like you've got through half my cellar already," said Victor, picking up the empty Sauvignon bottle.

"And why not," asked Lizzie, smiling. "We were celebrating my safe return."

"I'll drink to that," said Victor, smiling too. "We've missed you."

Lizzie chinked glasses with him and then leant across to do the same with Gaynor. "Well, I'm back now," she said.

They ate in the kitchen. Lizzie tossed a salad in a big Mediterranean bowl, warmed crusty rustic rolls from the freezer, lit candles and piled fragrant steaming pasta on to three plates. Gaynor, sitting on a stool at the breakfast bar, watched her gratefully. She felt safer with Lizzie here. She felt as though Lizzie would somehow get to the bottom of things. Above all, that Lizzie believed her. That Lizzie wouldn't tell her she was imagining things, like Sarah, or that she was somehow better off not knowing, as Sam had tried to suggest. Though Sam made her feel safe too. Thinking about Sam sent a spasm of something through her.

"Have you got a thing about him?" Lizzie had asked earlier. And Gaynor had shaken her head. She hadn't, had she? She liked Sam, appreciated him. Because he listened to her and took her seriously. OK, so she did think about him a lot but that was because she was so churned up and confused anyway. How could she say what she felt, when all this was going on? If she just knew what Victor was up to...

"So what have you been up to?" Lizzie asked him across the table.

Victor, screwing the cork from another bottle of Barolo, answered easily. "Still running the rat race, trying to earn a crust."

Lizzie laughed. "You poor old thing. So it's still big bucks, fast cars and loose women, eh?"

Victor grinned. "I wish. I've spent all day in a meeting about Homestyle Double-Silk Quick-Dry emulsion. Forty-four new colours for the style-conscious executive and about as gripping as watching the stuff dry."

"No exotic locations?"

"Thailand for a week. Weather was fantastic but the shoot was a pain in the arse – the models were all about fifteen and kept bursting into tears, and the photographer had a row on the phone with his boyfriend on the first night and got so drunk he spent all the next day in bed. Laurence and I were tearing our hair out. I was pretty glad to get home." He smiled.

Gaynor felt Lizzie's eyes flick towards her. Victor sounded completely genuine but then, what was he going to say? I took this great trout of a woman with me and we spent every spare second humping? She held out her glass to be refilled.

"You managed some shopping though, didn't you?" she asked deliberately, pushing her empty pasta bowl to one side. Victor nodded, still seeming completely at ease. "Some amazing boutiques," he said to Lizzie. "And markets to die for. Great silks and stuff. Got Gaynor a fabulous dress."

"Oooh, that reminds me." Lizzie jumped up and ran to the hall. "Look what I've got for you. She came back with her battered leather holdall. "Such gorgeous colours – I couldn't resist them." She pulled out a wad of tightly folded fabric which she began to shake out, unravelling yards of patterned silk in blues and greens and silvers. She held it out in her arms. "Look – saris – don't know what you'll do with them but they were so cheap…"

"Wear them!" cried Victor.

Gaynor stood up, gathering the silk to her, trying to fathom which way it went. "My God, there's so much of it – where's the end?"

"Here." Lizzie pulled at acres of material. "Come here." She began to wrap part of it around Gaynor. "Lift up your arms." She giggled. "I did know how to do this."

"So did I, once." Victor picked up another, vivid in burnt oranges and yellows, a splash of turquoise across it. "Remember when I did that video in Madras?" He jumped up and began to wind it around himself. "Does it suit me?"

"Very nice." Lizzie laughed and began to wrap more fabric around Gaynor's middle. "It's something like this."

"Isn't it supposed to go over one shoulder?" Gaynor unwrapped it again, dragging the heap of silk round behind her. "I think you do this..." She pulled a length of silk round behind her and down over her left breast. "Then you wrap it round you..."

"Sari race!" Victor tossed a third folded sari in vivid pink and gold at Lizzie. "First one to get it on and still be decent!" He pulled off his shirt and took a swallow of red wine. "Loser does the washing up!"

Laughing, Lizzie grabbed at the sari and began to wind it round her. "The Indian women wear a T-shirt underneath half the time," she said. "None of this topless stuff. Look – your nipple's showing."

Victor went on wrapping himself up. "Are you getting excited?"

"In your dreams!"

Giggling too, as she attempted to get her own slippery mass in some sort of shape, Gaynor looked lovingly at them both. Suddenly Victor was being his old fun self again, prancing across the floor tiles in acres of silk as Lizzie laughed helplessly. She looked at the empty bottles among the pasta dishes. Wonderful stuff, alcohol. Suddenly nothing seemed so bad after all.

She went out into the hall and tried to make sense of the winding process in the reflection of the long mirror. She took off her jeans, then holding the material over her shoulder like the end of a bandage, began to wind it round and round her body until she reached her knees. It was too tight to move in but sort of looked the part. Or as much of the part as she could remember, women in saris not being exactly thick on the ground in Broadstairs. She draped the rest around her.

"I've done it," she called, hobbling back into the kitchen in tiny shuffling steps, trying not to fall over. "Look at me!" She twirled, holding on to the end piece of silk. "I need to do something with this bit."

"You need to do something with all of it. There's a great gaping bit round your bum," said Lizzie, still struggling with her own creation. "You couldn't go out like that – we can all see your knickers."

"Nothing unusual," said Victor. "Look at me!" They both looked and collapsed laughing. Victor did seem to be the one who'd done it properly. The bright garment looked totally incongruous wrapped round his tall frame and bare male chest but it was over one shoulder in a most professional manner and seemed to hang and drape without showing any signs of slithering into a pile on the floor, as Lizzie's had just done. He jumped on to a kitchen chair and held out his arms like a diva. "TRALAA!"

"Looks great with the socks," said Lizzie, pointing at Victor's feet.

They all looked at the grey patterned wool and burst out laughing again.

"I give up." Lizzie tossed her sari into a corner and began to stack the supper things. "I'll show you how to belly dance instead."

She moved all the plates and bowls on to the breakfast bar, got up on to a chair and into the middle of the table. "Got any sexy music?"

She began to gyrate her middle. "There was this totally fantastic dancer in this restaurant I went to with Ravi. She moved round the tables and her stomach just went into hundreds of ripples." Lizzie thrust out her pelvis, rolling her own flat brown abdomen up and down, the red stud in her navel flashing in the candlelight.

Victor clapped enthusiastically. "Yeah!" he cried. "Yeah, yeah, yeah..."

"That was a great evening," Victor said, when Lizzie had eventually gone and they had weaved their way upstairs. He began kissing Gaynor's neck. "We need to do more of that," he said, as he propelled her along the landing. "Need to have more fun..." He was still wearing the sari half-draped over him and looked ridiculous. But there was no mistaking his passion. He pushed open their bedroom door with one foot, his hands moving over her. As he urged her backwards, she felt an urgency about him that hadn't been there for a long time.

"Come on ..." He pulled her down on to the bed, fingers undoing the button on her jeans, mouth moving down between her breasts. "Christ," he breathed, "I really want you."

Gaynor wrapped her arms around him, weak with relief, feeling the desire flow through her in answer.

"I want you, too," she said. "I want you too..."

13. 2000 Sauternes
Initial impressions good, but a weak vintage.

Gaynor sat up in bed, cup of black coffee in hand, watching Victor in the important task of tie selection. She waited patiently while he deliberated between a flowery number in various shades of purple and mauve and an elegant silver-grey with red polka dots. She brought her knees up beneath the duvet and carefully balanced the cup on top of them.

"You're going to spill that," Victor said, without looking round.

"I'm still holding it." She put the coffee on top of the bedside cupboard and put her chin on her knees instead, watching Victor carefully knot his chosen tie and reach into the wardrobe for his jacket. He turned and smiled at her. He always looked devastatingly attractive in a suit.

"Why don't I come to London with you?" she asked suddenly.

He carried on smiling. "Because I'm leaving in two minutes and you're still in bed."

"Very funny. I don't mean right now. I'll come up later on the train. We can go out for dinner tonight and…"

"Sorry, darling. I've got a client dinner. We're taking the wall-coverings lot out."

"Well, I'll stay in the flat, watch TV till you come home. I can do some shopping tomorrow and then…" She hesitated. Was she imagining it or had a flicker of fear crossed his face?

He turned back towards his wardrobe. "You don't want to stay in the flat. I let Laurence stay there a few nights last week when Paula kicked him out again – it'll be a right mess.

I need to get it cleaned and decorated anyway – it's really looking tatty these days. He gave a forced-sounding laugh. "A real bachelor pad."

"I'll clear it up while you're at work."

Victor gave his tie a final tweak. "There's no need. Look, come up sometime next week and we'll stay in a hotel and I'll take you out then, OK?" He buttoned up his jacket.

"I want to be with you now – we've had such a lovely weekend."

Victor didn't look at her. "We did have a good weekend," he said, a hint of impatience in his voice, "but I've already had an extra day and now I have to go to work."

"I know, but I wouldn't..."

"And don't you have to, too? Aren't you supposed to be working in that wine bar of yours? Fed up with it already? I thought the novelty would soon wear off."

"It hasn't. But it's not going to be that busy on a Tuesday and one of the students would cover, I'm sure. Look, I don't care about the state of the flat..."

"Gaynor, not today, all right? I've got a pile of work to do – I'll need to stay up late and get through it. I can't have any distractions."

He didn't meet her eyes. He opened the top drawer of his chest and pulled out a handkerchief, obviously desperate to be gone. "Another time, OK?"

She got out of bed, determined not to let him off the hook. "I don't see why I can't come tonight."

Victor looked really irritated now. "Just leave it, will you!"

"I'll bloody leave him," Gaynor said to Lizzie a week later. They were sat at a table in the window of Greens. Gaynor was supposed to be behind the bar but there was nobody in yet so she had time for a glass of wine first. She'd seen Claire and Sarah exchange glances as she poured two Frascatis.

"Don't worry – I'm paying for them," she'd said gaily, deliberately misinterpreting the looks. "I don't know," she said to Lizzie now. "I don't know what to think. He was absolutely lovely all that weekend and then he went back to London, stayed away three days, came home and was all peculiar again. He must be seeing someone. Mrs Voluptua with the big calves, I presume."

Lizzie shook her head. "I don't know. He seemed happy enough with you when I was there – distinctly cuddly, I thought. I know we'd all been drinking but he seemed really relaxed and happy – not like a man with a guilty conscience at all."

Gaynor sighed. "Yet the moment I suggest going up to town with him he makes all sorts of excuses."

"Like what?"

"First he said I wouldn't like it much 'cos Laurence – his sidekick at work – has been staying there and it's a mess and that he'd be home really late. Then he turned it all round and said wasn't I supposed to be working in the wine bar and he knew I'd soon get bored and how I never stick to anything and why didn't I stay here and do the job I was supposed to be doing and we ended up having a row and he walked out." Gaynor tugged at her hair. "As he does, the bastard. Leaving me somehow feeling it's all my fault."

"Well it isn't," said Lizzie. "I wonder if you should just turn up there – arrive at one in the morning and let yourself in and see what he's up to?"

Gaynor pulled a face. "If he's even there. Perhaps he's staying with her. And if I turn up and nothing's going on he'll really get cross. If I haven't phoned first it'll be obvious that I'm checking up on him."

Lizzie shook back her shiny hair. She'd had bits of it braided in yellow and purple and gold and the little beads at the end of each colourful strand jiggled together as she gazed at the ceiling thoughtfully.

"Shall I turn up?" she asked after a moment or two. "Say I was up in town and my date got cancelled and I wondered if he fancied a drink?"

Gaynor twisted her wine glass round and round on the polished table "But he can fob you off just as easily as he can me. He'll tell you he's with a client."

"I'll turn up at the flat – say I tried to phone but the line was constantly engaged. He'll just think it's faulty."

Gaynor gave a wry smile. "No, he'll think you're lying through your teeth. There's no line in the flat – he's never bothered to put one in. He just uses his mobile – keeps saying he must install broadband for his laptop but as he's only ever there to sleep…"

"Hmmm. So you can't even check he's really there at all?"

"No." Something stopped Gaynor telling Lizzie that she'd tried to phone him several times late at night recently but his phone was always off or just rang unanswered. That she'd sat clutching herself, feeling wretched, well into the early hours, trying every twenty minutes. It made her sound so desperate. So bloody sad.

"Look," said Lizzie, "I wouldn't mind a day or two up in the smoke anyway – want to catch up with Jules apart from anything else." Julie was Lizzie's older sister – a commercial lawyer and as respectable-looking as Lizzie was bohemian. "Why don't I just turn up at Victor's office while I'm there – say I'm at a loose end and see what I can find out?"

Gaynor hesitated. She knew she was being stupid but there was something in her that didn't want Lizzie going to find Victor. She knew if he was free he'd be charming – take her out to dinner, look after her. He might even invite Lizzie to join him if he wasn't free. Might judge she'd be good company for whatever fat cat he was wining and dining that evening. She could hear him now: And this is the lovely Elizabeth – a very good friend of my wife's – come to check up on me – ha ha ha. Peals of laughter all round.

She didn't want Victor paying anyone that sort of attention. Even Lizzie. Especially Lizzie. He'd never made any secret of the fact that he thought her attractive. She'd even found herself wondering if it had been the sight of Lizzie

157

cavorting about belly-dancing a week ago that had turned him on. He was never usually that passionate.

"Think about it." Lizzie got up to go. "Or we'll both pay him a visit. Say we're doing a spot of girly shopping. You've got a spare key to the flat, I suppose?"

"Um, yeah – well, I think I know where it is."

"We could check it out – see if it looks like she's been staying there. One thing's for sure," she picked up the empty glasses in one hand and then bent and put her other arm around Gaynor's neck, hugging her, "you can't carry on in this state."

Sarah had openly glared at Gaynor when she'd had a second drink but Gaynor ignored her. "I always say I do this job better pissed than sober," she'd told Lizzie firmly. Lizzie had laughed.

Still she felt slightly light-headed as the bar filled up and got hotter and smokier. She turned the extractor to full and poured herself a glass of water. She realised she hadn't really eaten all day. "Hey, Kate," she called, as the girl prepared to carry a pile of dirty plates down to the kitchen. "Can you ask Benjamin to send me up some leftovers?"

The bar was packed now. All the tables in the restaurant area were taken and Kate and Claire were constantly up and down stairs with trays. Jack was behind the bar with Gaynor who was halfway through a long round and had forgotten where she'd got to.

Shit! Two large Frascatis, a small Shiraz and how many bottles of Bud had they had?

"And a Diet Coke," said the guy she was serving, helpfully. "Oh, and a dry white spritzer. No ice," he added as Gaynor added a shovel-load to the glass. He turned to greet Maurice, one of their regulars, known to them privately as The Cappuccino King. Gaynor's heart sank.

"Oh how kind." Maurice did a little twirl. Gaynor tried frantically to get the adding-up back on track.

"Oooh, I just don't know." Maurice surveyed the wine list carefully as he did every time he came in. "Such a choice."

Gaynor tapped her foot as six girls came up behind him and the bloke up at the end of the bar waved an empty bottle at her. Jack had disappeared down to the cellar and not come back and the music had stopped.

"What are you having, Maurice?" she asked, forcing a smile. "Nice glass of Sauvignon? One of our Specials this week."

Maurice giggled. The guy ordering the round had wandered off somewhere. "Oh I know," he said, "I'll have a latte."

"He always does it when we're rushed off our feet," Gaynor complained as she banged the coffee grouts out of the steel filter. 'It's a bloody wine-bar – why doesn't he drink wine?"

"Lot of mark-up on coffee." Claire put two plates of nachos on the bar. Gaynor leant out and took a tortilla chip while her back was turned. She crunched it hastily.

"But it's always when we're busy. Where's Jack?"

"I think Sarah's got him helping her. She's doing her pieces in that kitchen." Claire shrugged helplessly.

"I'm doing mine. Look at all these people waiting."

And now there were two more. Gaynor looked across to where Danny stood grinning at her. He had his arm around the waist of a tall, model type in a tiny leather skirt and what looked like a bikini top, sporting acres of flat brown stomach and a large chunk of silver in her belly button. She glowered at Gaynor.

Danny winked. "When you're ready, gorgeous."

But Maurice was leaning over the bar. "I don't suppose," he said coyly, "I could have a little chocolate powder on my frothy bits?"

"Try being in here all night!" Sarah ran a hand through her hair. "It's so bloody hot."

Benjamin looked up from the dessert he was preparing. "It's been very warm indeed," he confirmed, as he carefully drizzled strawberry sauce in a lattice work around the edge of the plate. " Approaching intolerable."

"Lovely sandwich though." Gaynor put a friendly arm around his shoulders. "Just what I needed."

It had been a work of art – brown bread and tuna artfully decorated with swirls of cucumber and a lettuce leaf folded into the shape of a swan.

Sarah rolled her eyes. "Just what we needed when we were rushed off our feet."

She put the cloth down from wiping the steel tables and took a large swallow of water. "I'm going to have to talk to Claire about spacing the orders better. It's ridiculous – there's a limit to how much this kitchen can physically turn out. She needs to remember there's only me and Benjamin here!"

"The dream team." Benjamin lovingly placed half a strawberry on the top of a mound of whipped cream and scattered a little grated chocolate around it, standing back to consider his creation. "There!" he said. "Who could resist that?"

"They'll have gone home if you don't hurry up," Sarah said sourly. "It's all very beautiful but there are three other sweets on that list and one of them's a cheeseboard!"

"All in hand." Benjamin selected a stick of celery from the plastic box of salad and considered it. "And don't carve anything," Sarah snapped. She pulled a foil card from a drawer in the kitchen and emptied two tablets into her hand. Gaynor gestured to her.

"Come upstairs and have a drink if you're finished here," she said. "You need to relax a bit."

Sarah scowled. "And the floor will wash itself, will it?"

"I'm sorry." Sarah sipped at the glass of Beaujolais Gaynor had handed her. "That kitchen does my head in." She smiled ruefully. "Didn't mean to be an old bag." Claire whizzed past them with a tray of glasses. "Lots of ashtrays need emptying," she said briskly.

Behind her, Gaynor grinned and clicked her heels. "Yes sir!"

Danny placed a proprietary hand on her bottom as she bent over his table to clear it. "When's that husband of yours away?" he murmured. Gaynor saw the model coming back from the loo.

"New girlfriend?" she asked brightly.

Danny smiled. "You've got my number," he said.

I most certainly have. Gaynor carried handfuls of empty glasses to the bar. She couldn't think how she'd ever been attracted to him. He was so arrogant and shallow.

She thought fondly of Sam who was neither of those things and then of Victor who could, for all she knew, at this very moment be in a bar somewhere in London behaving just like Danny. One woman was clearly not enough for some bastards. But she thought it without bitterness. In fact she laughed to herself. She'd had enough to drink to have reached that happy state where she really didn't care. Let Victor do what he wanted. He could have his overweight fancy woman and when she finally caught him at it he could have a great big divorce settlement to deal with too. Sod him!

She hoped Sam would be up when she walked home. She'd take a bottle of wine and make him share it with her. Tell him what she was going to do. That from now on she'd live her own life and ignore Victor – let him bloody get on with it. Maybe have a little hanky panky of her own. Who knows, perhaps even with Sam? He might have all that moral fibre. But most men, when you got down to basics, wouldn't turn away a woman gagging for it. She giggled to herself, knocking an empty bottle over as she piled more empties on to the bar.

"Careful!" Sarah caught it. "What are you suddenly so amused about?"

"Just happy, that's all!"

Sarah smiled. "Oh good! Things better at home now, then? Are you…"

"Just resolved to make the most of life." Gaynor looked up at her mobile phone propped high on a shelf with the pint pots. She thought about phoning Sam and asking him to wait up but there was no signal at all tonight – even up there. And someone was using the main phone.

"He's been on there bloody hours," grumbled Sarah, nodding at the young man who was draped over the end of the bar, the receiver tucked under his chin. "We're going to have to get a second line in here. Oh damn it," she sighed as he dropped another coin into the slot. "I want to phone Mum to see how the kids are. Hurrah," she said, as he eventually put the phone down and sloped off.

It rang immediately. "Bet that will be her!" Sarah shot over and grabbed the receiver.

"Oh," Gaynor heard her say. She sounded surprised. "Of course, I'll just get her for you." She beckoned to Gaynor. "She's just coming," she said into the phone, adding in a concerned voice, "are you OK there?"

Gaynor frowned as she came across the room. Was it Victor?

"Who is it?" she mouthed.

Sarah ignored her. "Oh, I am sorry," she said to whoever was at the other end of the line.

"Who?" said Gaynor again, reaching her side.

Sarah handed her the receiver, looking serious. "Your mother."

Gaynor sat on a barstool, suddenly sober again, her elation quite gone.

"It's David," she said, as Sarah put a black coffee in front of her. "He's taken off somewhere. He does this when he's bad." She bit her lip. "My mother's so worried."

"Where will he go?" Sarah put a hand on her arm.

Gaynor shook her head, feeling suddenly sick. "Could be anywhere – he just gets a fixation. One time he went to the

162

Isle of Wight to try and find the cottage where we'd once been on holiday." She pulled a face. "Pretty bloody dismal it was too. Another time it was London. Got picked up by the police wandering about all confused. But this time –" she looked at Sarah anxiously as the full realisation made her heart begin to pound. "This time, Mum thinks he's coming to find me."

14. Pinot Noir
Appealing red though unbalanced.

She went straight home in the taxi Claire had called her. "Just go," Claire had said. "Don't worry about anything." But Gaynor *was* worried. David had disappeared some hours ago – for all she knew he could be waiting on the doorstep. She tried his mobile, knowing he wouldn't answer.

She wondered where he was – her mother had said he hadn't taken the car. On the train? The station was a fair walk from her house and it was beginning to rain. Her own mobile was full of messages from her mother who seemed to have been trying all evening before she tracked down the number of Greens. As she let herself into the house, she saw the answer-phone flashing. That message was from her mother too.

Pointlessly, she tried David's number once more. Still switched off. It was nearly half-past eleven. She sat on the stairs in her coat. Should she drive to the station and meet all the trains? But what if she missed him and he arrived at an empty house? What if he'd already been here and gone off somewhere again?

She sat looking at the small lamp on the hall table, the jug of flowers she'd put there earlier, the oriental rug on the polished wood floor. Part of her willed him to appear at the door, unable to bear the thought of him wandering about in the dark on his own, distressed. But a much bigger part longed for her mother to phone to say it was all OK, he'd arrived home. That she was dealing with it. Because that part of her, Gaynor admitted to herself, was scared.

She'd changed her clothes and was waiting for the kettle to boil for her third cup of tea when the doorbell rang. As ever, she steeled herself for what she'd see. However many times she saw David when he was unwell, it was always a shock.

And there he was on the doorstep. Beyond him the rain poured down. The shoulders of his duffle coat were saturated, the rucksack he held in one hand dripped. His hood was down – his brown floppy hair was soaked and droplets of water ran down his cheeks. He was shivering and behind the long wet strands of hair his eyes were huge and terrified. She was filled at once with that huge surge of feeling she'd had for him when they were children. When she just wanted to make it better. She opened the door wide and gestured him in. "It's OK," she said. "It's OK."

She'd finally got him to take his coat off. He stood in her kitchen in the familiar pose that sent a chill through her. His shoulders high with anxiety, hands in front of him as though he were holding an imaginary knife and fork in front of his chest. He was terribly thin. She put her arms around his bony shoulders. "Come and sit down," she said for the fourth time. "I'll make you some tea."

He shook his head silently, his eyes full of tears. When he spoke it was in such a low voice she had to bend her head closer to hear him. "They won't believe me," he said. "None of them. Not even Mum."

Gaynor led him towards the chair. "Sit down," she said again. "Tell me."

"I wanted to phone you," he said. "I wanted to warn you but the phone's tapped."

"I've been calling your mobile," she said.

His eyes flicked fearfully round the room. She saw them narrow at the microwave and kettle. "Not safe," he said.

"Tell me what's been happening." She pulled another chair close to him and sat down with a hand on his arm. She could feel him trembling.

"It's the council," he said. "They want to take my job away because I know what they've been doing. I am the enemy now. They want me out."

Gaynor spoke gently. "Are you sure? Do you think perhaps you've been getting very stressed again and everything seems..."

He shook his head vigorously. "They've put a virus in the system – it's all about me. It's in everyone's address book and in six days it will be all round the world." He suddenly jumped up. "Where's yours?"

"What?"

"The computer. Don't switch it on!"

Gaynor shook her head. "I hardly ever touch it," she said. "Only Victor uses it really."

David grew more agitated. His hands fluttered in front of him. "Don't trust Victor," he said.

I don't, she thought silently. She tugged at David's wrist till he sat back down. "How long has this been going on?"

He seemed to be thinking. "I didn't notice it at first," he said slowly. "Then they all kept coming to me. Problems with files, system crashing. They all kept asking me what it was."

"But that's your job isn't it?" Gaynor asked cautiously. "Aren't you there to trouble-shoot the problems?"

David gave a grim smile. "These weren't real," he said. "These were put there to get at me. They've been sending emails round. It looks like a virus – it says it's confidential information but really, inside, inside the return path, it's all about me."

Gaynor felt the old frustration rise inside her and took a deep breath, keeping her voice very calm. "What about you?"

David looked at her sadly. "Saying I'm evil. They want to get rid of me because I know what they do." He looked anxiously around again. "They might come here, I don't know."

Gaynor's mind raced. She was glad Victor wasn't here but she felt that frisson of fear she always did when David was like this. She knew from her mother that he hadn't been taking his medication, that he'd convinced himself that he was being watched and followed, that he refused to go to the doctor. He thought the medical profession were now in it with them.

"It sounds to me," she said carefully, "as though everything's been getting on top of you again. Have you been taking your tablets? Have you got them with you?"

His eyes narrowed again. "I don't need them. There's nothing wrong with me – it's them."

"What does Mum say?"

He shook his head again. "She doesn't understand, does she?" He spoke sorrowfully. "Mum doesn't know about computers. She believes what people tell her. Mum's too innocent. She just says I'm tired and I should go back to hospital!" He opened his hands and shrugged. "It's no good trying to explain it any more."

"What about Dad?" Gaynor asked warily

David's eyes flashed. He jerked back from her. "He's very two-faced!" His voice was high and loud. "Don't trust him either!"

"It's OK," she said, mind racing, wondering what to do. She should try to get him to go to bed and sleep – he looked totally exhausted. Perhaps tomorrow she'd be able to persuade him – God knows how – to come to a doctor with her.

"There is a conspiracy," he said urgently. "I know everyone thinks I imagine it but that's what you're meant to think. They want you to believe I'm mad and then they can do what they like. But things are really happening to me, they really, really are." He put his head in his hands and she watched a tear trickle down his cheek and slide through his fingers. When he raised his face again his eyes were pleading. "Do you believe me, Gaynor? You believe me, don't you?"

She heard her mother's voice in the back of her head, worn down with having the same conversations over and over, wrung out from the constant emotional rollercoaster of David, weighted down by disappointment in her husband who would have silently withdrawn, who would be sitting now, morosely looking out of the window into the garden leaving his wife to wonder what she had done to deserve this twice. A husband and son who found, in their different ways, reality so very hard to stomach.

But despite that, her mother would be remembering her reading and her experience and still, desperately, through her weariness, trying to do the right thing. "Don't collude with him," she would say, when later Gaynor found a way to make the whispered call that would let her mother know David was safe. "Try and get him to a doctor, make him take his medication…"

Gaynor looked at David, huddled in the damp clothes he still wouldn't take off, looked at his scared, wretched, exhausted face and she leant over the table and took his hand.

"Yes," she said, "I believe you."

She lay awake staring at the ceiling. David had finally been persuaded to take a shower and put on a big baggy sweatshirt of hers and some tracksuit bottoms she swore weren't Victor's, and had gone to bed in the spare room. She'd peeped in at him earlier and he was asleep, a glass of water beside him. He wouldn't have anything to eat and she wondered if he thought his food was poisoned. In his worst-ever illness he wouldn't even drink, convinced that the water was contaminated. He would take only carton orange juice from one particular shop he felt safe about. They'd had to sedate him and put him on a drip in the end.

She gazed upwards wondering what to do with him in the morning. She'd made the call to her mother, keeping it brief, just saying he was sleeping and she'd call again. Her mother had been anxiously listing things about social services and ringing the 'out-of-hours' team and how long it was since she thought he'd taken any tablets but Gaynor was barely listening. She'd told David he was safe here, that she would look after him. She didn't have a clue what to do next without letting him down.

She felt very alone. Though Victor would probably have made things worse. He didn't understand about David. They had nothing in common even when he was well. Victor found him hard to talk to, nervy and introspective.

"He's got a permanent chip on his shoulder," he'd said, disparagingly. "With good reason," Gaynor had answered shortly.

She couldn't explain to anyone the emotions David brought out in her – the blend of frustration and rage and pity and fierce, protective love. Victor had called David "that nutter" once. Gaynor had hurled a plate at him.

But lying here alone in the half-dark, she felt afraid. She'd left the lamps on downstairs and a soft glow came up the stairs on to the landing. She looked at the clock. It was nearly two a.m. She thought about ringing her mother back but she didn't want to wake her – she probably hadn't slept for the last two nights. She turned over.

She wished she could talk to Sam, but he'd probably be asleep too and if David woke up and heard her... He'd probably be better with Lizzie – he was always more comfortable with women – but Lizzie could go in too strong and alarm him. Her eyes felt gritty and she felt nauseous with tiredness. She'd sleep on it. See how things were tomorrow. She yawned and pulled the duvet more closely round her. She was getting warm and heavy. She'd drift off in a minute. She'd decide what to do in the morning. Maybe David would be better when she woke up...

She sat up with a start, as a high wailing noise came from down the landing. Heart pounding, she got out of bed and groped for her dressing gown. The green illuminated hands of her clock showed it was twenty past four.

She threw open the door of David's room. "What's the matter?"

He was sitting up in bed, hands waving in agitation in front of him. She went to him but he writhed away from her, still making the same desperate sound of despair.

"It's OK, it's OK." She sat on the edge of the bed, blinking, as he began to hold his head and rock back and forth, moaning as if in great pain. The awful thought that he had a brain tumour flashed through her head. "What is it? Does something hurt?"

"They won't stop," he cried, "they won't stop!" He turned and looked at her wild-eyed. "They keep on and on inside my head. They're here, Gaynor, they're outside, they're under the floorboards…"

"No, nobody's here."

He began thrashing about again, one arm flailing out and knocking the glass of water to the floor. It bounced on the carpet and splashed up, drops splattering against the wallpaper, the rest seeping across the crimson pile in a dark red stain. Gaynor looked at it uneasily.

He was still shrieking. "They want to get me, Gaynor! They're in this house and they're creeping inside my mind."

Gaynor stood up. "I'll call someone to help us then," she said. "I'll get the police."

"NO!" He stood up too, knocking into the bedside table, making the small lamp rock violently. "They're involved. Everyone's been told and everyone's in on it. Don't call anyone!"

He stared at her and her heart thumped again. He had that look in his eyes she'd come to dread. He was somewhere else entirely. He held his head to one side as if listening. Then he stared at her again, looking almost menacing.

"No police." One of his hands went to the lamp.

"David, sit down." She felt scared now. She was sure he wouldn't hurt her but she didn't know quite what he would do. Once in his teens, he'd knocked her mother's glasses off and their father had punched him. The most awful fight had broken out – Gaynor remembered her mother sobbing and wringing her hands while she herself huddled horrified in a corner, powerless to stop them. Her father had come off worse, Gaynor remembered, with satisfaction.

"No police," David said again. He stood in front of her rigid and trembling.

"I know a retired one – a good one – he left them – now he's just on his own – he'll help and protect us," Gaynor said desperately, wondering if Sam would come. She needed someone else here. She didn't like it and she didn't know what to do.

"NO!" David had hold of her arm. He still had a wild look in his eye. "You can't trust anyone. They'll take me away if you call."

"I won't let them!"

"You can't stop it! STOP IT," he screamed, letting go of her and clutching at his head again. "Stop it, STOP!"

She began to move towards the door.

He leapt after her and gripped her elbow again. "Don't go anywhere!"

"I need to go to the loo."

He looked at her suspiciously. "You can't." His voice rose. "You're going to call them and get me taken away."

"I'm not." She pulled her arm away from him. "Let me go!"

"No!" He picked up the red patterned lamp and hurled it at the wall. There was a tinkling of broken glass as the bulb smashed. The plug, wrenched from the socket, thumped down after it.

Real fear ran through her. "David, I have to go to the bathroom." She could hear her voice breaking.

He stared at the lamp and then at her. For a moment he frowned as if puzzled. Then his face closed in distrust once more. "Where's the telephone?"

"In my bedroom."

"You're not to use it."

"I won't, I promise."

"I'll sit by it."

"OK."

Her mother had reminded her about this. It was always a problem. Once, David had ripped the phone from the wall when she'd tried to call the doctor.

"If it gets bad," her mother had whispered down the line earlier, "keep your mobile with you. Call me!"

It was in Gaynor's dressing-gown pocket. For a heart-stopping moment, she thought David would want to search her but he seemed not to have thought about mobiles, or assumed hers was elsewhere. He sat stiffly on the edge of her bed, guarding the landline as she went into the ensuite.

Her fingers were shaking as she found the number. She flushed the loo and ran both taps praying the noise would cover her voice. Oh God, please answer, please be awake. At the other end, the ringing stopped. He sounded calm and alert despite the hour. Her mouth was dry. She could already hear David calling for her. There was a thump outside the door. Don't ask questions, just do it, she begged silently, as she managed to say, hoarse with panic: "Sam, please, please come."

15. Uruguayan Tannat

*Aggressive flavours with an
overpowering endnote.*

David seemed to have exhausted himself and agreed to lie on
her bed, holding the phone off the hook while she went down
and made tea. The house was cold. She felt sick and shivery.
She pulled her dressing gown more tightly around her and
flicked on the heating.

Gazing at the kettle, waiting for it to boil, she wondered
what would happen when Sam came and half-regretted calling
him out. Maybe David would fall asleep up there, maybe the
whole thing was best left till daylight. Till she could call her
mother and make a plan. A noise made her go to the hall. Sam
was tapping quietly on the frosted panes to the side of the oak
door.

"Thank you," she said in a low voice as she opened the
door. "Thank you so much."

Sam raised his eyebrows as he looked about him.
"Wow," he whispered. Then he touched her face. "Are you all
right?"

She silently shook her head, leading him through to the
kitchen before she tried to speak. He put his arms around her.
"What's been happening?" he asked. "What's going on?"

"I just don't know what to do now," she finished, wiping her
eyes, weak with relief at having him there. "He won't trust
anyone." She pulled a wry face. "Especially men."

She handed Sam a mug. "I don't know what he'll do if
he sees you."

When she went into her bedroom, David was lying back with his eyes closed, the receiver left dangling next to him. He snapped awake as she approached.

"Tea," she said brightly. He sat up, reaching for it, looking a little more normal than before. He peered into the yellow mug as if checking its contents but seemed prepared to put it to his lips.

"How are you feeling?" asked Gaynor carefully. She was aware of Sam waiting quietly at the top of the stairs, ready to spring into action if needed. They had agreed that if David was calm, it was better not to rock the boat, and Sam would stay out of sight. "I'll talk to him," he'd offered at first, but Gaynor had shaken her head. He didn't know what David could be like.

Now, as David opened his mouth to speak, there was a creaking on the landing outside. Gaynor grimaced. That bloody floorboard.

"Who's there?" David shot from the bed, the mug flying across the room, the contents cascading from it. "Who is it?" he shrieked.

"A friend of mine," she yelled back, thinking of Victor coming home to find tea all over the pale carpet and suddenly wanting to shake her brother. David came right up to her, putting his hands on her shoulders, gripping them tightly. "Who?"

"I'm Sam." His voice was quiet in the doorway.

"NO!" David howled, shaking Gaynor.

She shrank back, terrified now as David appeared to go totally out of control. He threw her away from him, turning and banging his own head hard against the wardrobe door. There was a sickly thud as he did it again against the tasteful grey and pink paper. Again and again, till he was literally bouncing off the walls, all the time making terrible noises of pain.

She was aware of Sam holding out his hands to him, saying something she couldn't hear. David's nose had begun to bleed.

"Stop it," she cried. "Stop it, stop it."

David appeared not to see or hear her. He picked up the velvet-covered stool from her dressing table and brought it high above his head. He was staring at a point somewhere in the distance but she realised he was going to hurl the heavy wood straight at her.

"No, David!" she shouted. She was shaking so much she thought her knees would buckle. The seat sailed past her as she ducked. There was a loud splintering sound as it crashed into her full-length mirror. She dropped to the floor, hearing herself shriek.

Then Sam was there, launching through the air, bringing David down in a rugby-style tackle on to the bed. Gaynor screamed again. Sam had his arms wrapped around David's, pinning her brother's limbs to his sides, the weight of his legs hooked over David's. David struggled, squeaking like a trapped animal, hands and feet flapping but Sam, breathing heavily, held the rest of him immobile.

Gaynor stood transfixed and horrified. She wanted to cry out to Sam not to hurt him, but then David went limp and began to shake with loud racking sobs and she heard Sam's familiar tones .

"Shhhh, Shhh," he was saying soothingly. "You're safe now. I've got you and nobody is going to harm you."

He looked up at Gaynor. "Ambulance," he mouthed over David's shoulder. "Ambulance now."

It was daylight by the time they'd all gone. Gaynor sat at the kitchen table, still in her dressing gown. She scrubbed at her face with a damp ball of kitchen towel. Sam came in through the back door, a warm waft of tobacco smoke coming in with him.

"You could have had that in here," she said wearily.

He shook his head. "You should get some sleep," he said, picking up his jacket from the back of the chair.

Gaynor rose and began to pace up and down the room. "Did you know the police would be called?" she asked accusingly.

Sam watched her. "I thought there was a fair chance, if he wasn't going to go willingly."

She stopped and glared at him. "Why didn't you tell me?"

"If I'd told you, you might not have called anyone and he needed treatment."

Fresh tears rolled down her face. "I've let him down now. I feel terrible." Sam leant out and took her hand, pulling her back to her chair. "What else could you have done?"

"I don't know. Kept him here, tried to get a doctor."

Sam shook his head again. "He was beyond that."

"But the police," she wailed. "Like he was a criminal." She saw David's face as they'd manhandled him into the back of the ambulance, heard the PC's flat tones as he'd stepped in after him. "We'll deal with it now, love."

"I thought the ambulance men would just sedate him," she said, "I thought they'd calm him down."

"You heard the bloke," Sam said reasonably. "They're not allowed to inject him without his permission. And he wasn't going to give that, was he? You can't blame the crew. Of course they want police back-up if someone's being violent."

"He's not violent, don't say that," Gaynor said hotly. "He's ill – he didn't know what he was doing."

"Maybe, but he could still have hurt you."

"He wouldn't do that!"

"He nearly did."

Gaynor turned on him angrily. "Not deliberately! He was frightened. Because you were there."

Sam looked steadily back. "And you called me because *you* were frightened."

"And you had him taken away!" She jumped up again and began to walk around the kitchen.

176

Sam sounded annoyed. "I didn't do anything except try to help you. The Mental Health team took the decision and, in my opinion, the right one. This wasn't going to get better on its own. He's in the best place now, with experts who can take care of him."

"He's been bloody sectioned!"

"It was the only way they were going to be able to get him in there. Under the Mental Health Act…"

She put her hands to the sides of her head, grimacing in frustration. "Don't quote that at me," she snapped. "It was bedtime reading where I grew up."

"Then you'll know I was trying to protect you," he snapped back. "Next time I'll let him smash your head in with the furniture, shall I?"

"Don't you dare say that." Gaynor rounded on him, shouting. "This is my brother we're talking about, you bloody bastard!"

Sam's face darkened. "It happens, Gaynor," he said coldly. "Whether you like it or not. I've seen it before. I've known people to be stabbed to death by relatives they swore would never hurt them." He put both hands on her arms and looked straight at her, his eyes angry. "So don't you dare swear at me!"

"Sod off." Gaynor brought her arms up hard, shoving him away. As she did so, her dressing gown fell open. For a moment they looked at each other, both breathing hard. Then she moved towards him and he slid a hand inside the smooth fabric. They both gasped. He took his hand away.

"You need to go to bed," he said with difficulty. "You're exhausted. Get some sleep, go and see David later."

She leant up and closed her mouth over his. He gave a sort of groan.

She was hot, molten, quivering with longing for him. She felt as though she were on the edge of ecstasy already and on the point of collapsing in tears.

"Please," she said desperately, "please, Sam, come to bed with me."

For a moment he was quite rigid, as if having some kind of struggle with himself. Then his hands moved again. He pushed the robe from her shoulders and, as it slithered down to a heap on the floor, swept her naked body up into his arms.

16. Malvasia di Cagliara
*Has a honeyed fragrance but
tends towards the flat.*

"Have a good day!" Jamie picked up his briefcase from a chair and leant over and kissed Claire's cheek. "I'll do my best to get the six-eighteen tonight but you know how it is..."

"No problem." Claire, dressed in tracksuit bottoms and sweatshirt, was sitting at the kitchen table, tapping at a calculator and frowning over columns of figures in a red hardback book in front of her. She sounded distracted. "I'll probably be in the bar, anyway."

Jamie stopped, one hand on the handle of the back door. "But I thought it was your night off. I thought we were going out."

"We are!" Claire glanced up at him. "Come straight down to Greens when you get off the train and we'll go as soon as you get there. I've booked a table at the new Thai at the top of the High Street – fantastic vegetarian selection apparently. We can have a drink on the way."

Jamie nodded. "OK. Perhaps we can have two. Then I might get my wicked way with you later..."

"Yeah, yeah." Claire waved Jamie goodbye, closed the accounts and gathered up the dogs' leads. The two Airedales leapt from the floor and threw themselves at her, nearly knocking her over. She grabbed at their collars, wrestling with them while she clipped on the leather straps. At last she got the door open. "OK boys! Let's hit that beach."

They tugged hard against her as she made her way down Harbour Street, under the flint archway to Viking Bay. Once down the slope on to the sand, she bent and released both dogs who bounded joyfully away from her.

It was supposed to be her day off but she wanted to get the VAT up to date. And she'd thought that this morning, while they were closed, she might just pop an extra coat of paint over the walls of the stone passageway to the loos. She told the others it was looking tatty already, not wanting to admit, even to herself, that she wanted everything perfect for when her parents visited later in the week.

Her father still hadn't been down to see her new business. He'd said he was short-staffed and couldn't to leave his pub in Norwich when it was the opening evening; had cancelled another visit since. Now he was supposed to be bringing her mother down on Thursday, but Claire wouldn't hold her breath.

She'd already invited them all down for Christmas – knowing you had to get in early for a fighting chance of any family gathering that wasn't on her father's own licensed premises. "That will be lovely," her mother had said, anxiously. But Claire wouldn't hold her breath for that, either.

She wanted her father, Grant, to see how well she'd done. She felt childish for needing it but she wanted to hear him say, just for once: well done! It was Neill he watched with pride. Neill – the big banker with the glittering future and his slick city life – who got the praise. Even though Neill had never given a toss about the family business and she had slogged her guts out, helping Grant build up one crumbling pub after another. Still it was Neill he clapped on the back and Neill he had the faith in. "You should get your brother to go in with you," Grant had said, on hearing about Gaynor as the third partner. "He'd know how to turn out the profits!"

Well, actually, so did she. Neither Sarah nor Gaynor showed any particular interest in the books but Claire pored over them constantly and, by anyone's standards, Greens was doing well. Despite the fact that Sarah seemed a lot more stressed in the kitchen than Claire remembered her and Gaynor could be irritatingly ditzy at times, she'd grown really fond of them both. Somehow it was working, though it could work even better perhaps if …

She walked the length of the bay and back, planning and dreaming. She had so many ideas for the future. This was just the beginning…

Reaching the jetty again, she whistled for the dogs. Wooster arrived first. "Come on!" she called to Henry who was still sniffing among the seaweed. Eventually he trotted towards her, something in his mouth.

"What have you got?" Claire bent down and retrieved a bashed-up fruit juice carton from between her dog's teeth. Henry was always picking things up on the beach. If she was lucky she'd be gifted with a piece of wood or chalk. But sometimes he'd have gulped down the remains of a picnic and would bring her the chewed packaging; on one charming occasion he'd bounded up with a condom dangling from his jaws.

"You terrible dog." She patted them both and clipped on their leads. Then she straightened and began to walk purposefully back up towards the wine bar. Sarah wouldn't be in till much later, Gaynor was still away. In the meantime, Claire had work to do.

Gaynor pulled out on to the M4, moved across to the outside lane and put her foot down. She felt a glorious sense of freedom. She turned the radio up. They were playing 'Young at Heart' and all at once it was exactly how she felt. She turned it up, feeling herself moving swiftly and smoothly away, leaving the stifling air of her parents' semi in Reading behind. David had seemed much better by the time she left.

"Thanks," he'd said diffidently when she went into his room to say goodbye. She'd hugged him. "Sorry," he added as she left.

"Don't be daft," she'd said. He wasn't back at work yet but he was taking his medication again. They hadn't really talked about what had happened. They'd managed to skirt round it in a way that enabled them both to express apology yet still feel their actions were defensible. She was relieved that any sense of betrayal David might have felt at her letting him be carted off by the burly arm of the law seemed cancelled out by his embarrassment at having tried to smash her house up.

She'd quietly closed his bedroom door. "You take care, eh?"

"Don't you feel like walking out sometimes?" she'd asked her mother downstairs as she kissed her.

And her mother had given a sad smile. "Sometimes," she said. "But then I remind myself they can't help it."

Gaynor privately thought her father probably could. He wore his depression like a badge. One that gave him total absolution from responsibility.

"Why don't you do something nice for her for a change?" Gaynor had asked him. "Buy her some flowers, take her to the cinema – Mum'd love that."

He'd looked at her in that half-patronising, half-disparaging way he'd looked at her all her life, and said, "I don't think it's any of your business how we spend our time, dear," the last word delivered with that blend of superiority and malice that made her want to hit him with something hard.

But she said nothing more. She had got through the whole visit by holding on to what she had inside – the memory of Sam, glowing like a warm coal. Each time she thought about the way they had fallen on each other, she felt a hot jolt of desire that almost made her cry out.

She was longing to see him again and in no rush at all to face Victor, whom she'd spoken to briefly on the phone and who had been largely uninterested in David's welfare but only too keen to debate the cost of new mirrors. "Seven years bad luck you'll have now," he'd said spitefully.

She was glad she'd emptied an entire can of 1001 mousse on to the bedroom carpet and he hadn't seen the tea stains.

She put in her earpiece and tried ringing Sam again. He still wasn't answering. She guessed he must be out or in the garden but she felt a vague unease. She'd tried a couple of times yesterday too, when she'd escaped her family for ten minutes, but he hadn't been there then, either. She wished he'd get a mobile but, when she'd suggested it, he'd looked at her askance. "What on earth for?" he'd asked. She smiled to herself. Perhaps she'd get him one for Christmas.

She remembered him saying Debra was coming down sometime. Perhaps she was there now and they'd gone out somewhere. Perhaps he had a sign to get finished and he was ignoring the phone – she'd known him do that before.

She'd try one final time and then leave it till she got home. She hoped he'd answer soon. She hoped Debra wouldn't be there. She wanted to meet her, but not just yet. She missed Sam and when she got back she wanted him all to herself.

But she got Victor instead. As she pulled into the drive she saw him getting out of his Jag and her heart sank. Damn it, she should have gone straight to Sam's cottage. But Victor actually looked pleased to see her for once, perhaps regretting his unsupportive attitude earlier.

"Hi," he said, warmly. "Shall we go out tonight?"

It was the last thing she'd thought of doing. She'd expected him to be home late, if at all, giving her the opportunity to hotfoot it down to Sam's. She'd have to wait till the morning now.

"Marchesi's?" asked Victor.

She smiled and nodded, unable to think of a single convincing reason not to. "Sure," she said, pulling her bag from the boot, going upstairs to unpack and get changed, wishing she could let Sam know what she was doing and deciding that she would buy him a phone tomorrow, never mind Christmas, so that at least she could text him at times like these.

Victor was at his most charming. She sat opposite him in the conservatory at Marchesi's, toying with her king prawns, listening while he spoke cheerily of the ad campaign they were doing for Easy-Chef Cook-it Sauces and the debate he was having with Laurence about the wisdom of having a Delia Smith look-alike wearing high heels and a bikini beneath her pinny as she stirred.

"I said," Victor explained happily, "that stuff is just too last century. It would be a lot more happening to just try and get Nigella."

Gaynor smiled, half amused, half irritated at his attempts to sound young and funky. Perhaps, she thought suddenly, Victor was simply having one giant mid-life crisis. Perhaps all this staying away involved nothing more sinister than him hanging round achingly-trendy nightclubs trying to kid himself he was still in the bloom of youth. She herself felt like a teenager. She felt the old affection for Victor she always did when he was nice to her but she was also thinking about Sam. She'd been to the Ladies twice so she could phone him but the loos here were in the basement and there was not a flicker of a signal either time.

Victor poured more Montrachet into her glass. "How was the trip? Are your parents well?" he enquired politely.

She nodded stiffly, sipping the cold white burgundy, usually one of her favourites, now barely tasting it, not wanting to think or talk about her family, not really wanting to talk about anything. She wanted to fling her arms around Sam – see his slow smile as he opened the door. Hear his voice, as he hugged her to him.

"Are you all right?" At the end of the meal, Victor peered at her.

"Just tired." She smiled brightly at him. "Just need to get home and have some sleep, I think."

Victor nodded. He was being solicitous. "Another coffee first? Herbal tea? Brandy?"

She shook her head, wanting to get out of the place so she could get home, hide away in the bathroom and try another phone call. She didn't want anything. No coffee, or after-dinner mints, or any more banal conversation.

Victor was being perfectly good company for a change, but she just wanted to see Sam.

Fate was against her. When Victor woke, he was still in born-again mode. He brought her tea, stood in the kitchen in his dressing gown scrambling eggs, smiled at her across the orange juice and munched toast with maddening slowness and enquired after everything from the progress of the wine-bar to Lizzie's love life and Gaynor's excellent judgement in choosing a new shade of nail polish at her last manicure.

She tried to look pleased. He was being the Victor she had craved for some months, but of all the mornings for him to return from the dead this was not the one she'd have chosen.

"I'm in no rush to get the office," he said, "I'm entertaining half the night, after all. Frankly I'd rather be here with you."

Hurrah! And Oh-for-God's-sake-go-to-work. Sam was still not answering his phone. Gaynor wanted to get to his cottage and track him down and very probably take him to bed. Her body still tingled at the memory of last time. Her mind was split in two with longing and guilt in equal measures. It would be so much easier if Victor was being a bastard.

"Love you!" he called as he slid into the Jag at around two by which time she could barely keep still.

"Love you too," she called back, thinking: it is true, I do love you. But can I trust you? Will you still be like this when you get back and oh – *Sam*...

The moment his car was gone, so was she. She didn't even walk today. She drove down to the seafront, parking her car on the esplanade, and ran the short distance along the cliff-top pathway to Sam's cottage.

She banged on the front door. And waited. Nothing. She walked around the back of the house, feeling uneasy. She hoped he hadn't gone out early. She still couldn't understand why he hadn't answered late last night. A sudden fear gripped her at the thought of him lying ill, or dead. Unless he'd stayed away overnight. Her mind slid away from the thought. She couldn't lose Sam. Victor, maybe, but please not Sam. Was he fed up with her? Tired of her weeping and wailing?

Brutus was sitting on the back step. "Hello, gorgeous!" She bent and stroked him. He stood up, arched his back and purred. He looked sleek and well-fed, so he clearly hadn't been left alone long. "What have you done with him?"

She tried the handle of the French window – it was open. Heart thumping, she walked into the back room. The piano was closed. The roses she'd bought him hung their heads in a vase on the top. An ashtray on the table next to the battered sofa was full of his tiny squashed cigarette ends.

"Sam?"

She walked through into the hall, looked in the kitchen. "Sam?"

She didn't want to go upstairs. She was suddenly afraid of finding him slumped in bed or the bathroom, Afraid, too, of finding some evidence that he had someone else. But not Sam, she told herself. Not in the space of a few days. I love you. He'd said it on Monday. He'd meant it – she could see he meant it. He'd almost had tears in his eyes.

He was in the front room. Sitting back from the window, looking out, his profile turned away from her as she walked in.

"Oh!" She gave a cry of pleasure and relief. "There you are." She rushed over to the big leather chair. "Why didn't you answer me?"

He went on gazing out across the garden. "Sorry."

"I was worried. What's the matter?"

He didn't reply. His face had a remote, haunted look – even the corners of his mouth seemed to be dragged down.

"What's happened?" She felt instantly guilty, as though she'd been caught out in a terrible deed, as though he'd found out something awful about her and was about to say that everything had changed. "Has something happened?" she asked again.

He turned then and shook his head. "No," he said, his voice sounding tired and beaten. "Nothing has happened – just me."

She sat on the arm of the chair, put an arm around him and hugged him, all her good spirits dwindled away to dismay. "I've been so longing to see you," she said. "I've missed you."

He looked round at her. It was an expression she hadn't seen before. "I've missed you too," he said tonelessly.

"Well, I'm here now," she said, moving closer.

He felt stiff and unyielding. "Not really," he said.

She moved round and knelt on the floor in front of him, looking up into his face. "I am – I am here. I've been thinking about you all the time, thinking about that night, knowing I just want to be with you."

Sam looked back at her. His eyes were sad. "Are you going to go home and pack your bags, then? Tell your husband it's all over? That you've met someone else? That you want a divorce? I'm not asking you to," he went on, as she hesitated. "I would never ask you to do that."

"So why…" She looked at him, confused.

"I've been sitting here doing a lot of thinking. Feeling badly about what we did. Badly for you, for your husband. And for me. I promised myself I wouldn't do that."

"I don't regret it," she said staunchly. "I think it was meant to be."

He gave a grim smile. "That's something people come up with to excuse their shabby behaviour."

The nails from one of her hands dug into the palm of the other. "Do you think what we did was shabby?"

187

He looked past her, out of the window. "I'm not very proud of it. Having sex with a married woman who's in a highly emotional state and suffering from lack of sleep, when her husband's away, in her husband's house – does that sound like behaviour to take pride in, to you?"

She grabbed at his arm and shook it. "It wasn't like that! I wanted it – I made it happen. You wanted it too, didn't you?" Even now the thought of his passion sent a shock of desire through her.

He nodded. "Oh yes. I should have controlled myself. It always takes two."

There was something about the way he said it. Gaynor looked at him and things fell into place. "Did your wife have an affair?" she asked suddenly.

He was silent for a moment. Then he reached for his tobacco. "I don't know. Part of me hopes she did. That I wasn't all she ever had. She threw out a lot of stuff before she died. Was very keen to clear everything up. Diaries, letters, cards. I don't know. I saw one of them. It just had kisses inside. I don't know who it was from. There was this black plastic sack full of rubbish waiting to go out. She'd tied the top up. I carried it downstairs to the bins outside the flats and I wanted to rip it open and take out all her papers and look for clues. But I couldn't do that to her."

He stared bleakly in front of him. "Though I sometimes wonder what would have lasted longer – the guilt at betraying her trust like that, or the unanswered questions that eat me now."

Gaynor took his hand, moved by his expression, and tried to sound reassuring. "I think you'd have known if she was having a long-term thing. Perhaps it was just a harmless little flirtation at work or something. I think you do know when your partner has someone else." Though did she? Sometimes she was convinced Victor was playing away. Other times, like last night, she wasn't sure at all…

Sam was talking again. "I don't know – Eleanor had this sort of closed air about her. You never really knew what was

188

going on with her. Even the kids will say that now. And yet she was a lovely mother to them – she'd hug them, laugh with them."

He looked away again. Gaynor couldn't work out whether it was anger or tears he was controlling.

"They'd all be laughing at something and I'd walk in and it would stop." He shook his head. "Debra says it wasn't like that but it was. Eleanor never laughed with me any more."

Gaynor said cautiously, "When did it start to go wrong?"

She always felt intrusive questioning Sam, as though she were probing somewhere he didn't want her touching, but she had a strong urge to hear more. A sense it was important. He turned and looked at her. His face had softened a little.

"It wasn't ever really right," he said matter-of-factly. He pulled a cigarette paper from the packet. "She was a WPC when I met her. We were partnered. We got called out to a party where a kid had been abused. You couldn't believe it. The bloke's family stood around him, shielding him. He was drunk, they said. They offered it by way of an explanation. He was drunk so he tried to screw his six-year old niece."

He stopped and began to roll a cigarette. Gaynor sat quite still, stiff with horror.

Sam went on in the same even voice. "Eleanor carried the child out while I arrested him. We couldn't look at each other afterwards. Back at the station, my mate Terry was suspended for throwing the bloke's hot tea in his crotch. I felt dreadful afterwards because I wished I'd done it…"

The light was going. Sam stared out at the garden, his expression in shadow. Gaynor sat on the floor at his feet, laid her head against his legs, leant up and took his hand. He squeezed it briefly.

"We shouldn't have got married after that. We were both doing it for the wrong reasons. We both wanted it for what we thought it stood for but not for each other. We did it because the church had been booked and the cake iced and her mother would have been mortified if we hadn't.''

"Did Eleanor say that?''

"No, Eleanor wouldn't say that. Eleanor didn't say much about anything.'' He sighed. "She was a lovely mother and the best wife she knew how to be, bearing in mind she wasn't in love with me.''

Gaynor searched for something to say that would make it better. "Perhaps she was but she couldn't show it.''

He laughed without mirth. "Or perhaps she just wasn't.''

"I think,'' he said later, as they sat quietly looking out at the blackness, "that she loved me in her way. She loved me as her husband, as the father of her children, as the provider, because that is what one does. She didn't feel passion for me and – in fairness to her – why should she have done? After the first, short, desperate weeks, I didn't feel it for her, either.''

Gaynor realised she was holding her breath. She felt as if she had to keep very still, that now he had started telling her this, she must not move and interrupt it.

"We ended up embarrassed for each other,'' Sam was saying. "I think there were times when she would have liked me to take her in my arms, when perhaps she even wished we could make love, but by then she couldn't approach me and I would never have made a move towards her, for fear of more rejection.''

He looked down at Gaynor and she saw the pain on his face. "It was the thing that grieved me most at the end,'' he said. "I did try and hold her then and I felt between us all that loss and remorse and regret.''

Gaynor twisted round and put her arms around his knees, hugging them. "I want you to hold me, Sam.''

He stroked her hair. "You belong to someone else.''

"Someone who is unfaithful to me.''

"You don't know that yet.''

"I'm going to find out.''

"And then?''

Gaynor sat back, throwing up her hands. "Tell him, leave him. I don't know. I thought I'd feel bad the next morning but I didn't. It felt right. It felt special. But..." She struggled to put into words how she felt – to even understand those feelings herself. "I'm confused about Victor. I was quite sure he had someone else – well, I am sure. I think he has. So what can he expect from me?"

Sam was silent.

"And although he has just been nice to me today, he spends more time being awful and I can't live like that. But then, when he is OK, I feel that I should..."

Sam spoke quietly. "I'm not going to be a weapon. Not something you use to get even with your husband. My feelings are involved here, Gaynor. I don't know what's bloody hit me."

She looked at him desperately. "Please give me time to sort it out. Please do that. You said you loved me. You said it. Do you love me, Sam?"

He leant down and pulled her up into the big chair with him, on to his lap, into his arms, held her against him.

Her heart stilled. Brutus appeared on the arm of the chair and rubbed his face against Sam's shoulder. She wished it could all stop here – that they could stay in this chair in front of this night-filled window, warm and safe, for ever.

"Do you still love me, Sam?"

He squeezed her tighter. "That is the problem. Yes, I do."

17. Vinho Verde

A young wine and missing some body.

"Who is it? Who's doing this?" Sarah appeared to be trying to pulverise the answer-phone as Gaynor walked into Greens.

"Not another one!" Gaynor dumped her handbag on the bar. "Play it to me!"

"I can't even understand it." Sarah hit the Play button. "Just the usual stuff – you bitch, etc."

They both listened. It was more indistinct than the others. "You're a fucking what?" Gaynor asked.

Sarah shook her head. "Dunno. Lezzo?"

Gaynor listened again. "Oh, could be. Well, it wouldn't be the first time someone had assumed that, now, would it? I still want to know which one of us is with who. I think I fancy you more than Claire." She grinned. "Or are we supposed to be a ménage à trois? I tell you, it's some pervert who wants to watch…"

Sarah glared. "It's not funny."

"What happened to the police?"

Sarah grimaced. "They're looking into it. Which they were doing three weeks ago. I phoned BT again. They say all they can do is give the police the number again. And they still won't give it to me!"

She rummaged under the bar and extracted a packet of pain killers. "My head feels like it's going to burst. I hate that kitchen – I fucking hate it. It's all very well for Claire to have all these great ideas about lunchtime specials but who's got to bloody cook them? It's only omelettes and salads, she says.

192

Omelettes are a pain in the arse when everyone wants them and Benjamin's on salads and it takes him all bloody day."

"They are lovely, though," said Gaynor. "That woman and her daughter who were in here yesterday said they'd never seen such beautiful –"

"Yes," Sarah interrupted, "but they were on holiday. Most of the people in here in the week have to go back to work in the afternoon. They can't spend their entire lunch-hour waiting while Benjamin carves a water-lily from a radish!"

Gaynor giggled. "Bless him."

"You wouldn't say that if you were in the kitchen," said Sarah darkly. "If you had twenty-seven meals to get out and his sole contribution was to colour-coordinate the veg."

"Can't we get another chef to help out so you can be up here more?"

"Claire says we can't afford it yet," said Sarah shortly. "Don't think I haven't tried."

"Can't she do more down there?"

Sarah shrugged. "She does what she can. She's made all the desserts this week and she did all the finger food for that engagement party we had last Sunday. She can do the odd evening if I've prepared it all but I'm the one who's supposed to be the trained chef." She pulled a face. "I'd just forgotten how gruesome it can be!"

She looked at her watch. "Paul's due to pick the kids up at eleven. I hope he's not late again. Charlie's been dressed since six."

Sarah looked incredibly stressed out. Gaynor switched the coffee grinder on. She felt worried about her – the long hours she was working, her headaches, her worries about Paul letting the children down.

"I'm sure he'll be here and we'll be able to get someone else to do the cooking soon, she said. "We must be doing OK – we're pretty full every night, aren't we?"

"Yeah, I suppose. I really must pay more attention to the figures. I've just had so many other things to think about, I've left it all to Claire. I mean she's so good at it." Sarah ran a hand through her shock of hair. "I used to be a capable person," she suddenly burst out. "I ran restaurants four times the size of this before I had the kids!"

"I know." Gaynor put down the coffee cups and gave her a hug. Sarah felt tense. "You are still capable. You're the most capable person I know – you've just got a hell of a lot on."

Sarah sighed. "Yeah. Bit tired."

In a gesture of support, Gaynor peeled potatoes, while Sarah made up lasagnes and Benjamin fashioned carrot twirls. "Just fluted edges is fine," Sarah said, "it's much quicker."

"Presentation," said Benjamin. "At college," he told Gaynor, "I got full marks for my scalloped celeriac."

"Put them in a real kitchen," growled Sarah, when he'd disappeared upstairs to oversee the flower arrangements, "and they wouldn't last five minutes."

"Shall I go and open up?" Gaynor put the last of the vegetables in water and looked at the clock. "Where's Claire, anyway?"

"Not coming in till later. Got to take one of the dogs to the vet. Let's just hope we're not too busy."

Gaynor picked up a bunch of keys and headed for the stairs. Overhead a pair of feet ran across the floorboards. Moments later, Bel appeared in the doorway holding her doll Rosie by the hair. Sarah looked up from her chopping.

"What's the matter, darling?"

Bel adopted a long-suffering expression. "Scarface has been sick on my bed," she announced importantly. "Daddy's not coming and Charlie has run away."

"Where's he gone?" Sarah switched off the TV and pulled the headphones from Luke who was sprawled on the sofa with his CD walkman and the remote control.

Luke shrugged. "I don't know."

"Couldn't you have stopped him?"

Luke sat up, sighing. "I didn't know he was going, did I? I was talking to Dad and when I put the phone down, Bel said Charlie had gone. It's not my fault," he said belligerently. "How come you always blame me?"

Sarah looked in their bedroom. Somebody could have died in there and you wouldn't know. It was impossible, from the widespread chaos and week-old washing strewn on every available inch of floor space, to have any idea if Charlie had taken anything with him.

"Why didn't your father come, anyway?" she asked sharply.

Luke lounged in the doorway. "He said he had to work."

Yeah, right, thought Sarah, as she dialled her mother's number. Bloody Paul. Bel was young and accepting, Luke in teenage-slouch mode didn't care much about anything, but Charlie... Charlie was the one who'd taken all this hard and he didn't deserve it. Paul had lost sight of everything but his next high at the bookies. No wonder he'd called Luke's mobile rather than her.

She waited impatiently for her mother to answer the phone, steeling herself for the inevitable diatribe on Paul's shortcomings. She hadn't really expected Charlie to be there but anything was possible. She explained as briefly as she could, shaking her head at Gaynor as she listened to her mother's response. "No? OK. No please, stay there. Just in case he comes to you..."

"Where might he go?" Gaynor was putting her jacket on.

"I don't know." Sarah was white. "I just don't know."

Richard, who'd fortuitously wandered in, mid-crisis, was attempting to interrogate Luke. "How long ago did he leave?"

Luke shrugged.

"Think!" Sarah shrieked at him.

"Bel came down about twenty minutes ago," said Gaynor. "He can't have gone far."

Richard picked up his keys. "I'll go and get the car. Has he got any money with him?"

Sarah shook her head. "I shouldn't think so,"

Gaynor squeezed her arm. "I'll go and check the beach."

"What shall I do?" Benjamin enquired.

"Hold the fort!" Gaynor called, as she headed for the door.

Poor, poor Sarah, she thought as she ran along the jetty. She'd looked as if she was going to be sick. Gaynor shaded her eyes and scanned the curve of Viking Bay, hoping to see Charlie kicking a rock somewhere. The tide was going out – ropes and chains stretched beneath the stranded fishing boats on the glistening sand. In the distance a couple poked about in the whelk-encrusted pools and someone wandered along with a dog by the pastel-coloured beach huts, all boarded up for winter beneath the cliffs, but the figures were all too tall to be Charlie. The wind whipped her hair about as she gazed at the white undercliff in the distance, curving round towards Ramsgate. Nobody there.

"It's not that I think anything will happen to him wandering about Broadstairs," Sarah had said, "but I worry about his state of mind. He's been withdrawn lately – difficult, you know. He could do anything. Suppose," she said, looking stricken, "he tries to find Paul. Suppose he tries to hitch a lift or something?"

"He's not that silly." Gaynor had tried to be reassuring. But really she didn't know anything about ten-year-old boys. Or have a clue what he might do.

"He hasn't caught a train," said Richard, getting back into the car. The bloke thinks he'd have seen him and no kid on his own has bought a ticket in the last hour or so."

Sarah blew her nose. "Oh God, where is he? You know, if it was Luke I'd know where to look – he'd be at Tyrone's house or at the skateboarding place or skulking round the arcade. But Charlie…"

She shivered, pulling her coat around her, trying to block out the horrible visions that kept crowding into her mind.

196

Richard put a brief hand on her knee before he started the engine again. "We'll find him."

Gaynor got back to Greens to find a small riot in the bar and Benjamin flapping about in an apron.

"I've got rather a lot of lunches on the go," he was saying apologetically to a group of impatient suits.

Gaynor cast off her jacket and slid behind the bar. "Can I help anybody?"

There was a clamour of voices. Benjamin beat a retreat to the kitchen. Gaynor switched on her hugest smile as she looked at the clutch of orders he'd stuffed into her hand.

She hoped Benjamin would be able to produce them without Sarah at his elbow.

She'd just about got all the drinks served when the buzzer sounded from the kitchen. Gaynor ran down the stairs.

"What is that?" she enquired, looking at a small, yellow rubbery circle richly garnished with frilly spring onion.

Benjamin looked downcast. "Sarah usually does the omelettes," he explained.

"With more than one egg, I should think," said Gaynor. "I don't think I can serve this – can't you make a bigger one? Three eggs and just flip it over while it's still…. Look," she said, seeing the expression of dumb panic that had crossed Benjamin's face, "I'll do it."

She grabbed an apron and thrust her order pad at Benjamin. "You get up there and calm the masses. And take that up – who was it for?" She nodded at the tray he'd loaded with a panini and a salad nicoise.

Benjamin looked at her hopelessly. "I'm afraid I have no idea."

"Goodness!" said Claire, arriving in the doorway half an hour later, to find Gaynor at the stove. "Never thought I'd see the day…"

"You nearly didn't. We almost set the kitchen alight with that chip fryer. Can you help? I haven't got a clue what to do with scallops and Benjamin's just taken an order for three of them."

Claire shook her head. "They're not even on the lunchtime menu."

Gaynor handed her the spatula she'd been prodding omelettes with. "I'll go and sort it."

She gathered up the Avocado and Mozzarella Surprise that Benjamin had created in frantic trips to the kitchen and threw her apron into a corner. She carried the salad plate and a bowl of soup upstairs to where an academic type with a silly goatee beard was sitting with his bored wife.

"Sorry for the delay!" She smiled brightly from one to the other. Goatee was not pacified.

"This is ridiculous!" he fumed. "We've been waiting for over half an hour." He glowered at Gaynor. "We've got a train to catch."

Hot, sweaty and frazzled from the rigours of the last hour, she put his plate down a little too hard.

"And my business partner's little boy's gone missing."

"Arsehole," she said, as she carried empty dishes through the swing door into the kitchen. Claire had confiscated Benjamin's vegetable knife and put him on washing-up. He looked round from the sink resignedly as Gaynor heaped more plates on the already-tottering pile. "I wonder if Sarah's called the police," Gaynor added.

"Perhaps she's found him by now," said Claire, deftly sliding apple pie into dishes.

Benjamin raised his pink rubber-gloved hands from the suds. Gravely, he said, "In my experience, they won't do much until he's been missing for several hours. And all avenues have been exhausted. They know that most children reported missing turn up perfectly safe and sound at a friend's or relative's within…"

"In your experience?" queried Gaynor, surprised

"It was on *Morse* last week," said Benjamin. "There was a case where a twelve-year old girl went missing. Now in fact she'd been murdered but first of all…"

Footsteps were coming down the stairs.

"Dishwasher's stopped!" Claire interrupted sharply. "Leave that stuff to soak and empty it, will you?"

Sarah appeared in the doorway and shook her head. She looked dreadful.

"We went to the police station," she said. "They were really kind. They're circulating his description and they said try not to worry, most children turn up on their own."

Gaynor glanced at Benjamin. She saw Claire do the same. His mouth opened and closed again.

"Sit down," said Claire. "We'll make you a coffee. Would you like a brandy in it? Benjamin, you pop upstairs and …"

"No, thank you. I'm going upstairs to see Luke." Sarah pulled her coat more tightly around her, shuddering. "We've left Bel at my mother's. Charlie could go straight up to the flat through the side entrance. I'd better go and wait."

"Is there anything we can do?" asked Gaynor, feeling helpless.

Sarah shook her head. "Oh," she turned to Claire, suddenly remembering. "The fish pies. I've done the base – it's in the fridge. But the potato…"

"Don't worry." Claire was already pulling the earthenware dishes from the cupboard. "I'll do it."

Sarah nodded, white and exhausted. "Thank you. Was your dog OK?"

"Yeah, Henry's fine. He's been a bit off colour and I was worried he was ill but the vet said –" Claire stopped abruptly. "Sorry, you don't want to hear all that."

Gaynor gave Sarah a little push. "Go on, you go upstairs. We'll be here. Charlie will be back soon and we'll see him, whichever door he comes in…"

When Sarah had gone, she said, "Oh God, I simply cannot imagine how she's feeling."

Claire tipped potatoes into the sink. "Poor Sarah. I've got no idea about the whole children thing but I know how bad I feel if anything happens to one of the dogs. Charlie will come back, though." She looked at Gaynor. "Won't he?"

"He'd better." Gaynor picked up a potato peeler. "Shall we take these upstairs in case he comes to the front door?"

They sat at the back of the bar, a pile of spuds between them. "It's really not fair of Paul," said Gaynor, dropping a skinned potato into the large pot of water. "He means the world to Charlie. He should be more reliable. He's his father. If he says he's coming, then he should damn well make sure he gets here."

Claire was silent. Her long dark hair fell over her face as she carried on intently peeling. Something about the way she kept her head down made Gaynor feel awkward. "Don't you think?" she added.

Claire tossed the vegetable away from her into the saucepan and picked up another. "Yes I do think," she said, tightly. "I'm a hell of a lot older than Charlie and it still hurts me when my parents can't be bothered."

Gaynor gathered up a damp handful of peel and put it in the carrier bag beside her. "Did your dad not come the other day?" she asked carefully.

Claire gave a contemptuous laugh. "No, he didn't. And more fool me for thinking he might! He's always much too busy to leave his own life to ever come and visit a bit of mine." She stabbed the peeler through the middle of the vegetable in her hand. " But, you know, I always believe him when he says he will. I run around and get everything ready – wanting him to be impressed – and then of course, the phone call comes. Always from my mother," she added bitterly. "Never from him. Saying they just can't manage it after all…"

She looked at Gaynor, rolling her eyes at herself. "Stupid isn't it?"

"No, it's not." Gaynor got up and went behind the bar to the coffee machine. "My father's completely crap but it never quite stops one hoping that he might suddenly be different next time. You want one of these?" She held up a coffee cup.

Claire nodded. "When do you stop caring? I wonder."

Gaynor thought of Sam. "I don't know if you ever do." She put an espresso down in front of Claire. "And Charlie's only ten," she said.

"Yes." Claire looked troubled. "Poor Charlie."

Upstairs in the flat, Richard put the kettle on. "I'll go back out again in a minute," he said. " I'll go up and down the High Street in case he's walking home."

"Where from?" cried Sarah, white-faced. "Where can he have been? Oh Richard, where is he?"

She sat down at the table and put her head in her hands, her fingers pressing against her tear-filled eyes. Richard went and stood next to her, patting awkwardly at her shoulder. "He'll turn up," he said uncertainly.

"All those questions," Sarah said bleakly. "Like it was really serious. Like they thought something terrible might have happened."

"No," said Richard, still patting her. "Just standard, just doing their job."

"Did you see?" Sarah looked up at him, anguished. "Did you see the bit of the form where they had to tick vulnerable or non-vulnerable?"

Richard shook his head.

Sarah began to cry. "Vulnerable, they said he was vulnerable."

Richard sat down beside her. "It's because he's a child," he said, trying not to look worried. "But he'll be home soon."

He made her a coffee and put his coat back on. "I'll keep looking," he said. Sarah nodded silently. She felt sick and cold. It was getting dark outside. She had a vision of Charlie sat on a doorstep, shivering and crying, not knowing how to get home. She closed her eyes as if to block it out but opened them again as she heard Richard say, "Oh!"

He had opened the outside door that led to the steps down to the street. Sarah sprang up from her chair and saw a tall figure coming towards her. She took one look at the uniform and felt her legs buckle.

"I wasn't going to steal it," said Charlie vehemently. "I was just seeing what it would feel like in my pocket."

"He'd been in the shop for sometime," said the PC who had accepted a cup of tea and made himself comfortable at the kitchen table. "They let him be for a while but then the manager saw him take one of the phones and called us."

"I didn't…" Charlie shouted.

"Shhh," Sarah said vaguely, so weak with relief she could barely follow what was being said.

"All right, son, we'll leave it now." The PC looked at Charlie and then turned to Sarah "I've got kids myself," he said. Charlie glowered.

"Dad said we were going to go there," he told Sarah when the policeman had left and Richard had tactfully disappeared. "He said we'd go to Phone World and get one today. He said." He looked up at Sarah, anguished.

She pulled him towards her, torn between wanting to rail at him for how badly he'd frightened her and still so grateful to see him that she wanted nothing but to cuddle him. "I know, darling. I'm sorry."

"I don't suppose I'll ever get one now," he said.

"Just buy him one, Mum," Luke had said wearily earlier. "I don't care if he gets one before I did. At least it will stop him going on."

"But I do," she'd said. "I care. I care about the principle and I have to particularly care about the money."

"Maybe Christmas," she said now. "I'll speak to Dad. But you really mustn't…"

"I was just looking," Charlie said doggedly. "I told the man in the shop. I was just holding it. He wouldn't believe me."

"I believe you," said Sarah.

"It was a 66X500," Charlie said, "with a camera. And Dad said..."

Bloody Paul! Sarah looked at her poor, bewildered middle child, and wondered how much to say. Much as she could cheerfully have taken a blunt instrument to her ex-husband right now, she still felt a perverse loyalty to him. But she could no longer bear Charlie's endless disappointment. "Dad's got some problems at the moment," she said carefully. "He's not very well, really."

Charlie looked at her. "Is he going to die?"

"No, no he's not going to die but he's finding things a bit difficult and that's why sometimes he can't come when he says he will and he can't always buy you the things he'd planned to."

Charlie continued to gaze at her. She could see the struggle playing out on his face. He shrugged as though he didn't care but the hurt and confusion was clear in his eyes.

"He loves you very much," she said, "but he's having some work problems." Charlie needed to be prepared for Paul to let him down, but looking at the little boy's expression she knew she must also do all she could to save Paul's image in his son's eyes.

Charlie frowned. "What did you mean he's not well?"

She wished she hadn't mentioned it now. "He's a bit stressed," Sarah said lamely.

But this seemed to satisfy Charlie. He nodded sagely. "Like you get," he said.

"I suddenly remembered I had this." Richard was casual. "They sent me a new one." He held a box out to Charlie. "An upgrade, they told me. But I don't like it much. It's got a camera and a radio." Richard shook his head as if this were a very sorry state of affairs. "And I don't know how to figure out things like that. I'm a boring old fart," he added, as Charlie's eyes widened. "Much prefer my old one. So suppose you use this new one for now?" He glanced at Sarah. "You know, just till your dad gets you a better one?"

Charlie stood quite still, staring and then his face split into a huge, disbelieving grin. Sarah's eyes filled with tears.

"We're going to have to have a budget," she said briskly, fishing in her pocket for a tissue and blowing her nose. "You can't use it all day long."

Charlie shook his head, eyes shining. "I won't, Mum. I just want to have one." He looked up at her joyfully. "And then if I ever run away again you can text me and I'll tell you where I am."

"You'll never do it again," she said sternly. "I was very, very worried."

"Don't worry about the money," Richard said to Sarah later as she poured him a drink in the kitchen. "It's pay-as-you-go and Charlie can clean my car if he wants. Earn his top-ups."

Sarah put the tonic bottle down. "Richard, you do not have to go to those lengths. Giving Charlie a phone is the most lovely and generous thing. Please do not put your car at risk, too. Frankly, I wouldn't let him loose on the litter tray."

Richard laughed, suddenly looking bright and playful. Younger. Sexier. Her stomach gave a little flip. "He's OK," Richard said.

Sarah leant forward and kissed his cheek. "You've been brilliant today," she said. "You didn't really have a spare phone, did you?"

He put an arm around her. "Got there just before they closed." He swilled his glass about, chinking the ice-cubes together. "I know I'm a funny sod. I know I'm strange." He suddenly looked embarrassed as he said gruffly, "But it's not because I don't care."

18. Chianti

Heavily fruited with a touch of acid.

Gaynor sat cross-legged on the sofa in the breakfast room and looked at her Gynae Chart.

She squinted at the blocked-in bits representing FLOW, which looked like a child's depiction of the New York skyline. She didn't seem to have plotted her last period at all. She frowned. She wasn't sure if she'd even had one. Everything seemed to be all over the place again.

A bit like her FEELINGS. She chewed at the end of her pen. How best to describe her current state? Weepy? Depressed? No. More *emotional*. Tearful. Now, through Sam, she'd "learned how to cry again" (Hurrah!), it was all she could do to bloody stop.

November 15th. Am snivelling idiot. Feel...

She paused. How did she feel?

1) Angry with Victor.

2) In love with Sam.

3) Guilty about Victor. (Sometimes. After all, I am cheating on him.)

4) Guilty about Sam. (Often. He doesn't approve of cheating. He is in love with me and I am still with my husband.)

5) Sad about my marriage going to pot (it was OK once).

Gaynor shifted position, brought her feet up under her, sucked the end of her biro a bit more and looked wistfully at her list.

205

I wish, she thought, I wish…

1) I could catch Victor out so I could leave him (after all, I know he is cheating on me too).

2) He'd be nicer to me. (`Cos even though I want to leave him, him being vile still makes my stomach churn.)

3) I could spend more time with Sam. (It just feels right. Except for problems above.)

4) I wasn't so damn horny because neither of them will sleep with me (one `cos he's shagging a hippopotamus and the other cos he's on a moral crusade). Grrrr.

Gaynor put her pen down. What would Mr Bradley-Lawrence make of that? She wished she could just have one set of feelings and hold on to them. When she was with Sam it felt so good. Most of the time. Except that it was so hard to keep her hands off him. When she was close to him she could feel the electric tension between them. She was longing to go to bed with him again and she was pretty sure that if he weren't so caught up with the ethics of it all, he'd feel the same. Sometimes, when she brushed a hand across his arm or kissed him hello a little too lingeringly, he'd abruptly move away, as if afraid of what might happen.

When he was down and withdrawn, he hardly even looked at her and it sent a chill through her every time, but then he wouldn't be depressed if they weren't in this situation. She hoped.

When Victor was revolting, she felt very sure of what she was doing – she needed Sam. How could she cope with all this otherwise? Her husband was still disappearing to London for days on end and quite often staying away at weekends too, and continuing to be very slippery and defensive if she tried to delve into what he was doing. He was short-tempered and spent much of the time making it very plain that he'd rather be anywhere other than with her. But then, inexplicably, he would suddenly be lovely, suddenly be the old fun Victor he once was, and apologise for his crabbiness, blame it on work or the universe in an entirely reasonable-sounding way, and she would wonder if she'd got it all wrong and she was doing a terrible thing to both of them.

"Yes, I do feel angry sometimes," Sam had said as they sat on rocks along Stone Bay and looked at the wintry sunshine glancing off the grey leaden sea. "I get depressed and angry with the situation. I feel that for both our sakes, I should tell you to go away."

"I know," she'd said, rubbing her gloved fingers together, hunching against the cold wind.

"But I love you, so I'm still here. You need to decide what you want, Gaynor." Sam stared at a cormorant skimming across the water. "I sometimes think you are looking for some perfect man to make it all come right for you. Some non-existent being…"

"No, I'm not," she'd said, pushing the toe of her boot into the sand, hoping it was true. "I was happy enough with my marriage in the beginning. I thought he was perfect for me. I thought it would be wonderful for ever."

Sam had shaken his head. "If he seemed perfect, then at what cost to himself? How long could anyone have kept that up? If he was perfect, what are you doing here?"

He didn't wait for her to answer. "I'm real. I am here for you. With imperfect, hurting, human love." He turned and took her hand. "There is always a price to be paid. Nothing is ever really perfect."

She wondered if Sam would like a quick wander along the beach now or whether he'd be out in the garden lovingly digging in more compost or whatever he'd spent the whole previous day doing.

"You 'av to put it in to get it out, me dear," he'd said in a bad imitation of one of the Archers.

She had to be at the wine bar by eleven to cover for Claire who'd taken Henry to the vet again. Claire had sounded uncharacteristically agitated on the phone. "He's not right still," she'd said when she'd phoned an hour before. I'm going to take him in and wait to see someone. He's just lying around and not eating. He's not being himself at all…"

Nobody was. Sarah was drifting around with a permanent glow ever since Richard had started staying the night, Lizzie had completely gone to ground since she'd scooped up Ravi from Heathrow and, as far as Gaynor could ascertain, had taken him straight to bed where they'd remained pretty much ever since, and she herself felt very peculiar indeed.

She ran a hand across her stomach, frowning at the chart once more. Then she looked at her watch. There was time to call in and see what Sam was up to.

He was painting. A huge sign was propped on his kitchen table. PEDRO'S PASTA, in bold red italics. Sam was putting the finishing touches to a steaming plate of orange spaghetti below the name.

Gaynor filled the kettle. "Where are they opening?"

"York Street." He glanced at her. "You OK?"

"Yes." She kept her back to him as she took mugs from the cupboard and opened the coffee jar. The lid slipped from her fingers and bounced to the floor, rolling away across the old, worn tiles. "Shit!"

Sam added a last tendril of pasta, sitting back to consider it. "You sure?"

"I feel funny."

Sam laid his paintbrush down and came over to her. He put a hand on her cheek. As always, when he touched her, she felt a jolt go through her body. "What sort of funny?"

"Oh nothing. I've just got PMT. I seem to have had it for weeks. But my hormones are in such uproar I don't know where I am. She laughed. "I almost wondered if I could be pregnant."

She felt his hand stiffen before he took it away and reached for his tobacco.

"And could you?"

"Well – I don't know."

His face was suddenly cold and closed – that same expression she'd seen in the beginning in the wine bar. She felt herself shrink back.

"Gaynor, you told me you couldn't have children."

She looked down, spooning granules into each mug. "I can't. Well that's what they've told me."

"So – how could this be?"

She kept her eyes on the kettle. It was beginning to boil. "I've never conceived in six years of trying. And they think I've got endometriosis again which can cause infertility, so the chances of me having a baby are pretty slim. So," she added lightly, as he remained silent, "there's no need to panic."

He lit a cigarette. "I'm not panicking, but it would be a bit of a mess, wouldn't it? I feel bad enough ever having made love to you – if you were pregnant too…"

"I'd deal with it."

"Deal with it? If you were pregnant after all this time, I'd hope you'd get great joy from it. Which means being pregnant by your husband."

The kettle turned itself off with a click. "Even if he doesn't give a shit about me and is shagging someone else?"

"You still don't know that."

She poured boiling water and stirred. "I do know that – I just need to prove it, since he's never going to admit it." She looked at Sam. "And when I do, I shall leave him."

He didn't reply so she went on. "And personally, I would think it some sort of wonderful gift if I found I were having your baby. Would it really be such an awful thing?"

"I think I'd find it pretty traumatic, yes."

"Right." She looked away from him feeling sick.

He spoke more gently. "Gaynor, I am your friend – I am here for you. But I crossed a boundary that I shouldn't have crossed. It was wonderful and magical but it shouldn't have happened. Not least because I have these strong feelings for you and you aren't free to be mine. And that hurts like mad.

209

But of course I'd support and look after you. You know I'm here."

She wanted to throw herself into his arms. Instead, she scowled. "As long as I'm not pregnant and don't cause trouble."

He sighed, exasperated again. "For Christ's sake, Gaynor! If there was any chance of you being pregnant then you shouldn't have had unprotected sex with me!"

"You didn't seem to mind at the time."

"No. I've just said. I behaved badly."

She pushed the mugs away from her – hot coffee slopped across the work surface.

"No you fucking didn't!" She was shouting. "We both wanted to and we did. I don't feel ashamed of it. I'd do it again. And if I were pregnant now I'd pray for the baby to be yours and not Victor's."

He stood rigid in front of her. "Why? Could it be his?"

"What? I don't know – my cycle's all over the place."

Sam flicked at his lighter. He was speaking very quietly now. "You also told me you don't have sex with your husband."

"We don't. We've done it twice in God knows how long."

"Since you've been trying to get me into bed, obviously."

"How dare you! I haven't been trying." She glared at him furiously, knowing that was exactly what she'd been doing. The thought brought a wave of humiliation and fresh rage. "You're making me sound like some old slapper."

He stared back. "I'm making you sound less than honest. 'We don't have sex' means no sex. When I didn't have sex with Eleanor we literally never touched each other for years on end. We didn't have it a couple of times in the space of one menstrual cycle."

"It's longer than that," she said angrily. "I've completely lost track of what my body's doing. I have been honest. He never wants to come near me now. We used to do it all the time and now…"

Sam's voice was cold. "Thank you. I really wanted to know that."

"I was just explaining…"

"Anyone else in the picture? Seen that Danny lately?"

"You bastard!" She lunged at him. He stopped her with one hand and held her away from him. "That's so unfair." She was sobbing now. "I trusted you when I told you that."

He let her go. "Sorry."

"Bollocks to you." She grabbed at her handbag. "You can fuck off."

She heard him say, "Sorry," once more. But he made no move to stop her as she ran out of the door.

19. Muscadet

A steely little number. Served chilled.

"Oh Gaynor!" Down in the wine bar kitchen, Sarah put an arm round her, a coffee in front of her and a tissue in her hand. "What have you been doing?"

Gaynor wiped her eyes, feeling about seven. She gave Sarah the edited highlights.

Sarah put on a pair of the thin rubber gloves that always reminded Gaynor of gynaecologists.

"Well, you've just got to forget all that. For God's sake don't make it any more complicated than it already is. It's crazy to have an affair yourself when you're all in turmoil with Victor. How's that going to help anything? And if you and Sam are not even getting on…"

Gaynor said nothing. Something had stopped her telling Sarah the full story and she didn't have the energy to go into more detail. She picked up her coffee. "He's been very good to me."

Sarah began to take plastic boxes from the fridge. "Maybe, but I think you should be making an effort with Victor."

"For God's sake," Gaynor exploded. "You are like a bloody stuck record. I have made an effort with Victor until I'm blue in the face. I am one big, walking, fucking effort! Right now, I'm upset about Sam!"

Sarah tipped grated cheese into a large bowl. "If you ask me," she said firmly, "having a row with him is a lucky break.

I think that's telling you something. To go home and sort things out once and for all."

"Look," said Gaynor loudly, stopping as Charlie appeared down the stairs.

"Can we have some crisps, Mum?"

Sarah shook her head. "No, go back up to the flat. I'll come and make you something in a bit."

"I don't know what time Claire's going to be back," Sarah said to Gaynor when Charlie had trailed away. "I know that dog's important to her but I'm trying to look after three kids here." She put a large carton of milk on to the work surface with a thump. "Bloody teacher-training days! Susannah's away and my mother's tied up with her Quilting Convention. It's all getting a bit much! Now about Victor..."

"Don't you get it? He doesn't want to know."

"What I've come to say," piped up Bel sweetly from the doorway, "is could I have some crisps please?"

Sarah swung round. "Did Charlie send you? Go and say Mummy says NO and she's getting cross."

Gaynor put a hand out and drew Bel on to her lap. "They can have a couple of packets can't they? We've got boxes and boxes of them."

"No, they can't," said Sarah sharply. "Charlie's been eating too much rubbish. He won't eat his lunch and then he'll be bouncing off the walls all afternoon."

Gaynor stroked Bel's hair. "Thought it was blue smarties that did that – not a bag of cheese and onion."

"Thank you for that expert advice," snapped Sarah. "How many children have you got?" She immediately put her hand to her mouth. "Oh Gaynor, I'm so sorry. I didn't think."

"It's OK."

"Pleeeeeese can we?" whined Bel. "Mummy? Crisps?"

"One packet between you. Go on, get them and take them upstairs!" Sarah ran her hands through her hair when Bel had gone, and looked at Gaynor. "It's not OK – that was really insensitive. I haven't even asked – are you still upset about Chloe?"

213

Gaynor shrugged. "I haven't been thinking about it. Though she's itching to come down for a weekend, so no doubt it will raise its ugly head again soon." She paused. "I don't know if I feel a bit pregnant myself." She winced at the way she'd blurted it to Sam. "I've been waiting to come on, I've got sore breasts and stuff – but nothing happens."

"Take a test," said Sarah.

"No, I won't be. I've been here so many times before – all hopeful and then a couple of weeks later my period starts. I've just got a funny cycle. I stopped even bothering to test in the end – I think there's still a kit in the bathroom cupboard, probably well past its sell-by date. That way I could keep the fantasy up as long as possible before I got disappointed again."

Sarah squeezed her arm. "It could still happen."

"Oh, I don't know if I'm even ready for children – I still feel like a child myself..." She thought of the feel of Sam stroking her hair. "I want someone to look after me." She laughed self-consciously. "Never mind caring for a baby twenty-four-seven. Sam said..."

"That's the appeal of Sam," said Sarah. "He's listening to you. Giving you some attention when Victor isn't. But you hardly know him..."

"I know him very well. We've talked for hours." *And we have made passionate love and he knows me and turns me on and I think about him all the time...and can't imagine life without him ...*

"Sam's a red herring," Sarah said firmly. "You've got to sort your marriage out one way or another." She picked up a large shiny garlic clove and pushed it into the crusher, closing the steel press down on to it and watching as the white sludge dripped into the bowl below. "I assume," she enquired primly, "from what you said about pregnancy, that you and Victor are making love again?"

"Only occasionally. He had a sudden flurry of interest after we'd had a nice evening with Lizzie – we all got drunk and had a few laughs and he was all over me when we went to bed, but since then…"

"There – I told you." Sarah was triumphant. "That's what you need. Some fun and laughter. He's probably stressed out of his mind at work and just needs to relax. Organise some nights out with people he likes. Dress up, flirt with him…"

"You sound like bloody Dear Deirdre – you've missed your vocation. You should be on *Trisha* doling out advice!"

"Anything would be better than this place. It's doing my head in."

She reached up to the shelf over the freezer and pulled down a foil pack of pills. "Not to mention making it hurt." She emptied two tablets into her palm and picked up her glass of water.

"You get too many headaches," said Gaynor. "I wish you'd go to the doctor."

"There's nothing really wrong. Just a tension thing," Sarah smiled. "Really – these will get rid of it and I'll be fine."

As if to prove it, she smiled when Charlie reappeared ten minutes later. "Your Auntie Gaynor says I should let you eat whatever you want," she said. "So you can take that cheese and crackers upstairs and share them with Luke and Bel."

Charlie grinned and put his arms round Gaynor's waist. "Thanks Gaynor!"

"But if you don't eat your broccoli, you're in trouble," Sarah called after him as he went back up the stairs.

"They're lovely, your kids," Gaynor said, "so affectionate."

"I know. And I'm just not there for them at the moment," said Sarah ruefully. "I think that was the problem with Charlie – Paul being an unreliable sod but also me simply not being there enough to make up for it. He likes Susannah and my mother's usually around but it's not the same…"

"Can I do something to help you have more time off?"

Sarah smiled. "Next week, maybe? Perhaps you can work Tuesday night … Oh hello!"

She broke off as Claire pushed open the swing door. Then frowned. "Claire what are you doing? You can't bring them in here."

Henry and Wooster were both on leads. They sat obediently on the kitchen floor behind Claire, who looked defiant. "I'll tie them up in the cellar. I can't leave them at home. Henry's not well – he's had blood tests and I've got to keep an eye on him." For a moment it seemed that Claire, unbelievably, might be about to cry. "And Wooster will pine if I leave him at home alone."

Sarah shook her head. "I'm sorry about Henry," she said firmly, looking at the two Airedales, who looked back longingly. "But you know very well we can't have dogs anywhere near the kitchen. You go home and look after him and we'll manage. Won't we, Gaynor?"

"Sure." Gaynor forced a bright smile. "We'll be fine."

Claire shook her head. "I need to be here," she said "We've got a delivery coming and there's the menu for Beaujolais Nouveau Night to sort out and the blackboards to do and …"

"And we can deal with it!" Sarah's voice was sharp. "For goodness sake, Claire, you're not the only one who can do things, you know. I'm perfectly capable of handling it all. I've already written out the menu and Gaynor can do the blackboard. Now go home. You haven't had a proper day off since we started. Have one now!"

Gaynor looked from one of her partners to the other. For a moment she thought Claire was going to start shouting but then she suddenly seemed to slump.

"OK. If you're sure," she said. "I can ring Jamie and see if he can get an early train and maybe my neighbour would come in and sit with them, she has before. I could come back later…"

Sarah crossed the room and put a brief arm across Claire's shoulders. "Just go home," she said quietly. "Gaynor and I will deal with everything."

"Right," she said, when Claire had reluctantly gone. "And now we've got to. I'll call Jack and get him to come in tonight, and you can go do your artistic bit with the blackboard." Sarah looked at Gaynor. "It will keep your mind off things," she said briskly. She held out a piece of paper.

"'C'est arrivé' in big letters across the top and then the special menu beneath. I thought we'd do French Onion Soup, Coq au Vin and Boeuf Bourguignon, maybe Tarte Tatin... Are you listening?"

"Yes, sorry." Gaynor took the paper and looked at it. She wondered what Sam was thinking.

Sarah was watching her. "Come on, Gaynor, we've got to get on."

"Yes I know. I'll get it..." She jumped up as, above in the bar, the phone began to ring.

"I think the answer-phone's still on...."

They heard it cut in as Gaynor pushed open the swing door and Claire's cool efficient tones floated down the stairs asking the caller to please leave a message after the tone. Then the click as a receiver was replaced.

"Talkative," said Sarah. She gathered up a pile of glass cloths and followed Gaynor up the stairs. "There are a couple of other messages on there. I haven't had a chance to listen yet. Can you write them down?"

Gaynor flicked the switch and reached for a pen, as a giggly female voice sounded. *Hen Party*? Gaynor wrote. *December 5th. Table for seventeen.*

"Oh joy," said Sarah, folding the cloths and putting them away in the cupboard beneath the optics. "Dildos at dawn..."

They both laughed. Then froze as the next message came on and a now-familiar voice began to speak. *"You've really done it now, Carrot-top, you ugly bitch. You'd better watch your back..."*

It was Gaynor's turn to get the tissues out. She shooed the kids back to the TV, made sure the door up to the flat was firmly shut and stood by feeling helpless as Sarah sat down at a table and burst into tears.

"And Richard's away tonight," she sobbed. "I've got to stay here on my own with some bloody madman after me…"

"I'll stay with you," said Gaynor. "He's just some twisted perve. He's not going to do anything."

"That's easy for you to say," cried Sarah. "It's me he's got it in for!" She tugged at her hair. "Carrot-top. Oh God," she said through fresh tears. "What I have done to deserve this?"

"Nothing." Gaynor was picking up the phone. "And I'm going to call the police and make them do something." She wished she could call Sam and ask him how best to do that. At the thought of him, her stomach twisted. Forget him, she told herself firmly. Look after Sarah.

She waited impatiently for the phone to be answered at the other end.

"Yes, hello," she said in the crispest voice she could muster. "I want to talk to someone about threatening phone calls…"

Sarah was out on the pavement calling Richard on her mobile when Gaynor came off the phone. She still looked white. "He says I can stay at his place with the kids until he comes back, but…"

Gaynor nodded. "Or you can come to me. We've got lots of room." She closed her mind to what Victor would think of it being filled with three children. "You're very welcome."

"I know, thank you. But it's a lot of palava moving three kids about and…" Sarah bit her lip, "I don't want to be driven out of my own home." She looked at Gaynor with huge eyes. "I might be afraid to ever come back."

"Then I'll stay the night with you."

Sarah looked at her gratefully. "Thanks." She looked up in surprise as the wine bar door opened.

"What are you doing here? You're supposed to be leaving for Bristol."

Richard shrugged. "I told them I had an emergency."

"What did the police say?" Richard asked Gaynor, as she lined up three cups beneath the espresso machine.

She pulled a face. "The usual. Said they'd look into it, send someone round. I laid it on thick – single mother, living alone, three children etc."

Richard glanced round to check Sarah wasn't in earshot. She was still upstairs with the children.

"Phone them again," he said. "Tell them if they don't trace that number today and get round here to tell Sarah they've done something about it, you'll be calling the local paper." He smiled grimly. "The *Thanet Times* would fall on a story like that. Police won't lift finger to help defenceless mother? Great stuff."

Gaynor poured a little milk into his coffee and handed it to him. "Do you want sugar?"

Richard shook his head. "The editor's a friend of mine. He'd enjoy phoning the sergeant in charge with a few pertinent questions. Put a rocket up someone…"

It was difficult to imagine anything moving PC Robertson very fast. He arrived about four p.m., grinned at Sarah and Gaynor as if this was all a rather jolly state of affairs and seemed in no hurry to tell them much at all. He burbled on happily about obscenities and the telecommunications act and looked around the bar and said what a nice place it looked and perhaps one evening he would bring his wife. Gaynor gave him her most winning smile. "And we'd be very pleased to see you. Anyway, have you..?"

"Caught him?" finished Richard.

PC Robertson guffawed. "I have been to see the individual concerned and made it quite clear they are committing an offence," he announced proudly. "They have been warned of the consequences of continuing with their actions. I don't think they'll be doing that again."

"Who is it?" Sarah was grim-faced.

PC Robertson consulted his notebook. "I'm not really at liberty… we wouldn't necessarily, usually…"

"Look!" Sarah's voice rose. "I need to know who it is. We need to know. We're running a business here that's open to the public." She gestured around her. "Anyone can walk in. This man could come in here, cool as he likes, and order a drink and if he does I want to be able to bar him. I'm frightened," she said, her voice suddenly breaking. "I'm frightened for my children…"

PC Robertson cleared his throat, suddenly serious. "I don't think there's any need to worry about that. I think we've put a stop to it."

Sarah walked away and sat down at one of the small tables, apparently unable to speak. Richard went and sat beside her. "The girls need to know what they're dealing with," he said, taking Sarah's hand. "It's only fair."

Gaynor remained standing and looked the policeman in the eyes. "We really do need to know who it is," she said softly, keeping her face fixed on his. "We'd be very grateful."

He looked at his notes again and cleared his throat. "The line used to make the calls is in the name of a woman. Do you know a Miss Tania Wilkins?"

Sarah and Gaynor gazed at each other, mystified. Both shook their heads.

Behind them, Richard put his in his hands. "I do."

"Poor Richard," said Sarah, as they got ready to open that evening. "No wonder he's so wary of relationships. Apparently he and Tania had a brief fling a couple of years back and she's still plaguing him. Every time he's seen with another woman she somehow finds out and makes obscene phone calls to him in the middle of the night. When she suddenly went quiet this time, he thought she'd finally left him alone – never dreamed she'd go for me instead."

"Bloody hell," said Gaynor. "She sounds seriously scary."

"Yeah – Richard says she's a bunny boiler all right." She suddenly laughed. "Thank God she didn't get hold of Scarface." Sarah wiped her eyes. "I'm sorry, I'm getting hysterical."

"I'll slap you if you get any worse," said Gaynor. "This bloke of hers must be pretty simple to have gone along with it. Imagine making calls like that!"

"Well, he'd be very stupid to do it again now he's been threatened with prosecution."

"Have they ever been in here?"

"Richard says Tania came in once when he was here but turned on her heel and walked right out again. She's obviously seen us out together or found out he's been staying here."

"What does she look like?"

Sarah raised her eyebrows. "Descriptions are hardly Richard's forte. Big hair, mad eyes and lots of lipstick, as far as I can work out."

"Sounds par for the course."

Sarah walked across the varnished floor and turned the Closed sign to Open. "How are you now?"

Gaynor straightened the beer mats. "I don't know."

Sarah joined her. "Remember what I said. Forget Sam and concentrate on Victor. Have another go. Organise a night out."

"Much use it will be. I may as well give up on the pair of them." Gaynor picked up the ice bucket. "I'll go and fill this."

Sarah remained where she was, blocking Gaynor's path, glancing at the couple just coming through the door, before speaking in a low voice.

"Gaynor, it's horrible getting divorced. Having to end my marriage was the worst thing I've ever had to do. Don't you give up on yours just yet."

Gaynor tried to slide round her to the top of the stairs. "But Sam…"

Sarah put a hand out to stop her. "He hasn't contacted you this afternoon to make up, has he?"

Sarah was being kind. She tried to give Gaynor a hug. But, feeling the lump rise in her throat, Gaynor slipped away and began to walk down the steps to the kitchen.

No, he hasn't.

20. Pouilly Fumé

Mysterious, smoky flavours.

Gaynor poured two glasses of Chablis and handed one to Victor. He looked up briefly from the newspaper.

"Thanks."

She sat down at the kitchen table opposite him. "This Friday, can you get home early? I'm not working so I've organised dinner out. Lizzie's game – she's got a guy over she met in India, who sounds great – and I thought I'd give Lyndsey and Roger a call. It's ages since we've seen them – it'll be fun."

He looked up again and she smiled at him. "I've booked the terrace at Marchesi's – they've got an opera night and...."

She saw his face shift – saw it for a moment, the discomfort, the way his eyes flicked away from hers. For a second she could almost see the pulsating of his brain as he formulated his excuses. Then it was gone and the easy, relaxed expression returned. It was over so quickly she could have imagined it.

"Oh!" He'd adopted his brightest voice. "I thought I told you – I've got to stay over on Friday. That's a shame. Got this boring bloody dinner with the Homestyle mob."

Her heart dropped. "Really? On a Friday?"

He sipped at his wine. "Yeah, well, you know the CEO? He's just split up with his wife. You know – going through the lad-about-town bit? There's some new restaurant in Piccadilly he fancies. And there's been a bit of trouble with the shoot for his new commercial – we've had to delay it – and the account chaps think we ought to take him."

Gaynor took a gulp from her own glass. She heard her voice get tighter.

"Can't Laurence go instead? You do so much and it's opera night – you loved it last time. I thought you'd be pleased."

"And I would be." He smiled at her. "I'm sorry, darling. I'll make it up to you. Why don't you go and have fun with Lizzie and I'll do something really special with you next week."

She was suddenly furious. "It's always next week – but next week never comes, does it? Send somebody else and do something for me for a change!"

Victor's smile had gone. "I can't. The shit has hit the fan. They're pissed off about the shoot and I've got to go myself."

"Why have you?" She was shouting now.

He looked at her warily. "Because I just have. I would rather be at home and take you out. Of course I would."

She banged her glass down on the work surface. "I don't believe you. I don't think you want to do anything with me any more. I think," she said, her voice dropping with quiet venom, "that you are full of shit!"

He put his own drink down and sighed. His voice was half-annoyed, half-weary. He didn't look at her. "Why do you always have to make me feel so guilty?"

She stood up. "Perhaps, because you are!"

Victor deliberately folded the paper and put it away from him. "What's that supposed to mean?"

"You seem to take every opportunity to stay away these days – there's always something to take you back to London. I rather wonder why."

His eyes were hard. "Don't start that again, Gaynor!"

"Why not?"

"Because it's just bloody paranoid. Look at you. You're shaking. DTs again? You ought to do something about your drinking, Gaynor – you'll end up a lush."

She felt her voice quiver with rage. "I'm shaking because I'm angry. I don't drink any more than you do."

"You're a woman – your body can't take it. Anyway, I'm cutting down, actually."

"Can't say I'd noticed."

"You don't notice anything apart from yourself."

She gasped at the injustice. "You bloody bastard. I'm the one trying here – I'm trying to get our marriage – our friendship – back again." Tears had sprung to her eyes. He stood up and picked up the paper.

She screeched at him. "That's right! Walk out like you always do! Don't discuss anything – don't look for any answers. You go to fucking London. See if I care what you do."

She heard him cross the hall and the front door open and close. Running into the sitting room at the front, she saw the Jag pull out of the driveway.

"Bastard!" she yelled again.

She drank the rest of the wine in the bottle, the unfairness of the situation becoming ever more apparent with each glass. There was she, organising nights out, trying to do nice things for him, to make him happy, and all he could do was accuse her of thinking of herself.

"Bastard," she said over and over again, her brain stuck on the word, finding some comfort in its endless repetition. "Bastard, bastard, bastard!"

She sat at his desk and leafed through his leather diary. Nothing written in for Friday at all.

"It's in the one at work..." She could imagine his smooth tones now. For a moment she thought about phoning Ziggy and asking her what Victor had scheduled, but no doubt Victor had that covered too. She was only the wife. No doubt Ziggy, with her silly neon hair and pierced nose, had been fully briefed not to tell her a bloody thing.

She hurled the diary to the floor and in a fresh fit of rage and frustration thrust her arm outwards and swept the rest of the desk-top clutter with it.

Pens, rulers, Sellotape dispenser, paperclips and Post-it notes scattered across the carpet. A blue willow-patterned bowl full of business cards sailed through the air and landed with a crack on the edge of the fireplace. It broke into several pieces, the cards fluttering around it like confetti.

"Bollocks." She put her head in her hands, suddenly in tears again, her anger thinning away to misery and defeat. She knelt down and began to pick up the broken pieces of china. Victor would be furious. She'd have to tidy up quickly, say she'd knocked it accidentally.

She could see his face. "What were you doing, anyway? Poking through my things again?"

She gathered up the cards, stacking them in her palm. The sort of people Victor met – media people, the creative and beautiful – seemed to vie with each other to have the wackiest, most off-the-wall presentation of their details and skills. There were plastic cards, metallic ones, some with fluorescent print, some embossed. Printers, photographers, illustrators. Here was a shocking-pink affair edged in green. *Daring Damien –Transformations Unlimited.*

She looked at it. Had Victor taken Damien up on his services? Asked for a total transformation from Wonderful-in-the-Beginning to Pretty-easy-going-puts-you-down-a-bit-and-doesn't-always-listen-but-you-can't-have-everything through to Completely-Selfish-and-Philandering-Arsehole?

This next one was on paper as thin as tissue crossed over with black spidery fibres – *Optic Design Dot Com.* Hmm. Very happening.

'Katrina Carpenter' had a photo of herself on her card – a gothic babe with black lips. She was a 'Life Coach'. Was she the one? Was Victor going to her 'studio' in Hammersmith twice a week for tuition on how to 'unlock his potential'? Gaynor grimaced. Yeah right. His potential to be an absent partner, pissing off for pretend dinners with clients, rather than spend a single evening with his wife.

But probably not, if Katrina was left languishing in the bowl. Gaynor had seen Victor empty his pockets and wallet here many times. Keys and phone in the top drawer, change in the little brass dish, important cards left on his desk to follow up. The remainder tossed into this bowl – just in case. She picked up the rest and flicked through them. PR people, media buyers, MDs of companies she'd never heard of, people Victor had met at parties and conferences. *Forever Fabulous Makeovers* – hmm, couldn't he have bought her one? And then, beneath a black card with silver writing – *Hassan Farquari Celebrity Agent* – was a small, credit-card sized piece of cardboard. She only looked at it idly at first but then frowned. It was an instruction card. Quick guide to the Speakeasy 3340.

She picked it up and looked at it more carefully. *Retrieving your messages*. There were some numbers in biro in the top right-hand corner in what seemed to be Victor's writing. She turned it over in her hands, running her eyes down the list of instructions. The operating instructions for an answer-phone. *To retrieve your messages remotely...*

Gaynor frowned. It wasn't the one they had. The one sitting on the shelf in the hall next to the phone. She began to read.

1) dial your phone number.

2) Wait for the tone and enter the four-digit pass code...

Gaynor frowned. Whose machine was it? The mystery elephant's? But why would Victor need to remotely retrieve her messages? Perhaps it was a work thing. It was a London number.

She hesitated. Suppose she called it and someone answered? She could always put the phone down.

Suppose it was Victor? She needed to know. Taking a deep breath and pressing out 141 first, she dialled the number. It rang three times then there was a beep and Victor's smooth tones broke in.

He didn't say much. Just gave the number and sorry there was nobody there to take the call. Please leave a message. Fumbling, she pressed out the four digits he'd scrawled on the card. Surely, if it was work, he'd have said his name or EBTD? She looked at the number again. A different code from the Soho offices.

There was another series of beeps. Then a robotic voice. You have TWO new messages. Gaynor's stomach tightened with sudden anxiety. In a split second she knew she was going to hear something she'd wished she hadn't.

But the first one sounded like Laurence. *Where are you, you old bastard? I've left messages everywhere. There's a load of problems with the Hampstead shoot. We're going to have to rethink. Can you call me?* Beep!

Then a second one. *Message left at nine-forty-five-pm on the twenty-second of...* Gaynor realised she was holding her breath. It was a voice she'd never heard before. A man – cultured, speaking with an amused drawl – maybe a bit drunk or stoned or something.

Victor baby. Are we going to see you at Tony's little soirée on Friday night?

Within the first few words she knew this was it. Her insides lurched as she heard the whole message. The voice paused as if sucking on a cigarette and then went on: *More to the point – will we be seeing the lovely Gabrielle? Starts at nine. Ciao...*

She gripped the back of Victor's office chair. Gabrielle? Was that the woman in Victor's life? Obviously. Quite clearly she and he had a circle of friends she, Gaynor, knew nothing about. A private phone line – presumably in the flat – she also never knew existed.

She swallowed, feeling her heart thump. The lovely Gabrielle. Dressed no doubt in three hundred pounds' worth of Voluptua lingerie. On Victor's arm, walking into a party together. Gaynor felt horribly sick. She replaced the receiver, trembling.

She'd known already, of course she had. It had been adding up for a long time. Even before the lipstick on his shirt, the lingerie in the wrong size, the constant staying away. Even before that, there'd been his funny moods and distance. His snide comments, his readiness to put her down one minute, to make it up the next. He'd obviously been struggling with guilt or just plain fear of being caught, for a long time. Yes, she'd known.

But it was different now – a deep shock to really know. Though it wasn't rage she was filled with as she would have expected, but misery. Misery and a deep, deep fear.

She suddenly hated him. Hated him for standing there in their kitchen – the kitchen in their joint marital home – where he was supposed to be honest and true to her and lying, blatantly lying, sipping at his Chablis and just making up a tissue of lies.

Gaynor took a swallow from her glass. He was clever, Victor, talking about his clients, mixing fact with fiction, spinning the sort of plausible story that meant he could never be caught out.

She looked at the phone card she was still holding.

Except this time, she thought grimly, he bloody well would be.

21. Zinfadel

Startling colour and depth.

She didn't tell any of them. Lizzie would have insisted on coming too, Sarah would have urged caution. She hadn't seen or spoken to Sam since she'd stormed out of the cottage. She had to sort this one out herself. She just told Claire and Sarah something had come up and she couldn't work on Friday night, turning away from the expressions on their faces at being short-staffed again, threw some things in a bag and called a taxi to the station. She felt purposeful and strung out, half afraid, half thrilled, with a huge dead space inside.

It was one of the old trains and someone had left the window open so the carriage was freezing. There was the usual collection of burger boxes and empty beer cans left on the floor and a scrunched copy of the *Evening Standard* spread across seats. Gaynor buttoned up her coat to her throat, wishing she had brought her pashmina. Who cared if they were passé – they were just the thing to huddle under on rattling, draughty trains when you felt like shit. Or better still, to put over your entire head when someone you didn't want to talk to got on at Margate and plonked herself opposite you.

"HELLO!" said the girl, pushing the newspapers to one side and sitting down directly across from Gaynor so their knees were practically touching. "How are YOU?"

Her voice was filled with the kind of surprised delight reserved for an especially dear friend one had been forcibly parted from for several long years. Gaynor didn't even know her name. She recognised her, with her Barbie blonde hair and Alice band, little glittery top beneath the black velvet coat, as having been into Greens a few times – possibly with a floppy-haired boyfriend who drank lager-shandies – but that was about it.

This did not stop the girl giving Gaynor a full resumé of her life to date, with particular reference to Andy (presumably the name of floppy-hair) and his new job, where her mother thought they ought to live and the difficulties of deciding what to wear when you were going clubbing in Leicester Square.

At this last nugget of information, Gaynor's heart sank. She'd been hoping the girl would hop off at Birchington or Herne Bay a few stops along, to visit an ancient aunt (which was about the best you could hope to encounter in either place) and leave Gaynor alone and in peace with her miserable thoughts.

"Are YOU going anywhere nice?" the girl trilled, breaking into them once more.

"Just to see a friend," Gaynor said, looking out of the window at the distant lights across the black fields.

The message had said it started at nine. The soirée. Victor probably wouldn't get there for the beginning but he was bound to go out for a drink first. Maybe even for dinner. She couldn't risk getting to the flat too early and catching him before he went to meet Gabrielle. She wanted to be there when he returned. When he brought Gabrielle back to take her to bed. She was imagining he would do that. Unless they were going to stay at Gabrielle's place instead.

At the thought of her plan being thwarted in this way, Gaynor felt deflated. The girl opposite, who was apparently called Amanda ("Mandy and Andy – it makes everyone laugh") was still talking. It was a hen night she was going on – wouldn't it be? The final pre-knot celebration of an old school friend who now worked in Harrods. Gaynor smiled vacantly.

She'd been so excited just before she married Victor. It had only been a small gathering. Lizzie, Chloe, a few friends from work. They'd gone to a restaurant in Canterbury. Victor had pressed a huge wad of notes on Lizzie before they left, telling her to buy them all champagne…

Gaynor swallowed. OK, then, if they didn't come home, she'd wait in the flat all night and see what time he did roll in. See how he could explain staying out all night when he was supposed to be with a male client. For the hundredth time her fingers closed around the key in her pocket. Suppose Victor had been telling the truth and Laurence was staying there? Well, she'd interrogate him – get some truth out that way. He must have some idea what was going on.

"I love a good wedding, don't you?" asked Amanda, happily. "Always makes me cry."

Gaynor's nerves were strung out by the time they pulled into Victoria. "Have a lovely time!" Amanda cooed as she searched in a small sparkly handbag for her ticket. "Ah, here it is! We'll be in to see you in Greens again soon…"

Can't wait, thought Gaynor as she waited in the queue for a taxi to Bloomsbury. As the cab wound past Buckingham Palace, she thought back to how much she used to love doing this. Once she'd met Victor, going to London was full of glamour and promise again instead of sleazy bars and dispiriting bedsits. Trips to the capital meant treats and luxury. Then they'd hailed cabs for fun restaurants, the theatre or ballet, going back to their pied-a-terre tipsy and giggly to drink more champagne and make love.

Now she was heading for that same small flat to try and find him in bed with someone else. The driver was the friendly sort. "What are you up to tonight, then?" he asked cheerily, raising his eyebrows in the rear mirror. "Out on the razzle?"

Gaynor shook her head, smiling. "I'm going to meet my husband."

Only, unfortunately for him, he doesn't know it.

Outside the mansion block, she felt suddenly sick. Suppose Victor was still there. She'd have to say she'd come to surprise him – that she missed him, that she was sorry they'd rowed. She'd have to say that if he came home alone, too. Or should she confront him anyway? Ask who Tony was? Who Gabrielle was? *More to the point...*

She slotted her key into the front door and hit the light switch inside. The interior was dingier than she remembered it. There was a slightly stale airless smell in the corridor. The drab green carpet tiles had become worn. She moved towards the lift finding the atmosphere oppressive, feeling suddenly vulnerable and alone.

She pressed the button for the fourth floor, holding her breath slightly as the lift jolted into action. She wasn't really claustrophobic, she'd never been trapped or anything, but she never quite relaxed in a lift, or anywhere she might be shut in, in the dark. She was always steeling herself for a horrible halt between floors and the lights going out.

She would look at the strangers around her, wondering who would become hysterical if they got stuck, which pair might want to have sex together to relieve the tedium, whether – if it went on long enough – anyone's bladder would give way...

But today she was alone, and the lift creaked to a standstill at the fourth floor. She got out and stepped across more of the hard green carpet, past more dull cream walls to their front door. Victor's front door. It must be over a year since she'd been here. She tried to remember the occasion. A dinner out or something – some sort of corporate entertaining. In the days when he used to take her with him.

She remembered one night, when they'd both been so drunk they couldn't get the key in the lock. First he'd tried, then she had, then they'd collapsed against the wall, laughing. Joking about how they'd have to sleep in the corridor. She couldn't remember who'd managed it in the end. She knew they'd both had hangovers. Victor's was so bad he'd admitted to it.

She looked at the lock now. She felt nervous. Afraid, as though she were doing something wrong. She felt as she had as a teenager when the girls from school used to shoplift and she would watch them sliding eye-shadows and mascaras down the fronts of shirts, or tucking them into their bras as cool as anything, while her own heart thumped so loudly she was convinced the shop assistant would hear it.

I have a perfect right to be here, she told herself, turning the key with clumsy fingers. This is our flat – I can come if I want to. The hall was in darkness. She called out Victor's name though she knew at once it was empty. Then she went through, flicking on lights, trying to feel safe.

In the kitchen, a bottle of whisky stood on the table, a used tumbler beside it. A mug was upturned on the draining board. The rest of the room was tidy and bare. So much for Laurence leaving it in a state.

She pushed open the door of the small living room. Victor had left a lamp on. There were a couple of newspapers on the dark blue sofa, his briefcase lay on the coffee table, with a couple of folders. It looked like the slightly spartan bachelor pad it was. Once, when Gaynor had stayed more often, there'd been flowers and candles; she remembered some beautiful embroidered cushions she'd picked up in Kensington High Street – they seemed to have disappeared.

No sign of Gabrielle so far then. She crossed the tiny hall to the bedroom and opened the door. Oddly, the cushions were the first thing she saw. Then she took in the rest and froze. She felt her skin tingle with little shocks that went deep into her solar plexus and down to her fingertips.

Her cushions were piled on the bed as though it were a lady's boudoir and that's exactly what the room was. Everywhere she looked was soft and frilly – undeniably feminine. There were candles and bows, drapes, and an ornate mirror on the wall. But there was worse to come. Across the bed was flung a black dress, a silver handbag tossed down beside it. On the floor, a pair of high-heeled jewelled sandals – the sort she might herself covet – lay discarded.

Over the back of a chair were tops and wraps and skirts. A pair of stockings dangled like two rats tails. The typical fallout of a woman getting ready for a night out. One who couldn't decide what to wear.

Gaynor's eyes swung round to the pine chest of drawers. There lay a hair brush, perfume, tissues, a jumbled selection of make-up. Gaynor breathed in sharply. Gabrielle had made herself pretty at home.

Shaking with rage and emotion she pulled open the wardrobe doors. There was Victor's dark suit, a selection of shirts, the normal cluster of silk ties, a pair of casual cotton trousers, a polo shirt and one in deep green silk that she had bought him. "Fucking great!" Gaynor said out loud. Bloody marvellous – she'd bought him a shirt and here he was, wearing it out with this fat tart he'd picked up from God knows where.

Alongside was a whole rack of women's clothes. She pulled at them angrily – they were all either brash, tarty, glittery dresses or rather dated flowing things in bright chiffon. A sort of Margot in *The Good Life* meets Patsy in *Ab Fab*. Where had Victor got this creature from? She snatched at the label on the nearest top. Yes – bloody size sixteen. Though the skirt next to it was only a twelve. So she wasn't huge at all. She just had great tits. Gaynor ran a hand over her own thirty-four inch chest. Bitch!

Madly she began to pull at drawers. There were a few pairs of socks and boxers but a whole heap of lingerie, including, Gaynor saw, the bile rising in her throat, the very garment she'd found that fateful day at the bottom of Victor's closet at home. She pulled it all out in handfuls and threw it to the floor. "Bastard!" she cried.

She was sobbing as she went into the bathroom. More make-up. She picked up a tube of foundation, a lipstick that was too bright. She examined it – was that the shade she'd found on her husband's shirt? Then she deliberately snapped it in half and threw the case in the bin. It was all here: nail varnish, make-up remover, tweezers, hairspray.

This woman wasn't staying the odd night, she was fucking living here!

A pair of earrings lay on a shelf below the bathroom mirror. Gaynor picked them up. And Victor had had the fucking cheek to call *her* Bet Lynch! She hurled them across the room.

What a charming creature Gabrielle must be – no taste, all that pancake make-up on her face, great big feet – Gaynor went back into the bedroom and picked up the shoes again.

Here and there were items of discernment. This footwear, a lovely silky wrap, an exquisite little beaded bag. These must be gifts from Victor – they were just the sort of things he would buy. The thought made her sob harder. "You bastard," she cried aloud, again. "You fucking, fucking bastard!"

She went into the kitchen and pulled open the fridge. There was nothing in it but a pint of milk and a bar of chocolate. Oh, so it was all right for the fat trout to eat it! Nothing to drink but the whisky on the table.

Gaynor hated the stuff. She poured some into the tumbler and took a mouthful, gagging as it hit the back of her throat. Spluttering, she drank some more. Needs must. She should have thought to bring some wine. There was a pub a couple of roads away but she couldn't face going there now. Not like this.

She looked in the bathroom mirror. She looked deranged; her make-up had run, she was still crying. She wiped her face on the back of her sleeve, and then swept her arm along the bathroom shelf in fury, scattering pots and tubes, picking up the heavy glass bottle of Victor's aftershave and flinging it into the old enamelled bath. It shattered with a huge noise – the smell was overpowering.

Choking, Gaynor stormed back into the bedroom, tearing the clothes from the hangers – his and hers – and flinging them about the room, actually ripping one of the dresses apart at the seams before collapsing on to the bed sobbing.

"Sam," she cried suddenly, longing for the safe feel of his arms. "Oh Sam, I so need you."

She'd closed the bedroom and bathroom doors and was sat in the little sitting room with just the small lamp casting a pool of light in one corner. She had got used to the warmth of the whisky as it burned a comforting path down inside her chest. But she had a headache now and the rest of her felt shivery and empty. It was nearly midnight.

She wondered when they would come home. What would Victor say when he saw her there? What would Gabrielle do? Did she even know about Gaynor? She wondered for a wild moment if Victor was one of those men who led a double life – perhaps he told Gabrielle he was away at work when he was with her? Though surely not, she thought, as she looked around the room. Wouldn't Gabrielle wonder where all his things were? There were no real personal possessions, just a couple of books, a couple of ornaments.

And where were Gabrielle's things if she lived here all the time. Books? Photos? Perhaps she didn't have any. Perhaps she didn't read – just lay about in frightful dresses and was too ugly for anyone to want to photograph. Gaynor reached down to the bottle of Scotch beside her.

She knew that really, Gabrielle wouldn't be ugly at all. Victor loved beautiful things. Gabrielle would be tall and majestic – the sort of Amazonian woman who brings a grace and beauty to her stature. She would have a way of wearing clothes. Those things might look gross on the hangers but they were all clearly expensive and Victor wouldn't be seen dead with her if she didn't look good.

Though this time he might have no choice, she thought, overtaken again with fury. Right now she could happily plunge a knife right through his treacherous heart. And then her own.

She'd got really cold now. The heating must have turned itself off. She should get up and switch it back on. She wanted to go and get something to put round herself, too, but she didn't want to touch any of their bedding. Didn't want to go into that room again. "Whore's parlour," she said aloud, hearing her voice slur. "A whore and a bastard. Fucking bastard…"

She sat up realising she must have dropped off to sleep. Her mouth felt disgusting and she needed to go to the loo. She stood up, shivering, looking at her phone for the time. It was quarter to two. Obviously they were having a good time at the party. She was stiff and chilled. She'd have to go and get one of Victor's jackets. As she flushed the loo, she saw his red striped dressing gown on the back of the door and suddenly felt a fresh shaft of pain as she thought of Sam wrapping her in his old towelling robe. Holding her gently. Loving her, respecting her. He seemed a very long way away now.

Tears ran down her face. When this was over, she would go and see Sam. Try to talk to him. She lifted the dressing gown down off the hook, checking to see that it smelled only of Victor. It did, which made her cry again. Wrapping it around her she made her way into the kitchen and filled a glass with water.

What would happen? Would Victor beg her forgiveness? Promise never to see this woman again? Or would he get angry – shout that he was in love with Gabrielle, that he wanted to spend his life with her? Would they sell the house? Where would she go? How could he have done this to her, so blatantly, just set this woman up here? She lurched slightly as she crossed the room carrying the glass. Then she jumped in fear.

There was a sound at the door, the key going in the lock. Panic-struck she shot back into the living room, spilling the water in her haste, switching the light off, huddling back in the chair, body shuddering with palpitations as she heard them come in. She could only hear his voice. He said something about a drink.

She heard a low murmur in reply but could not pick out the words. Then a switch being flicked, doors opening. Victor's voice in the kitchen, saying something about the Scotch. He must have moved into the bathroom. She heard him say, "Oh fuck!" Then feet coming up the hall.

They came fast but the moment seemed to go on for ever. Them coming towards the door, as she sat there behind it, her hand clutching the robe around her in the dark. Terribly afraid, waiting to see what they would do.

She had a sudden irrational fear that Victor would rush in and attack her. For a moment she wanted to call out but she couldn't make a sound. She just sat petrified, her heart nearly choking her.

And then the light snapped on and there were two people in the doorway. The first figure stopped and cried out in alarm. But Gaynor was looking past him at the tall woman. She gasped as she took in the short pink skirt and high heels, the odd thought passing through her head that the top didn't match, that the whole look was tarty, that Victor would never let *her* go out looking like that…

And then Gaynor looked up into the woman's face, saw who it was and screamed.

22. Hermitage
A stunning texture and finish

Victor came into the kitchen in a T-shirt and tracksuit bottoms. His hair stood on end and he hadn't shaved. Gaynor looked at him with a mixture of disbelief and pity. She poured him a coffee. "Why don't you go and have a shower?" she said. "It will make you feel better."

He took the mug from her. "I will in a while." He leant out and touched her shoulder briefly, tentatively. "You've been very good about this," he said. "Really."

"I still can't believe it."

She felt as though she was in some sort of nightmare. However hard she tried, she couldn't get her head round it. She'd woken this morning, back in her own bed, just wanting to feel normal again but clouded by a deep sense of unreality.

"I'm sorry."

They still hadn't properly talked about it. Her head was full of questions while her mind shied away from the answers she didn't want to hear.

"Who was that bloke? The one you brought home." She remembered the look on his face when she'd started shouting. He hadn't been able to get out fast enough. They'd heard his footsteps almost running down the hall of the flat and the slam of the front door. Then there'd just been her and Victor. Her huddled in shock and horror in the chair, him standing in front of her in full make-up and heels.

"I was just going to make him a coffee. That's all. I don't want to have sex with men. It's not about that."

"What is it about?

"It's about…" He fiddled with the handle of his coffee cup, suddenly diffident. "It's about being treated like a woman. He fancied me. He knew I was a bloke but he fancied me as a woman. I liked that feeling. I wasn't going to do anything."

"Really?"

"Really."

She'd ranted and raved. Filled with rage at his deception, followed by a strange relief, and then a deep fear. The flat had seemed small and claustrophobic – filled with the sickly stench of perfume and face powder.

"How can I trust you, Victor? How can I know you're telling me the truth? You've lied and lied to me. I've been to hell and back wondering what you were up to. Do you have any idea how you've made me feel? Do you know what it was like, thinking you were seeing someone else?"

He sat down and put his head in his hands. "I know and I'm sorry. But I wouldn't do that to you. Not that sort of betrayal."

For a moment her stomach twisted in guilt. That was the word Sam had used about what they had done. She pushed thoughts of Sam away – it was too painful and confusing. She had to sort out where she was with Victor.

"I didn't want to hurt you," he was saying. "I didn't know what you'd do."

She sat down opposite him, so many questions moving around her head, her exhausted brain still trying to make sense of the few answers she'd had already.

"Why did you stop having sex with me then? The only time you ever really seemed to want to was when Lizzie was here with the saris…" She stopped. "Is that why? 'Cos you'd been dressing up?" She looked at him, stricken. "Can you only make love to me now if you've got a dress on? Is that why you don't want me any more?"

He shook his head. "It's not that – though yes, it is exciting to wear feminine clothing, or imagine I am."

"And I thought it might be me turning you on," she said bitterly.

"It was you."

She got up and walked across the kitchen to the kettle. "Yeah, so much so that you kept avoiding me."

"Look." He held his hands out in front of him as if begging. "I've been confused, I've been feeling guilty. I didn't want you to see my legs…"

She looked at them bewildered.

"I'd shaved them once," he said, embarrassed. "Just to see how it felt – and I was afraid you'd notice. I tried to keep away from you till they'd grown back." He gave a self-conscious laugh. "I was going to tell you we were trialling hair removal cream – that the girls in the office did it to me for a laugh."

"You've got very proficient at making up the stories," she said grimly. "What else have you lied about?" She turned on the cold tap. "I want to believe you, but you haven't got a very good track record, have you? You're telling me all this stuff now but I'm afraid of what you're not saying…"

Victor sounded earnest. "I'll be honest from now on. I promise. I'll hide nothing. I'll tell you how I'm feeling, what I'm doing. Maybe we can work out a compromise." He looked at her pleadingly. "Maybe, if I don't do anything you're uncomfortable with. I'll just do it in London, never here. I'll spend more time at home with you. There are other guys – you know, with families and children and they work it out…"

"Do their children know?"

"Some do."

"Are you going to tell Chloe?"

His face clouded. "I don't know yet."

"Well, you need to think about these things – we both do."

"Do you think you can…?"

She looked at him and an awful certainty came over her. "I don't know," she said slowly. "There's something I need to do first."

She sat on the edge of the bath and breathed deeply. However much you imagined how you would feel in a given situation, however sure you were that you would have certain reactions, you could never really know. Nothing had prepared her for how she felt right now.

Her heart seemed enormous in her chest. She was in the grip of a dozen emotions and couldn't have named one of them. She shivered and pulled her dressing gown from the back of the bathroom door, pulling it round her, over her sweatshirt and jeans. Wrapping herself up.

As she went slowly downstairs, images chased their way across her memory. Sam here, casting off this very dressing gown, Chloe triumphant in the wine bar courtyard, Victor staring wide-eyed at her, lipstick smeared across his startled mouth. She felt she had to carry herself very carefully, as though she might split apart at any moment.

Victor was still at the kitchen table. Winter sunshine sent low beams across the soft sheen of the wood. She glanced around her at the gleaming kettle and toaster, the high-tech espresso machine, the designer tiles. She looked and it was all at once familiar and utterly strange, like someone else's kitchen. Her husband looked up miserably.

"There's something you need to know before we decide anything," she said. She felt tremulous. "It's the most incredible timing." Her eyes suddenly filled with tears. "I can't really believe it should happen now but it's a sort of miracle, too."

Victor sounded exhausted. "What are you talking about?"

She'd imagined saying the words so often – imagined her excitement and joy. Now she just felt scared. For a moment she couldn't speak at all and picked up her cup with its inch of cold coffee. She swallowed.

"Victor, I'm pregnant."

He sat bolt upright. "You can't be."

She smiled. "Yes, I am. I know. I thought it was like all the other times, too. That's why I wasn't going to bother but I just did a test and…" She grinned at him, the whole ludicrous truth of it sinking in. "I'm pregnant!"

She waited, watching him, and as she did so, fresh fear crept in. She'd imagined all sorts of reactions but not this one. He stared at her, going red and seeming to struggle for words. Then he went white again and his mouth hardened. He stood up and stepped back from her, eyes like flints.

She said, uneasily: "I know it's a shock, I wasn't expecting it either. I never thought for a moment…"

"Whose is it?"

She stared back. "Yours."

Inside her heart thumped. It had to be Victor's – for God's sake, there was only the once with Sam. You didn't get pregnant doing it once – not in real life.

He looked at her contemptuously and his voice was cold: "No, it's not. Who have you been screwing, Gaynor? Jesus – you were so suspicious of me – kept accusing me of having another woman, when all the time it was you. You're the one who's been sleeping around!"

"I haven't!" Her voice rose.

Once didn't count, did it? She felt her own conviction grow. She was upset – they'd got carried away. Sam said so. He'd said they should put it behind them, move on.

"This baby's yours, of course it is," she said, frightened. "We made love that night Lizzie was here and that other time before, when we'd been shopping. My periods have been all over the place. I don't know quite when it would have been but…"

"It's not mine." His voice cut through hers. "Don't lie to me, Gaynor. I've been through hell too and I have just been as honest with you as I know how. Don't insult my bloody intelligence. What have you been doing?"

His face was working in pain and anger. He threw the newspaper to the floor and banged his fist on the table. "Who is it?" he roared suddenly. "Who the fuck is it?"

"Nobody." She shook her head, heart hammering, not knowing what to say.

"I thought," he said, suddenly sinking back into a chair, speaking quietly again, "that there might just be a small chance. That maybe I could somehow work through who I am and have my other feminine life and still have you as my friend, my wife, who knows. I was so afraid of telling you but I still thought, clung to the hope that perhaps if I did it right, once you'd got over the shock, you might understand. Because once we were good, weren't we? We had something…"

She was silent – gripped with a sudden shame.

"But now, I find you were cheating on me all along." Victor's voice was cold. "You've been lying. You've been having an affair and you stand there and tell me…"

Rage filled her. "Hang on," she said furiously. "Hang on a bloody minute. You're the one who's been dressing up in fucking suspenders for months on end – you've lied and lied. You've been going out with other MEN for God's sake. How faithful is that? What could you have given me?" She clutched her stomach in panic.

"Nothing," he snapped back. "I've told you and told you, I haven't had sex with anyone. You obviously can't say the same."

"I can." She hesitated. Wondering for a moment whether to tell him. To say it was only once. But surely it had to be Victor's baby. She thought wildly about DNA testing. She tried to remember where her cycle had been when she and Sam had made love. Her mind was a blank.

"This is your baby," she said again. She felt sick. Never for a moment had she thought the announcement would lead to this.

"It is NOT!" He banged his hand down hard again, making her cup tremble in its saucer.

"How can you be so bloody sure?" she yelled back.

He stared at her. He looked like nobody she knew.

"Because," he said, suddenly icily calm again, "five years ago I had a vasectomy."

23. Trebbiano di Romagna
Unexpectedly bitter

"Oh Christ." Sarah put her arms around Gaynor. "I can't believe it – how absolutely awful."

"Bloody bastard!" Lizzie pulled the cork from a restorative bottle of Macon. "Wait till I see him."

Gaynor blew her nose. "You know, I think I just might have been able to put up with him prancing about in a frock once a week, it might have worked." She gave a bitter laugh. "We could have gone on girly shopping trips together and swapped mascaras." She snorted, half-crying again. "Bloody hell, I can't get my head round this."

"I should think not." Lizzie looked mutinous. "I'll tell you what I'd like to do with his mascara. The creep." She glanced around Gaynor's kitchen. "Where is he now?"

"I don't know – gone back to London I suppose. How could he do that to me, how could he?"

Lizzie poured wine into three glasses. "All that time making you worry he had another woman and was buying her racy little numbers, and he's bloody wearing them himself!"

"Well, I suppose he was afraid of what you'd do if you found out." Sarah tried to be reasonable. "And you can understand that. Lots of women would be horrified if they knew their husband…"

Gaynor shook her head wildly. "It's not that. It's not the dressing up – I could forgive that, I think – he can't help how he is. It's the betrayal. The vasectomy. All those years, when

247

he knew I was desperate for a baby." She burst into fresh tears. "Don't you see? He's stopped me having a baby."

Lizzie took a swallow of wine. "Except he hasn't, has he? You're pregnant, honey – and you need to start thinking what you're going to do about it."

Gaynor shook her head as a fresh wave of pain overcame her.

Sarah asked gently. "What does Sam say?"

"He didn't, really – he just said if I was pregnant then … He just made it clear that he wouldn't be very happy. He said he thought I couldn't, and I said I probably wasn't anyway, and…"

"You haven't told him?"

Gaynor shook her head again.

"Well," said Sarah. "That's the first thing you must do. Go and see him now."

"I don't know." Lizzie was doubtful. "He sounds a bit of a flake to me. I don't think you want to go through all that again, do you? It will only drag you down. Look – if you are going to keep it… plenty of women bring up babies on their own…"

Sarah frowned. "Of course she's going to keep him or her. And yes there are plenty of single mothers about, but it isn't ideal. And neither are most things. It's a matter of compromise. I thought Paul was the love of my life – well he was, but…"

Lizzie interrupted her. "Gaynor's lived with enough depressives to last her a lifetime. It's better to have a child on your own than hook up with some half-hearted father who doesn't give a shit."

Gaynor tried to get a word in. "Oh no, he's not like that – he's been a wonderful father to his kids. He's really…"

Sarah was still talking. "Richard's not perfect. He's frightened and he has all that baggage with Tania. But he's a good man. He's lovely with Charlie, and if there's one thing that being with Paul taught me is that sometimes you just have to hang on to the good things. If Sam…"

Lizzie gave an incredulous laugh. "I don't believe this. You were the one who told her to forget him and make it up with Victor!"

"I didn't know then," Sarah said heatedly. She turned to Gaynor. "If you'd told me, if I'd known you were pregnant..."

"I didn't know myself."

"Well, everything's different now." Sarah was firm.

"But does Gaynor want someone who can't cope?" Lizzie persisted. "If he's going to go into a decline every time things go a bit wrong, that's no good, is it?"

"You don't know him," Gaynor cried in frustration. "He's good and he's strong. It freaked me out the first time I saw him on a bad day but he fights it – he gets through. Perhaps if he were with me all the time...perhaps a baby would…"

"Totally finish him off," Lizzie said flatly.

Gaynor sat back, deflated. "Yes, maybe," she said.

Sarah glared at Lizzie before turning to Gaynor. "You won't know until you tell him."

Lizzie, unperturbed, topped up Gaynor's glass and held the bottle out to Sarah. "Are you sure you don't want one?"

Sarah waved it away. "I've got to get down to the wine bar and start the prep for tonight." She spoke to Gaynor. "Walk down with me and go and tell him."

Gaynor shook her head. "I did. He didn't want to know."

"You didn't – you said you might be and then you backtracked. You've got to tell him you are pregnant for sure, and it's his baby."

"No."

"You must – it's his right. You owe him that."

Lizzie poured more wine into her glass. "Bollocks to his rights – she owes him nothing."

"I think …"

"Stop it," Gaynor exploded. "Just stop! This is my life and my baby – mine and Sam's."

"Tell him then," said Sarah doggedly.

"I don't want to!" Gaynor shouted. She looked at Sarah in sudden panic. "And you mustn't either. Or you!" she added, turning to Lizzie.

Lizzie made a face. "I won't! I think you're better off without either of them, sweetie."

Sarah scowled at her. "Just because you have a problem with relationships."

Lizzie took another mouthful of wine. "I don't have any problem, thank you. I get shagged when I want to and I don't have all this crap to put up with."

Gaynor brought her hand down sharply on the table top. "Listen! I don't want him to know. You've both got to promise me."

Lizzie nodded. Sarah looked troubled.

"Please, please, promise." Gaynor was crying again. The thought of Sam's face the last time she'd seen him gave her a physical pain.

Sarah put a hand on her shoulder. "OK, OK," she said reluctantly. "I won't say a word."

"Why aren't they saying anything?" Claire demanded. Why don't they come and tell us what's going on?"

She stopped pacing the small square of vinyl flooring with its strong smell of disinfectant and sank down into a plastic chair and began to sob uncontrollably. Jamie, who'd been staring vacantly at the posters about vaccinations and roundworm, looked at her in alarm.

"It will be OK," he said helplessly. He patted her shoulder. "Henry's tough."

So was Claire too, usually. He couldn't remember ever seeing her cry like this. Privately, Jamie had wished she would sometimes. There were times when he'd have liked her to be the sort of woman you could protect or comfort or rescue in some small way – rather than being so strong and capable and so able to do everything herself that you sometimes wondered why she needed you at all.

But watching her weep now in this most un-Claire-like way he felt totally inadequate for the task. "He'll be OK," he said again, sitting down in the next chair and trying to hug her. Claire leapt up.

"Stop saying that!" she cried. "You saw him. Just lying there, not moving or eating, all weak…" Her heart twisted at the thought of Henry's eyes, clouded with pain, looking beseechingly at her from his basket while Wooster whined nearby. "Help me!" he seemed to be saying. "Make me better."

They'd struggled to lift the large Airedale into the car, his inert body weighing heavily between them. Wooster, left behind at home, had howled as they left.

"Oh God, what are they doing in there?" As Claire spoke, the door opened and a veterinary nurse came out wearing green overalls. She looked seriously from Jamie to Claire. "We've done some X-rays," she said. "And now we know exactly what the problem is…"

Back home in their kitchen, Claire blew her nose. "I was so frightened," she said. "I really thought we'd lost him." She looked at Henry lying in his basket with a martyred expression, and the shaved patch where the stitches were. "That will teach you," she said. "Teach you to go eating everything you find!"

The shadow on the X ray had proved to be half a red plastic ball that, the vet said, had probably been sitting in Henry's insides for some time. It was this that had caused the intermittent symptoms, that had caused Henry to feel so miserable and put him off his food as it shifted about inside and blocked things up. Now it was removed, the vet added, he would be instantly back to his normal self, if a little sore from the stitches and woozy from the anaesthetic.

Claire had cried again when they got home, this time in Jamie's arms, which made him feel better, though it made little impression on Wooster who had given up on them all in disgust at the attention Henry was getting, and had slunk off to the other room to sulk and debate whether his feelings would be better understood if he had a good chew at Jamie's briefcase.

Claire took Jamie's hand. "Thank you. I'm so glad you were here."

"I took the day off because I wanted to talk to you," said Jamie. "See you for a change."

Claire smiled at him. "And I want to talk to you, too. I've been meaning to for ages."

Jamie waited.

"I know we hardly get any time at the moment." She laughed, still light-hearted with relief over Henry. "Ships that pass in the night. Those little weather people in the old clocks. You come in and I go out. I get in and you're fast asleep having to get up early…"

"Yes," said Jamie. "That's what I want to talk about."

"Well I've been doing a lot of thinking," went on Claire brightly. "And I thought, you know, that things aren't really working out with Sarah. She's not happy. She's fed up in the kitchen and we can't pay a chef as well as both of us. Not yet. So I was wondering…"

"Yes?" Jamie suddenly looked hopeful.

"There's this place for sale over in Margate. A restaurant. It's a bit run down and old-fashioned but it could be fantastic. It's got great sea-views and if we stripped it out and did it up, it would make a great café-bar."

Jamie's face had fallen again but Claire went rapidly on. "And I thought, I'd still keep my share in Greens but Sarah could manage that – with a chef and maybe Gaynor helping out. I like Sarah so much, I really do, but I think, to be honest both of us are the sort of personalities that want to run the show." Claire smiled. "So I would take over the running of the new place. And I also thought –" Claire's smile widened into a positive beam. "You could give up work and do it with me!"

She jumped up and pulled open a drawer. "I've got the details here and I've done some figures. The bank seemed to think it wouldn't be a problem – there's already so much more equity in Greens from when we bought it, and then there's this house. And the way house prices have been moving! I think we could really make a go of it, it would suit everyone…"

"Except me," Jamie said.

Claire stopped. "But you said you wished we could spend more time together."

Jamie turned away from her and looked out of the window. "Yes. Proper time. Sitting talking to each other time. Not me trailing along behind while you build your empire."

Claire stared at him. "Is that how you feel?"

"Oh wow! You've remembered I might have feelings." Jamie turned back and scowled. "Do you know, I can't remember the last time you asked me anything about what I thought. Not that I ever see you to speak to. You're in that wine bar almost the entire time that I'm at home, except for the hour or so when you talk about it if I've stayed awake for you. You never ask how my job is or how I am. The only creature you've showed any care or emotion towards for months is that dog!" He jerked a foot towards Henry.

Claire looked shocked. "Henry could have died!"

"So could I, for all you'd have noticed!"

They stood gazing at each other, startled.

"Well, I'm sorry," said Claire, stiffly. "It does take a lot of work when you're trying to get a business up and running. Catering always means long hours. Of course I'd like to spend more time with you, but the wine bar…"

"Is so important to you, you want to buy another one."

"For us to do together," said Claire defensively.

Jamie put his hands down flat on the tiles of the work surface as if bracing himself. "Suppose I don't want to do that. Did you even think about what I might want?"

"Well, I thought…"

"You didn't think at all!"

Claire was silent for a moment. Jamie was never like this. She felt as shocked and bemused as if Henry had staggered from his basket and bitten her! "What do you want, then?" she asked tentatively.

Jamie looked out at the garden again. "The bank have offered me a transfer," he said harshly. "A two-year contract, promotion and lots more money. It's a fantastic opportunity." He swung back round to face her. "It means leaving here. And that's what I want."

"All right," she said faintly, her mind racing. She suddenly realised how much her heart was hammering. She needed Jamie. She supposed it didn't have to be Margate. She could get another bar somewhere else, get more staff, make sure she spent some evenings at home with him. She didn't want to leave Broadstairs but they could rent the house out, two years wasn't a lifetime. She didn't like the expression on her boyfriend's face or him talking like this, she wanted the easy-going, accepting Jamie back.

"All right," she said again, more loudly. "Take it then. I can adapt my plans if I have to." She forced a smile. "Where is it?"

He looked at her hard. "Tokyo."

24. Cerveteri
Severe and lacking a good bouquet.

Richard shook his head. "Sarah does too much already."

"Well, I think it could all work out brilliantly," said Gaynor. "She'd be much happier if she wasn't down in that kitchen all the time. She's so lovely with people, she should be behind the bar more anyway."

Richard put the pint glass he was polishing back on the shelf and picked up another one.

"And maybe, when you're not at work, you could help out yourself." Gaynor smiled at him brightly. She found if she just kept pretending everything was OK, if she just kept smiling and talking briskly, she was able to keep it all suspended. That first day, when she realised she'd lost Victor for ever and there was no longer Sam to run to, she had been racked with such pain she was quite unable to see how she would ever manage anything again.

There was still a constant gnawing in her solar plexus and she knew she would have to face things soon, but there were now whole patches of time when she was able to distance herself so firmly from the awful reality that she barely felt a thing. She upgraded the smile to a grin. "Now you've proved yourself such a dab hand with the glass-washer…"

From thinking Richard the most terrible stiff, she'd grown fond and appreciative of him. Since it had come out about Tania he had changed out of all recognition – smiling, cracking jokes, being wonderfully helpful with little things around the place, even – according to Sarah – cleaning the oven the afternoon Claire was in crisis with Henry. Now, however, he looked worried.

"She'll be a great manager," said Gaynor firmly. "That's the thing about Sarah – she might put on a show of moaning but she takes things in her stride. She's so grown up, so sorted. She's a year younger than me but she often makes me feel like a child. She's a great mother, she's –"

"Addicted to codeine." Richard's voice was flat.

Gaynor looked at him, stupefied. "What?"

He put his cloth down. "Haven't you noticed how she knocks back those painkillers all day long?"

Gaynor frowned. "Yes, well, she gets headaches, bad period pain. She's just trying to…"

Richard picked up another glass, looked at it and sighed. "She's got a problem, Gaynor. Believe me, I know about this stuff – we've done studies of it at work. See how she gets so tense and irritable and then she pops a couple of tablets and she's all smiles again?"

"Well – I thought…" Gaynor's mind was reeling. At the same time, a kaleidoscope of images flitted across her mind and things clicked. "Are you sure?" she asked Richard, knowing he was.

He nodded. "She needs help." He picked up the tea towel again and slowly began wiping around the rim of the wine goblet he was holding. "I'm just wondering how best to go about it…"

"Are you OK?" Gaynor smiled at Sarah who was putting on lipstick in front of the small pine mirror on the wall of the flat kitchen.

Sarah smiled back at Gaynor's reflection. "Yes, I'm fine. Now you know we've only got one Lamb Stroganoff left and two Dover Soles. The soup is Carrot and Coriander for the moment and when that's gone I've got some Leek and… Gaynor, are you listening to me?" Sarah turned her head and looked at Gaynor directly. "Are you all right? Are you sure you're OK to work?"

"Yes, yes, I'm fine."

"I don't have to go out. But I think it will be quiet tonight and if you and Ben and Claire really can manage…"

"Yes, yes we can. I just wondered…"

"Yes?"

"If you were all right?"

Sarah laughed. "I'm fine. Looking forward to getting away from this place for a bit. Though whether Richard is, is another matter. He's never had the kids in his place for the night before. Baptism of fire, eh?" She stuck her head out of the kitchen and yelled in the direction of the sitting room "We're going soon!"

Gaynor laughed. "Shows he's keen."

Sarah looked pretty and happy. Her hair shone very red under the kitchen spotlights and her eyes were huge and luminous, matching the green of her softly-clinging wool dress.

"Richard thinks I'd feel a lot better about everything here if I wasn't literally living on top of it. Will you be alright sleeping here on your own?"

"Of course!" Gaynor replied, making a mental note to leave some lights on. "I'm waiting for you to move in with him permanently. I've got half an eye on the place myself!"

Sarah was suddenly serious. "You know you're welcome here as long for as you need to be but – please go and see Sam."

Gaynor turned away. "No."

"Let me, then."

Gaynor swung back round and looked Sarah in the eyes. "You promised! Don't forget that."

Sarah picked up mugs and plates from the table and piled them into the sink. "Sorry about all the mess," she said shortly. "I'll just wash these up before I go."

"Leave it, I'll do it." Gaynor put a hand on her arm. "Look, I know you mean well…"

257

Sarah went out of the room. Gaynor could hear her telling Luke and Charlie to hurry up. She knew Sarah only wanted a happy ending for her, but the thought of her friend going cap-in-hand to Sam, pleading with him, filled her with complete horror. Sarah reappeared with an armful of clothes and began to push sweatshirts and socks into the washing machine.

"I know you care," said Gaynor. "But I just feel…"

"Ugh, you should see their bedroom," interrupted Sarah. "I wouldn't be surprised to find something nesting in that lot!"

She pulled the remains of a chewed and squashed Twix bar from a pocket. "Lovely."

She picked up another pair of jeans as Bel appeared in the doorway, Scarface dangling unprotestingly from her arms. "Those boys won't get ready, Mummy," she said sorrowfully.

"We're going NOW!" Sarah bellowed. She pulled a crisp packet from the denim in her hand and felt about for more debris.

"What's this?" She looked quizzically at a crumpled white envelope and frowned at Gaynor. "It's got your name on it."

She held it out. Gaynor saw the lettering on the outside and her heart jumped.

"What's it doing in Luke's pocket? Luke!" Sarah marched into the other room, still holding the letter. Gaynor dashed after her.

Luke looked blank.

"How did it get there?" Sarah demanded.

The boy shrugged until light dawned. "Oh yeah," he said yawning. "Some bloke brought it up."

"What bloke? For goodness sake, sit up and concentrate," said Sarah. "Why didn't you give it to Gaynor?"

Luke shrugged again. "Sor-ry," he intoned, bored.

"I'm so sorry, Gaynor." Sarah glared at her son who was absorbed in the TV once more. "He's away with the fairies most of the time."

Luke looked up. "Sorry," he said to Gaynor in an ordinary voice. "I forgot."

Gaynor ripped open the envelope and pulled out the note inside. It was on a sheet torn from a lined pad. A single line of black biro in Sam's large untidy scrawl.

So sorry. Please come back. I love you xxx

"When was it, Luke?" she asked, giving him a friendly smile.

The boy screwed up his face as if trying to remember. He shook his head. "Dunno."

"I wonder why he came up here," Gaynor said to Sarah. "Am I that scary?"

Luke sat up, suddenly inspired. "Oh, he said he could see you and Mum were busy with the police and he didn't want to disturb you. So he said to give it to one of you later."

"So why didn't you?" asked Sarah exasperated.

But Gaynor nodded. That was the day she'd told him she might be pregnant. He'd come down after her. Written to her straight away.

"It's OK," she said to Luke, squeezing the paper in her hand. "It doesn't matter. I'll sort it out."

She felt suddenly light and hopeful. She fingered the envelope, thinking of the words it held. *So sorry.* She gave Luke a forgiving beam. *I love you…*

"There!" said Sarah, satisfied. "Now you've got to go round there!

Claire said it was fine if she wasn't too long. Nobody had come in yet except Lizzie who'd arrived on the dot of opening time. Who, although she had pulled a face on hearing where Gaynor was going, said she'd do the honours if anyone needed serving before she returned. "So no need to rush back," she added with a wink.

Gaynor ran up the clifftop path. She wondered what he'd thought when she hadn't been in contact. Did he imagine she was still upset? That she'd decided not to see him again? He wasn't the sort of bloke to chase her. He'd just stay at home, hurt and withdrawn.

She prayed he'd be in now – she wanted him to know how she'd been hurting too, every second, how much she'd wanted them to make it all right again.

She reached his front gate. She'd give him a hug, tell him she'd be back later when the wine bar had closed. She shifted impatiently, both nervous and excited. She'd have to tell him about the baby... later, when they had time. Her stomach flipped over as she knocked hard on the door, willing it to open quickly.

It did. A young woman stood there in a white linen shirt and black trousers. Gaynor looked at her, startled, then took in the neat clothes, understated make-up and dark shiny bob, and held out her hand.

"Hi," she smiled, hoping her disappointment didn't show. "You must be Debra. Is Sam here? I'm ..."

Debra looked at her coldly. "I know who you are."

"Is Sam in?" Gaynor asked again, pleasantly, not knowing what to do but repeat it. For a moment, Debra surveyed her in silence.

"He's been very upset." She obviously had no intention of letting Gaynor over the threshold. "He's been through a lot, losing my mother and adjusting to his new life down here." She made it sound as though it had all happened a matter of weeks ago.

"I know," Gaynor said earnestly, not wanting to antagonise her further. "But we've become good friends and..."

Debra snorted. "Good friends? It doesn't sound to me like you've been much of a friend." She folded her arms. "I think you've caused a whole lot of trouble. You're married and you've just been dangling him on a string."

Gaynor was speechless with shock. She looked beyond Debra at the softly-lit room, glimpsing its old leather chair and drawing board, wondering where Sam was. "Did he say that?" she managed eventually.

"He didn't have to." Debra's voice was curt. "He's been through hell because of you and he knows now he's better off without you. So just leave my father alone."

"But he wrote me a note," Gaynor said desperately. She held it out to Debra. "He asked me to come."

Debra took the piece of paper and scanned it briefly. She was closing the door. "Well, he's changed his mind."

"Stupid bitch," Gaynor said to Lizzie. "How long's she going to be hanging around like a bad smell? Leave her father alone! Anyone would think he's a bloody child. What shall I do?"

Lizzie, at the bar with a large glass of Chardonnay, waved a dismissive hand. "Phone him and say what is your witch of a daughter playing at? Call his mobile!"

"He hasn't got one! And if I phone the land line, she might answer. I bet she doesn't even tell him I've been round. He'll think I'm ignoring the note and then…"

She stopped as two couples came into the bar. She shook her head at Lizzie and sighed. Then she switched on a dazzling smile for the customers. "Yes, good evening and what can I get you…"

There was no more chance to talk. There were lots of drinkers in as well as a few tables ordering food. The evening whizzed past in a frenzy of dashing up and down stairs with trays of pasta and garlic bread, opening bottles of wine with one hand and writing out bills with the other.

Looking round at several people waiting, Gaynor thought about asking Lizzie to come behind the bar but she was deep in conversation with a hippy-looking guy with a beard and already on her second bottle of Chardonnay.

"I won't keep you a moment." Gaynor nodded at a middle-aged man who'd been sitting at the bar on his own for some time. He'd told her he was called Gary and was an electronics salesman. Quite who he was selling to in Broadstairs, she had no idea but he seemed to have a fairly hefty expense account. He'd already had a bottle of Chilean red and a couple of vodka cocktails; now he was on neat vodka on the rocks and looking slightly bug-eyed.

He winked at her. "No problem," he said. "Whenever you're ready." He held out his glass. "Make it a large one. And one for yourself," he added expansively. "Can never resist a pretty face!"

Yeah, yeah. Gaynor smiled absently. It was nearly half-past ten and she just wanted the hands of the clock to whiz round to closing time so she could get cleared up and decide what to do about Sam. She wondered what exactly he had said to his daughter. She knew they were close – he'd said he could talk to her about anything, but this…

She thought she might just phone and see who answered. She could always put the phone down if it was Debra.

Claire had finished in the kitchen and had come behind the bar. "Is he all right?" she asked, nodding at Gary.

"He's being pleasant enough," said Gaynor as she looked at Gary's grinning face. She'd wondered fleetingly if she should have served him last time but she didn't want a scene and there'd been other people waiting. So she'd dropped ice-cubes into a tumbler and deftly pressed twice at the Smirnoff optic.

"Don't give him any more," said Claire in a low voice.

"Can we have another one?" Lizzie was waving an empty bottle from the other end of the bar. "Have you scored?" enquired Gaynor, raising her eyebrows in the direction of her companion.

Lizzie leant towards her. "Getting a bit boring now!" she said in a stage whisper.

Behind Gaynor, Claire spoke sharply. "Look over there!"

Gaynor looked round. Gary was beginning to sway. He grinned and held up his empty glass. "Vojka," he slurred. "Another one pleeesh…"

"He's got to go," said Claire. "You should have stopped serving him ages ago."

She walked round to the front of the bar. "Time to go home now!" she said briskly. "We're closing soon."

Gary giggled. "I don't shink I can move," he said, with difficulty. He gave her a large, drunken smile. "I shtuck here."

"Oh no, you're not." Claire pulled at his arm. He toppled forward. One of the blokes in a group next to him put out a hand and yanked him back up again.

"Want us to throw him out? he enquired cheerily.

Gaynor shook her head, feeling responsible. "No, no I'll do it."

She came round to stand beside Gary, too. "I'll deal with it," she said to Claire. "Come on now," she told Gary. "Get off the stool."

With the help of a couple of the men nearby, she got him on to his feet. He slung an arm around her shoulders and let her lead him, meandering drunkenly, to the door.

"Goodnight," she said, as she disentangled herself. "Time to go home."

"What's going on?" enquired Claire, when she came outside, five minutes later.

"Every time I let go of him, he falls over," said Gaynor.

Gary giggled. "I don't shink..." he said, "I don't shink..."

Claire rolled her eyes. "We can't leave him here. It doesn't look very good to have someone passed out on the doorstep. Shall we try and get him to the top of the road?" She looked back over her shoulder at the still-crowded bar. "I'd better not leave the place – I'll see if I can get someone..."

"It's OK," said Gaynor. "He said he was staying at the Grand. I'll walk him up there."

Claire looked doubtful. "Are you sure you'll be all right?"

"It's not far."

The Grand Hotel was only round the corner and along Albion Street. It was the town's best and she could imagine how delighted they would be when Gary graced reception.

But that was their problem – it wouldn't be the first time they'd had to deal with an inebriated guest.

"Come on," she said. Gary began to giggle again. With a huge effort he straightened himself and began staggering forward up the hill.

"I like you," he told her loudly as they weaved their way to the top of Harbour Street. "You are a bish of all right."

He was leaning most of his weight on her and as they rounded the corner, he crashed into the lamp-post and nearly knocked her flying. "Stand up straight," she cried in alarm. "Keep walking!"

If she could just keep him moving, she could propel him forward. It was when he stopped that his knees sagged and then she couldn't get him started again. A group of youngsters emerging from the Dolphin Pub nudged and pointed as they staggered past. Gaynor made an exasperated face at them, hoping it would be apparent that she doing her good landlady duty in dragging the old drunk home and he wasn't her hot date for the night.

They'd got halfway up the road. Her back was hurting from supporting him and he seemed ready to sink to the pavement. She stopped outside the Albion Bookshop and tried to prop him up against the entrance. He slumped against the glass and pointed a finger at the window display. "I sh' read that," he told Gaynor. "Ish very good."

"Great!" she said through gritted teeth. He still had an arm wrapped around her. "Come on, Gary," she cried, in desperately jolly tones. "Let's get you home!"

He shook his head with an idiotic grin. "You're very beau-shi-ful," he said.

She heard footsteps come along the pavement behind her and tried to move him out of the way. "Gary, please…" She turned and stopped, startled, as she found herself looking up at Sam. Debra was beside him.

"Sam!" she said in surprise, smiling with relief. "I'm so glad to see…"

She trailed off at the look on his face. He glanced coldly from her to Gary and then stepped off the pavement and walked into the road to skirt round them. Debra put her arm through his, shooting Gaynor a poisonous look as she hurried her father past.

"I shink I love you!" Gary shouted, draping himself back over Gaynor as she looked after Sam. She saw Sam look back but couldn't see his expression in the darkness.

She heard Debra though. Her voice floated back to them, loud and clear and deliberate. "Well, it didn't take her long, did it?"

"You are a bloody nuisance," Gaynor said to Gary when she'd got him moving again. As if in answer, he promptly fell over. She stood watching him giggling on the pavement with something approaching despair.

"Please!" she called out to three guys, swinging along in leather jackets on the opposite side of the road. "Please could you come and help me?"

They sauntered over – they were in their mid-twenties and sniggering at Gaynor's predicament. "Where are you trying to go?" one asked.

"In there." Gaynor nodded to the illuminated hotel sign twenty metres away.

"Come on, mate!" Two of them took an arm each and hauled Gary to his feet. "Bedtime."

The third fell into step beside Gaynor. "What have you done to him, to get him in such a state?" He grinned at her as they walked up to the double doors of the hotel.

"Nothing to do with me," she said, shortly.

"You want to give him a bit more love and attention," said the one on Gary's right arm, as he pushed open the door with one foot. "Look after him! Be a proper wife!" They all laughed loudly.

"He's not my husband!" Gaynor said hotly. "I don't know him from Adam." They stopped in surprise just inside the foyer.

"In that case, love," the young man said, "I should fucking leave him to it."

They both let go of Gary. Gaynor clapped a hand to her mouth as she watched him plunge forward into the hotel's giant cheese plant. There was a snapping sound as leaves and compost scattered across the pale carpet.

Gaynor fled.

Lizzie was fast approaching a similar state by the time Gaynor got back to Greens. "I'll take her upstairs with me," she said wearily to Claire who had done all the clearing up and was jingling her keys impatiently.

"I wondered what on earth had happened," said Claire. "I was just coming to look for you."

"I've bought us some wine." Lizzie was gaily waving yet another bottle of Chardonnay. "Come and tell me all about it."

Gaynor sat on the window seat among Sarah's cushions and watched Lizzie pull out the cork.

"You should have seen the way he looked at me," she said, morosely. "Like I was a piece of dirt."

"Bastard," said Lizzie succinctly. "Come on, have a drink."

Gaynor looked down. "I'd better not."

Lizzie glanced at Gaynor's middle. "Suppose," she said grudgingly.

Gaynor had changed into a pair of pink pyjama bottoms and an old T-shirt of Sarah's. She put her arms around her knees and sighed. "I must go home and get some more stuff soon but I can't bear the thought of bumping into Victor."

Lizzie looked around the sitting room. "Where are you sleeping?"

"In Bel's bed – poor little thing is on a put-you-up in with Sarah. Sarah's been so good…"

"You know you can stay in mine when Ravi and I go off travelling again."

Gaynor smiled. She'd tried staying in Lizzie's spare room, but the sounds of Lizzie and Ravi locked in passion coming through the thin walls had kept her awake and made her utterly miserable. "Sorry," Lizzie had said sheepishly when Gaynor gently explained that she thought she'd be better off above the wine bar.

"When are you going?" Gaynor asked now.

Lizzie shrugged. "I don't know. This temp job ends at Christmas. I quite fancy hitting the sunshine then. It'll depend on money and stuff. Ravi's broke too."

Gaynor smiled again. Lizzie was always broke, always in temporary jobs, but somehow it never stopped her doing what she wanted.

"Where is Ravi, anyway?"

"In Hull seeing his mum. He was supposed to go last weekend, but he couldn't tear himself away from me." Lizzie lay back on Sarah's sofa with a smirk.

"I think you've fallen for him," Gaynor said, seeing if she'd confess, now she was three sheets to the wind.

Lizzie sat up and swigged at her glass of wine. "Not me!" she said, with mock bravado. Then she wrinkled her nose. "A little bit, maybe." She giggled. "Still don't really know him, but hey…" She fell back into the cushions.

"I'm beginning to wonder if we ever know anyone," said Gaynor, sadly. "Everyone seems together on the surface but scratch it and there we all are – as flaky as hell."

She turned sideways and stared down at the street lights below. She was still reeling from Richard's revelations about Sarah. Now she thought about it, it all made sense. The way Sarah would be crabby and uptight and then swallow a couple of pills and be all smiles and light again. The way her headaches were constant. Richard had said that if you took too much, the codeine itself gave you headaches, so there you were, taking tablets for a headache that would give you a headache, so you had to keep taking more and more…

He'd said he'd talk to her about it. Gaynor wondered how Sarah would react.

"And look at Sam," she said to Lizzie now. "I would never have had him down as a bloke who'd let his daughter send me packing."

She thought painfully of the expression on Sam's face, the way he had stepped round her as though she were infected.

"Told you he was a flake," Lizzie said disparagingly. "Though, in fairness," she added, a slight doubt in her voice, "perhaps he really wasn't there and doesn't know what she said."

Gaynor shook her head. "I saw his face tonight. He's not interested any more. There was no love or affection there. I'm really gonna be Mother of the Year, aren't I? No money, no home, no father for the poor brat..."

She suddenly felt her chin tremble. "Oh Lizzie, what am I going to do?"

Lizzie sat up again. "You are going to get yourself together, sweetie," she declared, slurring slightly. "You've got to sort Victor out – your house up there must be worth a fortune by now. You want half of that for starters – then you can look for a place of your own. And the sooner the better. Nine months isn't very long."

Gaynor felt panic rising inside her. "I know, but I can't cope with seeing Victor right now."

"Is that all it is?" Lizzie looked at her. "Sarah thinks you're in denial. That you're not facing up to being pregnant."

"Well, I am, but..."

"Do you still want it?"

Gaynor looked at her friend in anguish, feeling the tears come into her eyes. She hugged her knees tighter. "I don't know – I've waited for this for so many years and you know how you imagine a moment. I thought when I finally discovered I was pregnant, it would be so magical. I imagined telling Victor and him cracking open champagne. A bit like he did for Chloe, really," she added bitterly.

At the thought of her step-daughter, the panic increased. She didn't want to lose Chloe too – not any more than she had already. But…

"Have you spoken to her yet?" Lizzie lay back down, hands behind her head, her bare feet up on the arm of the sofa.

Gaynor shook her head. "No. She keeps phoning. I haven't answered – she's had to leave messages. She's obviously in a terrible state. Can't really work out whether she wants to blame me or commiserate." Gaynor looked shamefaced. "I know it's awful but I can't face going to see her either – I don't want to talk about Victor and she's really pregnant now – she's seven and a half months, she'll be huge…"

Lizzie frowned. "So? Why's that a problem? You will be before you know it."

"Yes."

"Gaynor," Lizzie said again deliberately, "do you want this baby?" She propped herself up on one elbow and took another swallow of wine. "It's a big undertaking. It's a huge, life-changing thing. Never a moment to yourself. Total commitment. Can't send it back…" She shuddered.

Gaynor sipped at the tea she'd made. "It's not that I don't want a baby," she said slowly. "It still seems such a miracle that I'm pregnant after all this time."

"Nothing wrong with you after all!" said Lizzie crossly. "That bastard…"

"But I wonder if I'm up to having one on my own…As you say, it's a big commitment." Gaynor chewed at her thumb. "I might give the poor little thing a terrible time. Is it fair?"

Lizzie flapped a hand. "I'm thinking of you. Is it fair on you?" She was really slurring now.

"But I don't think I could – you know – not again…" Gaynor bit her lip, trembling.

Lizzie shook her head. "That was a very long time ago," she drawled. "It's all quick these days – in, out and home again. Steffi had one in that new clinic out at Ashford. Said it

269

was nothing. Said it was much worse the next day when she had to have a filling replaced."

Gaynor wrinkled her nose. "I wouldn't feel like that. I know I'd..."

Lizzie sat up and wagged a finger at her. "You have got to sort yourself out," she said drunkenly. "You go and see Chloe, you face up to things. You've got a problem if you can't look at a pregnant woman!" She leaned forward and waved her hand a bit more. "Go and look at Chloe and face it, then you'll know... It's not good," she slurred, "putting it off. You've got to go and see her and tell her what really happened with Victor and then make a decishhon..."

"There isn't really a decision to make," said Gaynor bleakly. "I'm having a baby."

Lizzie slumped back among the cushions. "It's not a baby yet," she said loudly. "It's only a, it's only a .. phew," she said with difficulty, "a phew cells..."

Gaynor fetched a quilt from one of the children's beds and put it over Lizzie. As she leant out to switch off the light, Lizzie's eyes suddenly snapped open again. "And no father," she said, and passed out.

And no father. Gaynor got into Bel's bed, pulled the pink-patterned duvet up over her shoulders and thought about Sam. She thought about his slow, thoughtful way of talking, the way he would listen intently, would lean out and stroke her hair. "I'm here for you," he'd said.

And then she thought about Debra on the doorstep and the way she'd hurried Sam past. He hadn't resisted. Hadn't tried to stop.

He wasn't here for her anymore. Nobody was. There was just her and this little creature growing inside her that somehow she must look after for ever. Lizzie's words crowded in. Gaynor turned over and over, trying to get comfortable.

*   *   *

270

At first, the ringing was part of a dream. Then she woke and saw her mobile flashing. Trying to get her eyes open properly, she picked it up in time to see 'missed call' appear. She looked at the display. 7.02 a.m. It still wasn't light. Ugh. It had been well after two when she'd got into bed. Nearer three by the time she'd dropped off. Her head flopped back on to the pillow.

The phone rang again. Gaynor stretch out an arm for it, answering with her eyes still closed. "Yes," she said sleepily, "who is it?" It was the robotic woman telling her she had voice mail. Gaynor yawned as she listened to the message, but then, as her befuddled brain began to make sense of what she was hearing, she was suddenly awake.

She lay staring at the ceiling, tears in her eyes, suddenly knowing what she should do but feeling paralysed and quite powerless to do it. She knew she should. It was simply a matter of getting up, going to the station, doing what had to be done. For a moment she hesitated, feeling sick, clutching at her abdomen, as everything Lizzie had said was re-played across her mind. Then she switched on the bedside lamp and got out of bed.

25. Côte Rôtie
*Hot and Racy with an unusual
combination of flavours.*

Lizzie was still out cold on the sofa when Sarah returned.
Sarah looked at the empty wine bottle and threw open the
curtains.

"What are you doing here?" she asked, as Lizzie slowly
came to. "Where's Gaynor?"

Lizzie sat up groaning.

"I don't know. She went somewhere."

"Where?"

"I don't know. I feel dreadful."

"I'm not surprised," said Sarah, collecting up glasses.
"She's supposed to be helping out at lunchtime. Did she say
when she'd be back?"

"She woke me up and said, um…" Lizzie shook her
head. "She had a bag with her."

"What sort of bag?"

"A holdall thing – an overnight bag. She said she might
have to stay."

"Where?"

Lizzie struggled to remember. "I don't know. She was
talking about her baby. Something about hospital."

"Hospital?" Sarah cried. "Was she OK? Did she think
she was losing it? Was she bleeding?" She looked at Lizzie as
if she'd like to shake the answers out of her.

"No, I don't think so. She said I was right and she had to
do it…"

"What?"

Lizzie frowned, then suddenly put her head in her hands. "Oh God, Oh no, I think I might have…"

Charlie and Bel appeared in the doorway. "Mum, there's no cornflakes."

Sarah didn't look round. "You had breakfast at Richard's."

"And there's no milk."

"Then go and get some from the kitchen downstairs."

Neither child moved, sensing something interesting going on. "Go now," said Sarah sharply, turning back to Lizzie as they reluctantly shuffled away. "Tell me what's happened," she demanded. "What did you say to her?"

Sarah glared at Lizzie, when Lizzie had finished piecing together as much as she could remember. "We've got to stop her. She's wanted a baby for years. Mind you, she'll only be able to make an appointment. They won't do it just like that…"

Lizzie shrugged. "They might. It's pretty quick these days. Spot of counselling which basically amounts to 'are you sure?' a couple of doctor's signatures and show us the colour of your Barclaycard."

Sarah scowled. "How do you know so much about it?"

"I just do."

"How are we going to find her – where would she be?"

"We talked about the clinic in Ashford." Lizzie rubbed at her temples.

"Oh bloody brilliant, so you got as far as actually telling her where to go! Don't you realise how vulnerable she is?" Sarah's voice was raised. "She's not thinking straight if she's even considering anything like that. You are fucking unbelievable," Sarah finished furiously. "I'm going to get Sam."

Lizzie leapt to her feet, wincing as she did so. "But you promised. You gave Gaynor your word you wouldn't say anything."

Sarah picked up her coat from the back of a chair. "Then I'll write it down for him!"

Sam accelerated as they left Canterbury behind and joined the road to Ashford. "Try her again," he said to Lizzie, sitting beside him.

Lizzie hit the redial button on her phone, glancing sideways at him. He'd barely said a word since they'd driven out of Broadstairs. His profile was set as his eyes flicked back and forth in the rear view mirror, his jaw rigid.

She listened for a few seconds. "Still going straight to answer," she said to Sam, saying in completely different tones into the receiver: "It's Lizzie, sweetie, We're worried about you, please call me when you get this message." She pressed the button, to end the call. That's three we've left now," she reminded Sam. "She's obviously switched it off."

It was the first thing Gaynor had seen when she went through the automatic glass doors: *The use of mobile phones is not permitted anywhere in*.... She wondered if she could sneak in a quick call to Sarah – just to let her know – but as she pulled the phone from her handbag, a nurse walked past and gestured towards the notice. Oh well, Lizzie would have told her when she woke up.

Gaynor wondered how her head would be. She'd been practically incoherent when she'd crashed out last night and hadn't made much more sense when Gaynor had tried to wake her this morning. She knew Lizzie was right though. Sometimes you had to face up to things.

Still her stomach churned as she walked towards the Reception Desk. A middle-aged woman wearing a blouse and navy cardigan was sat in front of a computer screen, a white-uniformed nurse seated beside her. They both looked up as she approached.

"Yes?" asked the nurse pleasantly. "Can I help you?"

*   *   *

Lizzie was out of the car before Sam had even parked. She shot through the glass doors, past a young girl who stood crying by one of the potted palms, and up to the desk. "I'm here to see Gaynor Warrington," she said.

The woman looked at her levelly. "And you are?"

"I'm her sister," Lizzie said firmly. "And it's very important I tell her something."

The woman looked at her again. "Is she a patient here?"

"As far as I know, yes."

The woman raised her eyebrows.

"She told me she was coming here," improvised Lizzie, "and I said I'd meet her. I really have to see her straight away."

The woman pressed a few buttons on her computer. "There's nobody of that name here."

Lizzie tried to lean over the counter to see the screen. "Is she booked in for later? Has she got an appointment or had one already? I need to know – it's very urgent."

"I'm sorry," the woman said severely, twisting the monitor so it faced away from Lizzie. "We cannot discuss patient appointments. We have a code of confidentiality. It's one of our regulations." One, her tone suggested, that she took great pleasure in upholding.

"So what am I to do?" Lizzie cried, "She said she'd be here and I need to see her."

"I'm sorry," the receptionist said again, firmly. "I can't help you any further."

Out of the corner of her eye, Lizzie saw an older man arrive and lead the young girl outside.

"Where've you been?" she said crossly to Sam as he joined her. "They say she's not here but I bet she's booked in under another name. The old bat on the desk isn't giving anything away. Can't you get in there and impersonate a police officer?"

Sam looked at her impassively.

"You've got to do something." Lizzie's voice rose. "I feel terrible. Please go and try."

"No point," said Sam shortly. He held up Lizzie's mobile phone. "Sarah called. She's heard from Gaynor – she's at St Saviours. That's Highgate."

"Highgate?" Lizzie said again, as Sam joined the M20. "What's she doing there?"

"I've no idea."

"Didn't Sarah question her?"

Sam looked in his mirror and moved into the outside lane. "It was a text. Gaynor just said she was at St Saviours, waiting, and had to keep her phone turned off. Sorry she wouldn't be able to work today."

"Waiting for what?"

Sam turned his head briefly to flick her a hard look. "Who knows."

"Shall I call them?" Lizzie asked, as the red car in front moved over and Sam put his foot down.

Sam shrugged. "They won't tell you anything. They'll ask what ward she's in and if you don't know you won't get anywhere in a place that size. That's if they even answer the phone. Tell me again what you said to her," he added coldly.

"I don't know, it's all a blur. We were just talking about whether she was really doing the right thing keeping the baby since it didn't have a father and she didn't have a home. Which are perfectly valid points," she added defensively.

Sam was terse. "No wonder she was upset."

"She was upset," said Lizzie loudly, "because you gave her a dirty look when you met her trying to get rid of that drunk."

Sam reached out and pulled his tobacco pouch from the glove compartment. "Is that what she was doing?"

"For Christ's sake, what did you think she was doing? Going off into the sunset with him? Very likely isn't it? Her husband turns out to be a quasi-woman. The bloke she thinks she's in love with lets his daughter send her off with a flea in her ear. You think the first thing she's going to do is hook up with some soak who's had twenty-seven vodkas and fallen off his perch?"

"I didn't know any of that," said Sam, trying to roll a cigarette with one hand. "First I heard of it was when Sarah banged on the door this morning."

Lizzie picked up the tobacco pouch. "Well you know now. And you ought to tell your bloody daughter to butt out."

"I expect she meant well," said Sam, in a controlled voice.

Lizzie opened a paper, put in a pinch of tobacco and began to expertly roll. "She devastated Gaynor."

"I'll put it right."

"She thinks you don't want anything more to do with her."

"I'll put that right, too."

Lizzie handed him the finished cigarette. "I told her you were a worthless flake."

Sam gave a sudden laugh. "And you probably got that right." He was suddenly serious again. "I wouldn't do anything to deliberately hurt her. That's why I wrote her the note apologising, that's why I wanted to see her. It's all been a misunderstanding. I thought she didn't want to see *me*."

"I expect Debra made sure of that!" said Lizzie, meaningfully.

Sam accelerated up behind a white van and flashed it to move over. "As I said, I'll sort it."

"All of it?" asked Lizzie boldly. "I mean, now you know, do you want to keep the baby?"

Sam kept his eyes on the traffic ahead but she felt him tense.

"I want," he said tightly, "to talk to Gaynor."

They'd sat in silence for the best part of an hour. The traffic was horrendous. "I'm glad you're driving," said Lizzie eventually, as they came up against yet another diversion and Sam expertly took a back-double somewhere behind

Whitechapel High Street. "I wouldn't have a clue where I was going."

Sam pulled out and indicated, looking in his rear view mirror as he turned into City Road. "I spent a lot of years tramping the streets round here," he said, flicking ash out of the open window. "Not a time I look back on with much pleasure, but it means I know the way to St Saviours all right. It's not far now."

"I don't understand what she's doing there," said Lizzie again. "You can't just walk into a hospital and get an abortion can you?"

Sam shook his head. "I hope she's all right," he said. As they slowed at the lights he turned his head and looked directly at Lizzie for the first time. She saw the anxiety in his eyes. "That's where the big A and E department is."

"If she's OK to text then she can't be that bad," said Lizzie logically, as they crawled along the Holloway Road past the grimy shop fronts with their shutters and grilles and dispirited-looking shoppers. "Nice round here, isn't it?"

They stopped at a red light and a grinning black guy with dreadlocks sprang forward with a plastic bucket and grey-looking sponge which he aimed at their windscreen. Sam waved him away.

"Perhaps," said Lizzie imaginatively, "she was on her way to a clinic and she fainted and someone took her there. Perhaps she was waiting to be checked out. Pregnant women often pass out, don't they? Or perhaps she started to bleed or something and panicked. Anyway," Lizzie said, with forced cheer, "if she's there, then we're probably not too late. Unless she's lost it naturally, of course…"

"Bloody hell!" Sam suddenly exploded, banging his hand on the wheel as the next set of lights changed to red too.

"Sorry!" Lizzie looked out of the window. "I was just thinking aloud."

"It's OK," said Sam, sighing, as they crawled forward a foot and stopped again. "I just want to get there."

278

Gaynor wondered if they'd all forgotten her. She sat on her plastic chair and twisted her wedding ring round and round on her finger. She supposed she should take it off now she'd left Victor but she felt strange without it. Sort of half-dressed. She looked at the door nervously. She knew he wouldn't – it was totally illogical – but part of her kept half-expecting Victor to burst through the door, to demand to know what was happening. She cringed at the thought of seeing him. She'd have to at some point, of course. Would have to sit down and sort out the details, talk about what they were going to do financially etc. But not yet. Not till this was over.

A nurse put her head around the door. Gaynor jumped as she spoke and the nurse smiled kindly at her. "Mrs Warrington? All ready for you now…"

"How bloody ridiculous!" fumed Lizzie as they drove round for the second time looking for a meter. "What's one supposed to do in a crisis?"

Sam shrugged. "Always been like this. You can only park in the hospital itself after six and even then you can never find a space. Ah, someone's going. It's a huge place," he warned as they waited for a blue Ford Escort to squeeze its way out of the gap ahead. "I hope we can find her."

"We just won't leave till we do," said Lizzie determinedly. They walked rapidly down Highgate Hill. "She's got to be in there somewhere."

The hospital was huge and sprawling – an unhappy mix of old Victorian brick and glass and steel extensions. As they crossed the packed car park an ambulance came in a side entrance, blue light flashing,and disappeared around the back of the building.

Lizzie stopped and looked at the bewildering array of signs. "Where?" she said.

Sam began to walk purposefully on. "This way."

They went through big main entrance and up to the reception desk where there was already a small queue.

Lizzie walked to the head of it, tossed back her glossy black hair and swung her patchwork bag about with authority. "Excuse me," she announced to the column of waiting people. "This is an emergency."

Sam handed Lizzie a strange-smelling coffee in a polystyrene cup. "There's not a lot else we can do," he said, sitting down in a plastic chair next to her. "If she's not anywhere on their computer, then they can't help us."

"But it doesn't make sense," said Lizzie, taking a sip from the cup and grimacing. "Why tell Sarah she was here if she wasn't? Why say anything? Or has she lost her marbles completely and is wandering round the corridors somewhere in a white coat with a stolen stethoscope, thinking she's a brain surgeon?"

Sam didn't laugh. "I don't know," he said, shaking his head. "Doesn't make any sense to me either."

Lizzie stirred the sludgy brown liquid with the plastic stick Sam had brought with it, in the hope it might taste better. "We'll just have to keep phoning her," she said. "Presumably when she leaves here, she'll switch the phone back on – then we can grab her."

"I suppose," said Sam slowly. "It was this St Saviours."

Lizzie stared at him, "Oh, fucking wonderful," she said loudly. People around them turned their heads. "You said it was Highgate," she said, lowering her voice.

Sam nodded. "It's the only St Saviours I know of in London."

"But suppose she wasn't in London?"

"Why would she go anywhere else?"

"I don't know," hissed Lizzie. "But we'd better find out how many other flaming St Saviours there are in the country. She could be back in Ashford, after all." Lizzie got up and swept towards the desk, prepared to barge her way to the front of the queue once more.

A voice made her swing round. "Lizzie?"

Appearing from a corridor on her left, Gaynor stood, looking tired and forlorn, her hair unbrushed, clutching her handbag in front of her like a shield. Her face was blotchy as if she'd been crying.

"Sweetie…" Lizzie started to rush towards her but Sam got there first.

"Oh darling," he said, voice breaking in remorse. "What's happened?" He wrapped his arms around her, pulling her head on to his chest, stroking her hair.

Gaynor raised her eyes to look at him. "Chloe's had a boy," she said. And burst into tears.

26. Millennium Claret
A vintage with potential.

Gaynor lay on Sam's sofa wrapped in Sam's towelling dressing gown, her feet in his lap.

"I told Lizzie I was going to Chloe," she said. "And I told her to tell Sarah." She picked up the cup of tea Sam had made her. "I didn't realise she was so pissed she wouldn't remember."

Sam massaged her toes gently. "She felt pretty bad about everything. Thought she'd talked you into something you'd regret for ever."

Gaynor shook her head. "I was getting a bit maudlin but I wouldn't do that. Chloe phoned at seven and woke me up. She'd gone into labour suddenly and couldn't get hold of anyone. Oliver was away at a conference and didn't hear the call. Marie, her mother, is on holiday in France and she hasn't spoken to Victor since he told her he was also Gabrielle. Oliver got the message and made it to the hospital eventually, of course. But Chloe was panicking, so I went."

Sam stroked her instep. "You're lovely."

"I was ever so worried about seeing her," Gaynor said. "But when I got there, I was just worried *for* her. Oliver was in there and I was waiting outside and it just went on for hours. I heard her screaming at one point. She looked at Sam, stricken. "I felt so helpless."

"But the baby's gorgeous," she went on in softer tones. "Ever so tiny of course – he'll be in an incubator for a few days, but he's perfect!"

"And so will yours be," said Sam. "Ours," he corrected himself gruffly.

She pulled her feet away. "Look, you don't have to…"

He grabbed both ankles and pulled them back again. "Don't be silly."

"What about Debra?"

"I'll tell Debra."

"What did she say to you?"

"Nothing much. She just made it sound as though you'd come round, shoved the note back at her and didn't want to see me."

"She told me you didn't…" said Gaynor indignantly.

"I know and I'll speak to her. She's very protective but this is my life. Mine and yours. She'll be fine when she sees how happy I am."

"Will you be happy?"

He hesitated for a moment, and then gave a long, thoughtful sigh. "I can't tell you I shall never get low, Gaynor. I am, as your friend Lizzie so eloquently puts it, 'a flake'."

"You're not, she didn't mean that!"

"I am and she did and that's OK." He began to roll a cigarette. "I do get depressed. It's usually worse in the winter. It's like the light goes out. Everything is suddenly grey and bleak and my mind is clouded. It's a sort of blindness. I know the sun is there, colour is there. But I can't see it. It's a strange feeling." He paused. "But I come back out of it. I fight it. It may never happen again. Or it might. But I will still love you. I will still be here."

"It frightened me," she said. "It frightened me when you were sitting there in that chair when I came back from taking David home. When you were talking in that voice."

"I know." He began to stroke her feet again. "But all I can say to you, Gaynor, is that I am not David, I am not your father. I am me, and me is different."

He turned his face to look into her eyes. "You see, I understand it now. I know what happens. And that's how I know I am getting better. For years I didn't realise what it was. At times, especially at the end of my time at work, I could feel myself spinning down and a great fear would engulf me. I'm sure now I was badly depressed in my teens but nobody noticed. And then my marriage and Eleanor dying finished the job."

Gaynor leant out and took his hand. "You don't have to say all this."

Sam nodded. "I do. You need to know everything – what you are taking on." He reached for his lighter.

"Anyway, to help yourself with depression, you've got to accept it, which is the reverse of what you might think. So I do. But I fight it as well. Not by trying to walk through walls but by realising what is happening to me, then trying hard to go on again. Learn to live with it, not in it, they told me. I try to do that."

"I know." She felt guilty, as though she had been selfish and unsupportive.

"I get depressed and I wish I wasn't, but the great thing is I can say that to you. Even a few months ago, when we met, I was just belligerent and would have gone into denial rather than have this conversation. Now I can admit it and tell you what's going on, or try to."

"Yes," said Gaynor. "And then I can cope with it."

"I do understand your position," he said seriously. "Your history. Your present as regards David. And your fears for me and you and the fears you must have for our baby. Given both sets of scars and the history, there are going to be times when our needs clash – that's inevitable."

He was holding her hand tightly. "But I am always here for you. I hope you know that. I'm very much in love with you, Gaynor. With you I think I will be OK. I think I will find contentment. I think I will play music again, see the sun and feel its warmth…"

He smiled at her. Tears were running down her face. She nodded.

"I'm in love with you too," she said.

Sam had lit a fire. "I should really get this chimney swept," he said, as a belch of smoke came back into the room. They both sat looking at the flames.

"I felt terrible when I was so awful to you when you told me you might be pregnant," he said. "I felt a real bastard."

"I think that was the expression Lizzie used."

"I bet it was."

"It doesn't matter now."

Sam picked up another log and tossed it into the smouldering grate. "It does. But it was only because I hurt so much. Sometimes with me, that turns to anger. I wanted you so much. I couldn't bear the idea of you with Victor. It was just a shock, the thought of you still having sex with him. I'd been in your house. I'd seen your bed…" He stopped and said more quietly. "And I shouldn't have said that about Danny. I'm sorry."

Gaynor suddenly giggled. "He came in the wine bar the other night and still tried it on. He is such a dick! Ooooh!" She squealed as Brutus leapt on to the sofa and landed in the middle of her stomach. "Oh you darling," she said with real pleasure. "I've missed you."

"Why haven't you got a cat, if you like them so much?" Sam asked, leaning over and stroking the grey furry head.

Gaynor pulled a face. "Victor isn't an animal person. Thought a cat would leave hairs on the furniture." She ran a hand down Brutus's spine. He purred loudly. "But I always wanted a Burmese. I told you, my Godmother had one called Sidney – he looked just like this. He used to chase bits of screwed-up paper all over the room."

Sam leant out and tore a corner from the newspaper on the small table next to them. He scrunched it up in his hand, watching as Brutus immediately sat up, alert. "Go on!" he said tossing it away to the other side of the room. Brutus leapt after it.

Gaynor smiled. "I used to do that for hours with Sidney. I used to love going to stay with Eve. She was my absolute refuge from home. The person I could turn to when everything got too awful."

She suddenly felt sick. "Sam – there's something I have to tell you too. It's horrible and I'm ashamed of it but you have to know. So you know what you're dealing with, as well."

He looked at her calmly. "Go on."

"I was pregnant once before."

He sat very still. Just his fingers moved, gently caressing her ankle.

She said quickly: "It was when I had started my relationship with Victor. You know, just started – I was still in this grotty bedsit and I don't know how it happened – I was on the pill – but I think I'd had a bug or been sick or something and anyway…" She stopped. Sam's fingers went rhythmically on.

"Anyway, I told Victor and he said straight away he'd pay for everything – it was like there was no question and I did say, perhaps… but he said we'd have one later – that he wanted to have some time first with just the two of us. Because we were so special…"

Her voice broke a little. "And I told myself that was best too because I didn't know what was going to happen then – if we'd even last – and I had no money and nowhere nice to live and…" She stopped once more and gave a bitter laugh, trying hard not to cry, "…funny how things come round again. And then, back then, it seemed more important to keep Victor – I know that sounds awful."

Sam shook his head silently.

"And then later," Gaynor rushed on, "when I thought we were trying to have one – when I thought that it was my fault that we couldn't, that there was something wrong with me, then I thought it was my punishment… I don't know how he could do that to me…" She began to sob.

Beside her Sam's hand had stilled. She looked up, dreading the expression she might see on his face. But he had tears in his eyes too. "Oh you poor, poor thing. He took her in his arms. "It's OK, darling. It's OK…"

"Why did he do it?" Sam asked, when Gaynor had blown her nose and he'd piled more wood on the fire. "To have a vasectomy without even consulting you? It's pretty unforgivable."

Gaynor shrugged. "Said he didn't want any more children and couldn't trust me not to get pregnant. He was too busy working through his 'gender issues' to have a screaming brat in the house. I don't know…" She shook her head. "I still can't believe it either."

She lay back in the cushions. "But I don't want to think about him. I feel like a drink. I haven't had a glass of wine for weeks."

"I should think not." Sam looked ruefully at his tobacco. "I suppose I'll have to stop smoking."

Gaynor suddenly sat up again. "Sam, what are we going to do?"

"Looks like we're going to have a baby."

"I'm a bit scared."

He leant out and pulled her towards him again, putting her feet gently on to the floor so he could put his arms right round her.

"So am I," he said.

27. Dom Perignon
Smooth and full-bodied with a lasting finish.

Happy Christmas from Greens. Kiss. *Happy Christmas from Greens.*

How lovely to see you. Kiss. *A happy Christmas from Greens.*

Happy Christmas to YOU. Kiss. *From all the management.* Kiss.

Mulled wine on the bar. Kiss. *Do help yourself to a mince pie...*

"Can I have one?" Sam appeared at Gaynor's side, holding a large orange juice. He put it in her hands. "Got one of those kisses for me?"

She put her arms around his neck and hugged him. "Not half."

Sam kissed her lips. "Sarah says there's no need to stand here for hours – she says go and circulate and enjoy yourself."

Gaynor raised her eyebrows. "And?"

"She wants you to hand round the mince pies."

What was left of them. Down in the kitchen Bel and Charlie stood with bulging cheeks over a large plate of pies that Benjamin was trying, unsuccessfully, to decorate with icing sugar before they took any more.

"Richard's got an ENORMOUS Christmas tree," said Bel with her mouth full.

"And," said Charlie, excitedly. "We've opened our presents from Dad already. He said we could. I got a Playstation Two and Luke got an iPod!"

Gaynor put her arm around him, catching Sarah's eye over the top of his head. "How lovely!"

Sarah nodded meaningfully. "Did you see Luke upstairs? I told him to help clear some glasses – do something useful. I bet he's slunk off instead."

Gaynor shook her head. "Didn't notice him." She smiled at the two smaller children. "Would you both go up to the flat and see if Chloe's OK? Ask her if she wants a drink or anything?"

"Oh, she said to tell you she'll have to go as soon as she's fed Edmund," Sarah said. "Isn't he adorable? It's made me all broody again."

"That reminds me," Gaynor said, when the kids had scuttled off for a last glimpse of the baby and Benjamin had ceremoniously borne another tray of sausages up the stairs, "you still haven't told me what the doctor said."

Sarah pulled a rack of garlic bread from the oven. "He was really nice. Very understanding. He said it's more common than you'd think and not to panic or anything. I think Richard thought I was on the road to junkydom but I've got to just try and cut down."

She laughed and said, in exaggerated tones, as if reciting, "I must not do it suddenly. I am on a 'reducing regime!'" Then she grinned. "I've got this chart to follow…"

Gaynor grinned too. "Not a chart! We could have filled them in together. Except mine's rather academic now." Gaynor ran a hand over her stomach. "I'm so glad you went – I was really worried about you."

"I'm fine, honestly." Sarah took off her oven gloves and gave Gaynor a sudden hug. "In fact I'm happier than I have been for ages. The kids are more settled, Richard's wonderful and roll on January the fifteenth."

Gaynor looked at her quizzically. "What's happening then?"

"The new chef arrives. Roderigo! Sexy, Latin and with a filthy temper, he tells me." Sarah looked pleased. "He will probably give Benjamin a nervous breakdown, but I..." She held up her hands in a gesture of triumph and delight, "will be out of this fucking kitchen!"

Chloe was sitting on the window seat with Edmund asleep against her chest. Gaynor sat down beside her and looked at his blissful little face and tiny curling fingers. "I can't imagine what it's going to feel like," she said.

Chloe yawned. "Totally shattering," she said. "Oh, for a night's sleep. Thank God Ollie does the three a.m. shift."

Gaynor smiled. "I'll get you some more of that eye-lift gel – extra strength for the new mum."

"Can you get me some for my stomach and bum too?" said Chloe. "Everything seems to be sagging. As for my breasts –" She looked ruefully at her firmly-encased bosom. "Don't even go there."

"Ah, but he's worth it, isn't he," said Gaynor soppily, sliding her little finger into the baby's tightly-closed fist. "I can't wait…"

Chloe nodded. "I'm pleased for you," she said, stiffly. Then in a sudden rush she went on: "We're having Christmas dinner with Dad tomorrow."

"Good," said Gaynor, still gazing at Edmund's sleeping face. "He's still your father, after all."

"I've told him I don't want to see… you know…"

"That's a part of him too," said Gaynor. "It wasn't that Chloe, that made me leave him. If it had just been that…."

"He wasn't even going to tell me at first," said Chloe, "he was just going to let me think you'd gone and got pregnant with someone else."

"Well, I did but…"

"I wish I didn't know," Chloe burst out. "I can't really bear it."

"Give it time." Gaynor put an arm around her shoulders. "And thank you for coming to see me."

*　　*　　*

Gaynor stood on the pavement and kissed Chloe as Oliver brought the car up alongside Greens. Chloe hadn't wanted to be introduced to Sam and Gaynor hadn't pushed it. It was enough for now to have Chloe back in some way. Whatever had happened with Victor, Chloe still felt like family.

"I'll visit in the New Year," Gaynor said, touching Edmund's pink cheek beneath his designer wool cap.

Chloe looked emotional. "Shall I say anything to Dad?" she asked. "Shall I give him a message?"

Gaynor nodded. "Wish him a happy Christmas."

Inside, Claire looked equally watery-eyed. It was the first time, Gaynor reflected, that she had ever seen her standing still. She stood by the fireplace with a mince pie and a haunted expression. Above her the speakers banged out the collection of festive songs and carols that she had insisted should be played non-stop.

"Making the most of your last traditional Christmas?" Gaynor said chirpily, and immediately regretted it.

"It's going to be very strange, but we'll come home for visits of course," Claire answered, with forced cheer. "And to see how this place is getting on."

"Of course you will." Gaynor matched the tone. "With air travel these days, the world's really very small." She squeezed Claire's arm.

"Apparently," said Claire brightly, "Kyoto is very pretty."

Gaynor leant out and picked up some glasses from the mantelpiece. "What happened to Tokyo?"

"There were several cities Jamie could choose from. There's a bit more space in Kyoto and the Emperor lives there and he has lots of dogs."

"Oh yes, I meant to ask. Who's going to look after Henry and Wooster while you're gone?"

Claire looked horrified. "They're coming with us."

A short, stocky man in his late fifties joined them. Claire sprang into action. "Gaynor, this is my father, Grant. Dad – Gaynor." She disappeared to empty ashtrays.

Grant looked Gaynor up and down appreciatively and then let his eyes travel around the bar. Gaynor followed his gaze. It looked good. Holly and ivy festooned the beamed ceiling, a Christmas tree decorated in red and gold filled the front window. Tiny white lights sparkled along the top of the bar. All around them, clusters of glittery-topped young women and whackily T-shirted guys, in groups and couples, were laughing and chinking glasses. There was a warm and festive buzz to the place. Many of their regulars had turned out to have a Christmas Eve drink with them. She gave Maurice a brief wave – noting that he was at least drinking the free mulled wine and not demanding fancy coffees tonight. Neville Norton looked as though he'd got the Christmas spirit about three weeks ago and hadn't stopped drinking since. Amanda was wearing a fuchsia pink dress and clutching the arm of her hapless boyfriend as if she were afraid he might try to escape.

Gaynor blew a kiss towards Jeffrey, the chartered accountant who'd had Sunday lunch here every week since they opened, and raised a glass towards Terrie and Anita – the two glamorous women of her own age who could always be relied upon to work their way through the entire stock of Cloudy Bay the moment it hit the Specials board.

"Lovely, isn't it?" She waved a hand around her and smiled at Grant. She thought with his thickset shoulders and rounded stomach, he looked the archetypal landlord. "First time you've been here?"

"Yes, hasn't she done well?" Grant said. "She's always been a business woman. Could tell it even when she was a little girl. Always been clever. She can succeed at anything she turns her hand to." He winked conspiratorially at Gaynor. "I wouldn't tell her that, of course."

Gaynor remembered Claire's face on their opening night when Neill had told her their father was too busy to make it. The tone of her voice when he'd cancelled the last visit.

She gave Grant a penetrating look. "Well, perhaps it's time you did!"

"Are you OK?" she asked Jack, who was giving his very best attention to three blondes who had come in decorated with flashing seasonal lights and wearing tinsel in their cleavages. "Need any help?"

"I'm lovely, sweet-pea!" he called, while not taking his eyes off the nearest plunging neckline. "Maybe get some more glasses?"

Claire, behind him, was pulling the cork from a bottle of Bollinger. She folded a white cloth over the ice bucket and reached up for champagne flutes. "Oh yes, Gaynor, please. We've got almost none of these left."

Gaynor began to skirt the room, collecting empties, stopping to kiss and chat to those she knew. Squeezing through to the bar, her hands full, she felt a hand on her bottom. "Hello gorgeous! Mmmm..." The hand felt around a bit more. "You're not putting on weight, are you?"

"Do you mind!" Gaynor turned crossly on Danny. He had on a new leather jacket and a deep tan and was looking exceptionally pleased with himself.

"Have you missed me?" he asked, "I've thought about you every day." He tried another experimental fondle.

Gaynor stepped back, holding the glasses out in front of her. "Keep them to yourself."

But another arm had already wound itself around Gaynor's waist and a different hand stuck itself out in front of her.

"I'm Sam and you must be Danny. I've heard such a lot about you..."

It was nearly midnight and everyone was in Christmas mood. Gaynor smiled as yet another couple did a spot of profound snogging under the mistletoe that Sarah had strategically dangled.

"Am I really putting on weight, already?" she asked Sam, smoothing her hands over her hips. The slinky silver dress did seem a bit tighter than the last time she'd worn it.

"Not that I can see," he said. "But you're bound to, sooner or later, aren't you? After all, you're carrying someone else about too."

She smiled at him. "Victor always went on about how heavy I was."

Sam kissed her ear. "I'm not Victor."

She was flagging by the time they rang last orders. Everyone in the place seemed to close in on the bar and she and Claire and Sarah all found themselves behind the bar helping Jack serve.

"Hubble, bubble, toil and trouble…" Claire's brother Neill called out wittily.

"The Witches of Eastwick…" His friend Seb lounged across the bar, grinning.

"Do you want to get served or not?" asked Gaynor, severely. "It doesn't do to upset the management."

"Come and give me a Christmas kiss," said Seb, unrepentant. "Since Sarah has spurned me."

Gaynor leant over the bar and brushed his lips lightly with hers. "She always did have good taste."

It was a minute to time. Gaynor was adding up seventeen drinks in her head. "Don't speak to me," she instructed Jack as he leant round her to open the till. "And don't even think about a cappuccino," she said to Maurice who was dithering over what to have for himself, now he'd bought a round for his entire end of the bar.

"I wouldn't dream of it," he said, dancing from foot to foot and looking fetchingly at the blackboard. "I'll you what," he said, through lowered lashes. "I'll have a hot chocolate."

"I thought they were going to be here all night," Gaynor said to Sarah when she'd kissed the last giggling customer and propelled them gently through the door. "I am totally kissed out."

"I hope not," said Sam, squeezing her.

Gaynor yawned. "I think I need to go to bed."

"Mmmn," said Sam softly in her ear.

"Not yet!" said Jamie. "We're having champagne."

"I can't really…"

"A bit won't hurt," said Sarah authoritatively. "You can drink in 'moderation'." She grinned at Gaynor. "Though I'm not sure you and the medical authorities would share the same interpretation of that phrase. When I got pregnant with Bel I told the midwife I was going home for a bottle of bubbly and she just said, "Well, don't get too pissed."

"We've got through our first six months," said Claire. "That's worth celebrating. And then there's Gaynor's baby and Jamie's new job…" She flashed a huge, brave smile as Jamie took her hand, "and Sarah moving in with Richard and…"

"Poor old Seb without a woman for Christmas," said Seb, sadly.

"Come clubbing in Margate," said Jack, putting on his jacket. "Never mind this girly champagne stuff – let's go and find some totty."

"Totty?" said Sarah. "What sort of an expression is that? Those lucky girls, eh?" She grinned. "Seeing you two coming…"

"I can't stay too long either," she said, when they'd gone. "Richard is at home with the kids. We've told them HE won't come if they don't buckle down and sleep but that's no guarantee of anything."

"We've got my parents waiting at home for us," said Claire as they all sat round a table in front of the fire and Jamie popped the cork from a bottle of Bolly. "But hey, I want to have a drink with you all."

"Yeah, when did they go?" Neill nudged at his sister.

Claire gave him a look. "Mum was tired," she said, her voice loaded.

Neill nodded. "Dad had had enough, in other words."

"He's so proud of you," volunteered Gaynor. "He told me – he thinks you've done brilliantly."

Clare gave a humourless laugh. "I've spent my whole life trying to impress him. But golden boy here has always taken the biscuit."

Neill shook his head. "I don't know why you think that. He thinks I'm an idle loafer most of the time. I've never been forgiven for not going into the licensed trade and getting a beer gut to match his."

Jamie leant out and patted Neill's middle. "Oh, I don't know." He looked at Claire. "He is proud you know. He told me I had to be very sure I knew what I was doing – taking you away from your glittering career here."

Claire looked embarrassed. "Happy Christmas, everyone!" she said, raising her glass. "Here's to us and Greens and the future and a very happy Christmas." They all drank. "And," Claire went on, "Thank you, Sarah and Gaynor for a successful partnership and, look after the place, eh?" Her voice wobbled and she took another big swallow of champagne. Jamie hugged her. "And happy Christmas!" said Claire again.

They all laughed. Gaynor leant over and chinked glasses with her, then turned to Sarah. "Happy Christmas!" Then she stopped, looking stricken. "Oh Sarah, what's the matter?"

Sarah gave a sort of choke, half laughing as she sniffed. "Oh God, I don't know, Christmas is like children's birthdays – if you're not careful you always start blubbing. I cry every year at the nativity play," she told them all, shame-faced. "The minute they start 'Away in a Manger' I'm off."

Claire jerked her head towards the speakers from which 'Frosty the Snowman' tinkled out for the thirty-seventh time. "Oh dear, I think it could be on in a minute."

"You've got all this to come," Sarah told Sam and Gaynor. "Birthdays are just as bad. Every year, I used to tell myself I wouldn't cry when the kids blew out their candles, but I always ended up grizzling."

All at once, Gaynor felt that peculiar feeling in the pit of her stomach that was half nostalgia, half self-pity, laced with fear. A baby. A grown-up life where you went to school plays and had birthday parties and sang over candles. She glanced at Sam, wondering if he too had suddenly faced the enormity of what they were doing. He looked perfectly relaxed, sitting there with his largely untouched drink in his hand, listening to whatever Sarah was saying.

Gaynor stood up. Of course it would be all right, she told herself. They were going to be together and have a beautiful son or daughter. It was just that the champagne had gone straight to her head and she felt slightly disorientated and a little faint. She stepped behind Sam towards the door to the loo, praying she wouldn't be sick.

She could hear them behind her, laughing, singing along to the strains of 'I Wish it Could be Christmas Every Day'. She walked down the corridor, breathing deeply, suddenly wanting to be at home, snuggled up with Sam in bed. Just the two of them.

As she washed her hands, feeling cooler, she thought how cheerful he'd been since he'd finally stopped smoking and how passionate...

She smiled as she reached out to unbolt the loo door then screamed, as she was plunged into darkness. She heard a far-off shriek echo hers. Heart beating, she fumbled with the door in the blackness, feeling the panic rise in her chest as her fingers felt for the cold metal of the catch.

The swirling dark pressed in on her and she found herself gasping, as if short of oxygen, as she stumbled out into the corridor beyond, eyes struggling to focus on anything in the windowless passageway.

Faintly she could hear them – "Get that candle! Bloody trip switch again! What's Benjamin doing down there?" – but she couldn't reach the door, the door that would open on to the light of the fire, Claire lighting the restaurant candles,

Jamie poking in the fuse box with a torch, Sarah rolling her eyes as Neill sat back and simply lit another joint…

She knew they were only yards away but she felt trapped and powerless. She tried to keep calm as she felt her way along the cold stone walls. "Sam?" she called, frightened. "Sam, where are you?"

And then the door to the bar opened and a shaft of light came in and she heard the music come back on. Hark ye Herald Angels Sing! And Claire calling: "Crisis over – more champagne, Jamie!"

Sarah's kind voice: "Benjamin, they're beautiful – I've never seen chocolate-covered Snowman Crème Brulée before, but you really must be careful with that hairdryer…"

Gaynor stopped, heart pounding with relief, as Sam came towards her, tall and strong, holding out his hands.

"I'm here," he said. "I'm here."

The End

Also by Jane Wenham-Jones

Perfect Alibis
Infidelity for women – a survival guide

Stephanie – bored housewife and disillusioned mother – wants a job, and Madeleine's recruitment company appears to be the ideal place to go. Except that Pas isn't quite what it seems.

Far from providing companies with Personal Assistants, the agency offers Perfect Alibis to unfaithful women. And, as Stephanie soon discovers, there are lots of them about!

Founder member Patsy is a serial philanderer and there's a dark side to her best friend Millie. For the well-heeled ladies of Edenhurst, Pas is a ticket to risk-free adultery.

When slacker Troy, Stephanie's first love, returns unexpectedly to town, even she is tempted. But her life is soon in turmoil, and that's before the tabloids get involved…

Published by Bantam Books
Available from www.accentpress.co.uk

Raising The Roof, published by Bantam Books, was Jane's acclaimed first novel.

Jane Wenham-Jones features in:

Sexy Shorts for Lovers

"A fine collection of heart-warming stories." WOMAN
£1 per copy sold goes to the British Heart Foundation. As part
of their Real Valentine Appeal it will help to raise £1 million
to fund more BHF Heart Nurses around the UK.

ISBN 0954489926   RRP £6.99

Sexy Shorts for Summer

"Sexy, funny and page-turningly good." KATIE FFORDE
Another sizzling collection of short stories this time in
support of Cancer Research UK, helping promote their 'Sun
Safe' campaign.

ISBN 0954489934   RRP £6.99

Sexy Shorts for Christmas

"Sparkling stories. Perfect entertainment."

JILL MANSELL

The ultimate stocking filler in support of Breast Cancer
Campaign.

ISBN 0954489918   RRP £6.99

Remembering Judith
By Ruth Joseph

"This hauntingly moving tale of a daughter's devotion to her anorexic mother tugs at the heartstrings and plays on the mind long after you've finished it."
PRIMA MAGAZINE

"Elegantly written, atmospheric, nostalgic and full of trapped emotion. One of those books that manages to be both harrowing and elegant."
PHIL RICKMAN, BBC RADIO WALES

A true story of shattered childhoods...

Following her escape from Nazi Germany and the loss of her family Judith searches for unconditional love and acceptance. In a bleak boarding house she meets her future husband – another Jewish refugee who cares for her when she is ill. Tragically she associates illness with love and a pattern is set. Judith's behaviour eventually spirals into anorexia – a disease little known or understood in 1950's Britain.

While she starves herself, Judith forces Ruth, her daughter, to eat. She makes elaborate meals and watches her consume them. She gives her a pint of custard before bed each night. As the disease progresses roles are reversed. Ruth must care for her mother and loses any hope of a normal childhood. The generation gap is tragically bridged by loss and extreme self-loathing in this moving true story of a family's fight to survive.

ISBN 1905170017   RRP £7.99

The Boy I Love
By Marion Husband

The story is set in the aftermath of World War One. Paul Harris, still frail after shellshock, returns to his father's home and to the arms of his secret lover, Adam. He discovers that Margot, the fiancée of his dead brother, is pregnant and marries her through a sense of loyalty. Through Adam he finds work as a schoolteacher, while setting up a home with Margot he continues to see Adam.

Pat Morgan, who was a sergeant in Paul's platoon, runs a butcher's shop in town and cares for his twin brother Mick, who lost both legs in the war. Pat yearns for the closeness he experienced with Paul in the trenches.

Set in a time when homosexuality was 'the love that dare not speak its name' the story develops against the background of the strict moral code of the period. Paul has to decide where his loyalty and his heart lies as all the characters search hungrily for the love and security denied them during the war.

ISBN 1905170009   RRP £6.99

Paper Moon
By Marion Husband

The sequel to *The Boy I Love*

"*This is an extraordinary novel. Beautifully controlled
pacy prose carefully orchestrates the relationships of many
well drawn characters and elegantly captures the atmosphere
of England in 1946...This novel is perfect.*"
Margaret Wilkinson

Paul's son Bobby escapes Thorp to become a Spitfire
pilot during World War Two. When his plane is shot
down he learns to come to terms with the terrible burns
he suffers even as his past returns to haunt him.

Paper Moon is a passionate love story set in 1946 that
explores how the sins of the fathers can have far-
reaching effects on their sons.

ISBN 1905170149   RRP £6.99
AVAILABLE APRIL 2006

Raffy's Shapes
By Tamar Hodes

Bizarrely beautiful, pure escapism. It's simply wonderful.

Raphaella Turner is a best-selling painter who lives beside a lake. Inside her cottage, everything is white. When she is not creating her huge, brightly coloured abstract paintings, she swims in the lake and changes shape. Sometimes she is a bird or sometimes a fish. Unknown to Raphaella, her real mother, Martha, lives on the other side of the lake with her husband Richard and four sons. Martha also changes shape as did her mother Helga, escaping from a difficult life in Nazi Germany as a Jew, and an unhappy marriage.

The title *Raffy's Shapes* refers to Raphaella's collection of shapes in jars, her paintings, her shape-changing, and the two sand-world's she creates, one to live in and one to draw away the unwelcome attention of the people who want to understand and cash in on her genius. The novel explores, among others themes such as deceit and truth, the complex nature of creativity and the desire to make shapes.

ISBN 1905170173   RRP £6.99
AVAILABLE JULY 2006